ALPHA CENTAURI

Previous Collaborations

IRIS
FELLOW TRAVELER

Previous Books by William Barton

HUNTING ON KUNDERER
A PLAGUE OF ALL COWARDS
DARK SKY LEGION
YELLOW MATTER
WHEN HEAVEN FELL
THE TRANSMIGRATION OF SOULS
ACTS OF CONSCIENCE

Previous Books by Michael Capobianco

BURSTER

ALPHA CENTAURI

William Barton and Michael Capobianco

AVON BOOKS  NEW YORK

This is a work of fiction. Names, characters, places, and incidents either are the product of the author's imagination or are used fictitiously. Any resemblance to actual events, locales, organizations, or persons, living or dead, is entirely coincidental and beyond the intent of either the author or the publisher.

AVON BOOKS
A division of
The Hearst Corporation
1350 Avenue of the Americas
New York, New York 10019

First Avon Books Trade Printing: July 1997
First Avon Books Hardcover Printing: July 1997

AVON TRADEMARK REG. U.S. PAT. OFF. AND IN OTHER COUNTRIES, MARCA REGISTRADA, HECHO EN U.S.A.

Printed in the U.S.A.

OP   10   9   8   7   6   5   4   3   2   1

A special acknowledgment is due Matthew Barton,
who helped us do some of the arithmetic.

ONE

Mother Night fell from a star-filled sky bearing a fragile cargo of lost souls, souls locked in an iron darkness of dreamless sleep.

Maeru kai Ortega awoke suddenly, staring at the gray inner surface of his transition shell, unmoving, unthinking, not really aware that he was awake, listening to the soft whisper of his own breathing, not even wondering what it was. Lassitude. Quiet lassitude. The pleasure of renewed existence, after . . .

Oh, right. Self-awareness trickling through like the first rivulets in a dry desert riverbed, thunder echoing hollowly up in the mountains, presaging a flood to come. Right. Still alive. It *worked*. He moved, just one arm, just a little bit, and heard himself make a distant whine, muffled, yet sharp, insistent. Hard splinter of pain down his spine. He whispered, "Please. Open the shell." It came out as a series of thin, cracked, inhuman sounds, just creaking noises, like some corroded brass hinge. The eyebubble core understood him, nonetheless.

Soft hiss, like compressed air, like hydraulics, and the transition shell's cover swung up and away. Cold air from outside flooded in, like a billion trillion tiny needles, like a spray of ice-water on sun-burned skin. And Maeru kai Ortega thought, *Fuck. We're here!* He sat up suddenly, daring the pain, defiant, one hand clawed against the shell's rim, the other pressed to the side of his head, and thought, God damn it, this doesn't matter. I'm here.

And all alone right now. Right now I'm the only one here.

Somehow, he got over the side of his coffin and stood wobble-legged on the floor. Already getting used to it. Already moving again. From the feel of it, the system's rule sieves had the centrifuge running at about .05 gee. Not far from Titan normal. The high-gee types would feel like they were floating away. Kai looked around, stretching, feeling all the aches and pains break down, becoming part of the background. Inside him, the resurrection hardware would be working furiously, modules working from their own memory of the standard model of Maeru kai Ortega, the Kai who'd lain down to sleep fourteen years before. Earthside, it would be sometime in March, 2239 A.D.

He walked up the gently curving floor, past ten more coffins, paying no attention to panels of blue, green, and amber lights, an occasional cluster of red here and there, walked to the foot of the ladder and hauled himself upward, pace quickening as pseudogravity diminished, ignoring a little wave of coriolis-induced vertigo.

None of this is important. Not now. Not when we're *here*. . . .

Mother Night's command module seemed dim and shadowy, with a faint, indefinable smell, as if no one had been here for a very long time. Still, there were lights on the board, a slowly blinking cursor on the center console's flatscreen. He waited for a second, then snapped his fingers soundlessly at the local bubble's sensor. "Hey in there. Wake up." The sensor lit, pale blue, and a cluster of interface routers shifted, aiming at his face. "That's better. Open the window."

There was a faint, shuddery sensation, then the external shield segments over the command module's windows swung open on night: Stars. More stars. Familiar stars. Bright stars. Dim stars. So many stars the constellations were hard to make out, though they were still there. The Milky Way was a long, clotted river of light, just now a diagonal swath through the heavens. He said, "Turn the ship so I can look toward the system's barycenter."

There was a distant, rumbling whine as the eyebubble tilted

the ship's gyro platform and the stars rolled slowly to one side. Reassuring to think that the subsystems still work. A brilliant star appeared; no, a sun. Too small to show a disk but impressive nonetheless. Then another, this one much dimmer, but still bright, incandescent-seeming. More than eighty AU away, Alpha Centauri A and B shone like jewels, washing out the starfield around them. Kai felt the breath stop in his throat and stared, transfixed, feeling as if he could reach out and catch them up.

I am, he thought, the first man to see this. *I alone.*

Remember. Remember this for as long as you live. No one will ever again have a moment like this. Not like Balboa on his peak in Darien, looking out over the wide Pacific. Not like Armstrong stepping down onto the charcoal dust of Luna. Other starships would fly, were already flying, en route to other stars, would arrive, so other men and women could stand transfixed by wonder. But *Mother Night* was the first such ship, and Maeru kai Ortega the first to see. He wished, briefly, that there were someone, some thing perhaps, to thank for his good fortune, but could think of nothing and no one. Almost regretfully, he got down to the work of completing the mandatory systems check. With sinking heart, he noted anomaly after anomaly in the tables and abstracts the eyebubble fed through his eyes and ears. Although the ship was in a safe condition, and obviously still stable and functional, something was wrong.

Hell, the shield didn't come off . . . they were still carrying its mass. This was serious, would require immediate repair, but was not immediately life-threatening. We'll have to see. . . .

Back down in the bottom of the artificial gravity well, he stood for a long moment before a full-length mirror, staring again, this time at himself. Maybe, he thought, it was heartless of them to put a mirror here. Supposed to reassure us, I suppose, but *this* . . . The being in the mirror was still Maeru kai Ortega, but his fourteen years as a dried-out mummy were yet to be erased. The basic shape, then: tall, slim, pale, hairless body, the pretty, narrow face, pale gray eyes, short, straight, lustrous gray hair, growing into a natural shag cut that never needed trim-

ming. This was the Kai he'd had made on the first day of his
majority, when his parents could no longer dictate that he wear
the form and figure of a stockily muscular, handsome blue-
eyed, blond boy. They'd been so angry they'd refused to see
him for years. Angry at the slim, under-muscled arms and legs,
the delicate bones of his narrow hips, the hairless little-girl
vulva peeking from between his legs . . .

Kai tried to extrude his penis, felt a sudden pang when nothing came out. Oh, hell, don't worry. The repairmen aren't done
yet. Look at all those wrinkles and puckers, hanging pads of
skin yet to fill out. It takes a little time. And if anything's
wrong, Doc will fix it. He said, "All right. Wake them up."
The panel lights of the coffins began coming up, first one, then
the next, then the next, *Mother Night*'s ten remaining crew
members, sleeping across the long gulf to Alpha Centauri.

Virginia Vonzell Qing-an first, her panel of indicator lights
blinking once blue, then again, all green, amber lights starting
a count-off row down the left-hand side, one, two, three . . .
Ginny'd wanted to wake up first, be the one summoned by the
insensate will of the machines, had wanted to be first to *see*,
had claimed it as captain's right. The central committee of the
Daiseijin had decided against it. Engineer first. See to the ship.
Then captain. Ginny's lights. Then Doc, who'd be on hand to
see to the rest of the crew, then Sheba Zvi. . . .

The lights on Sheba's blinked hard, fast, on–off, on–off, some
green, others blue, a few amber, most of them red. Kai walked
over, suddenly short of breath, and looked at the readouts. Rean-
imation failure. Simple as that. There were details to be had,
but they meant nothing. He popped the emergency override,
lifted the coffin's lid, and peered in.

Sheba Zvi's corpse looked anything but peaceful. Leathery
black skin shriveled against twisted bones. Mouth open, yellow
teeth corroded away to black stumps. Eyes gone, leaving behind
dark and hollow sockets, hair lying loose on the padding around
her head like a worn-out feather duster. She looked like she'd
been dead for ten thousand years.

He shut the lid then, feeling empty, and rubbed the tips of

his fingers over a complex pattern of control lights, telling the coffin subsystem to restore the interior of the transition shell to full stasis. Maybe Doc . . . No. He won't be able to bring her back from *this*. Maybe, when the main fleet gets here. If it does, in twenty or thirty years. . . .

A coffin lid hissed open and Kai turned to watch. The top of Ginny's head appeared first, her straight black hair, as always, looking freshly combed, then the broad, tawny forehead, narrow, moderately slanted eyes. Black eyes. Looking at him. A barely comprehensible whisper: "Good morning, Kai. Ship works, I take it."

He nodded slowly. "Seems to."

She got out of the coffin, wincing, and leaned against it, as he had, looking down at herself. "Hell." She lifted the empty skin that had been her breasts. "I don't think I was expecting this." She looked at him. "You seem all right."

Kai patted himself on the lower abdomen and said, "Seeming is not being."

A thin grin from Ginny, wry, affectionate. "Well. Let's hope Doc is feeling up to a little repair work."

"Sheba's dead."

A blink of shock, of momentary disbelief. Ginny looked at the lights on the woman's coffin, then at a coffin a little farther up the row. "Uh. Shit. Andy's not going to take this well."

"No." That was a strong memory. Andy Mezov and Sheba Zvi, both from Mars, bonded into an old-fashioned permanent-exclusive marriage; he balding and muscular, she short, plump, and always merry, the two of them laughing together, holding hands as often as not, old-style humans exemplifying the tenets of their Natural Physical Culture religion.

No, Andy would not take it well.

The next coffin lid hissed open and Kai stepped forward, looking in at the occupant. "Morning, Doc. Jeez, you look pretty good. . . ."

Ernesto Matel smiled up at him, pale face bland, dark eyes bland, a hairless, sexless mannequin of a man who lay quietly, waiting for the vitality he knew would return. "There are times," he said, "when my rather more simplistic lifestyle choices are a distinct advantage."

Kai said, "Maybe when I'm a hundred I'll feel the same way. . . ."

Ginny, standing beside him, put her hand in the small of his back, fingers gentle on his spine, and said, "Then again, maybe you won't. . . ."

Cold, cold, cold. My God. Everything hurts. Thoughts so confused. Everything hurts, and I'm . . . confused? Is that the word I want? I . . . I, who? David? No, not right. God damn it, that's not my name. Thoughts flat and without texture, like cold, dry sentences written in dusty chalk on an old, warped, too-shiny blackboard, chalk hardly able to stick at all.

Who the hell am I?

Click. Mies Cochrane. Yes. That's the right name. Not David Gilman, whoever the hell . . . brief image of a tall, bony Asian woman, Japanese? Reiko Somethingorother. No, that's not right. Somethingorother Reiko, lying on a sweat-wet bed, spreading her legs for . . . Dark shadow. Fear driving him away. Not me! Somebody else's memory.

Oh. Awareness flooding in with the pain of awakening, shoving aside confusion. *God damn it, boy, get with the program. Indigo* trusted *you. Trusted you.* Sounds now. Voices. Ah, yes. *Time to get up, little David. Time for school.* But, Mummy, I . . .

Very low gravity. Could be anywhere. . . . Not alone. Lying in his coffin, snarled still in the shadowland of death, Mies Cochrane concentrated and . . . a voice, nondescript, inhuman, like static, said: "Time to get up. Rise and shine."

He opened one gummy eye, a wisp of pain lancing down his cheek from even that small movement, forced himself to smile, perhaps more of a grimace in the frozen musculature of his face. "Good morning . . . Can you help me . . . get out?" Shivering slightly, he tried to sit up. Everything felt wrong, his body violated. Not an unfamiliar sensation, really. This is my second time back from the dead. Or is it the third?

Outside the coffin, three bland shapes wavering in the light:

Ortega, Matel, and the captain. Waiting for him. He thought, My God, I wish they'd done a better job of integration. All these . . . things, lining up, just as if they *were* me, waiting their turn. David Gilman, mostly a little boy now, doppelgangered to the grown-up Gilman who labored for the Human Matrix, who played with Indigo until . . .

Hide! Hide, Mister Mies! If they catch you, they'll . . .

Indigo hid him, all right. Hid him inside the woman-body of Harada Reiko, hid him in Tokyo Metropolis, hid . . . The girl again, spreading her legs for . . . He reached up, put his hand on the edge of the coffin, felt Doc's hand pat ·his knuckles. "Doing okay, Cochrane?"

Compulsively, Mies tried to meet the man's gaze, instead saw he was examining him. His body, so shriveled now. Looking at . . . Oh, God. Little prick nestled in brittle brown hair, like a half-full sausage casing, but still there. Still a man. He suddenly realized how comical he must look.

Kai snickered. "Don't worry, Mies. You're not missing anything."

Not surprising we'd be this way, after all that happened.

Suddenly, as though brought back to health, he sat up. The others were already beginning to turn away to tend to some other coffin, laughing to themselves, shutting him out. Just as well, he thought. All right now. We're here. The resurrection was successful. Safe at last. Free from Indigo, safe from ICOPOSI's agents. Hidden. Perfectly hidden. Not like before. . . .

Fourteen years. Two stars in the sky. A star system to explore.

The scientist in me loves that idea. Hell. Little David does, too. Despite his fears, he loved exploring. You remember that much, don't you? Somewhere, deep inside, he could feel the tattered remains of little David smile. Yes. He loves the idea.

So all right. Here we are at Alpha Centauri. Nothing can spoil this for you, can it? The dark eyes of that other David Gilman, grown up now but still a child of sorts, looked back at him somberly. *Have you forgotten, Mister Mies?* The autoviroids . . . No. Put that aside.

You're here. Here among the new worlds. New worlds. Consult the timeline. First stop, Nephelë. Nephelë, mother to the centaurs, herself just stray fog molded into Hera's likeness by a jealous Zeus. Outermost of the two A/B gas giants, about twice the mass of Jupiter but much colder, little more than just discernible from four light-years.

The planetologist Mies Cochrane, personality construct, seemed to swell, doing its thing, calculating, conveying the thrill of being here to his jaded consciousness. Yes, that's me. Yes, it is. But the other ones . . . *The other ones never quite go away, do they?*

Mies found himself floating in the wardroom hatch, blinking at the bright lights, looking at all the others. All of them there, clutched by zero-gee chairs, eating, spooning up thick gruel, sipping from tubes of clear soup. Eating breakfast, that's it. My God, did I black out? No. No, I remember. Getting out of the coffin, watching them awaken one by one, helped from their coffins, standing in the low gee of the centrifuge deck, gagging and yawning and blinking and . . .

"Are you all right, Mies?"

He twitched, holding onto the door frame, looked down at the soft, concerned woman-voice. A jolt of hard awareness. Rosamunde Merah. Of course. He'd watched them put Rosie down, comforting her with a last tender caress, waiting his turn as she closed her eyes, as the coffin lid closed over her. Calm. Knowing she'd awaken again in fourteen years, untouched by his own fears, his doubts.

And floating beside him now, recovering quickly from the years of suspended animation, almost herself again. Still radiant, her sallow, rather bony face somehow improved by its current gauntness, touch of Malay bluntness accentuated by a delicate smile. A smile that comes from loving me. Though love isn't exactly the right word.

"Breakfast," she said. "I like the sound of that. And it's been a while."

Sudden hollow pain in his stomach, almost like being out of breath. Been a while? Christ, we haven't eaten in fourteen years. He smiled. "Where'll we sit?"

Kai, Ginny, and Doc clustered round one small table, eyes only for each other, the three of them talking, serious, as always, captain, chief engineer, ship's surgeon. The real crew, the rest of us specialists, mere passengers.

At another little table, Izzy and Metz, in charge of *Mother Night*'s data processing systems, the essential expedition programmers. Everyone's assistants, a finger in every pie. And so very much in love with each other. Izzy, Belgian Isador Feldschuh, a tall, slim, intense man, dark of hair and eye, pale of skin, his matching Asian bookend Metz, Orang Metzalar Ho, just the same, but dark of skin as well. Look at the way Izzy touches his hand. I'm supposed to touch Rosie that way, when we sit together. Look at them making moon-eyes at each other, feeling it, not just playacting. Not showing a hint of their long history together, when they lived on the Moon, before joining Daiseijin, when they'd been partners in a remarkably successful datagrooming venture. Successful yes, bright, cheerful little Izzy and whiny little Metz. Their tithe added mightily to Daiseijin's coffers.

At the next table? Spence Warvai and Linda Navarro, Warvai already plumping back up, face waxy and decorated with that sharply cut brown beard and mustache, slotlike mouth cutting through the oval of exposed skin, idiotic looking. Doesn't he know what he looks like? Glaring at Linda, just now, surly, but afraid to let loose in front of the others. Angry with her about something. Always a trifle. Linda holding her ground, attractive mouth set, washed-out green eyes calm. Something always coming between them. They don't belong together. Stuck together by default, in each other's beds as we trained, calling it love, no doubt.

Poor Linda. Look at that face. Compelling. She couldn't be an easier target. Woman-eyes, holding forth the promise of fulfillment. The preliminaries are already over, done long ago, as we geared up for the mission. Well. Just a few well-practiced phrases . . . I can just see myself, facedown in her luxurious brown-haired cunt. I can . . .

Short, sharp shock. Indigo eyes looming out of the depths. NO, MISTER MIES. NOT WITH YOUR MOUTH. VISUALIZE YOURSELF *IN* HER, THRUSTING, THRUSTING, SEMEN JETTING, AUTOVIROIDS ON THEIR WAY . . .

And over in one corner, Andy Mezov, looking like a redheaded historical re-creation, like an actor made up to play Lenin, sat alone and contemplated an empty chair, eyes shining, as if with unshed tears. Andy Mezov, expedition physicist, specialist in particles and fields, Mies Cochrane's other half. Staring at nothing. Why is he staring at the chair? Of course. I remember. Remember awakening with the others on the centrifuge deck. Ten people rising from their coffins. One. My God. He's looking at the ghost of his wife. In his mind, only an hour ago, they kissed and hugged and went off to sleep. Now . . .

Rosie said, "Oh, Mies. I feel so bad for Andy. Let's sit with him."

Mies felt a touch of cold horror, other personalities boiling up, ruthlessly suppressed. "Yes. Let's." But. Andy? No. Image of living Sheba, clothes off, in the moment of their tryst. How do I feel about her? Do I feel bad about her being dead? Do I feel sorry for Andy? No. Just sorry about wasting autoviroids. Visions of her dark-haired crotch fading into the grave, carrying them with it.

Hanging suspended in one corner of Ginny's cramped quarters, one leg looped around part of the bed's support structure, Kai watched the woman float before the flush-set wall bureau and fuss with her belongings. Mutterings about dust and degradation, and how could it have *gotten* like this in only fourteen years?

As beautiful, he realized, as the first day I saw her, repair modules already finishing up their work, smoothing out puckers of flesh, reinflating those sleek, tan breasts, leveling the contoured planes of her face. I thought she was so unique when I first saw her, Virginia Vonzell Qing-an, who would command the first interstellar flight, half Chinese, half Azanian, that latter half subdivided between blond Dutch Afrikaaner and pure black Xhosa genes. Unique and beautiful. Slender seen from the back, waist flaring out into hips and muscular buttocks. Almost enough to make me wish I was fully male again. Almost, but not quite.

He was floating free now, drifting across the room, drifting up behind her, touching her on the shoulder, still remembering that first day, at the merchant commerce academy, then remembering the night they'd gotten together in her dorm room. The grin, looking over her shoulder, was still the same. She turned and gave him a hug, flattening still-baggy breasts against his smooth chest. A whisper: "I think I missed you, Kai."

Missed me. Just a thing to say, of course. A nice thing. No memory at all of those unconscious years. No, it's only been a few *hours* since the particle beam catapult shut down, since we checked our bearings, gave the computer systems their marching orders, and, Now I lay me down to sleep . . . Memory of Sheba Zvi, dead before she woke. Memory of Andy Mezov's tears when they told him.

Sound of the door opening behind them, a faint techno-whisper. And a soft, neutral voice, "Well. Should I leave you two alone, or can an old sod like me join in?"

Looking over Kai's shoulder, Ginny said, "Hi, Doc. Just getting reacquainted."

"I gave Andy a light hypnotic and set him to putting the galley in order. I, uh, think he'll be all right."

Ginny nodded. "For now. You think he'll be able to adjust to this? He and Sheba . . ."

Too right. Of all the people on board, they were the two who'd depended most on each other. For pretty much everything.

Doc shrugged, holding onto the door frame with one hand, bracing his feet on the floor. "Hard to say, of course. I've . . .

taken a quick look at Sheba. Nothing I can do. Quite possibly nothing anybody can ever do.''

''Christ.'' Ginny's face was serious, biting her lower lip, gaze turned inward for a moment. Captain's duty, after all . . .

Doc said, ''Everyone else is fine, more or less. A few major repairs here and there, nothing I can't handle. You two came through about as well as anyone.'' He looked at Kai. ''How about you? Back in working order?'' Brief grin, a bare showing of even white teeth in that nondescript face. ''Or did I come in too soon?''

''I don't think that's what we were up to, but . . .'' Kai sat down on the edge of the bed, ankles locked under the ledge, knees apart and looked down at his crotch. Probing with gentle fingers. ''Seems like the passive parts are all right. I can't make anything else happen, though.'' Would I miss it if it stayed this way?

Doc floated over to the bed, holding him by the knees, leaning in for a closer look, sighed and shook his head. ''I checked your tagalong records. There's nothing mechanically wrong. Probably just synaptic disconnect. If it hasn't, ah . . .'' quick look at Ginny, ''cleared up by tomorrow, I'll get into the hardware and see what's wrong.''

Wry grimace. ''Thanks.''

Ginny looked away, rolling her eyes in exasperation. ''If you two *fellows* are through making plans for my nightlife, there's still work to be done.''

Kai nodded, pressing his knees together, holding himself in a seated position by grasping the undersides of his thighs. ''Right. Primary systems check is all done. I've got Mies going over the records right now. Andy's job, of course, but . . . He'll track back through the whole entry sequence looking for trouble before he pulls the particles-and-fields data for the preliminary science net.''

''You think there's something wrong?''

A quick nod. ''The chromobraking shield should've come off right after we emerged from A's corona and before the engines blipped, putting us in the first ellipse.'' The image, just the image of what had really happened, lying behind those dry words:

Mother Night falling out of the starry sky at better than a quarter the speed of light, impulse applied at Sol by a particle beam catapult acting on her magnetic sail. Starship falling from the sky, from an infinite depth, brushing right by interloper Proxima Centauri, scraping across the face of the class M dwarf, losing energy to the chromosphere. Then off into the sky again, crossing the 13,000 AUs to Alpha Centauri, chromobraking at A, chromobraking at B, emerging on a steep trajectory around the double star's barycenter, arriving intact, fully fueled, ready to explore.

A brilliant plan. One that let the Daiseijin's dedicated Ten Thousand fund humanity's last hope of salvation from their own pockets, while all the unwashed, unthinking billions walked blindly toward oblivion, while their government collected taxes that went toward its own preservation, though the species' terminal event-sequence had already come over time's horizon. Ghost of Thomas Malthus, three centuries dead: *I told you so. . . .* Ghostly murmurs of satisfaction.

Starships, they said, are impossible. No civilization disposing only the resources of a single star system can leap the gulf between the stars. But it had been possible for a hundred years, *easy* for a generation. A commercial powerplant, bought by the members' eighty-percent tithe. A military particle beam, bought at the cost of huge bribes to elected officials. The same magnetic sail system used to retrieve inanimate cargoes from the Kuiper Belt. An ablative heat-shield system, cooled by laser radiators developed for use at the Cismercurian power complexes. And a fully fueled, completely equipped, manned cargo freighter of the sort used by the Oort Cloud mining operations, projected to the stars.

Kai said, "Once we identify the causative event, it should be possible to predict where systemic damage took place. That'll make it easy enough to fix."

A nod from Ginny. "You think this had anything to do with Sheba?"

Doc shook his head before Kai could answer. "I backtracked through her records. Programmer error. Her maintenance modules were shut down by mistake about six years ago."

Kai felt a cold hand slide invisible down the back of his neck. An error lurking in the software that could've taken us all. "She didn't, uh, wake up, did she?"

Ginny gave him a momentary, peculiarly horrified look.

Doc said, "Um. I don't . . . think so."

Don't think so. But not *sure*. Sheba Zvi awakening in darkness, locked in her coffin, alone between the stars. Wondering for a while, hours, days, maybe weeks, just what had gone wrong.

Things always go wrong, thought Kai, technology the mirror of our lives, resurrecting the dead past and throwing it in our faces. It's been like that for a long time. Forever for me. Growing up on Titan, I don't think I *ever* thought about where I was, where we all were. Ever thought about what might happen if . . . if the machines let us down. Life on Titan just like one more sunny day in the springtime. . . .

In his memory, it had always been warm under the dome, warm even when you came right up to the end of the universe, put your back to the domepark's rolling yellow-green landscape, trees and lawns and dark trails paved with sharp-smelling pine-bark mulch, flooded so brightly with the light of a hundred big multispectral lamps, warm when you came and looked out into the world.

The thing you looked at, of course, was always the sky. Sky defined not by the low, rolling gray hills of the horizon, not by the slow, wispy boil of Stataera's white-lit habitation fog, but by its own clear remoteness. Dim orange murk layered so far overhead. Layers delineated by striations of dark indigo. The fat, fuzzy pink blotch behind which lay the faraway sun.

Sky marked by Kai's age-old desire to . . . see. See right up into that black sky of glittering stars, black sky of faraway worlds. I want, he thought, to look back on Titan, watch it recede, fuzzy orange ball turning to a red marble, to a speck in the sky. To nothing.

When you're eleven years old, it's just a dream. You know it'll come . . . someday. But that someday is a forever away. Turning away from the dim sky with a sigh, Kai put his back to the dome's warm anchorwall, hard gray plastic vibrating softly against his bare skin, looked back out across the parkscape, wishing he were alone.

If I was alone, I could take off my shorts and sneakers, run naked through the grass, go swimming in the duck pond. Even play with the ducks if I wanted to. . . .

He was walking now, hands behind his back, following the anchorwall, going behind the trees, parkscape blotted out, with it the sounds of children playing. All alone here on Titan. So few people. So much space. . . . Smiling to himself. The lies they tell in school, when they tell us how lucky we are. But I'm not playing outside now, naked and free, outside where the cold winds howl. Stataera wasn't very big, after all, people cheek by jowl, living in cubbies and warrens while they pretend to be free.

Walking down into the woods now, not on one of the carefully maintained trails, but between the trees. Walking where you're not supposed to walk. A whipping from my parents if I bring home a trespass ticket, but . . . whippings worth what you get them for. Worth the freedom to . . . do. Standing still now, still in the forest, pretending it was the forest primeval, standing flat-footed, listening to the wind in the treetops, pretending it didn't come from those fans you could hear thudding away in the distance.

Someone whispering nearby, spoiling the illusion that he stood in a terrestrial forest, stood alone, savage, naked, no more than warpaint on his skin, stood flat-footed and firm under a natural one-gee with muscles grown for the task. But, someone whispering. Whispering softly . . . Kai crept forward, crept slowly, mouth slightly dry, wanting to swallow, not wanting to make a swallow's little cluck of sound. Kneeling now, leaning forward, reaching out, carefully parting the underbrush, looking into the hardly lit space below.

Girl in a short green playdress, kneeling, bending forward,

back of the skirt rising up smooth thighs. She had her shoes off, toes digging into the chunky loam the gardeners had so carefully smoothed, long, straight black hair flowing down off her head, hanging in the boy's face as she kissed him, kneeling between his denim-clad legs, boy's bare feet motionless, pointing upward.

Boy with his back against the smooth gray trunk of a birch tree, kissing his girl, head tipped to one side, face invisible behind the black ball of her skull. One hand on her arm, steadying her. The other reaching down to stroke the inside of her thigh, reaching up under her dress, moving smoothly back and forth, girl rocking her hips a little, arching her back a bit, then bowing it. Boy's hand coming off her arm, sliding down the long curve of her back, down to the back of her thigh. Resting there. Helping her move, perhaps.

Through her legs, you could see the front of his jeans humped up, something moving there, like an animal trying to get out. Kai could feel the same animal coming to life in his own shorts. New sensations, that had grown increasingly frequent over the last year or so. Some of the boys, in secretive whispers, claiming they could *do it* already. Most of them, probably all of them, lying.

Boy's hand on the move again, moving back up her buttock, this time under the dress, pulling the dress up over her hip, bunching it up onto her back, girl's buttocks smooth and round under sleek white underpants, smooth and round, dark shadow in between. Boy's hand going up to her waistband, feeling around, rubbing softly at the base of her spine, all this going on while they kissed and kissed. Boy's fingers getting under the waistband, while his other hand continued to palpate the cloth between her legs. Boy's hand going back down her buttock, dragging underpants along with it, exposing her bare skin, other hand coming up to help, panties now no more than a roll of cloth stretched around the tops of her thighs.

Kai staring, mouth open, breath falling shallow from his lips. Watching the boy hold the girl's buttocks, pulling them apart, almost as if pulling them apart for him, showing him the dense black hair between her legs. Boy's hand reaching down there, smoothing the hair, boy's fingers feeling around, finding, evidently, what they were looking for. Kai's breath stopping entirely as one of the boy's fingers found the right place, seemed to slide on in, up to one knuckle, then another . . .

A stiffening then, girl reaching under, between her legs, grabbing him by the wrist, making him stop. Boy's voice a querulous little murmur. Girl saying, "It hurts a little bit. I don't think I'm ready yet."

Boy: "In a few minutes? Or . . ."

Girl, shaking her head, black hair rolling on her shoulders: "I don't know. It scares me a little, Jerzy."

Boy, whining: "But Neeshah . . ."

Girl sighing, sitting back, naked buttocks resting on naked heels: "Oh, Jerzy. It'll be okay. You'll see . . ."

Kai backed out of the bushes, slowly, cautiously, silently, just as silently walked away, uncomfortably conscious of his own little erection. Walked away into the shadows, found his own birch tree to lean against. Pulled down the front of his shorts, took his dick in his hand, started doing to himself what the girl had been doing to the boy, eyes shut, head filling up with visions of the endless vista between her legs.

Dark places there, shadows beneath the hair, boy's finger sliding in, first to one knuckle, then the next . . . Sudden scald of something like nausea, muscles clenching at the base of his belly, penis hardening up in his hand, expanding in his fist, muscles clenching one, two, three . . . *Ow.* Something like hard pain between his legs, something clenching in the space between his asshole and his nuts . . .

Kai opened his eyes, heart pounding hard in his chest, astonished, a little afraid, and stared at the hot white puddles scattered across his stomach, at the white thread connecting the little opening at the end of his dick to the last and smallest of the puddles.

Oh, he thought. Of course.

Mies sat alone in his cubby on the ship's science deck, clutched gently by a zero-gee chair, going through setting-up exercises with the eyebubble remote. God damn Rosie, he thought. Unfathomable. People just unfathomable. Memory of her coming to his room, of putting her arms around him, refusing to be pushed away. Floating beside him, like a fish in a sea of air, trying to kiss him. Some part of me trying to say, But, I can't . . . *Can't? Of course you can. You always can.*

Rosie fumbling at his zipper, getting the fly of the coverall open, putting his shriveled little prick in her mouth, sucking on it, like a baby sucking a nipple. God damn it. Mies willing himself flaccid, willing himself numb.

Dark Indigo eyes staring at him out of the depths. IF THE AUTOVIROIDS GO DOWN HER THROAT, THEY CAN'T GET TO HER OVARIES. UP HER VAGINA, MISTER MIES. THAT'S WHERE THE AUTOVIROIDS GO.

But she's already infected. Revulsion. Induced revulsion. Already infected. Don't want her anymore. Remembered image of Rosie crying, shouting at him, as he pushed her away, tucked his little red prick back in his pants, zipped up, bobbing in air, bobbing out through the door, deaf to her fury, coming here. Coming here to be alone.

Get the information synthesized. Get ready for the meeting. Inquiring minds will want to know . . . God, just *do* something. *Doing* will help, will . . . take you away from all this . . . bullshit.

Soft voice: ''Mies?'' Almost a whisper. A male whisper. Tentative. Helpless.

Mies jerked, looked up, swallowing convulsively. ''Oh. Ah, hi, Andy.''

Balding redhead floating in his doorway, eyes glassy with hypnotic sedatives.

''What is it?'' *Shit. You know the right words. Say them.* ''Can I help?''

A pale imitation of a smile. ''I heard you were assigned to do the data search. I'd like to help. I . . . I'd just like to get back to work. Do my job.''

Of course. She's dead. Dead and gone, you poor bastard.

And . . . yes. *Doing* will help you . . . escape. Mies said, "Sure. Come on in, Andy. Sit down."

His scientist persona was now gaining control, losing interest in everything else. Enormous amounts of data for him to analyze. And, of course, his identity and future depended on his ability to manage this challenge, already parsing out the results of the experiments, generating a degree of self-maintaining interest, the afterimage of wan self-disgust fading slowly. He quickly became little more than an interested observer as they began their discussion with the complex computer systems and memory overlays that made up the ship's eyesystem, the AI-driven network of local databubbles, quasi-independent subsystem motes, and packet-switched information floaters that ran just about everything.

It presented him with data about the planetary systems first, knowing that they were where his primary interests lay. From Earth, no planets had been detected around Proxima, and their quick passage through the system had only turned up a handful of Ceres-sized objects in extremely irregular capture orbits. Clearly, something had disrupted the little system at some time during its early history. Perhaps an encounter with a different star, perhaps some chance event in its nursery days.

B and A both had regular systems of terrestrial planets, four each, easily detectable from Earth and already named after centaurs and other creatures from mythology. No surprises there, though he would have to study the images taken during distant flybys in greater depth. The A/B gas giants, first of the planetary bodies discovered from Earth, were coming up, their numerous moons prime sources of materials for the colonists to come. Nephelë was already growing in the real-time televid, bands and belts nearly lost in deep, blue-white haze.

Backtracking through the stellar passages, each one distinctive. A's measured in minutes, B's lasting tens of seconds, and back to Proxima, its eight-second-long encounter recorded in a short but extremely detailed portfolio. Of course, no instrumentation could survive outside the shield during chromobraking, so the encounter itself was observable only through field-dynamic changes on the barrier's inner surface.

Ah, yes, an anomaly there. Pretty severe, too. The particle counts were orders of magnitude higher than expected. The maximum temperatures were much higher, as well, as though they had penetrated much deeper into the chromosphere than planned. Or that dim little Proxima's chromosphere deviated spectacularly from the predictions.

As soon as the shield temperature dropped, two banks of instruments had opened out, and he looked at a captured visual image from the rearward-facing set. Less than two minutes after the corona passage was over, they were already more than 1,800,000 kilometers away, showing the diminutive star as a small, mottled disk in the wide-angle vid.

The eyebubble supplied him with needed information to develop the scale of the image. Diameter at chromosphere boundary 459,720 km. Mass within 0.09 of Earth-based estimates. No problem there. But what in the hell was that? Protruding from the star was a slightly curving filament of light, a prominence of sorts.

Out of the electronic deeps, Andy's voice, bemused, still hypnotized, said, "Well, there's one reason the chromobraking shield didn't come off. It's a miracle we're here at all. The interaction of an induced field in the ship's structure with Proxima's own magnetic field had an unexpected effect. We somehow caused the field lines to cross."

Mies said, "Not good."

"Fucking lucky is what we are," said Andy, voice filling with something like . . . life? "Proxima's a flare star to begin with. Its field lines are hopelessly tangled, and every so often they intersect, short-circuiting the magnetic flux and releasing enormous amounts of energy. No one predicted this effect, though. We must have dragged the field lines across one another and generated a flare as we passed out of the corona. It looks like it propagated along our magnetic wake, following us like lightning up its return channel. If we hadn't been going so fast, it would have vaporized the ship, shield and all. As it was, the shield must have sustained heavy damage."

Transfixed by the image, Mies said, "We would never have known."

The meeting came, Mies and Andy floating together in the hatch that led to the main science deck compartment, the one with the big light table surrounded by zero-gee chairs. Ginny, Kai, and Doc, the ruling triumvirate, sat there now, sat in chairs, looking down through the light table into a 3-D starfield. The scientist persona took note with interest: *Yes, the stars were just for show, for flavor.* What was in the stereo tank was a schematic of the Centauri system, A and B, with planets and moons, in neat orrery array.

Doc was reviewing the data, bland face serious, expressionless. He looked up at Mies. "Okay. Do we have to change the mission plan?"

This was the question he'd been expecting. He glanced at Andy briefly, then channeled into his science self and let it take over. "Well, yes and no. The unforeseen events in Proxima's magnetosphere pose the most serious questions. Certainly the colony ships, when and if they come, will have to take a different route across Proxima or bypass it entirely. We'll have to do an analysis of our pass and the flare it generated before we can hazard a decent guess. Andy's compiling a real-time soft x-ray map of the star's surface. We appear to have passed directly over the major starspot group, and in retrospect that doesn't seem to have been wise."

"What about chromobraking across the polar regions?" asked Ginny.

Andy said, "That could pose additional problems."

Kai: "In any case, the good news is that while our ship was damaged by the flare, we weathered the remainder of deceleration, the braking episodes at A and B, fairly well. There was no real damage aside from what happened to the shield structure itself, and that appears to argue that the Proxima encounter can be jettisoned."

"Well, yes," said Doc, mannequin face unmoving. "The extra stars are a luxury." Other starships, going to single stars, Tau Ceti, Epsilon Eridani, would have to take their chances with a deeper plunge into the stars' chromospheres, much shorter, sharper braking encounters.

Listening, somehow excluded, Mies felt a small quiver of resentment. "Remote observation of the principal planets is also ongoing. The quick-pass reconnaissance done before and after the chromobraking phase has given a glimpse of both the A and B planetary systems. As suspected, the surface of Pegasus, A4, is completely hidden by aqueous clouds. Though the evidence is mounting that Pegasus has entered its greenhouse period, it's clearly the place to look for biological activity. Pegasus' large retrograde moon, Bellerophon, also looks quite interesting. The new observations have confirmed our decision to explore the A system first."

Doc: "Nothing new on the other worlds?"

"Some things, of course. Eurytion, B4, is beginning to look like a place worth visiting. The surface, though dominated by water ice, shows a surprising degree of variability. It may in fact have one of those elusive sub-ice oceans that never materialized in the solar system. The other interior worlds increasingly appear to be analogous to Mars or Venus. Not to say that they won't be fascinating in their own right and very useful as resource supplies." A quick glance at Rosie, seeing her frown. Of course she'd frown. Analogs of Mars and Venus? Then . . . no life. Nothing for the biologist to do. That makes you supernumerary, Rose. Doc's PA, Kai's assistant engineer, looking after our life support.

Ginny sighed, released herself from her chair, and floated, looking down through the light table at ersatz stars. "So. The upshot is that a first-look analysis indicates Alpha Centauri is all the things that we thought from Earth-based observations. The possible loss of our return ability is no big deal."

Mies had a brief memory of his early days with the Human Matrix, compiling the first big population/resources spreadsheet, realizing just how short a period the human race had left. That one thought, borne home so viscerally, had brought him here inexorably, though the side-trips had been far afield and stranger than he could have anticipated.

It still seemed so *odd* to work side by side with these people, who'd reached the same conclusion, but then stepped back from the obvious solution and devoted themselves to this ultimate delaying tactic. Not that he hadn't gone through the same logic-train, thinking that humanity's only hope was to spread among the stars. But Indigo's Malthusian equations had taken him further, to a vision of hundreds of worlds in agony, thousands perhaps, millions . . . each one shutting down in succession to the accompaniment of a hundred billion screams.

And the autoviroids inside him were waiting. Waiting for the next sexual encounter, programmed to go forth and hide themselves in the woman's genome, with only one goal in mind, the termination of meiosis, the halting of conception. Birth control. Definitive. Undetectable. Involuntary. Irreversible. Self-propagating. The only sane answer. And just as necessary here among the stars as back on Earth.

The next morning, morning by the clock, drifting in the strut-obstructed red-lit darkness between *Mother Night*'s superstructure and the hull of the chromobraking shield, Kai could almost make believe they were back in the Solar System, that the adventure had yet to begin. Somewhere inside the ship, then, Sheba was still alive, red-cheeked, happy, Andy Mezov by her side.

Right now though, Andy was floating beside him, holding onto a frame member, waiting, silent. You'll get over this, Andy. But not now. And the interim will be difficult. Ginny's voice in the earphones: "Okay. Life-support local copies you cycled out the midships airlock and transited back aft."

As they made their way aft, the space widened out a few meters. Before them, the translucent blue bells of the ship's four reaction-plena projected from the ship's body, piercing the shield to the outer void. Christ, it'd be a hell of a sight, being in here with the engines firing.

Most of the ship was a huge boron carbide sponge filled with a two-percent water solution of ninety-percent-enriched uranium bromide. When the valves opened, when the plena filled with that hot salt water, neutron inhibitors left behind . . . Call it a continuous nuclear explosion, violet light flooding out through the walls of the sapphire plenum piping, flooding the space inside the shield, nuclear plasma rushing away into space with an exhaust velocity of 4,725 meters per second, just under 1.6 percent of light speed.

Not enough to get us here. Not in under a hundred years. But the ship's 27,000 tons of fuel and ten-to-one mass ratio translated to 12,000 kps of delta-vee. Delta-vee to burn while exploring an entire virgin star system. Kai said, "We'll exit through the magnetic sail containment structure . . . Andy?" He could see the man looking at him through the faceplate of his helmet, eyes liquid highlights in the semidark.

"All set. Let's go." Not quite without affect, but close.

Kai anchored himself beside the circular access hatch and began ratcheting the lock-lever mechanism, momentarily wishing it was plugged into the core's command circuit. But only wishing, and only for a moment. These things were left off the circuit, were actuated with three-century-old mechanical technology, for a good reason. Imagine then, *Mother Night* sliding across the very photosphere of a living star. And just then the computer system decides it's time to pop the aft access hatch and take a look outside. Programmer error. Or even just a magnetic-induction glitch. And the surface of the star comes pouring right in.

Outside, the night sky was, as before, black and full of stars. If you didn't look at Alpha Centauri, if you didn't know to look for that first magnitude star in Cassiopeia, you'd never know we weren't still home. Kai kicked himself away from the hull, whispering brief instructions to the suit's operational remote, then looked at the extra star. The famous "W" had an extra jag, connecting it with the Perseus star-stream. Right. Sol. Just a star with a name. He turned around his long axis and

looked back toward the ship, back past the crouched, drifting
shape of Andy Mezov. "*Jesus.*" No more than a murmur.

Ginny: "What is it?" A hint of nervousness in her voice.

In the beginning, on the day they left, *Mother Night* had
looked like the starship of everyone's dreams; sleek silver cigar-
shape, encapsulated by the chromobraking shield, the four arms
of the magnetic sail support structure projecting from the aft
end, surrounding the four muzzles of the nuclear engines. Like
a living thing. Like an iron hydra. He said, "Scorched all to
hell and gone. One of the sail arms is bent forward in its mount.
There's a, uh, buckled segment along one side of the shield. Not
quite enough to rupture the containment seam. Close, though."

Over the comlink, he could hear Andy whisper something,
almost like a prayer.

Ginny said, "What was that?"

Andy: "We'll never get it apart now. Probably jammed for
good."

Kai nodded to himself. They could fly the ship with the shield
still attached, of course, but getting the landers out, proceeding
with their mission . . . "It's not as bad as it looks, Gin. We
can cut the sail support structure off and back the ship out
through the hole."

Moment of silence, then, "Yeah. I see. Tight enough
squeeze, though."

Another whisper from Andy.

"What was that?" Ginny, worried.

Soft voice: "It's beautiful out here. Sheba would've loved to
see this." She would indeed. Kai looked back at the sibling
stars, now less unequal in brightness and closer together.

Ginny said, "Might as well get to it. And make up our minds
we're not going home anytime soon, no matter what we find
here."

There was that truth to be faced. What if the star systems of
Alpha and Proxima Centauri had nothing to offer, despite the
bright promise of two centuries' telescopic observation? The
contingency plan called for *Mother Night* to refuel among the
ice-moons and asteroids sure to be here and head for home,

burning all her fuel on the way out, chromobraking at Sol a hundred and thirty-five years later. Sol or some other star, depending . . . If, a cold voice whispered, if and only if we find enough radionuclides to salt the water. Well. Not now, though. Not now, in any case. Kai floated in space, looking at the crumpled spar, at the dented hull, and sighed. "I guess we'd better get busy."

Alone in his room, Ernesto Matel flagged the security interleave system, overrode the safety parameters, locked his door, and had the high-level command interpreter display his notes. All right. We're here, everything's working, more or less. Erasmus will be glad enough when he hears. Image of the old man smiling, yellow face a maze of wrinkles, bright eyes barely visible for all the flesh surrounding them. Image of him clapping me on the back. *Good work, Ernesto! Well done.*

He cracked open the ICOPOSI personnel files and began annotating, adding to the impressions he'd been building up, the personality profiles he'd been revising for the past five years. Wouldn't old Erasmus Hiraoka be in for a shock if he saw *this*! Well, maybe not, though he'd never said a word. . . . He's just too damned intelligent to think a generation of Daiseijin operations would go unpenetrated by the government. The shock would be finding out it's *me*. So many false operatives in the system just to provide cover. So long as they keep finding them, here and there, at various levels, they'll never think to look . . . up here. Or out here.

He started folding up the files, putting them away, stopped when he came to Mies Cochrane. All right, so you know it's there, even if you can't put your finger on it. After five long years of training, observation, of getting to know a man, however closed and self-contained . . . hell. It ought to be more complete than this. Cochrane's file is less than a quarter the length of any of the others. Even mine.

Thin smile. Hell of a thing, that. If someone, Kai or Metz perhaps, ever runs a really *thorough* router trace on the data processing core, winds up unferreting these files . . . Well, there'll be a file on everybody, unbiased. Maybe they'll just think it belongs to the eyebubble's command interpreter. It'll make fascinating reading for them.

Mies . . . god damn it. Too many axes. Not enough data. Like there's an undiscovered personality disturbance. Passive-aggressive, yes, like a good tenth of the human population. But . . . not quite. Something off here. Whatever it is, it doesn't interfere with his work. Damned good at it. Kai seems to like him.

He finished folding away the files, restructured the interleave protocols and released the packet. System motes drifted back in, safing his little hidey-hole behind layers of false programming.

Doc undressed, attaching his clothes to the closet rotisserie, drifted over to his sleeping net, slid into the mummy bag. Cold comfort. Go to sleep now. We'll be busy tomorrow. He ran his hands down his sides, liking the way the once-again smooth skin felt, paused to scratch an itch in the almost-featureless place between his legs.

You still miss her, don't you?

Yes. I still miss them all. Marianne was only the last. There was a brief, detached memory: He and Marianne in bed together, the night before she was killed. Making love. I can remember the way her eyes looked, staring up into mine, unfocusing as her orgasm began, expression half smile, half grimace.

Then she died in that senseless wreck, because somebody with an ideological grudge decided it was time to put a wooden shoe in the machinery. . . . Nothing left of her. Nothing to bury. Nothing to see, to trigger my grief. As if she went away and decided she just wouldn't come back. Like there was something wrong with *me*.

And so to work. Agent of the government embedded in the Daiseijin organization, almost from the beginning. I remember hoping, when I volunteered for the first deanimation reference shot, wishing it would fail. So what if ICOPOSI needs me? And waking up, of course, the technicians telling me, Well, there's a few bugs to iron out.

So easy to die. Why haven't I?

Because there's work to be done. You joined ICOPOSI sixty years ago, because you believed in its mission. Do you still? Good question. In some ways, ICOPOSI, silly acronym for a silly bureaucratic name, International *Command* Organization, for God's sake, Organization for the Promotion of Scientific Investigation, like something from some ancient spy movie, was the human government's only functional agency, mandated by the old UN to monitor the evolution of science and technology, to make sure nobody accidentally put paid to the human race.

Go to sleep, you old fool. Work to be done.

TWO

Ginny held Kai in her arms, smooth skin to smooth skin, as they floated gently inside the sleeping bag affixed to her bunk, in the darkness of her cabin. Held him in her arms, face nuzzling against the side of his neck, breath warm behind his ear, hands trailing down his back, down across his buttocks, massaging the outsides of his thighs.

Waiting, he realized. Waiting for me to do my man's task. Waiting for me to act, so she can react. No sign of it yet. And Ginny, culture-changed from the Person in Charge, bold captain of the First Starship, to a woman breathing softly, a little quickly, waited for him. Her heart was a gentle rhythm against his chest, transmitted through soft, newly resurrected breast tissue. He could feel her nipples on him, stiffer, rougher than they usually were. If we had light, if we were looking at each other, I'd see them pulling together into little almost-black bunches, dark skin puckering, rising up, as if telling me what to do. He stroked her back gently, scratching here and there at imagined itchy spots with his own well-manicured nails. Waiting. I'm waiting, too.

Ginny pulled back in the darkness, holding him away for a moment, seeming to assess the situation, then leaned in again and kissed him, tongue turning in her mouth so it could slide rough-textured across his own, one hand stealing up against the back of his neck, holding him just so. And that other hand coming between them, fingers moving on his chest, hand turning, creeping downward, careful not to tickle, across his stomach, pausing on his hairless vulva, fingers almost recoiling, a tension forming between them.

She took a deep breath, and whispered, "When it's like this . . . when we . . ." A breathy sound, almost like laughter. "I feel like I'm seducing a little girl."

Tension. Because I feel like a child? Or like a girl? Maybe both. Because Ginny always used him like a man, expecting him to be ready. He said, "Sorry. I . . . I guess I'll have to talk to Doc again in the morning. If you'd like . . ." He made a move as if to draw away.

"No!" She held onto him hard, showing the force of the muscle that underlay her sleek skin. The hand was moving down between his legs, not quite shaking, knowing what to do because they'd done it before from time to time, for variety's sake. "Whatever happens is all right. It's . . ." A moment of silence, words failing to form themselves, then she leaned in again, renewing the kiss.

Kai put his own hands in all the right places, familiar places, warm and damp places, feeling her breath quicken on his face, feeling her slide closer, pressing herself against him. And waited. It works this way. Reason unknown. Let her go at her own pace. Form and figure of a woman, no, a *girl,* coloring expectations, but the hormones, the mind, the inner clockwork. Male mammal.

Ginny's fingers slid between his labia, rubbing the little nubbin that could pretend it was a clitoris, slid further back, finding the vestibule of his vagina, sliding in, finding moisture, palpating the forward wall . . . Kai felt a sharp lance of pain, abrupt and hard, and grunted, felt his penis extrude suddenly. He felt Ginny's grin against his face, felt her pull back, hand reaching for a more familiar object. Felt his own brief moment of regret, but then . . .

She was smiling, kissing him, already at work on him, back on familiar ground. You could feel the roles switching back, assuming their established polarization with an almost audible snap. He heard her whisper, softly, "Afterward. Afterward, I'll sleep. Sleep and dream."

I wish I could see into those dreams.

Drums hammering in the Antarctic night, *boom, boom, boom, boom,* slow drums, monotonous drums, deep-pitched kettle drums, hammering home their message while the winds of Antarctic midnight, the high winds of June, shuddered and moaned without. *Your time has come,* the Mother had said, and stripped her bare and hung the chains round her neck . . .

Little Ginny at twelve, chained naked to the Family altar, waiting, afraid, staring up through the skylights of the hypocaust, wide-eyed, at the black night of the cloudless midwinter sky, cloudless, bare black sky of a billion, trillion bright stars, black sky with a slow-moving, folded curtain of pale green rays, southern lights shifting back and forth, back and forth, dreadful, anticipatory rhythm, slower than the drums, far slower than the hard drumming of her heart . . .

You knew it was coming, you knew it was . . . but. Only the knowledge, not the real thing, head sunk in comforting old stories, escaping, escaping real life until they let you hide no longer, snatching you, snatching you from your bed, snatching you away . . .

Ginny tied down with silver chains, face up to the midnight sky, listening to the drums and the wind, arms stretched apart over her head, legs stretched apart, as far apart as they would go, splinters of pain in her hip joints, Mother shushing her when she cried. *Be strong, my babe, your time has come. . . .*

Time and . . .

" . . . reallydoreallydoreallydoreallydo . . ." Women's high-pitched chant a steep-rising shock in her breast, Mothers dressed all in gauzy white dancing round the dark hall of the hypocaust, bare feet on steam-warmed floor . . .

" . . . stop, stop, when will it stop . . ." Deep-pitched bark of the Fathers a hard counterpoint, Fathers stamping their heavy heels, *thud, thud* on the floor . . .

" . . . alwaysdoalwaysdoalwaysdoalwaysdo . . ." Mothers'

voices a thrilling shriek, riding up and down her spine, making her feel so cold, while sweat started on her belly, rolled over her sides in big fat drops, wetting the altar's black leather upholstery . . .

Sudden clench of belly muscles as the Senior Mother danced up to her, danced up between her legs, reached out and touched her, leaving behind a dab of sharp-smelling, vinyl-smelling ointment, there, *right there,* ice-cold between her legs, cold on her tenderest place . . .

'' . . . neverdoneverdoneverdoneverdo . . .''

Then the Fathers, always, '' . . . stop, stop, when will it stop . . .''

Mothers dancing past, one by one, reaching in to smooth the ointment, touching her there, one by one. Then the Fathers, heavy dancers, thumping by, bending low, standing tall, like dark fires, shadow in place of flame, one by one doing the same, until the ointment was spread everywhere . . .

Fathers and Mothers mingled now, dancing around her, dancing together, Mothers' gauzy shifts whirling high as they danced, whirling high, exposing sleek thighs, thighs dark and light, exposing their hips, exposing their patches of womanhair, hair light and dark . . .

Senior Mother dancing up between her legs, dancing while the drums drummed and the men's heels stamped, Mother whirling slowly, slowly, slower than the music, slower than the heels, seeming to fall in a swoon, Mother falling to the floor between her legs, long pause . . .

Sudden shock, Ginny straining against the chains, shivering, hearing the Mother's faraway voice: *Your time has come, no use in fighting it* . . .

But . . . fighting the chains, fighting . . .

Sudden shock of the Mother's mouth between her legs, woman's face rolling between her legs, rolling in the ointment, smearing it around with her face . . . Ginny's soft grunt of dismay as the woman's tongue, Mother's tongue, pushed into her, plunging deep into her, then out again, tongue sliding up and down, round and round on that little button . . .

Ginny thinking, It's punishment. Punishment because a Mother walked in on me last week, walked in on my bath, caught me fingering myself there. Idle moments, grown from childhood, the discovery, so long ago, that there was a secret place down there, a secret nice place that enjoyed being touched, a place that felt nicer, ever so slowly, as she grew older . . .

Place warming now, despite her fear, as the Mother's tongue rubbed and rubbed, as the cold ointment grew warm between her legs. Mothers, of course, knowing, just knowing what to do and how . . .

Mother rising now, dancing away, other Mothers falling between her legs now, one by one, for a quick nuzzle and a lick, a nuzzle, a lick, a dancing away . . .

Mothers and Fathers dancing round her, dancing round and round, the space between her legs seeming to grow cold again . . .

Senior Mother leaning down, bending over her face, Mother's face smelling of cold ointment and saliva, smelling of the place between her legs. Mother kissing her on the lips, gentle good night . . . Mother's tongue forcing its way in, tongue on her tongue, forcing her to taste . . .

Ginny tried to turn her head away, turn it away gagging, turn away from her Mother's smile, but . . .

Hands, big hands, Father's hands on her knees, Ginny looking down to see the Senior Father, pale hair and eyes gleaming in the auroral light, pale hands on her dark thighs, sliding toward her . . .

Mother took her by the chin, Mother's dark face and dark eyes hardly visible, just shadows in the night, Mother taking her by the chin, tipping her head back so she could see . . .

Ginny stunned, facing the dark place between her Mother's legs, Mother stepping forward, dark hair on Ginny's face now, Ginny's face forced between those soft, strong thighs, place between her Mother's legs, smelling so much like the place between her own legs, musty-sweet smell . . .

Mother's hair . . . damp. Slick wet coming from her opening.

Slick wet getting on her face.

Father's hands on her down below, hands on the place between her legs, blunt fingers feeling around, looking for *her* opening. . . . Ginny's heart hammering in panic now, Ginny smothering, gasping for breath, Mother's wet getting in her open mouth, Mother's wet going up her nose . . .

Father's blunt fingers replaced by a bigger, blunter thing, panic leaving her will-less, building her fear, knowing just what was happening, mind-voice going no, no, no, but . . .

Stretching down there, stretching of skin, faint burning of skin, as if someone was touching her with an invisible hot coal. . . .

Sensation of her Father's hard thing sliding into her opening, sliding in and in, seeming to disappear from her consciousness, sliding in so she could feel its length, but . . . going where? Nowhere. Just sliding in. Father pausing. Father sighing. Mother laughing as she rubbed and rubbed that wet hair in Ginny's face. Mothers dancing, shrieking their chant, Fathers dancing, barking, stamping their heels on the hypocaust floor.

Senior Father sliding out. Cool sense of relief . . . *no!* Belly muscles clenching as he slid back in, pain a bit less, but still there. Then out, then in, out, in, thrusting to the rhythm of the drums, Mother rocking faster and faster on her face, getting wetter and wetter . . .

Mother's voice, suddenly hissing, "Stick out your tongue, little bitch. Stick it out or . . ."

Fear. Hard fear. What could they do that was worse than this? All sorts of things. . . . Ginny stuck out her tongue. Put it where her Mother's hard-swollen button could get on it. Mother sighing, sighing, a whisper of, "Thank you, Daughter . . ."

On and on and . . .

Father suddenly jamming himself in hard, jamming himself in as if he wanted his whole body inside her delicate little hole, jamming himself in, holding still, hard rod of flesh growing harder still, growing impossibly bigger, a dense agony of stretching and . . .

She felt it jerk inside her, jerk again, again, as if trying to lift her off the altar, lift her against the silver chains. Warmth in there somewhere, not so different from when she'd lie back in the bath, open the hole with her fingers, let a little hot water inside, let it in for just a moment, warm inside her, then pushed back out with a little belly clench . . .

Belly clenching now, involuntary, triggered by memory, Father gasping with something like joy . . .

Mother wet on her face, wetter, wetter, rubbing, rubbing . . .

Mother crying out, woman-voice bell-like in the night, *Oh*. Hot, slick wet cascading over Ginny's face, running across her cheeks, getting into her hair and ears . . .

Then they were off of her, Father withdrawn, Mother stepped away, cool air on her wet face, on the wet place between her legs, stars and southern lights visible once again.

Ginny lying sprawled on the altar, stunned, unthinking, in the silence after the drums had gone.

Mother's voice, whispering softly, "There now, my babe, my own. You're a woman now, forever more . . ."

Woman?

Hard anger suddenly burning in Ginny's chest, drowning out the softer burn between her legs.

Enclosed in the sleeper, cradled in Rosie's hot embrace, Mies closed his eyes once more, trying to relax. The ship surged slightly, faint, distant movement, an infinitesimal change, pushing them against the netting. Soothing probably, for someone used to it. But his mind was seething . . . seething with . . . No, I can't call it thought.

Dark eyes on him, out of the depths.

Rosie's hands on him. Not caressing him, you see. Nothing so bold and deliberate. Just holding him as they floated together in the net, pretending to sleep, her breath long and slow, inhalations deep, long pause between this one and the next. Arms around him. One hand on his chest, breasts pushing into his back.

The other hand drifting somewhere near one hip. Touching him, floating away, touching again. Fingers chancing to brush against his pubic hair. Once, just once, delicately scraping along the length of his flaccid prick. Image of the damned thing in his eyes. FULL AGAIN. REAL AGAIN. FULL OF MEAT AND FAT AND BLOOD AGAIN. RISING UP TO CONFRONT HIM AGAIN. YES, MISTER MIES, whispered by the voice-no-voice, Indigo eyes on him in the dark. READY TO GO AGAIN, MISTER MIES.

Image of Rosie's hand, small, soft, delicate, approaching him in the night, unbidden. Hand curling under, palpating his scrotum, caressing the cargohold of universal death. What does she think when she touches them, feels the soft, almost untouchable roundness, maybe notices the other tiny structures, maybe feels me wince, anticipating. Once quick, hard squeeze, that's all it'd take, Rosie dear. You don't know what you've got in your hands.

Image of her small hand, curling round his soft prick, massaging, thumb on one side, the upper side, since she was behind him now, reaching round, thumb pressing an unsuspected implement of universal destruction down into her palm, the warm well of her crooked fingers. Image of his erection building itself, tension deep inside, reservoirs spilling open, seminal fluids mixing with deadly sperm cells, flagella whipping, sending them on their way.

To his amazement, he found the earlier distaste, induced revulsion, giving way to something akin to desire. Just the right touch, light as a feather, with the suggestion of warm heft behind it. An autonomic response, nothing more. Certainly Rosie's willingness had nothing to do with it. Ah, yes. Maybe, just this once. Imagine her continuing. Imagine her finishing you off this way, semen jetting away uselessly into the air. NO. NOT THAT WAY. TURN AROUND. PUT IT IN HER. THRUST. THRUST. SPURT. SPURT. ANOTHER ONE BITES THE DUST. But she's *already* infected. Rosamunde Merah can breed no more. The autoviroids have done their job. Sudden revulsion, rising up out of the depths.

Her breathing quickened. "Mmmmh." A little smile played across her lips. "Now, Mies?" She stretched luxuriantly, netting catching them again.

"Sorry," he said, "Sorry. I . . . still don't feel quite right."
He felt her fingers, toying with his hardened penis. Not quite
right? you could hear her thinking. Sense it in the way her
fingers rubbed and kneaded. He said, "I don't know how to
explain it."

Another long moment, then the fingers moved away, hand
gliding back up onto his hip. A waiting, then the hand moved
away, Rosie releasing him, turning away, rotating in the air
until only her back was touching him. He listened to her breath,
faster, then slower. Crying? Maybe. Or maybe just lying there,
staring at darkness, sullen, angry. No way to know just *why*
I've pushed her away. Or why I wanted her in the first place.
How much of you is left in all this mess? A thousand eyes
staring at him out of the imagined inner darkness.

Mechanically, he moved away from the woman, found the
slack opening in the netting, and pulled himself out. The lights
started to come up, anticipating his needs, but he shut them
down again and made his way to the little bath cubicle, closing
the curtain behind him. Very dark in here. Sympathetic darkness. I've got to think my way through to a conclusion. Got to
work it out. This is no damned good. I should have anticipated
what would happen, but . . . I just wanted to escape. Get away
from all the things that ever happened to me. Away from Indigo. From the world.

Why was it all right in Arizona, all right during all the years
of training? A thin smile. Of course it was all right, fucking
my way through whole regiments of Daiseijin technogirls. Ah,
that cocksman Mies! What gives him such a fatal attraction?
SO, DON'T KNOW WHAT TO DO? FOLLOW THIS RULE SIEVE.
WE EVOLUTIONARY BIOLOGISTS HAVE IDENTIFIED A WOM-
AN'S EMOTIONAL BUTTONS. PUSH THEM, ONE, TWO, THREE,
IN THIS ORDER, AND SHE'LL BE ON HER BACK, QUICK AS A
WINK, WHILE YOU SLIDE IN, SLIDE OUT, THRUST AND THRUST.
SPURT. SPURT. DONE.

NOW GET OFF HER, MISTER MIES. SHE'S INFECTED. GET
OFF HER AND GET ON TO THE NEXT. Memories of orgasms.
Memories of that inner voice springing up at just the right

moment, egging him on. COME ON, MISTER MIES. THE QUICKER YOU'RE DONE, THE QUICKER YOU CAN MOVE ON. The memories made him conscious of his persistent erection. Autoviroid-driven libido wanting him to get out there, get to the hustling, cruise the bars, cruise the dormitories. This one, that one, little swatches of hair and heat like impossibly powerful magnets.

Hand on his erection now, just like Rosie's hand, just like every woman's hand. Brief, uneasy memory, of that earlier time in Tokyo. An experiment, they said. Mies the man, made to look like a woman. All the while a man is screwing you, specialized autoviroids will be crawling up his urethra, crawling down his seminal vesicles, crawling inside his testes, setting up *new* little death factories and . . . a new soldier. Soldier of Indigo who doesn't even know.

Memory of how other men's pricks had felt in his hand. Just the way my own feels. So confusing. When I feel this, it's me making myself happy. Hand on prick, going up and down . . .

Indigo eyes in his head in the stygian here and now. NO, MISTER MIES. NOT THAT WAY. NO. But the familiar sensations were there already, defeating the Indigo eyes, that strong, triumphant feeling of inevitability, a tingling at the base of his spine, sense of gathering storm in the muscle behind his scrotum . . . uncontrollable pulsing, a drumbeat of ecstasy, quickly ended. The Indigo eyes closed and the voice went silent, personalities going away, folding themselves up, going home, leaving Mies alone in the dark. "Light," he whispered.

The infinite darkness became a tiny white room, Mies floating in the enclosed space, orbited by wriggling amoebas. Autoviroids wasted, going to their minuscule deaths. *Indigo.* Somewhere, they make new autoviroid soldiers. Somewhere, the drug factories build their tailored brew. . . . Maybe the reversal experiment worked, too. Maybe, somewhere, there are men posing as women, infecting other men. Maybe there are even women . . .

No, the mechanics of female biology weren't so conducive to building new autoviroids. At least, not without risk of detection. Only testes were suited for the job. That's why they gave up on the ersatz female notion. Besides. The whole notion was against everything that Indigo had come to stand for. Against the sacred rules of evolutionary biology, you see. Man the predator. Woman the prey. Always been that way. Always will. Anything else is . . . heresy. So much appeal for little lost David Gilman. He always wanted to be a predator. Poor David. Always the victim, never the perpetrator. . . .

A casual glance at the eyebubble sensor brought hot water cascading onto him, drawn by a sudden wind of circulating air, enveloping his body in its clean heat. He pulled down the respirator and hooked his left arm around the handhold, then began scrubbing his body according to the well-worn ritual. After a few more moments of savoring the shower, he shut it off. I still won't be able to sleep, he thought. Can't let those thoughts get started again.

He pulled on shorts and T-shirt and slipped out of the room, making his way up through the lab deck and docking cylinder to the command module. As he swung from handhold to handhold, his scientist persona began to come alive, a comfortable mask to hide behind. Images from his recent memory emerged in stately procession.

Ah, yes, he said to himself. *Context. Yes.* Remember an arresting image of an excessively bright world, shrouded by featureless white cloud, and in transit across its face an intriguingly complex moon, almost a quarter as big, reddish yellow like Mars, blotched with darker areas, some of them fascinatingly regular, his eyes playing the old *canali* game. They'd come off chromobraking at A on a heading for Nephelë, the closer of the two outer gas giants, but fortune had provided a hasty flyby of the giant terrestrial world Pegasus and its wonderful moon Bellerophon. This was the best of the images, taken from nearly two AU away.

Unfortunately, the inner worlds, however interesting, would have to wait. Now they were boosting into the shallows of the joint A/B planetary system, the realm where stable orbits were possible around the two stars. Here, more than a hundred AU from the barycenter, the detritus of the whole system had formed into an outer solar system analog, two Jovian worlds in nearly circular prograde orbits, each with a retinue of ice-moons of various descriptions.

Named Ixion and Nephelë after the putative parents of the centaurs, these two planets had beckoned to humanity for nearly a hundred years. And though telescopic evidence of satellites had eluded the most careful searches, we knew they *must* be there. It had been the moons of the outer solar system that had provided the wherewithal to make the final jump to a spacefaring species. At Alpha Cee, they'd expected no Oort cloud because of Proxima. These moons would have to do.

Old these stars might be, eight billion years and more, but the moons would be waiting, in deep freeze, as they had been since the far gone day of their birth, volatile moons with their cargo of raw fuels and organics.

The hatch to the command module was open, and Mies swam through, kicking against the rim for a little extra speed, changing course to end up holding onto the back of the pilot's chair. In a few hours Ginny would be sitting here, directing their braking maneuver into high-Nephelë orbit, Kai in the flight engineer's chair to her right.

Just the two of them. Two people and a big computer system all that was necessary to fly humanity's first starship. And the rest of us? We've come here to see to a host of new worlds, see if there's a place where the men and women of the Daiseijin can come and live and escape the long-ordained fate of humanity. . . . Even now, that little particle of anger coursed through him. *Escape.* Dirty word to the men of Indigo. Escape, run away, let all the endless billions go down to dust and decay, when the solution was so damned *simple.*

They were only a few hours out now, and Nephelë was naked-eye visible, a big gray-bright fleck against the dark of deep space. Technically, the ship was still hyperbolic, closing in fast, would cover the last million miles in just under an hour and go whipping down through the gravity well, down and out, on its way back to the interstellar deeps.

Above the double horseshoe of the command console, the huge world was visible in telescopic view. The scientist snatched awareness, studying it with rapt interest, automatically noting similarities to and differences from Jupiter. Out here, so far from either star, it was much colder, and the system's greater age meant that the planet had lost much of its heat of contraction to space. The result was a dim, hazy world, its clouds buried deep under a thick atmosphere of hydrogen contaminated with aerosols and, most importantly, methane.

Far down through the bluing layer, there were still belts and bands more or less tinted with the ruddy compounds that gave Jupiter its color, but here the total effect was one of colorlessness, the reds neutralized by the preferential scattering of shorter wavelengths. More oblate than Jupiter, Nephelë looked squat indeed, like a leaky gray basketball squashed at the poles. Data in his eyes. Mies noted that the fast rotation was almost exactly in the plane of the two stars, and the orbits of the moons, for moons there were, were also in this plane. Some dynamicist would spend his entire life trying to figure out just how such a star system could develop. It was difficult to visualize a protostellar nebula with all these countervailing forces. *Perhaps the cluster-capture theory will prevail after all.*

Now the moons were coming into view: working inward, Atalanta, Deianeira, tongue-twister Mnesimache. Three maidens who'd met with foul play at the hands of the rude centaurs, placed here at a comfortable remove from their tormenters, protected by a nebulous mother.

Atalanta, about three-quarters the size of Earth's moon, was quite distinctive. Bright water ice, very lightly cratered, not even as patterned as Europa's crack-ridden surface, but at both the leading and trailing points were continents of dark rock, giving a first impression that the thing had wide-spaced caterpillar eyes. The real-time images, in which the trailing hemisphere had rotated into view, showed a considerable gray transition zone, a mixture of dissimilar terrains.

Deianeira was a Callisto-sized object with a smooth surface of water ice contaminated with silicates. An albedo in the 0.4

range meant that the ice was considerably darker than the equivalent Jovian moons, but there was no clear evidence of geology: at ever increasing resolution Deianeira showed no distinctive terrains at all.

Mnesimache, almost as large as Mars, was also craterless, and the terrain varied in both albedo and color in an almost regular pattern, giving the impression of an already variegated marble that had been crazed by heating and sudden quenching.

The spectral readings of the moons presented a true puzzle. All three seemed composed entirely of water ice, with none of the more volatile ices that would clearly be expected in an environment this cold. That none of them had a palpable atmosphere was no surprise, since even nitrogen was quite hard at these temperatures. But where were the craters? When Proxima dispersed the Oort, thousands of comets should have pummeled these worlds. No clear signs of recent geology on the inner two, either.

Mysteries indeed for the scientist to ponder. And what about the others? David Gilman, cowering in the dark? Reiko-chan, moving in horror through a woman's world? All of them stark with amazement, struck dumb with fear at the notion of being . . . here.

By the time Nephelë bulked large in the control room's windows, Kai and Ginny were strapped in their seats. Kai watched his displays, watching the numbers build, particles and fields sizzling beyond the hull, deflected by shielding by deft lines of magnetic force. Okay for now, but soon energetic particles would start leaking in, breaking reaction chains in cellular machinery, kicking the hell out of nucleic acid codons.

Reminding us, he thought, staring out the window at the soft, blue-gray gas giant, that our technology is not at all magical. We can be here for a little while. We can't stay. Strange to place such a limit on a species that can aerobrake through the winds of a living star, but . . . no technology is indistinguishable from magic. Technologies have limits. Magic does not.

"Planetary insertion tee minus one minute."

Ginny said, "Acknowledge. Fifty seconds, *mark.*"

High-energy radar scan showed a clear path ahead. Not much we can do if something gets in the way now, moving at close to three hundred kilometers a second. I wonder if the explosion would be visible from Earth? A seventy-two hundred megaton fission explosion, plus whatever fusion gets cooked off in the water . . . Maybe. With a *real* good telescope?

"Thirty seconds," said Ginny.

Kai motioned to the turbopump start sequencer. There was a faint vibration in his chair, transmitted through the ship's structural members. Picking up clutter on the forward-looking radar now, sideband scatter off the clouds. Smearing, too. At this velocity, we're getting a little inadvertent synthetic aperture.

"Five seconds."

"Go for main engine start." Another control called up, the valves snapped open, hot salt water starting its short journey.

"Three."

"Commit to ignition sequence." Kai imagined he could hear the water gurgling as it flooded into the turbo pumps, pumps spinning up, forcing it through valves into the engine plenum reaction chambers.

Zero. Ignition . . .

A brilliant blue-white patch suddenly flared on top of the cloud deck directly underneath their track, bright light that swept along with them, and a giant hand grabbed Kai's chest, forcing him back into the seat padding.

Ginny said, "Plus five."

"Systems nominal. Minus twenty." And fifteen and ten and five, numbers flickering in his eyes, graphs renormalizing every few milliseconds, dancing against a flickering display. Zero and silence. Ship shuddering under them as the continuous explosion of the engines' firing sputtered out. Behind them, nuclear fire was a long, fading red arc against the night, dissipating as it lifted above their orbital track.

Kai said, "Okay, that's it. Atalanta orbital insertion in two hours five."

*   *   *

Seated in the command pilot's chair of planetary lander *MN01*, Kai could feel his heart pound. All right. You've done this a thousand times. So this rocky ice moon is named Atalanta, rather than Europa, rather than Ariel, rather than Triton. So it circles a planet of Alpha Centauri rather than Sol. So what? It's just a world, under a wide and starry sky. Four people headed down to land on the first extrasolar world. World of another star . . .

From the copilot's position to the right of the center console, Mies's voice was dry and calm. "Flight systems are at norm status. Go for undock."

Kai glanced over at him, at that face with its familiar guarded expression, always behind a gauzy curtain. He thought of the German word *scheide,* a word Ginny'd taught him one dark and happy night, and smiled. "Ginny?"

Her voice whispered in his ear: "Go for separation. Wish I could bend the rules." Over the radio link from *Mother Night*'s command module he could hear someone laugh softly, briefly, a sound quickly suppressed. No one, he supposed, really wanted to hurt her feelings, but she'd voiced her wish so often. From the backseat, Linda and Spence were muttering to each other, a brief distraction. Excited about the landing to come? No. For Christ's sake. Arguing. Spence mad at her about something. Something about no sex last night.

Kai checked his own instruments. Hydrogen slurry stable. Compact fusion reactor ticking over at hot idle. Propulsion turbine spun up and waiting for someone to feed it reaction mass. Soft eddy currents running around the compensating toroid's racetrack. "Okay," he said. "We're off."

Like that, the lander undocked, vibrating gently as the double ring rotated and disengaged, little pulses pushing them forward in their retaining harnesses as the RCS system fired, puffs of cold hydrogen backing them away from the mother ship.

MN01 and its sister ships were among the few items unique to the starship's equipment, developed by Daiseijin engineers because nothing like them was needed in the long-settled solar system, so nothing like them could be bought off the shelf.

Seen from the outside, the landers were fat disks, moderately convex on the bottom, flattish, rounded cones on the top. Two holes: an engine nozzle on the ventral side, docking adaptor at the dorsal apex.

Inside, it was clever: the bottom half of the capsule was engine, fuel tanks, control gyros, whatnot. The top half was a mere framework, supporting the docking adaptor, surrounding a space that held the pressurized control room/surface rover. After landing, the upper part of the hull would unfold like four great petals, leveling and stabilizing the lander, extruding a ramp down which the rover would roll.

In the vidscreen, the outer wall of *Mother Night*'s forward engineering space suddenly started to recede. Linda whispered, "It's hard to believe we're out here all alone."

Spence said, "Hell, you're almost as far away, out in the Oort. I mean, thirty thousand AU? If something fucked up, you'd be just as screwed."

Good old Spence, always the pudgy little tough guy. Kai rolled the lander into a heads-down attitude, jerking the controller so *MN01* made crisp movements around her axes and heard Mies gasp softly, breaking character just a little, for just a moment. Atalanta, all brilliant white ice and jagged black mountains, filled the sky overhead, rolling past, shadows shifting, like ghosts in some chiaroscuro kaleidoscope.

Beautiful. He said, "Okay. Let's go down." He hit the throttle, turbine whining hard behind their backs, blowing out a long, dense plume of cold hydrogen, and then they were falling toward alien ground. A minute, two, three, building to ten, while the land flattened under them, horizon losing its curve, changing from image, to world, to flat reality, then the engines were pushing again, settling them in their seats as they hovered above a motionless plain.

Mies said, "The surface ice is fairly cohesive. Not much dust. . . ."

Kai chopped the throttle and the lander shuddered as they touched down, shuddered, and was still, relaxing metal creaking softly around them, fading into silence. "Ginny?"

Her voice again, colored with a faint tang of envy: "Copy you down, *MN01*."

Kai sat quietly for a few seconds, absorbing the slightly canted view out the window, across a smooth, white-bleached plain, at the distant summit of a broken nunatak, almost as black as the sky. Beside him, Mies was sitting forward, glassy-eyed behind his faceplate, looking at data, at Kai. "Um . . ."

Linda said, "Look at these readings! The percentage of deuterium in the bed ice is . . . zero. And the ratios of the salts are all screwed up, too.'"

Mies: "This material was sputtered off the trailing hemisphere, and there's been little meteorite infall to remix it."

Kai motioned the chair arms to let go, getting to his feet, bobbing on his toes in the ice-moon's low gee. "All right, then, let's get the rover unlocked."

Another minute, swelling to five, petals opened and the rover rolled down onto crisp, icy ground, then Kai and Mies were standing together on the platform outside the rover airlock, looking down at the surface, a little more than a meter away, Lin and Spence behind them, inside the airlock, waiting for them to get out of the way.

Kai turned and looked at Mies, peering into the darkness inside his helmet. "I, uh, don't want to be, uh . . . *first*."

There was a brief, puzzled look. "You want me to . . ." He gestured at the surface.

Spence's voice rustled in his ears, exasperated. "Will you guys just fucking go down the ladder?"

Kai watched a sudden look of amazed hope wax and wane on Mies's face, quickly replaced by a sterner look. Suspicion? Something. Impulsively, he reached out and took Mies's gloved hand in his own. "Ready?" And, "One, two, three . . ."

Together, they jumped down to the ground, loud, brittle crunch coming through the suits as boot soles broke through dendritic ice. Still holding hands, looking up from the simple landscape into the starry sky, up where *Mother Night* and all their friends waited for them to speak.

Some words, some significant words, *something*—That's one

small step . . . Lafayette we are here . . . *Anything*. But all Kai could do was search out Cassiopeia in the midnight sky, look at the bright, glittering diamond of Sol, and whisper, "You know, from here the sun doesn't look like a place where you could hide two hundred billion human beings."

The other man let go of his hand and turned to look at him, face somber and unreadable. Up on the lander/rover's porch Spence and Linda appeared, bulky in their white spacesuits, looking down at them, faces invisible behind glassy faceplates.

Spence said, "Cute. Very cute. Can we get to work now?"

"Well," Kai said finally, "we're not going to get much closer than this in the rover." He stared up at the nunatak, trying to gauge the size of the thing. It was an enormous, faceted jumble of rock, almost like row on row of smashed dominoes. They were parked among small, dark lumps of stone sitting on the ice which gave way to a clutter of larger rocks and then finally to the apron of talus which buried the base of the mountain.

Crouching behind him, leaning over his shoulder so he could peer out the window, Spence said, "Talus can be better for prospecting than bedrock. The hammering's already done."

Mies, softly: "These rocks are all igneous, extrusive, mostly plagioclase, broken away from the nunatak by the action of small meteorites long ago. The bedrock facies may give us a hint of Atalanta's early history, but this doesn't look promising."

Kai said, "I keep forgetting this place has been sitting here intact for more than eight billion years. The micrometeoroid flux must be quite low." More time for the meteors to be swept up.

Mies said, "That's what's odd, Kai. We should be seeing signs of Proxima disrupting Alpha Centauri's Oort. More craters of all sizes, impact gardening of the surface, but it's just not there."

"Might as well get outside." Spence straightened up, looking down at Linda. "Plagioclase, eh? Not likely to be any ore deposits, then."

She shrugged. "We can bulk process, if we have to. It's been done before. I'd be happier if the radionuclide salts weren't absent, though. We won't be able to use our autonomous systems."

Ginny's voice said, "Kai? We're coming up on horizon intersect and LOS. We'll pick you up again in about forty minutes, hopefully post-EVA."

"Okay. That ought to do it." Kai called up a dosimeter and internal monitor. Interesting. An unmodified human would be in deep shit already. Two-sixty rem, despite the fact that they'd spent most of their time in the relatively well-shielded rover. "Much more than an hour outside, we'd probably start to feel a little queasy anyway."

Mies said, "I'd like to get up-slope and take a look at the stratigraphy of the formation."

Kai looked up at the summit, angular black rock against a starry black sky, and thought about some of the things Ginny'd told him about her Antarctic childhood. This must be like that. I wish she'd been willing to go sightseeing down there, while we were on Earth. "All right. I'll go with you. Spence and Lin can stay with the rover and do the slope cross-section sample run. Okay?"

Linda was already on her feet, heading for the inner airlock door.

Twenty-seven minutes later, EVA time almost half gone, Kai stepped into shadow and looked up. Alpha Centauri A had slipped behind an outlying peak, and it took a moment for his eyes to adjust. They were several kilometers from the rover, higher up among a jumbled disarray of boulders. Here, the nearly vertical cliff face of the nunatak filled the sky. Mies was some distance behind, muttering about pillow lavas, investigating something or other.

When he'd found a good, level spot, he turned and looked into the sky. B was hardly bright enough to matter, and the sky seemed filled with stars again, everywhere but down by the horizon, where the whiteness of the ice washed them away. There was Proxima, bright as Aldebaran but much ruddier, not far from the Pleiades. He tried to judge how far Sirius was out of true.

A sense of discovery, of exhilaration. Only now it's real. No sentient eye has looked upon this scene before. The edge of the shadow was sharp, like a silhouette image cut by an artist's knife, with hardly any sense of the double-exposure effect he expected. Beyond it, the granular ice surface was like clean and creamy paper, blackness of the shadow wiping away that faint grayish tinge it had when you saw it under the right conditions.

Kai glanced to the right, along the shore of the mountain, where it disappeared under debris. In the distance, out beyond the edge of the pediment, there was . . . something. Kai went over to the edge, straining to see, climbed out as far as he easily could.

"Uh."

Mies' voice in his helmet: "What?"

Kai stood transfixed, listening to the faint whisper of his suit's air circulation system increase as his skin flushed slightly. An odd numbness started up in his face, a prickling sensation in the shorter hair at the back of his head. "You'd, uh, better come here. There's . . ."

Exasperation: "I'm right in the middle of taking a sample, Kai. This outcropping shows a big discontinuity. We're finally getting somewhere."

No shit. Kai was afraid to blink, afraid the thing would turn into a mirage, would ripple like something seen through a window covered with flowing water, would fade slowly away, leaving empty ice behind. "You'd better come anyway . . ."

"Goddamn it, Kai . . ."

"Get the fuck over here!"

There was a long moment of silence, the sound of Mies's agitated breathing loud enough to activate his helmet pickup, then, tightly, "All right. Coming."

Kai stood quietly, waiting, drinking in the scene. In a few

minutes Mies came up behind him, muttering under his breath. "Okay, what the hell's so—" A sudden choking sound, then, whispered, "Holy shit . . . is that a crater?"

"A mighty strange one, if you ask me. It looks like a god-damned swimming pool."

A swimming pool that had melted under some strange, intense heat, square sides sloping inward, patches here and there catching the light from the suns behind them, shiny, as if the ice were still wet. Which was, of course, impossible. In the middle of the square crater was what looked like a pile of rubbish, black material forming a kind of central peak, oddly shaped, a little too tall and square to be a natural formation.

Kai said, "Ginny, are you picking this up?"

Static. "*Mother Night,* do you copy?" They'd still be occluded, but the ship had sensitive ears and a computer system that could pick wheat from chaff.

A fuzz of static in his ears, a crackle, then her voice came in, somewhat patchy. "Yes. No video . . . can't really make out what . . . out of the core shadow in . . ." There was a long, heavy burst of static, then her voice came in clear: ". . . telemetry. You should be back at the rover by now."

"No. Not an option, Ginny. Mies, we're going down to take a look."

Mies said, "Well. As long as we don't get *too* sick, we can recover back in the rover."

Spence said, "Kai? Mies? We're going back in the rover now. We'll tap your video feed."

Standing at the smooth rim, the thing was big, maybe a half kilometer square. The bottom was perfectly flat, marred by two or three small craters, almost translucent white. The central peak was even less regular than it'd seemed, incredibly pitted and broken, parts looking like they'd flutter away in the slightest breeze. If there was any breeze here.

They began picking their way down the inside slope, which steepened to about forty degrees. Mies said, "You know, I keep expecting it to be slippery, it just looks so unnatural . . ."

Kai, who was from Titan, where there *were* slippery slopes, had been feeling the same way. "What natural process would form something like this?"

That got a snort of laughter from Mies. "Nothing *I* ever heard of. But there must *be* one, and I will be damned interested to find out what it is."

Spence's voice: "You're not the only one. It *looks* like what old mining processes leave."

Linda: "In the old days, back in the eighteenth, nineteenth centuries, ad hoc mining groups would be afraid to shaft mine. Afraid to go under the ground. They'd dig down to the ore and get some out. Move on down the deposit a bit, dig down again . . . It'd leave a line of holes a bit like this."

Now they were walking across the floor of the crater, which, from the bottom, looked even more like a concrete swimming pool, or . . .

Mies: "Hey. This looks like an old limestone quarry I once saw in southern England."

Kai looked around, surveying the walls. "I guess so. No terraces, though. There're a few things like this out among the moons of Saturn, of course. All man-made."

Mies, deadly serious: "It'd be funny if this turned out to be the work of natives."

Kai said, "Don't be silly . . ." Why are we so *interested* in this, then? "If there were natives able to get out to their own ice-moons, we'd've detected them from Earth. Nobody's been here before."

"*We're* here."

"Yeah, but we—" Kai stopped suddenly, letting the implication sink in. Right. But *we* came from another star system. He turned suddenly and started walking quickly toward the central peak, thinking, Craters this small don't *have* central peaks.

Ginny's voice in his earphones: "Video signal acquisition coming up. Kai could you . . . *what the hell is that?*" The microphones compensated for the sudden increase in her voice's volume, but there was some distortion, dramatizing the exclamation.

Mies, standing beside Kai now, said, "Yeah."

Flaky black stuff, like metal from the bottom of the sea. Long, regular, curving lines, all sagging downward, as if under the force of Atalanta's small gravity. Things that were obviously separate structures, again regular, again sagging . . . add-ons. Separate components. Places where the thing appeared to have dripped, making little black splashes on the white ice.

Mies said, "Well. What do you think? Natives who don't use radio? Starfarers who beat us to the punch? Back at the end of the American Ascendancy, in the mid-twenty-first . . ."

Ginny said, "This thing looks older than that."

Kai nodded, inside his suit where no one could see. None of these people really here anyway. Just me. And Mies. "Yes. It does. No easy way to tell, though. I can't even *really* say it's artificial . . ."

Doc said, "Jesus, Kai, *look* . . ."

"I know, I know." Long slow exhalation, like the ghost of a sigh. "It looks like there's an inhabited star system somewhere in our neighborhood." But not the one *we* were sent to. "It looks like one or the other of the expeditions will be finding something interesting." One of those other Daiseijin starships that went out in their wake, looking for a new home for humanity.

Quietly from Ginny: "Yes. That is a possibility."

Mies said, "More than just a possibility." He reached out and touched the thing, watching as tiny bits of black dust, almost like ash, tumbled slowly to the ground.

Linda suddenly said, "Is Rosie on the link yet?"

Doc: "Uh. Just a minute."

Mies: "Wait'll she sees . . ."

Kai thought, Unexpected. Too unexpected. The expedition's putative xenobiologist is going to be . . . Image of Rosie, quiet, staid-seeming Rosie, jumping for joy, forgetting everything else. He said, "We'll have to go back to the rover and get a scanner head. Doc, you'd better get Izzy and Metz started on setting up the SAE interface. The RAMload takes a while."

Ginny: "Get a contingency sample first."

"Right."

Reluctantly, they turned away.

Finally, they were back at the crater, all four of them now, puffing from the labor of carrying inertially massive crates up the long, steep slope to the icefield by the foot of the nunatak. They set up the scanner head so its multiple, overlapping fields of view could take in the "central peak," attaching sensors, aiming particle beam devices so their tracks would intersect at various points inside the thing. Setting up the direct beam link to *Mother Night,* which had gone into a tall elliptical orbit so it could loiter over the research site.

When everything was ready, Kai plugged the scanner's waveguide connectors into the special jacks on his suit, glad he'd been part of the team that had selected the ship's hardware. Hell of a note if we'd packed an SAE, then made no provision to use it! Mies and the rest, monitoring the feed through his bubble's interface circuitry, would need no direct connection.

Ironically, the Synchronoptic Analysis Engine had almost not come along. It was a massive, power-hungry experimental device that could consume up to ten percent of the ship's total power output, and synchronometric analysis was a new bit of science, one not everyone could believe in. But a time machine of sorts *would* be useful for the location of geological resources.

He powered up the scanner heads, watched them started to nod and twist, back and forth, up and down. No sense invoking the particle beamers. We shouldn't even have brought them along. Not enough battery power to run the bastards here. Need to run a bleed off the rover's reactor. He began feeding raw data.

Science is based on theories, one succeeding the other at ever increasing levels of precision. Quantum Electrodynamics leads to Quantum Chromodynamics, to the twenty-first century's Transformational Dynamics to the twenty-second's Holotaxial Dynamics.

It wasn't a theory of everything, but it was pretty close, accounting for everything we could see, on every scale. The universe is composed of myriad tiny things that once were called particles—quarks, leptons, various intermediate vector bosons, a few peculiar things that seemed to have no function, or even nonexperimental reality. Perhaps the particles, which could participate in wave phenomena, were not solid things at all, but tiny propagating fields? Okay. Fields of what?

It made the universe seem like a phantasm, a complex moiré pattern of interacting ghosts.

But the particles were tiny physical objects after all, n-dimensional closed loops that came to be called superstrings, every one just like the next, their differential characteristics determined solely by patterns frozen in the particle's vibrational energy. It turned out that when two superstrings collided, they could trade energy patterns in a zero-sum interaction. They could change, even go into association, so long as the sum of both objects remained the same. That was Quantum Transformational Dynamics, in which gravitation and light and matter were equivalent.

But what was a superstring? What was it made of?

The answer, embodied in Quantum Holotaxial Dynamics, was, "Nothing." A superstring is the n-dimensional endpoint of something called a hyperpipe, an n^n-dimensional channel that unfurled from . . . someplace. Unfurled from a dimensionless entity embodying the sum total of all properties, all particles, time, space, energy, everything. Someplace without a name.

Which was when the long-neglected pure mathematical theoreticians stepped forward and said, *We've* been calling it Platonic Reality for a long time now.

And every particle in the universe is connected to every other particle, across all space and time, as if they were all the same object, everything in the universe just local manifestations of the same transfinite surface.

God plays at dice with the universe. And throws the dice where we cannot see. And lets us look at the end result. If the dice are thrown enough times, you begin to understand what's going on inside those hidden hands.

Kai said, "Iz? How're we doing up there?"

The man's voice said, "Spooler's loading now, Kai. Metz says we can offload into the top of the sieve chain in about . . ." Another voice, Metz's, said, "Now."

Through the interface, the scene in the crater was unchanged. A sense of movement at first, gone in a second. Kai looked around, exploring the dimensions of the artificial imagery. The corroded black hulk sat there, unchanging; in the middle distance were the slump-sided, translucent crater walls.

The nunatak also had not changed. Alpha Centauri made two bright trails across the sky, spreading and coming together, spreading and coming together. The rest of the sky was streaked with impossibly precise lines of light, some bright, most spider-web thin. The brightest of them, undoubtedly Sirius, was . . . fuzzy. He found others that were fat and blurry, spread out across the entire curve of their parallax.

He whispered, "Okay. It's not ours." A careful look. No blurring at all on the machine, if that's what it was. "It's been here a hell of a lot longer than two hundred years."

Ginny: "I see. Go a little deeper. Extend the reach to a few thousand years. . . ."

The star lines began to smear, tracking overhead as Alpha Centauri fell back through the galaxy. The crater walls seemed to shimmer and sharpen, but the black hulk was unchanged.

"Nothing. Christ. Take it back a few million."

Mies suddenly whispered, "No, more than that. Hundreds of millions, at least." His voice was eerily crisp, as if he were suddenly more . . . *focused.*

Ginny said, "We shouldn't—"

Kai: "No. He's right. Here, let me. . . ." Two nearby microcraters seemed to come into focus, then suddenly vanished. The walls began to flow, steepening, disappearing in a fuzz of probability mist. The nunatak began to look sharper, less eroded, but there was still no change in the black mass before them.

Doc said, "Hardly seems reasonable that it's older than, uh, geological events."

Linda Navarro said, "You know, if it's much older than a

few million years, it can't have been made by anybody we'll be able to find.''

Spence: "Right. If they came from another star, that star's no longer in our neighborhood. I mean, billions of years ago, how far was Sol from here?''

Mies: "That's assuming they *weren't* from somewhere in this star system.''

Assuming. But then . . . No. We weren't able to detect *anything* more than . . . Kai said, "I'm not sure I like the implications of that. Well.'' He upped the gain past the billion-year mark.

Mies grunted loudly as a blue monochrome rainbow suddenly painted itself across the sky.

"What the hell's *that?*''

A frightened whisper: "It's Nephelë. Kai, Atalanta is rotating.''

"Um. What does that mean?''

"I don't know. Kai, it's *not* possible!''

"Nevertheless . . .'' He turned up the gain, going into the billions of years past.

Snap. The machine was, ever so briefly, a thing of gleaming metal, exploding into a silver cloud, gone. The crater suddenly filled in, leaving them in opaque blackness, sightless, helpless, but in a moment the murk cleared, still dim, and they could see it again, encased in a sheath of boiling mist. Above, the sky was strange, an obscure distant surface netted with intersecting ripples.

"Stop.''

Kai said, "All right. We'll pull it forward slowly. . . .'' Boiling cloud, silver machine, surrounded by a faint tracery of flickering ghosts, nothing they could quite make out.

Izzy's voice: "Okay. That's it. Datatrack reads one hundred percent.''

Kai said, "All right. Record what you've got and kill the feed.'' He unplugged and the world was real around them again.

Silence.

And then Doc said, "What d'you think, Kai? Three, maybe four billion years?"

More silence, and Kai looked at the black ruin, thinking, Not possible. Just not possible. Not fucking *possible*. And then, in his own words, *Nevertheless* . . . "That's the implication, but . . ."

"Mies?"

A sigh. "There's nothing in the planetological record to rule it out. I . . . I'm just not qualified to speculate about the rest of it."

There was a brittle laugh from Ginny. "I don't imagine anyone is."

Kai floated in the half-darkness of Doc's cabin, huddled with the old man in his sleeping bag, eyes open on dim, bluish light, reviewing a long day of meetings, meetings and arguments. So now they'd power up the ship, head on down Alpha Centauri A's gravity well, skipping the rest of the outer system assessment, skipping the double star's sparse asteroid belt, skipping everything else, going directly to A4, Pegasus and its big retrograde moon Bellerophon.

That's where we'll find the planetary engineers, Mies had said. Emphatic. Insistent.

And me, wanting to believe in the ultimate coincidence. Wanting to believe we'd stumbled, right off, on the work of some other star-faring civilization, people who'd come to Alpha Centauri billions of years ago. Me, wanting to resupply the lander, load on more equipment, more personnel, and go right back down. Establish a surface base, start beaming findings back to Sol.

Imagine. Alpha Centauri is an *old* sun; we've known that for centuries. It's been circling around the galaxy in its orbit for eight billion years. And somewhere, somewhen, people with minds like ours came to a nearby star, just to have a look. Maybe to save themselves, just like us.

Why just like us? Because they were *here*.

Even if they *did* come from Pegasus, they're still our kindred.

Because they came this far, even if they never went on to the stars.

He felt Doc stir beside him and turned to look. The old man's bland brown eyes opened on quasinight, looking at him. A faint smile touched mannequin lips.

"Can't sleep?"

"No. Too excited. Thinking about . . . what's happened."

Doc said, "I used to be like that, too. I used to think, when I got a little older, when I'd gained a little more wisdom . . ."

"And?"

Soft laughter. "Never happened. It's in your gonads, Kai. Not your heart. Not your soul."

Kai put his hands on Doc's chest, looking into fathomless eyes. Let the hand trail downward across delicate abdominal muscles, sliding across a thick-bladed hipbone, downward between his legs. Sometimes, dropping over that pubic ledge, it felt a little bit like a woman down there, but . . . No vulva. No vagina. Just a few folds of skin, a little urethral opening.

More gentle laughter, Doc stretching slightly, arching his back just the tiniest bit. "There are moments when I enjoy having you do that."

And other moments, Kai knew, when Doc would relate to him as a woman, would relate to him physically, with hands and tongue. . . . Searching look, prying into those empty eyes. Sigh. Not tonight, though. "Think you'll ever change back?" Always that option. Or had been. Stuck out here now, until the fleet comes. If it comes.

What if the colonies are planted elsewhere? Tau Ceti. Some unsuspected planet of Procyon. What the hell would we do then?

Doc seemed very distant. Finally, the tiniest of shrugs. "I don't know. Maybe. Someday. When I've put all the old feelings away. I . . ." Expression then in the eyes, for just a moment, a long sagging moment of sadness. "I guess when all the old wounds have healed and all the scars faded. When I've lived so long I can believe I'm truly somebody *else*."

Kai put his arms around the old man, leaning in, pressing a

gentle kiss on soft, pallid lips. Doc smiled at him, holding him gently, and said, "Go to sleep, Kai. Or go see Ginny."

He closed his eyes. After a while, so did Kai, knowing morning would come.

In the cramped, red-lit spaces of the aft engineering deck, Mies and Linda moved slowly, handhold to handhold, Mies following the woman at a respectful distance. They passed through a series of tight spaces, slipping between complex metal surfaces like fish through coral. Here the soft hum of the life-support system filled the silence, masking other, internal, noises.

"Here it is. My baby. The most advanced piece of technology on board, except for the SAE."

She had stopped before a structure that, at first, reminded Mies of *Mother Night*'s habitat structure, or, he realized, a funny-looking hat—a cylinder topped by a spherical head sitting on a broad, circular brim. Around the rim sat four segmented conelike structures, each with a set of grapples. Mies looked up at it, impressed despite himself. Fully self-contained, loaded with a third generation nanobiotic computer mind, able to independently process the resources of any, well, almost any, ice-rich body, producing energy enough for itself with plenty left over. "Under the right circumstances, and with a little help from its friends, it can replicate itself."

"Amazing." He circled it, looking for signs of function in its form, found startlingly few. "Is it on now?"

She had moved to a position just to the right of the upper sphere. "You might be able to shut it down, but for all practical purposes, it's alive."

"And you're its . . . keeper?"

"Darn right."

Mies moved nearer, feeling exceptionally warm, smelling the thin, metallic tang in the air. "Truly impressive. Linda?"

She looked down at him, and once again, their eyes met. She didn't try to look away. He said, "Things haven't changed. I'm afraid they never will. I'm terribly unhappy."

Linda broke his gaze, looked away, then, reluctantly, back.

"I'm . . . I'm an engineer, Mies. To me, if something's broken, you fix it. Go back to her. Apologize. Work on your relationship, and you'll be rewarded."

Mies came closer. "I can't stand it. The pressure of . . . all this . . . only takes my mind off of you for a while."

"Your attention is very flattering," she said, eyes still unable to light anywhere.

Close enough, he caught hold of her hand, felt the smoothness of it, blood beneath. "You told me that you don't feel that much for Spence."

She pulled back feebly, weightlessness giving the tug little force. "He's so oblivious . . ."

He pulled her toward him, and she didn't struggle. Now he was a few inches higher than her, looking down at her, seeing in her face the inexpressible desire within him. A kiss, and then there was even a tacit consent.

Inside her, Mies spasmed his orgasm almost immediately, terrible pleasure electric current in every part of his body, flooding from his core in rhythmic pulses. It was done. Indigo rules, whispering like the wind. IT'S IN HER NOW. SHE'S FIN-ISHED. MAYBE SHE'LL GO BACK TO SPENCE NOW. GUILTY THAT SHE LET YOU DO IT. SHE'LL GO BACK TO SPENCE, FULL OF GUILT AND SYMPATHY . . .

Mies could imagine the scene. Would Spence notice the smell? Or would he just stick it in her and wonder why she was so hot, so hot and slick? Oblivious, she said. He's so oblivious. Oh, God. The scientist snickered. *If he fucks her soon enough, your little wrigglers'll crawl right up his dick and make themselves at home. Indigo always counted on that sort of secondary vector effect.*

Mies, feeling himself grow flaccid inside Linda, wished he could drag the rest of his body inside as well. That way he wouldn't have to see the look in her eyes, the look sure to be there, woman-eyes full of scorn as he pulled out and turned away.

THREE

In orbit around Bellerophon, Ginny and Kai sat in the control room with the full core-driven VR display filling their heads, getting a perfect view of the alien yellow landscape rolling by. As if we and the control panel, our chairs, bits of floor, no more than that, skimmed in orbit, two-sixty klicks up, just above the big moon's tenuous atmosphere. No walls. No windows. No ship. Just us. Sliding along in orbit, feet toward the planet so we'll feel comfortable with the view and . . . When she tipped her head upward, Pegasus was a bland white crescent in the sky, hanging just to one side of the hot blinding-white ball of Alpha Centauri A.

B, the dimmer star, was a small, tawny bolus of bright light far across the sky, and . . . Sudden startling realization that the dark part of Pegasus wasn't dark at all, but lit up pale gray by B and the light of its enormous moon. This will make for interesting nights, doubly lit, thick clouds parting occasionally to reveal *this*. . . .

Beside her, Kai was leaning forward in his seat, as if trying to get a better look at the curved surface of the little world by leaning closer.

Swirls of color, dark russet and orange and turnip yellow, defined the world. Deserts, low eroded mountains, all very natural looking. Things that might once have been rivers. Patches of white that could even have been small seas. Mies will know. "Well," she said, "I guess that settles it."

In the highland now coming toward them, under the unmistakable yellow line of a dusty atmosphere, there were the remains of what was clearly some technogenic construction of enormous proportions. *Canali,* and more than *canali,* a deep, square-bottomed trough cutting across hundreds of kilometers.

"Maximum magnification. Generate stereo view." Suddenly, the canyon yawned all around them. At higher resolution, some of the symmetry of the canal was lost. Wind erosion had worn the sides into elaborate, fluted curtains, and the bottom was filled with lumpy depositions of sand carved into slender yardangs by the wind. At this scale, it was difficult to tell that this shape was created by intelligent creatures. "Back off. Mono view. Mag less fifty times."

Ginny whistled softly. No, she thought, they don't make square rilles, however eroded. "You think this is where the . . . explorers came from?" Came from. Implied meaning. Because, you see, there's nobody down there now.

"I don't know. Pattern match . . ." A small globe of Bellerophon, integrated from the many photos they'd taken, during their first pass through the system as well as on the way in today, spun in the air between them. "Match to sequence 'ruins,' please."

A few dozen blotches formed in a regular pattern. Ginny said, "They're all scattered around the limb of the Pegasus-facing hemisphere, clustered around the huge shield volcano at its center."

Kai nodded "When the Americans first explored Earth's Moon, they were afraid to set down on the farside, too. I guess most of the ruins, the really important ones, are buried under that volcano now." You could hear the regret in his voice.

Ginny tipped her head back again, looking up at Pegasus. "You think . . ."

A sigh. "Whatever the answer is, we know one thing: We fucking missed them. Pegasus has been uninhabitable, by *any* sort of life, for something on the order of eight hundred million years."

The phase of terrestrial planetary evolution called "Mature

Steamhouse.'' Venus when young. The Earth, grown just a little bit older. Pegasus, circling Alpha Centauri A, just now. So they left a few old ruins on their moon. And up there, the graves of our missed First Contact.

Kai loosed his restraints and floated up out of his seat. ''I'll go down and talk to Mies. We'd better get started.'' He disappeared through a brief hole in the air.

Get started. Hurry. Hurry. What the hell's the rush? We aren't going anywhere. We've got all the time we need. All the time we feel like taking. She noticed an enormous ocher bulge distorting the horizon. The volcano, sliding toward her, two complex, multiringed, multileveled calderas at its summit. Did this bring about their demise, hot lava flooding into their houses, poisoning their atmosphere?

I wonder if there used to be ice caps at the poles. This must have been a nice world, once upon a time. Dark blue skies maybe, indigo or violet. Probably could have gotten by in an insulated mountaineering suit, maybe even those cheap things we used to wear in Antarctica. Yes. Cheap winter gear. Maybe an oxygen mask.

Brief memory of cold winter winds, sky not indigo or violet but dead black, freckled with a thousand bright stars. Brief memory unfolding, then, stretching out in all directions, blotting out the Bellerophon of here and now, bringing back . . .

Black and starry night, a crisp, clear sky above the white plains, dark jagged mountains remote on the horizon. No wind, nothing, no sound, motionless air. Ginny huddled snug in her cheap exosuit, frosty breath captured by the suit's mask, warm breath diverted down to circulate around her body. Down below was the collection of domes and bermed buildings the Family called its Manse, buildings soft-lit from within, escaped light making the pale habitation fog glow where it rolled along the ground.

Ginny wished she could open the suit, could reach down and scratch the insistent, crawly itch between her legs, dig at a place she'd already scratched raw. Probably another yeast infection, one last gift from Grandfather Dietrich. . . .

Old man with spiky white hair, eyes agleam in the half-light of her room, pushing her back onto the bed, shoving up her thin white nightie, slipping down her panties. You could see his teeth in the dark, white porcelain glowcaps catching the light of the stars, starlight flooding in through her little triple-paned window.

Old man whispering, You smell, little girl. Ought to take better care of yourself. . . .

Grandfather Dietrich paying the smell no mind, it wasn't his face going down there just now anyway, Grandfather standing on the floor by a bed that was, oh-so-intentionally, just the right height, fumbling with himself, getting the blunt end of his prick lined up, shoving it on in.

Ginny in the bed biting her lip, trying to relax, ignore the soft burn of his thrust into a too-dry vagina, reaching down to hold herself under the knees, hold her legs far, far apart. Relax, relax. Try not to let it hurt.

Grandfather Dietrich grinning as he humped, teeth about all she could see of his face, soft voice going, That's nice, little girl. Nice . . . Grandfather crooning as he came, prick jumping inside her.

Ginny now, outside in the snow, looking down on the Family's Manse, wishing she could open the exosuit and scratch her crotch, knowing she couldn't. Seventy below just now, maybe seventy-five. Freeze my damn pussy right off. . . .

Fumbling with her pack, then. Fueltabs for the heater in her exosuit. Some coldsnacks, enough to keep her going as she walked through the hills to Sevensee, which might take three weeks in this kind of weather. A little nodetap so she could track that weather, make sure she didn't get caught walking through a storm. A little exotent, stolen from supply only an hour ago. And the Sevensee JobService chicklet.

If this doesn't work out, I'm more fucked than ever. . . .

Soft, soft panic but . . . Three years. Three years since the altar. Every night for three years. No more. No fucking more.

Ginny slid the slim fiberglass canister from her pack, held it up to the starlight, looked at the setting ring. Gave it a twist and thought, Ninety minutes ought to be enough. . . . Down the hill, then, running, running, habitation fog swirling around her, dropping the canister off at the base of the hypocaust wall, thinking about the altar platform inside.

Tomorrow night, it's supposed to be little Millie's turn, pale little Millie, so very forlorn, lying in the little girls' dorm, sucking her thumb, twisting a lock of her pale yellow hair around one finger. Little Millie, only nine years old, for some reason known only to the Mothers and Fathers, judged to be fit and ready. . . .

Dropping the canister, then, dropping it and running on, running away into the darkness.

She was five klicks away before the sky lit up bright magnesium white behind her, before she heard the *thump-hiss* of the thermite canister's ignition. Ginny smiled, imagining their panic back there, smiled, and thought about the Manse burning down.

Outside the lander, the panorama of Bellerophon was breathtaking—low dunes of dark sand, each one topped with a delicate tracery of white, reaching in monotonous profusion to the flat horizon. The sky reminded him of a strange twilight, bright white blending slowly into yellow, thinning out as you looked up into starless blackness. Alpha Centauri A, bright-seeming as the sun, hung effortlessly in black sky, nearly overhead.

Out of this sea, a wall of hard white stone protruded, big, big enough to be seen from far out in space. The top, thinned to translucence, was broken and arched in graceful curves, bites taken out here and there. A corner, softened to near indetectability by time, stood near at hand.

Kai took a few steps, sinking in and leaving vague pits in his wake, looking toward the wall. "It almost looks like a natural formation."

Studying a spectrum of the material, Mies said, "Extremely unlikely, I'd say. I know of no natural stone anything like this. Especially unlikely in these type of facies."

Up on the lander's porch, outside the yawning airlock hatch, Rosie said, "I guess this has the chance to be what Mars was not. At least we *know* life once existed here."

Kai said, "You think this place never developed an active soil chemistry?" A chemistry that would have eaten away any lingering trace of microbial life.

Rosie, climbing down the ladder, eyes on the world; not looking at Mies, he noticed. "Oh, I'm sure it has to be a lot like Mars. The UV will have seen to that. Not to mention the atmosphere. Still. We'll see something." A gesture at the wall, at the bright world beyond.

Low rolling hills, rising more toward the east than the west. Sky pale yellow in the east, where he expected, incongruously, to see the shield volcano poking over the horizon, though even its basal scarp was hundreds of kilometers away; darker in the west, where night was receding, because they'd landed near the big moon's leading edge. Leading edge in its retrograde orbit around Pegasus, which was quite high, filling more than six and a half degrees of the eastern sky, looming near the nightlike zenith, bright crescent enfolding a dim gray circle. What do they call it? Old moon in the new moon's arms? I'd *really* like to be here during an eclipse.

Soft noise, just barely audible through his earphones, sensors reporting to him the amplified hiss of the wind-driven sand. Mies standing beside him now, looking around, face expressionless through the clear plastic visor of his lightweight environmental suit, thinking what? Just thinking about *facies,* not about . . . grandeur. About the glory of being here? Maybe thinking about what this place would be like during one of the late-summer sandstorms he was certain must occur? A vision of this pale yellow sky obscured with a dense brown haze.

Spence came out of the lander's airlock and let the hatch swing shut, came and stood heavily beside them. Like me, thought Kai, never liking the molasses-thick gravitational field of a "real" world. Heavy like me, not bobbing lightly like earthborn Mies. And not looking at the scenery: engineer Warvai instead looking at the ruin. If you could call it that. From far away, even in magnified views, it had looked something like a building. Here . . .

Spence's whistle was soft yet sharp in their earphones as he stepped toward the wall, reached out to touch it with his thinly gloved fingers. High, reedy, mechanical-man voice saying, "Damn. Polished like someone went over it with an old-fashioned drum sander. If you guys weren't so certain someone built this . . ."

Mies laughed. "This wall's only recently been exposed after aeons of burial. Otherwise it couldn't have survived so long."

Rose turned to stare at him, face somber through her faceplate. Angry? Or just sad? She said, "The walls are what give me some hope. If there are fossilized biochemical traces left anywhere, it'll be inside the building material."

Kai said, "All right. Let's go look for that radar hollow."

The four of them walked forward, boots cracking the surface crust of the sand, sliding on loose patches, as they went around the wall. Nothing much here. Eroded vertical walls. Crumbled piles of old talus. Steep slopes of wind-blown sand.

Mies put his hand on Kai's shoulder, pointing. "There . . . "

Like an archway cut in the bottom of one of the walls, only darkness beyond. Looking so very much like one of those natural bridges you find here and there, on Earth and Mars. But no blue sky beyond. He said, "Ginny? We're going in."

Clear voice from *Mother Night*: "Okay. I think the radio'll punch through just fine. Spence, your sensor's not on."

A grated, "Sorry." Fumbling at his chest panel. "Better?"

"Good enough."

They went through the hatchway, line abreast, stood blinking together in the dusty gloom. "Warmer here," said Spence.

Kai called up the suit's eyebubble interface and watched yellow letters scroll against the darkness, blinked them away, and said, "Can get an infrared scan . . ."

The core's node on the lander heard and lit up their suit lights, reading the data with its sensors and reporting the result into their eyes, to Kai much as if the room suddenly flooded with pale reddish light. Heaps of sand in the corners of a more or less empty square room. Nothing. "Well . . ." Not quite nothing. He gestured at two black lumps in the corner. "What do you make of those?"

Mies was already walking over, looking down at the things. A shrug, plainly visible through the translucent material of his environmental suit. "If I had to hazard a wild guess . . . billion-year-old Victorian armchairs?"

Kai said, "Might as well go get the scanner head. Ginny?"

"Right." You could almost hear her grimace. "I'll power down everything but life support and attitude control while Izzy and Metz start loading the SAE software. Forty minutes."

Rosie said, "I'll want to take some samples first, before we disturb the environment with a technogenic radiation flux."

Kai nodded. "Cut through an exterior wall. That way we'll be less likely to interfere with each other's dataset."

A little more than an hour later, they were back down in the gloom, scanner head for the ship's synchronoptic analysis engine on its little tripod, waveguides jacked into the sides of Mies, Spence, and Rose's helmets, Kai with a thick bundle of them plugged into the special fitting mounted on his suit's right hip. Too bad about Rosie coming up empty. Nothing in the stony building material that indicated it'd ever been in contact with life. Nothing macroscopic, other than the fact of its existence. Nothing microscopic, down to molecular level. If we were restricted to preholotaxial technologies . . . ah, but then we might not be here at all. He said, "Ready."

Izzy's voice said, "All right. Power to scanner head. Control to Kai."

A horseshoe array of imaginary instruments suddenly seemed to appear in the air below Kai's chin, visible even through the opaque parts of his suit. Disconcerting sometimes, even after a lifetime of VR, even in a culture that's been immersed in it since my grandparents were babies. . . . He nodded and blinked, setting things up, waited while the commands routed through the lander and back up to the ship, where the SAE would be programming itself. More computing power in the SAE than in the ship's eyebubble core by far. Hard to imagine what data processing will be like when they've got that kind of raw muscle into a typical portable core, much less. . . . "Okay. I'm going straight for the same era as the unmanned probe we found on Atalanta . . . *now*."

Blink. The building was gone, vanished in a twinkling, the three of them standing in a little knot around the scanner head under a pale cornflower blue sky.

"Fucking hell," said Mies. "How'd we get outside?"

And clouds, drifting serenely, high above, possibly an artifact of the analytical software. Brown desert around them flatter and . . . was that a river in the distance, that little twist of silver?

Spence, whispering, as if someone might be listening, said, "Pegasus is a lot smaller now." Still high in the sky, still in the same place, still a crescent, but . . . plenty of blue and brown showing through the cloud cover.

Mies said, "Been spiraling in for a long time."

Spence: "So where is everybody?"

Kai said, "Probably wherever they came from. Maybe up there." Pointing at Pegasus. Probably beyond the power of the SAE to let them know. Have to keep reminding myself we're not really here. Scanner head reading the data headers from subatomic particles that get in its way, synchronoptic analysis engine doing its best to extract information from chaos.

Rosie said, "We sent manned expeditions to Luna years before we got probes landed on the moons of Jupiter and Saturn."

Kai thought, *Manned.* Interesting notion. "Apollo was an aberration." How would we know? Until just this instant, we've had nothing to compare ourselves with . . .

Mies: "Let's slide forward a bit."

Kai glanced down at his "instruments." Things in good shape here. The data flow was sparse, but was pretty much intact. These surfaces hadn't been disturbed in a long damned time. "Okay. I'll try to run us fifty years into the future. I think the SAE can handle that kind of discrimination." Walls. A floor. A door leading into another room. A glass window where the eroded archway had been. Kai thought, The door must be under the sand heaped by the wall, I . . .

Mies said, "Look!" pointing through the glass, out at a landscape that had started to ripple as though seen through clear and turbulent water.

Kai tried to steady the image. Data from the windowpane is embedded in the back wall of the room. Goddamn it . . . One clear flash, the thing Mies was pointing at . . .

Spence said, "Looks like a turboshuttle to me . . ." White-winged technofact slipping up into the sky on a bright spark of clear blue flame and . . .

The window shimmered and turned into a black square, flickered and replayed the same snatch of rocketship taking off. Kai sighed. "That's all there is. Some image fragment left by chance embedded in the wall surface."

Mies said, "Why hasn't the wind scraped it away? That's not the originally exposed layer."

Kai shrugged. "Probably was exposed just long enough to collect that image, then covered up."

Spence snorted. "Putting on a new paint job that day, maybe? Patching a banged-up spot?"

Kai turned and looked at the empty door. Nothing but mist beyond. A room filled with pearly gray fog. "Let's see . . ." Fog swirling, swirling, growing structure and . . .

Rosie, voice vibrant with joy, cried out, "Oh, my *God!*"

Mies: "That's not a man."

Kai stared at the shadowy figure. "No. Not that we should be expecting . . ."

Spence said, "Looks like a goddamned frog."

Well. Sort of. Mostly shadow, but . . . The image suddenly sharpened and froze as the analytical sieves collected all their data into one spot and imposed possibly specious order on chaos. All right, thought Kai. A blotchy yellow-and-green leopard frog, eyes rotated forward for binocular vision. A tall, skinny, bipedal frog, dressed in floppy gray boots and pastel pink jockey shorts. Carrying a machine gun with an octagonal drum-clip. Looking right at me . . .

Rosie said, "Is this real or just a hypothetical image? It looks so . . . *authentic.*"

Kai could feel the hair standing up on the back of his neck. He whispered, "I wonder if he had a name."

Mies laughed softly, "He? You think that bulge is a prick, do you?" Frogs, of course, have no . . .

Kai checked his instruments and said, "The data is accurate, but that's all there is."

Mies turned and stared at him, looking like a ghost standing in the middle of the SAE's displayed image, looking as if he were, somehow, standing behind everything but the faint remains of the real-world, eroded structure of the wall. He said, "That's enough."

Hours and hours later. Back aboard *Mother Night* . . . scientist persona to the fore, full of anticipation. Others no more than tiny figures. As if they were no more than memories. Indigo eyes? Shut. Mies thought, I can help, you know. I know how to *be* Mies Cochrane. You . . . Angry: *I am Mies Cochrane. The role of planetologist defines him.* But . . . if we work together. Maybe . . . *No. This is my job. Stay out of the way.*

Mies hesitated, floating in the science deck's aft hatchway, remembering the magnificent desolation of Bellerophon. Too much to think about, images too disorderly. He shook the disquieting pictures away, donned his imaginary armor, and went on in.

Linda and Spence were together, just as before. No surprise there. Mies could still see the expression on her face as she left him: shame, mostly, with more than a little disgust thrown in. She wouldn't be revealing what had happened to anyone in a hurry. A momentary pang of delight passed through him, almost as intense as the physical orgasm had been.

He looked for Rosie, found her nestled close to Kai next to the waveguide housing. Hmm. That would be a strange pair. He didn't really like the implications, somehow. But no, the proximity was coincidental; Rosie was looking off in another direction. I wish I understood what went on in their heads. *Why* is she attracted to me? What can she possibly *want*?

Look to your evolutionary biology, simpleton. Your phero-

monic output accelerates her *reproductive cycles. And Indigo saw to it you'd be hormonally attractive to fertile women.*

But she's *not.* Not anymore.

"Time to begin." Ginny was floating in front of them. She said, "It seems our coming here, to A's inner system, was justified—" a nod to Mies "—but any real understanding of what happened here in this system is little closer. Kai, the SAE was tantalizing, but I can't make heads or tails of what it meant. Your conclusions?"

"Contradictory. I'm convinced that the creatures we saw possessed a technology somewhat *less* advanced than ours. Nothing in the image, real or otherwise, unfortunately, suggests *where* they came from, but it seems very unlikely that they represent the interstellar explorer scenario."

Mies smiled. "Which leads directly to the Pegasus hypothesis. It seems extremely unlikely that Bellerophon spent enough time as a watery world to produce the possibly amphibious alien we saw."

Ginny called up a shadowy image of the creature built from a hastily constructed database, and instructed the eyebubble to display it in realspace. Suddenly, the alien stood among them, seeming fragile yet powerful. "This doesn't look to me like an inhabitant of a two-gee world like Pegasus to me. If one of them managed to stand up, they'd be blown away."

Got you there, thought Mies. The scientist persona snarled, in control, "I've been thinking about that. I think they must've been an aquatic species, unable on their home planet to support their own weight unless buoyed up by water."

"Yet there are no signs of a water-breathing apparatus on this specimen," Izzy said. "What are we to conclude from that?"

Rosie suddenly said, "Amphibious, Iz. Able to breathe the air of long-ago Bellerophon. Given our dearth of information, and the limits of our window into the past, virtually anything is possible. Call up an image of your average life-long Oort Clouder from an anthropometric database, and she would appear incapable of standing on the surface of the Earth. We don't know what we'll look like a hundred zero-gee generations down the road.''

Doc said, "Not to mention artificial genetic adaptation. We have to think about what we'd be like if we'd had a point-three-gee world a couple of hundred thousand kilometers overhead.''

Ginny stretched, grabbed a handhold. "What's our next step? There are plenty more ruins down on Bellerophon.''

Got them. "Most eroded, much more deeply than the wall and room. The answer to all our questions must lie on Pegasus. Although Pegasus's active geochemical cycle has certainly erased any signs of the creatures' technological past, signs of the biosphere that once existed cannot be so easily swept away. I remind you of Hiraoka's famous maxim, 'Look around you. What you see is that which has persisted.' It appears that these froglike beings never reached the stage of adaptation necessary for long-term persistence on Bellerophon. Such can not be the case on Pegasus, where the creatures developed.''

Bravo, thought Mies. And bringing in a "famous maxim," at that! Bitterly: They always have maxims. Maxims for everything. Who can recite some Indigo maxims for us now?

Indigo eyes on him, full of suspicion. MAN. WOMAN. BIRTH. DEATH . . . A WORLD OUT OF BALANCE. PREDATOR AND PREY. DAVID GILMAN, PREDATOR. HARADA REIKO . . . PREDATOR DISGUISED AS PREY. To save the world, said the secret Indigo masters, we must first destroy it.

"All right," said Kai. "Once again our resident planetologist holds sway. Despite a few reservations, I concur. On to Pegasus.''

You see. They're not really as smart as you think they are, ninny. We can *defeat them.*

Mies thought, Why do you think of this as conflict? We're all in this together.

Indigo eyes opened, baleful. ALL LIFE IS STRUGGLE. STRUGGLE IS CONFLICT. IT'S US AGAINST THEM. Interesting. *Us* and *them*? Do they have no legions within? No, of course not. Just natural beings. Not . . . made, like me. But . . . but . . . I remember. Little David briefly looking up at him.

Ginny said, "Okay, everyone. Meeting's over."

People began to move, pushing off, following clumsy trajectories. Mies noticed that Rosie was glaring at him, dark determination evident on her face. This was it. The explosion that had been brewing between them ever since they had been demummified.

Fear sparking through him, the group flying apart. Well? How are you going to handle this one?

Task set complete. Job well done. This is your *business, and none of my own. Turning away, fleeing down into the darkness.*

Indigo? Eyes on him. WE'RE FINISHED WITH HER. Eyes folding shut.

He looked around for a place to escape to, in vain, of course. There were damn few places for private conversation in the upper decks, and certainly no way to maneuver her into one. She'd want it public, having exhausted her full repertoire of private persuasions. He began to back off as she approached, backpedaling, moving through the hatch in the direction of the command module. Maybe he could get far enough away to keep their conversation semiprivate.

No. She was propelling herself across the room expertly, would be upon him in a moment. Nothing for it but to turn and face the tiger.

She caught a hold on the lip of the hatchway, just a meter from him. "Mies," she said, her voice unnaturally loud and forced, "you can't get away. Oh, I see that look on your face; I'm not going to hurt you."

He showed her his teeth, a poor excuse for a smile, noticing that Doc was not far away, staring at them. "Come on, Rosie. What's wrong?"

She grimaced at him, a facetious grin, but tears were building in the corners of her eyes, catching the light. "You know damn well what's wrong," she hissed. "You've been trying to avoid me for days now. Every time we meet, you put me off with a delaying tactic."

Why am I all alone here now? Not quite alone. Little David, cowering in his corner. A larger David, the one who'd looked on Indigo as a way to . . . a way to be in control, to *control* the world that made him feel so helpless. Rules. Yes, rules to follow, simple rules, a consultable table of rules. Do *this*, Mister Gilman, and those women will be putty in your hands, bending over at your whim and . . .

Rules. Indigo rules. Rules for the handling of women.

Indigo eyes opening. WE'RE FINISHED WITH HER.

But, the rules.

FINISHED.

If I only had some rules to follow, I could read her, read her just the way I could when her cunt was my only object. Read her now and control her.

NO REASON. FINISHED.

But if I could *understand*, I could get us out of this.

Eyes, staring. JUST WALK AWAY. THAT'S THE ONLY RULE. WHEN YOU'RE FINISHED WITH THEM, YOU WALK AWAY. THE WORLD IS FULL OF THEM, MISTER MIES. WALK AWAY AND FIND ANOTHER.

Not in the world now. Voice from nowhere. From above, perhaps. The voice of some unreckoned god.

What do I say then? *Think.* He said, "But I've been extremely busy, dear. You know."

"You fucking hypocrite." She wiped her eyes with the back of a hand, voice hoarse with emotion. "Where are all your pronouncements of love now that we're here? Huh? Just what in the hell were you trying to *do?* You can't just flick me off like a piece of snot, ignore me after the things you said."

"We can discuss this in our—"

"No, we fucking well cannot. We'll have a resolution to it, and we'll have it now. Let's just run down the list of lies, shall we? Did you *ever* love me?"

No rules for this. Jesus, I'm an intelligent man. Why can't I understand what's going on here? I ought to be able to . . . Nervous sweat gathering at his hairline, Mies backed against the hatch, trying to get away from this confrontation. Nowhere to run. For the briefest moment he saw an image of Kai, unsullied, able to pursue a goal that required no treachery, clean and pure. Envy washed through him, almost causing a little sob.

"Mies!" Rosie pushed closer, hand out as if to slap. He ducked inadvertently, panicking. "Answer me!"

"Of course I loved you. I still do. Nothing can change that." The words came pouring forth, lies linked like a little chain. "From the moment we first met, I knew. You are special to me, more than words can say. It's just that I've been so busy."

"*Liar!*" A silence, anger curling in her eyes, then she said, "You *hurt* me, Mies. I *still* hurt. What in the name of God did you think would happen? I, I . . ." She stopped, made a guttural cough that mutated to a snivel.

Lost in her emotions. I think you can get away now. Feeling safe for the moment, he wriggled like a fish in a net, looking for a way to escape. He found an opening, and cautiously began to creep upward. As Mies swam away, he could feel Linda Navarro's eyes on him, slitted, emotionless. Like times past, he thought. Like times lost and gone forever.

Spence and Linda were together in their little stateroom, riding a moment of silence, Spence waiting for the anxiousness that seemed to dog their relationship to die off.

Linda had been acting strangely for the last few days, troubled in some way, so unlike the woman that he had come to know during the brief weeks before the launch. As their closeness had grown, he often found himself just *looking* at her, trying to puzzle out just *why* she was so attractive. By most standards, she was nothing special; dark-skinned face more square than oval, plain eyes defined by eyebrows that quirked up strangely, lank bangs curtaining her high forehead. Still . . . "Hey," he said softly, "something's not working." Echoing *her* oft-repeated phrase.

Her glance flitted around the room, and she caught hold of the bedding, twisting herself away from him. "I know. I . . . know. Something we may not be able to fix so easily."

He held off reaching for her, something almost palpable holding him back. "What's wrong? We've *fixed* so much. Mostly in me, I've got to admit."

Coming around in her rotation, she smiled a little, downward, not at him. "I'm afraid I'm not perfect. In fact, far from it. This is something that . . . that I can't even tell you about." Now the emotion he'd been feeling resolved itself into fear, pure and simple. Fear that it was over. He remembered the end moments of his two previous marriages, just like this—silence filled with portent, then the Announcement. What was it that they said? *When you least expect it.* That hardly applied now, of course. They were too early in their relationship, still bumping into the hard corners. He always expected it.

"What are you saying, Linda?" The pragmatist in him couldn't resist proceeding. No one ever told you they couldn't tell you something without knowing that it must ultimately come out. "You've got to tell me."

She began to reach out a hand, drew it back as though by reflex. "I thought I could keep it from you, hide it away in its own little cubbyhole, more gone than there. But, Spence, I can't. Everytime I look at you it's like I'm transparent, like you can see it if you just open your eyes. I can't live like that anymore."

Spence shook his head, more frustrated than anything else. "See what? See what? What do you want, my forgiveness? I'm prepared to forgive just about anything, you know that."

She sniffed. "How can you forgive without an explanation?" She was crying, he saw that now, looking at him imploringly. "But an explanation is just what I don't have. That's what makes it so maddeningly, ridiculously stupid."

"Goddamn it. Tell me."

"I slept with someone, well, not slept, you know what I mean. Screwed them. So stupid."

Spence squinted, confused, dry pain welling up under his Adam's apple. This had taken an unexpected turn. "So what do you want *me* to do? Forgive you?" Hard anger. "I forgive you. I *forgive* you. *Te absolvo.*" He kept his eyes on her face, expecting . . . "So who was it? Truth now. You've got to tell me everything."

She peered up at him sheepishly, as though she had been expecting something else. Perhaps, her eyes said, I have found out what I wanted to know. "It was Mies. He was . . . attentive to me, despite his work. You, Spence, you haven't . . ."

Somehow he found himself suddenly plunged into a sort of moral dark place, where the simple ideas he entertained about the world had vanished, with Linda at the dark pole of it all, hand out, beckoning. He understood, even if she did not. Their relationship would go on, but it would be empty.

Now she was pulling off her loose cottonette blouse, breasts little teepees of flesh erected on the brown earth of her chest, speaking to him as always in the language of desire. Tangled up in the netting, Mars-born never quite getting the hang of zero-gee, she unfastened her pants, jerked them down with effort, bringing up her knees and beginning to spin chaotically. His eyes followed the thin fringe of dark pubic hair curling down and between, and, hollow, he reached out to her.

Spinning slowly in the air, clutched together, he spread her legs and achieved penetration; wet, she was so wet. Innocence lost, he felt a growing sense of power. And there *would* come a reckoning. Of sorts.

FOUR

Sitting in the command pilot's chair of *MN01* again, Kai watched *Mother Night* recede and glanced at the little radar-based reference globe hanging amidst his instruments, mostly featureless ocean except for two widely spaced continents. Pegasus was truly enormous for a terrestrial world, five times as massive as Earth. Orbital mechanics were the same, though. In the center of the globe, a long, curving land mass, giving way on either end to arcs of islands. Hutton, Mies had named it. Their destination. He rolled the lander heads-down, making Pegasus a fuzzy sky rolling by above them.

Mies said, "The stratosphere is pumped full of water vapor. At this altitude, it looks a lot like Venus."

In one of the rear bay seats, Andy Mezov, voice singularly wistful, said, "Sheba and I never got as far as Venus, only Earth. Sometimes I regret that we stayed on Mars until . . ."

Kai remembered the way they had been, all smiles, eyes only for each other. Hard to imagine plump, smiling, shy Sheba Zvi a mummified corpse, though he'd seen it himself. . . .

From the other rear seat, Izzy Feldschuh said, "You wouldn't have liked Venus, anyway. Nothing but old mining tunnels. Quite dreary." Some talk of Izzy bringing Metz along for the ride, Ginny demurring at the risk of *both* the ship's programmers. Metz, whiny and glad at the same time: *You go, Iz. I'll make the next trip.*

On the next trip, they'd bring down Rosie and her biolab. She's awfully excited about this. A feeling in her, I'm sure, that at least *fossil* life will turn up. It has to, she would say, eyes shining, trouble with Mies forgotten. We *know* there was life here. A glance at Mies. Wish I knew what the hell I was feeling. Hell. Maybe nothing at all. Time will tell. Kai rolled the ship around its axis, pointing the engine muzzle along their orbital vector, slightly elevated toward black space. "Braking burn."

Ginny's voice said: "Roger, burn. Time on target."

The engine grumbled somewhere, faint, like someone dragging a heavy piece of furniture in another room, inertia forcing their rear ends down into the chairs. Kai said, "Here we go."

Izzy said, "Well, let's hope there's something other than murk here."

Memory of Titan. Right. The engine quit, popping them back into zero-gee, and Mies, suddenly angry, said, "Fucking high pressure at the surface, Izzy; no steam."

Longish silence, while Kai watched the cloudtops flatten slowly, slowly grow closer. Such a strange set of contradictions, this Mies Cochrane. I think I know him, and then he changes, sometimes into someone I know, sometimes into a stranger. Something gnawing at him all the time.

Ginny: "Everything's nominal, Kai. Have a nice trip."

Kai let his head rest against the seatback, watching out the window, keeping the ship oriented manually, though, in truth, aerodynamic forces alone would do it. We could all be dead. The ship could be dead. It'd just fall and fall and smack down on its rump at the end of the journey at no more than a few dozen meters per second, probably survive the impact nicely. Some techie would come along, fix what broke, and fly her right away into the sky. Take our corpses home.

Streamers of pale salmon light out there now, compression plasma forming around them. Kai thought of seeing the ship from outside, from far away. Like the bright-tailed meteors that cross the starry sky in all the children's stories you find on the net. Every now and again you'd see a meteor crossing the sky on Titan. No starry backdrop, though.

Behind him, Andy muttered, "Good grief."

Kai glanced at the deceleration figure picked out in pale golden letters in the corner of his eye: 1.04 gee. Oops. I must be getting used to this. He rolled *MN01* around its center of gravity, shallowing the trajectory's phase diagram. "Better?"

A grunt from Andy. Maybe 0.85 gee wasn't much better at that.

Izzy said, "Thanks, Kai. I got flabby living up on the Moon all these years." The Moon. Earthman's conceit, as if there were only one, and it was theirs. Kai thought about how he and the other low-gee types would feel, flattened by Pegasus's two Earth gees, and said nothing.

The lander was starting to shudder now, encountering turbulence as they got into the stratosphere, started falling through thermoclinic discontinuities, through denser and denser layers of air. And surrounded now by layers of darkening clouds, surrounded by moisture. Kai stole a glance at the black sky above. Stars already vanished, the darkness . . . going and gone. Replaced by dim, subtle, blue-green-gray.

The phase diagram had them dropping at a forty-five degree angle now, forward velocity already killed by aerobraking, wisps of pink outside fading away, insubstantial gray taking their place. Vertical component? A quick glance: 557 meters per second. Well, a little speedy, perhaps.

Suddenly, they fell out of the clouds.

And Mies, voice flat, empty of affect, said, "My God." Twenty kilometers of clear, shimmering air. Low, rolling gray clouds stretching out on both sides, but beneath them, dark stone mountains, mountains besieged by dark sea on all sides. White breakers rolling in from far far away onto narrow black beaches. A primordial scene, incongruous on this old, *old,* world. Izzy let out a long breath. Kai tipped the lander, using its intrinsic lift to shift their path inland, away from the seashore, toward the high plateau they'd picked out during the orbital survey. All right now . . . The blinking amber crosshatch cursor caught his eye, directing him toward the landing site: a broad, slightly cup-shaped valley surrounded by volcanic edifices. Doesn't look like much from up here, but . . . "You really think we'll find something here?"

Mies said, "At seven-point-two kilometers up, it's as close to an Earthlike environment as we'll find: if any life still remains, that's where it'll be."

Earthlike. *The* Earth, center of the universe? Pegasus under blue skies, rolling hills covered with green, green trees? I lost all that before I was born, hardly gained it back by moving to Earth, by living there for those few years. Green trees, rolling, verdant hills, to me no more than just one more big man-made park. Finally, they were hovering over the crude monochromatic valley, littered with boulders of all size and defined by the places in between, black crags of worn basalt in the distance filling perhaps a hundred degrees of horizon. A scene of utter desolation.

Mies said, "There's work to be done. Let's be about it."

Kai thought, He doesn't see what he wanted to see here. This is it for him. If the Frogmen came from Pegasus, we've lost them. "Right." He throttled back *MN01*'s engines and set them down in a spray of fog.

Standing at the foot of the lander's debarking ramp—no sense in opening the aeroshell, rolling the rover off—Kai found that he needed the Class 2 worksuit's powered exoskeleton system to stand, much less walk. Two gee. At least I feel a little like I'm sitting down.

Listening to the comforting whisper of the suit's ventilation system, cool air blowing softly under his chin, Kai turned, looking into the distance, where the faraway seeming lip of the valley had been swallowed by cloud. Just gray sky and gray clouds, no real horizon. Somehow like being at sea on Earth. Memory of the week he and Ginny had spent sailing the Indian Ocean, driving a wingsailer across the summery equatorial seas west of the Maldives. What was it she said? Yes. Remarking that, somehow, the superposition of colorless blue sea and sky put her in mind of certain Antarctic white nights, when land and sky seemed to merge, when the horizon seemed to slip away from you, slip away toward eternity. Here, though, there were many distinct clouds, almost-Earthlike tropospheric clouds rolling and boiling in the wind, forming themselves like white shadows against the remote gray sky.

Izzy, standing back up at the top of the ramp, said, "Huh. Looks like rain."

Does it rain here? No telling. A quick glance at the sensor, calling up controls, blinking up the environmental data. Atmospheric pressure, just now, just under three atmospheres. Hmh. Nitrogen, like what I was used to on Titan, with a lot of CO_2 and H_2O vapor as well. He swished his arm back and forth, trying to feel the air's resistance. Hard to tell what was or wasn't masked by the suit systems. Temperature? Three-seventy kelvins.

Earthlike? Is Mies crazy? He pulled up the suit's calculator. Just shy of the boiling point of water at this pressure. Like being inside a pressure cooker whose valve is about to pop.

Mies and Andy appeared at the top of the ramp as well, carrying the folded-up scanner head between them, and started walking it down to the ground. Kai said, "Set it up anywhere. This landscape is all of a piece."

Izzy stepped on a small angular rock, teetered for just a second. "God. This gravity makes everything treacherous. I'd hate to fall down."

Class 2 suits were heavily armored, designed to protect the wearer from accidents, but . . . Kai imagined his head whacking around inside the helmet, imagined himself with bruises and a bloody nose. "Well, let's be careful. I don't think this place is worth . . ."

Mies grunted as he put his end of the scanner head down, helped Andy push it upright. "Let's see what we find out before we write Pegasus off as a waste of time." A touch of anger there, perhaps. Turning away, reaching out for his leads.

Kai picked up his own waveguide bundle and started plugging it into the fitting on his hip harness. "Hmh. Hard to do in this kind of suit. Somebody screwed up, somewhere.'' Me, maybe. I was the one who proposed this harness pack. ''Andy?''

''Sure.''

When they were all plugged in, Kai called up to the ship: ''Ready on the surface. Ginny?''

Her voice said, ''We're all set, Kai. Transferring control now.''

Kai said, ''First run, we'll go to the same integral variant as the structure we looked at on Bellerophon.'' He nodded at the sensor. Waited. Looking at the twisting lines on his graphs, he said, ''Data's all screwed up. I see at *least* seven chaotic attractors.''

A sigh from Mies. ''We may not be able to get much from a site like this, which has been through hell.''

''All right. I'm going to run a full sieve on it. We may see a shadow or two. Or not. Ginny?''

A long pause, murmurs in the background from others on the ship, then she said, ''Kai, I'm going to have to cut power to attitude control for this. Hold on . . . all set. You've got five minutes, then we'll have to recage the gyros.''

''Right.'' And one, and two, and . . .

Nothing at all. Mist as impenetrable and featureless as Pegasus's stratosphere. Whisper from Izzy, ''No sign of a signal at any scale . . . this is useless.''

Disconnecting from the scanner, reeling the waveguides in, Mies felt a sort of dejection set in. They're not from here. I can see that, just from the geology. Was it really possible the Frogmen had come from the stars, too? A mental shrug. *Kai knows this isn't starship quality technology. Where else but Pholos? Pegasus isn't the only world that has changed.* Mies felt a giddy sense of pleasure. Very nice, working with scientist, knowing him. Indigo eyes opened on the dark and stared at them silently. Reminding us, thought Mies, about the why and how of our presence here. Will it really not rest until . . . my

God, is Ginny really all there is left? What will it do when we've finished her off?

Leave us the fuck alone, maybe, let us do our work.

Baleful eyes, saying nothing.

Let us do our work, or . . . *Just let it* try. *Meanwhile* . . . Mies felt the two of them suddenly jump together. Speaking with a single voice, addressing reality: "Okay, we'll have to do it the old-fashioned way. Spread out. If anyone finds anything unusual, let me know."

In some sense, the geology of the landing site could tell them just as much about the past as an SAE scan. If it could be interpreted correctly. Somewhere inside him, the romantic notion of this little field trip par excellence took hold. In the pressure suit, of course, it would be difficult to do anything other than look. He blinked away the fields of numbers and graphs obscuring his vision. Only the tiny suit monitors remained, a bank of telltales like an archaic UFO in the sky. *Now look, damn you. See.* He wiped his mind of preconceived notions, pushed down on the little fragment of himself that wanted to run back to the ship.

He turned from the others, away from the lander, taking cumbersome but power-aided steps, riding in his little harness, feeling the extra gravity as a kind of pleasant languor. There was an insignificant, glassy glare mark on the upper part of his helmet visor and a slight grayish tint that annoyed him, but otherwise it was as if he were standing there helmetless, in direct contact with this alien landscape.

The volcanic structures in the distance were clearly very young, considering the corrosive nature of the carbonic acid rain, no more than a few million years at best. The boulders around him, though composed of the same dark rock, were certainly different ages, many showing signs of the coarse texture associated with chemical weathering.

A slow but powerful wind carried fine particles about, ruffling the intermittent regolith, the only movement aside from the shuffling gait of his now greatly separated companions and the eternal parade of low clouds. He studied the clouds for a moment. There should certainly be topographically controlled weather variations here. Since it was local late afternoon, about ten hours from sunset, temperatures should have equalized somewhat, land warming slowly in the diffuse sunlight.

"Mies." Andy's voice. "I found a deep fissure filled with broken boulders. There's a small, clear creek visible at the bottom. It must've rained here sometime recently."

Mies nodded, looking at the clouds again, imagining where Alpha Centauri A and Bellerophon must be in the sky. He wished his helmet was totally transparent, resisted the temptation to switch to eyebubble input. "Good. I'm coming over."

The four of them met by the crack, a broken "V" zigzagging across the lava field in the direction of the low point of the valley. From here, the lander was a bright, squat cone standing at the brow of a boulder-obscured low ridge. Somewhere down in the dark, hardly self-aware, little David Gilman was imagining that a colorful fluttering penon at its tip would not be out of place.

"Where does it go?" asked Kai. "The creek seems to just vanish about halfway to the edge."

Izzy said, "Can't tell. Probably disappears behind another ridge."

"There is something not far from there," said Andy. "From the imagery we took while landing, it looks a little like a crater. Bottom hidden in shadow. Just a depression, I guess."

Mies tapped the data Andy was viewing, angry at himself for not noticing anything unusual. "No shadows here. It's more than that. It looks like some kind of sinkhole."

"Look at those clouds." Kai was pointing at the wall of gray he had noticed before, closer now, more structured: convecting upward, cauliflower-turreted pillars went up and up until they disappeared into the featureless upper banks. "I'm not an expert on hydrometeorology, but I don't like the looks of it."

Izzy started moving. "We'd better get back."

"Why?" asked Mies. "These suits can take a few drops of rain."

Kai said, "No sign of radio wave emission from lightning,

but radar seems to indicate a heavy wall of precipitation moving our way. Can't really get a good Doppler on it.''

Izzy turned back to them. "Look," he said, irritation plain, "I don't mean to wuss out here. But we're talking *unknown* in capital letters. I don't care *what* these suits were made for.''

Mies was watching the storm. No cirrus anvil, of course. The height of the cumulonimbus was impossible to estimate, but it clearly was many times the size of a standard terrestrial thunderstorm. Afternoon storms were a feature of many tropical environments; perhaps this was the regularly scheduled presunset storm hereabouts. Memory of young David waiting for an August thunderbumper, enjoying the cool downwash of the storm, frightened by its violence but unwilling to go inside. No. Can't afford that luxury here. "Right. Let's get back.''

The auditory feed from the helmet was very sensitive. Halfway back he heard the first *pock,* then another, a third, before he saw one of the large, fast-moving raindrops impact with a little explosion. The dark wall of the mountains began to lighten slightly, and a patch of whitish streaks showed where the storm was most intense. Buffets of wind bounced off his suit, and not so high above dim shreds of cloud fled across his field of view. A heavy raindrop splattered against his faceplate, followed by a steady spatter of smaller precipitation.

They were most of the way back to the ship when the full force of the deluge struck. It was as if the world had suddenly been blotted out and replaced with a dim gray-streaked miasma. The sound had steadied into a muted roar, and Mies fancied he could feel the water pouring over his suit integument. Kai was close enough to see as a dark-misted silhouette; Izzy and Andy, farther ahead, were gone. He continued to walk, general eyebubble feed still off, bumped into a boulder, fell halfway across it with a dull grating noise. It took nearly twenty seconds to right himself.

Kai's cameo appeared in the emergency locus, complex pattern of light and dark from the light coming through his faceplate revealing a crooked grin. "Guess we should've been more cautious. Are you all right, Mies?''

Upright now, but a little shaken, Mies nodded, turned on his suit interface, called up a barely intelligible multispectral view of his surroundings. At least he could see them all and, in the distance, a flattened cone that must be *MN01*. Through the face-plate there was nothing but the heavy wash of the downpour. Boulders here and there. He began to move again.

Izzy's voice: "Look at your feet!"

Mies leaned forward from the waist, looking downward, inadvertently forming a little clear space shielded from the rain. Around his feet surged a swirling torrent of muddy water, moving downhill, toward the fissure. As he watched, it deepened, now covering the ankle dovetails.

"This is turning into a real gulleywasher," Andy said, unnaturally loud in his ears. "We'd better call the ship."

"*Mother Night*," said Kai, "this is *MN01* landing party. Ginny, we've got a developing situation here. Do you read?"

"I'm here, Kai."

Mies activated his comcam. "Didn't quite expect the severity of this thunderstorm, Captain. The water is rising. We may need some assistance." His own voice cracked, sounded desperate, a signal from another him, almost powerless in this emergency. He looked down again, saw the water rushing around his thighs. He took a few steps, amazed that he couldn't feel it at all; the suit was compensating.

He scanned the rainscape looking for signs that the cloudburst was tapering off, but, as far as he could tell, it was actually growing in intensity. Even with the decreased visibility, though, he could see the water surface around him, chest high. Another step, and he felt a slight subsidence under his foot, the barest sense of loss of traction.

"We may need a rescue party, if this keeps up," Kai said.

Ginny: "I'll get *MN02* ready, Kai. Just remember, those suits are supposed to make you invulnerable. Manufacturer's guarantee."

"I'm not especially worried about getting hurt. It's just that this is damn embarrassing. I'm going to—whoops. Lost my footing there for a moment. This water's moving *fast*."

Andy: "Izzy and I have made it back to the lander. Can't see you. Mies, are you okay?"

"Yeah. I think so," said Mies tentatively. "But I've suddenly decided that it's not such a good idea to try to walk. Uh-oh."

"Mies, what happened?" shouted Kai. "Jesus, he's adrift; the water must've dislodged him. Goddamn it, me too. I'm going . . . shit."

"Hang on, Kai," said Ginny. "I'm coming down."

Mies was underwater, unable to see through the turbidity, feeling his orientation change quickly, swinging about in his harness. He felt a series of sharp impacts on his posterior, then, turned over, a sharp rap on his chest. He cursed the suit for not letting him know what was happening, then cursed it for not protecting him enough. The fear in the back of his mind built slowly. He tried to send a message, but only a hoarse croak came out.

Crack. Mies felt himself come apart and . . .

Scientist letting him go, reaching for the system's control interfaces; scientist grimly striving to save them all. Mies thought, the others. The others will get in his way. Turning, turning to suppress them and . . .

Baleful eyes opening, cold, calm, empty. YOU KNEW, it whispered. YOU KNEW WHEN THE LAST ONE WAS TAKEN . . . YOU KNEW WE'D HAVE TO DIE. YOU KNEW.

No. No I didn't.

Scientist, distracted, turning, astonished, full of angry, futile accusations. Little David crying out his terror. Wishing himself safe in bed. It's only a dream. I'll wake up soon, safe with Mummy and Dah and Seesy and . . . Image of Seesy, stripped naked, in the land of little David's dreams.

Reiko-chan moaning, **Oh, thank God. The end. Thank God.**

Grown-up David Gilman wakening from his long slumber, looking around, bemused. What? *Again?* Everyone looking. Just looking.

For a moment, his head broke free of the water, and he saw light, but it was gone before he could make out anything definite. He thought that the rain must've stopped, but he couldn't be sure. The next time his head stayed out longer. In the middle distance, the pool was swirling in what appeared to be a concentric set of waves; in the center of this disturbance the surface appeared to be below him slightly. As he watched he was carried some distance around, then plunged once more into darkness.

It was a whirlpool of enormous proportions, the maelstrom of legend come to life. Mies began to laugh. Silly, silly Mister Mies, to have come this far only to be swallowed up whole by the monster of his dreams. *As unlikely as it seems, this whole plateau feeds into that damn sinkhole, one great drainage system with an enormous drain. It makes a sort of sense, really, the acidic rain breaking through the resistant basalt to softer, more erodable materials below, taking the shortest route back to the ocean from whence it ultimately comes.*

Oh. Thanks. He braced against the inside of his suit and felt himself fall.

Falling, Kai looked upward through the foggy faceplate of his worksuit and watched gray daylight drop away into the darkness above, shiny wall of water almost motionless beside him, boiling globules forming, breaking up, coalescing, but falling right along with him. Mies was a bulky, struggling, gray-white figure in the near distance, arms and legs flailing in helpless, useless circles, amplified by his suit's exoskeleton, voice loud but damped down, a wordless, chaotic babble of barely formed sounds.

Izzy and Andy? Nowhere. Darkness growing as daylight became an irregular white blotch far above. Izzy and Andy on their hands and knees, beyond the little waveshock where the scanner head had fallen, was being swept away. Strong, earth-born Izzy clinging to a ridge of stone, boiling water a clear shell over his round white helmet; Andy under the water, no more than a shadow, seeming to cling to Izzy's legs . . .

Impact.

Kai felt his legs crumple, heard the suit hydraulics grunt, somewhere down one of his arms heard a servomotor scream and die. Sharp smell in his nostrils. Burnt-out motor. A brief flicker of amber numbers down by his chin, suit's eyebubble interface reporting damage control, but . . . primitive numbers. Simple graphs.

The core link is cut! Hard heart-thud of fear and . . .

Impact.

Kai's chin slammed down into flicker-fading numbers, slammed down on the lower edge of the helmet's hard structure, teeth snapping together. Taste of blood. Head rebounding, bouncing off the little pad in the back of the helmet. Something starting up in his nose. A faint smell of blood now as well.

Vision hazed, as if . . .

Droplets of blood, maybe, on the inside of my faceplate and . . .

Darkness. Darkness complete now.

Mies still crying out in his ears. Calling out for a savior? Some little god perhaps?

Impact.

Kai's face jammed into the faceplate, sliding around in greasy wet. Hydraulic fluid? My blood? Hammer of ghastly terror. Boiling water inside here with me? Cooking and dying like a lobster in my shell?

Face down on a hard surface, water pouring over him like slick oil, dragging him, arms and legs outstretched, like a limber starfish being dragged along the bottom of the sea by some powerful, implacable current and . . .

Impact.

Impact from above, hardly felt, something falling on him, bouncing away and . . . Kai reached out to grab whatever it was, powered suit limbs reacting perfectly, grappling with it, suit's touchsensors revealing a manshape, glassy outline trying to form in his eyes, struggling manshape outlined in a wireframe of amber and gold. Forming, flickering, dying.

Suit node overwhelmed and . . .

The man-thing got away, tumbling away into darkness, then Kai was falling again, falling, tumbling, whirling about three axes at once, heart seeming to stand still, to hang suspended and hopeless in his chest.

We'll never get out of here.

Falling and falling and . . .

Impact. Sliding. Rolling across some not-quite-motionless obstacle, suitnode, fed a morsel of raw data, forming the manthing again, very briefly, out of lines of light and . . .

"Mies!" Shout into the suit's sensor, hoping . . .

Wordless cries, resolving into Mies's voice.

"Where . . ."

Then they were falling again, rapping, over and over, against invisible black walls, just falling, voices become grunts of effort as the walls reached out to strike them again and again, until Kai wondered if he would ever breathe normally and . . .

Going to die. A very quiet voice, somewhere inside his head.

Going to die.

Not my voice.

Not Mies.

Not anyone.

Not even the voice of God.

Just the voice of realization.

Going to die.

Impact.

Kai lying, stunned, caught in an ice of total darkness, water boiling over him like a rock embedded in a stream. Like the rock that had caught him now, was holding him still against the flood. Heart hammering, slowing, weight of the water crushing him against a succoring stone. My God, my God, I . . .

Darkness.

Kai tipped his head up and to the right, looking toward where the input sensor should be. Must still be. My helmet's not broken. I'm still breathing. Air puffing from vents under my chin. My God, I . . . "Light. Light, please . . ."

Wan amber glow from the sensor. Kai, inside a tiny, featureless space, looking at the black dot that was all that linked him with the suit's node, node a tiny bubble of data processing capability, all that was left to him of human civilization just now.

A nod.

Numbers scrolling up around his chin.

My God. Everything works.

One hydraulic line in my left leg clamped off, oil leaked into my left boot. Kneeseal intact. Left elbow servomotor burned out, backup taking its place. Exoskeleton functional. Life support undamaged.

A whisper: "Uh. Radarlight?"

Scroll of numbers, node reporting external sensor conditions to him. "Radio link?" No.

He nodded at the sensor, struggled to his hands and knees, head breaking the surface of the water, water a rush of force at his elbows, up around his hips, and waited. Suddenly, the world outside his helmet filled with gold-orange light. Cavern. River in a cavern. Kai stood, teetering, force of water now directed only at his knees, looking around at an artificial image being projected into his eyes by the suit's eyebubble.

My God.

Hot yellow-orange tunnel, stretching away to the fore, radarlight dying out in a cacophony of echoes, curving upward aft, disappearing in a radar-bright wall of falling water, rushing river a mirror surface of burnished gold all around his feet, boiling at his knees like molten metal.

Black patches here and there around the walls. Radar absorbing regions. Or empty holes swallowing the signal . . .

Whisper in his earphones: "Kai . . ." Voice barely recognizable.

"Mies?"

Voice like a lost child, child whispering in the clutches of an invincible nightmare. "Kai. My God, Kai. Help me."

Kai glanced at the sensor, calling up a shimmer of appallingly simplified controls, blink at the radio direction finder. Signal indicator turning. Useless. He stepped to one side, watched it arc back and forth. Stepped again, watching the arc narrow. That way.

"Hang on, Mies. I'm coming."

Horrid whisper, full of despair: "Oh, Jesus. Losing my grip . . ."

Kai splashing forward, slipping, almost falling down, feeling the river bottom shallow under his feet, the current grown stronger and rougher and . . .

Suddenly falling to his knees, intestines cramping as he stared over the bright radar image of the water's curving surface, looked down into a black abyss lit only by the pale twinkles of false reflection. Dense air molecules down there, wisps of steam.

A long God-damned fall.

"Mies!"

"Hurry . . ."

"Where the hell are you?"

"Don't know. Slipping . . ."

"Are you under the fucking water? I'm on radar."

"Yes. Underwater. On a vertical . . . Ohhh!" A hard grunt then.

Kai crept to the edge of the waterfall, felt his hand grip the ledge, mechanical strength multiplying the force of his fingers a thousandfold, until the smooth rock seemed to deform, though it was probably only the structure of his worksuit gloves giving way, pushed dangerously close to their failure point.

Red numbers blinking in the corner of his eyes, warning him.

All right. All right. A nod to the radar control panel, pulling power from life support and sending out a pulse of power, like a brilliant flash of light, driving radio waves through the uppermost layers of the water.

There!

Briefly glimpsed shape of a man, about three meters to the right, about one meter down, hanging under the face of the waterfall. "Mies?"

"Hurry."

"All right. I see you. Hold on."

"I'm not going to fucking let go . . . " A trace of exasperation? A trace of humor? Mies calming right down, with the prospect of rescue. All is not lost after all. . . .

Kai crawled over until he was directly above where the suit remembered the glimpse had been, manufacturing an image of Mies. Well. If he's moved, the suit won't know, so . . .

He lay down in the water, clinging to the lip of rock, radar light suddenly snuffed, inner surface of his faceplate suddenly glaring bright, blinding him with its dazzle before the suit realized it should stop putting data in his eyes, replaced it with a wireframe of the rock face, the undersurface of the water, the outline of Mies Cochrane.

Good suit. Good damned suit. Well-written goddamned emergency sieve-matrix. My compliments to the fucking manufacturer.

He reach down, sliding his arm down the face of the cliff, reached out to touch the image of a spacesuited man. There. There. Rapping Mies on the helmet. "Okay. Here."

And Mies reacting like a demon, snatching at his arm before the falling water could snatch him away, swarming up his arm like Tarzan up a jungle vine. Then the two of them standing, knee-deep in radar-imaged golden water, Mies holding onto him, holding on as if the spacesuit were really a man.

Kai said, "Let's get the fuck out of here."

Away from the waterfall then, back up the bright river, angling toward one of the dark patches in the rough yellow-orange wall. Groping with outstretched hands. An opening . . . Turning the corner, new orange cavern opening up before them.

Mies, leaning against the nearest wall, then slumping to the floor, though his suit's exoskeleton needed no rest. "Where the hell are we?"

Kai suddenly looked at his controls, called up a schematic of the batterygraph. Forty-seven hours remaining. A very good suit, indeed. Kai slumped to the ground beside him, realizing how glad his body was, how relieved, to assume a posture of rest. Hell, even in zero gee, we used to pretend to sit down.

Here, two hard gees were crushing him into the bottom of his suit, feet swollen, feeling raw, abraded by the softest of socks, by the inside of his powered boots. "Under the ground. Under the fucking ground."

Silence, crackle of radiostatic in his ears.

Mies suddenly said, "*Mother Night,* this is *MN01* EVA-2, do you copy?" Nothing. "*Mother Night, MN01.*"

Nothing.

Kai said, "Radio's bouncing around in here just like the radar."

Silence.

Mies said, "You think we can . . . climb back up?"

Silence.

Kai said, "We'll have to. They're not going to find us before our batteries run down."

Silence.

Then Mies said, "Christ. I've only got forty-four hours left."

Silence.

Mies again: "You . . . want to go now?"

Kai said, "I'm fucked up, Mies. It's this gravity. I've got to rest a bit."

Silence.

Mies: "Yeah. Me, too. Maybe. Rest a while. Then we'll have to get moving. . . ."

At precisely forty hours of remaining battery power, Mies's alarm began to sound, a loud, repeating pure tone A. He awoke from a deep, deep sleep, opened his eyes on the virtual world of his suit readouts, nothing but blackness beyond. Icons mixed with the random firing of his optical reference system, the latter a swirling jumble of almost coalescing images. Where? Memory of getting lost under the covers, in bed at home, looking for the scrap of light that would tell him he was not blind. Memory of washing up on the beach, struggling a little, letting the breakers carry him, Robinson Crusoe, to land.

All alone?

Who?

Me. That's it, I'm . . .

Dry, whispery chuckle from the scientist. *You and I have a lot in common, don't we, Mies? I wish I was me as well.*

Soft throb of terror, followed by memory and refragmentation.

I like you, Mies.

Quirky, peculiar thoughts, an emotion coursing through him that was almost like amusement. A slightly sarcastic, Well, isn't *that* convenient?

Dry, bemused: *I suppose it is. Sure as hell convenient if it lets us work together. We're in a hell of fix, just now, you and I . . .*

''Christ!'' He sat up with a start, his swaying harness driving home the point. ''Anyone here?''

A small face appeared in the darkness, as if across a room, floating. Friend or foe? Tedious but friendly Kai. ''Turn on your radar vision. It's better than nothing.''

It was. Much better. The world was limned all around him, a world of gold, stretching out in all directions, complex but nearly monochromatic. Sitting on a ledge, with another bright, curvilinear suit. Ledge ending, opposite wall 1.5 kilometers away, honeycombed with what must be deep, tapering caverns. Upward, columnar basalt tapering inward, almost like a forest of closely spaced trees, leaning forward ominously. Above that, blocky strata of more quickly cooled rock formed a ceiling maybe half a kilometer distant. No sign of any opening, but a thin ribbon of gold appeared from nowhere and fell past them, the remains of the torrent. The water's motion seemed unnaturally fast, two gee making a substantial difference. And . . .

Kai. Yes. Good old Kai.

You like him, too, do you?

I do, yes. He's a rational man, way down deep.

Mies smirked. Way down deep? I didn't think you had it in you, scientist.

It's in both of us.

So. What kind of rational man cuts off his cock and balls so he can walk like a woman in the world? Indigo rules lighting up his path. Rules of behavior. Manufactured worldview, giving David Gilman a way to . . . to judge.

We can't help the way we are formed, Mies. Kai was born to be what he is. Which is more rational, having your biochemistry adjusted to drown the misery, or having your body adjusted to match your heart's desire?

A quick zoetrope of memories. Mies sighed. I wish I knew.

That's where Kai is superior to us. He knows. And knowing, he acted. That is the very definition *of a rational man.*

Is it?

Thinking of Kai now, picturing his slim, delicate form. Thinking of those few times he'd chanced to see the man naked. *Man?* Slim hips, like a teenaged girl at the very doorstep of puberty. Hairless slit of a vulva, like a girl younger than that. Kai batting gray eyelashes at him . . .

Throb of revulsion, turning away.

Indigo eyes opening on night. NOT A FERTILE FEMALE. WORTHLESS. FORGET HIM.

I wonder, Could *we infect him? If we wanted to?*

Mies feeling anger and despair. That again? I thought we'd escaped.

Indigo eyes cold and silent, staring.

The rules are still there, Mister Mies.

Anger. Hatred.

We could *infect him, you know.*

Impossible. His vagina's just a blind sac.

Oh, sure, but . . . get him to give you a blowjob, come in his mouth. Then get him to kiss you before he can swallow it or spit it out, get some of the semen in your mouth. Then give him a blowjob, with the semen still in your mouth. Some of the autoviroids would find their way up his urethra and . . .

Mies suddenly felt sick.

But the Indigo eyes were still watching, still listening. With evident interest? No telling.

Anyway, here we are, in our little spacesuit, far, far under the ground and not *likely to survive.* Somewhere, far away, little David started to whimper.

Out in the real world, Kai stood up and looked around. "What do you make of it?" he asked.

"Well, not a whole lot is clear from this vantage point. We appear to have been deposited in the neck of a gargantuan basaltic sinkhole unlike anything in my experience or, I think, my database." Mies slowly righted himself and stepped toward the ledge's edge, close but not too close. Of course, rocks usually persisted in relatively stable configurations, but you couldn't be too careful. "Down there is a cavern without parallel on the Earth, angling away from us about forty-five degrees from the level. I can only see about four kilometers, but there's no sign of a far wall."

"So what're we looking at?"

"We're almost through the volcanic caprock and into what appears to be much older, heavily stratified sand and siltstone. I'll bet in visible light that whole section beneath us would look like a Grand Canyon analog. It's spectacular, even to radar."

A moment of gawking, straining wonder. Mies tried to count the obvious separate formations going down, down, but lost track before reaching the limits of his radar. "Temperature's a lot lower in here, barely three-fifty kelvins. From the pressure reading, I'd estimate that we're a little under six kilometers above sea level.

"Looks like we're going to have to go down there to get out. Six klicks isn't that bad."

Mies felt a surge of something unexpected. "That'll be a challenge. But look at the bright side. We'll be climbing down into Pegasus's past. This erosion has uncovered what must be nearly the whole geologic record of the proto-Huttonian craton. Somewhere down there perhaps are the fossils we've been looking for."

"I don't think I'm ready for much in the way of falling. I'm pretty comfortable in my harness now, and my body seems to be making pretty good adaptation to the higher gravity. But. Let's take it slow, okay?"

Mies grimaced. "We haven't got a lot of time, otherwise

the prudent thing might be to wait for rescue from above. I don't know."

"What'll we find at the bottom? Is there any way to tell?"

"The water has to emerge somewhere. Whether the opening is above or below water . . ."

"Well, no sense standing around." Kai raised a leg and planted it firmly on the rim of the ledge. With a facetious scream, he leapt.

The journey was much easier than it had appeared at first. The suits, when prepared, could absorb the impact from a three-meter jump with no problem. They picked their way with care, moving slowly at first and then gaining momentum. At one point Mies looked back and could no longer find the little ledge where they'd slept.

After about three kilometers, the cave wall they were descending leveled out slightly, still inclined twenty to twenty-five degrees from horizontal, but much easier to traverse, though the suits were not well designed for the sort of sideways, one-foot-after-another, style of locomotion necessary. They paralleled the descent of the stream, one spectacular waterfall after another, its voice a subdued splashy roar that filled the cavern with sound.

Mies continually inspected the strata of rock through which they passed, taking samples every now and again, picking apart rocks to see what was inside, laughing to himself periodically. At a point where the cavern leveled out still further, he stopped, looked back. Kai, a couple of steps ahead, missing the *clump-clump-clump* of his companion, turned, came back.

"What is it?"

"Every scrap of information we need to interpret the last billion years on this planet is here, if we could just read it. If we had the scanner along, we'd know exactly what happened here. Even without doing a sample analysis, I can tell you that this continent has risen and fallen several times. We started off at what amounts to the present, the basaltic eruptions being certainly no more than a few million years old. Clearly, tidal forces from the downspinning of Bellerophon created or maintained a plume of hot mantle material in this part of the planet.

"The part of the cavern we've been in so far represents the offshore deposition of sediments in the hundreds of millions of years prior to the beginning of subduction. As we've moved downward, we're moving into the past, and we're beginning to come to the epochs when Pegasus was much more Earthlike, prior to the general hardening of the crust that halted plate tectonics and heralded the end of the geochemical cycle."

Kai said, "Interesting. No wonder the SAE scan was negative. Let's keep going."

A crackle of individuals separating out.

Interesting, he says, thought the scientist. *I like a man who can go to his death, admiring the scenery on the road to Hell and suggesting we press onward.*

Maybe just a fool?

Maybe we're all fools. Why the hell are we here, *after all? Not escape. That's just the excuse we made up! Escape from Indigo? Fuck. Indigo is inside us.*

Indigo eyes.

You see*?*

Mies looked at the battery monitor. God. Thirty-seven hours! Ahead of him stretched a surface, mirror flat, colored gold by the radar. For a moment he wondered inanely if it was some sort of weird rock formation, but when he stepped on its edge, little ripplets rushed outward in a spreading circle. Water. He surveyed the cave vault ahead of him, which had been narrowing for the last hour or so, the character of the rock changing slowly. *No way around it, the pool extends to the walls on either side.*

He said, "We have a complication."

Kai, who'd been lagging behind, appeared beside him. "I see. No way to tell how deep it is. Well, aside from being temporarily radar blind, this shouldn't be much of a problem."

Mies took another step into the pool. A wild moiré of intersecting ripples began to distort the smooth surface. The third step was unfortunate. Mies began to fall backward, legs disappearing deeper into the water, arms upraised in alarm. For a long moment, he teetered, center of gravity apparently in his favor, then slowly, as if one outcropping of rock after another was giving way, he began to sink. In a moment the golden water closed over the helmet.

Falling. Even through water, the sensation was clear; two gee made sure of that. Mies tried flailing, felt pain as the suit tried to respond. In his eyes, a blur of icons and the meaningless jumble of radar distortion. Falling. Not slowly, as in a dream. Quickly, accelerating. Panic receding, though. Get out of the way, little one.

He was just about to get a lock on his situation, bringing his arms in and resettling himself, when his feet struck hard, suit compensating, but not enough. Crushed into the harness, various body parts making sharp contact. No pain, that would come later. Stunned, he lost control of the suit, and it toppled forward, crunching when it hit.

Hanging prone, feeling like an abandoned marionette, Mies pulled together his jangled senses slowly. First, take stock, try to move. Nothing feels broken, but how can I tell for sure? He had an image of blood pooling beneath him in the suit, pushed it away. "I'm . . . I'm okay. I think." He smiled, blinked a little. Nothing better to do.

Kai's voice said, "Your telemetry indicates you've fallen approximately three hundred meters. That's one hell of a drop. But your life signs are okay."

"That's good to know. I should've been a little more careful, I guess. Hold on for a second. I'm going to try to stand up."

Mies shrugged his shoulders, repositioned himself in the harness, finally felt almost comfortable. He pushed himself up, brought a knee under. Damn, the radar was worse than useless. He extinguished it, found himself a little afraid of the darkness that resulted. "All right, I've got both legs under me. What the hell is *that*?"

As his eyes became dark-adapted, something was appearing beyond the bubble icons. Something pink. Light! "Suit display off. Kai, there's light down here!"

Kneeling there, slowly, so very slowly, his eyes became used to the low level of light. The water was as clear and clean as a lens, slight turbidity from his movements subsiding rapidly. The bottom of the pool looked like a crystal graveyard, covered to some depth with translucent, dagger-shaped crystals of all sizes, some shattered, most intact. Behind them, through them, around him, there was pink. Pink everywhere, coming from nowhere.

"Look at it! Kai, can you see?" Transferring the images.

"Goddamn it," the other whispered. "Yes. I can see. Look at 'em."

"I was expecting to run into fossils sooner or later. Nothing like this." Mies stood, feeling pain for the first time, bloody strong twinges in both knees. He looked upward toward the surface, where Kai must be, saw only pink.

Mies moved through the water slowly, carefully dipping his feet through the layer of crystals. "Kai, if I'm right, we've stumbled onto our first examples of genuine Pegasian life. The water temperature here is just under three-fifty kelvins, and I don't see why you couldn't have some kind of phosphorescent algae feeding off the heat and dissolved nutrients."

"Not much of an ancestor for a spacefaring race. I still can hardly believe we're talking about the same things."

Mies picked up a particularly large crystal, a milky-clear lanceolate structure perhaps a meter long, and examined it carefully. "These fossils are truly remarkable. Under close inspection, they appear to be composed of woven glass fibers, pure SiO_2, which would explain their resistance to weathering. If this were Earth, I'd speculate that this formation was originally composed of limestone or some other calcareous rock especially vulnerable to the acidic erosion. The fossils, originally embedded in this matrix, are now all that's left."

Kai said, "Hmh. Okay, Mies, that's fascinating, but what do we do now? I sure as hell am not going back."

"You're not going to like this, but . . . as I see it, this level is the natural continuation of the cavern we were following. There's only one answer."

"I was hoping that wasn't what you were going to say. However, I see your point. Here I come."

A moment later a hulking missile came plummeting downward encased in a shroud of bubbles, landing feet first, perfectly balanced. Mies heard the *oof* as he hit. "That wasn't so bad. You're right, this illumination is surreal."

Mies started off, noted that the other was following slowly. "I wonder if we would have found it sooner if it weren't for our dependence on the radar."

"Still, we can only see a few tens of meters. No way to tell what lies ahead."

"One way."

"Well, onward, then. If the batteries go, it won't really matter whether this is a dead end or not."

What seemed like days passed as they continued their erratic course downward. When the crystals began to grow sparse, they gathered up as many as they could fit into their sample pouches, algae-filled water harvested automatically. The temperature and light levels slowly decreased, leaving barely enough illumination to maneuver by.

The appearance of the water was slowly changing. Minute particles were scattering the light, and big strings of some white, gooey substance began to float before their faceplates, tangling around them, breaking as they brushed them away with a glove. Not life, perhaps, but something like it. The temperature began to rise.

Mies thought, I can't . . . quite come to grips with what I'm seeing here.

Life. Unmistakable. This is the evidence we were looking for. We'll get our samples back to the ship and . . .

If. If. *This makes our survival . . . necessary.*

Wistful: Rosie would've wanted to be here. If she'd come along . . . if she was here now, I might have a chance to . . . repair the damage I've done.

INFECTED ALREADY. NO INTEREST.

Fury. Shut *up*, you fucking bastard!

Not a person, Mister Mies. Not a person at all. Just god-damned rules. Save your anger.

Despair: But Rosie would *love* to be here now. This would have made her . . . happy.

All the more reason for us to survive. Onward.

For the first time, the cavern began to ascend, which made progress even more difficult. The rock was gnarled and studded with multiple hand- and footholds, and they climbed and climbed until it seemed they must be undoing the progress they had made. Abruptly, Kai's helmet broke the surface of the water and he found himself looking up into an enormous chamber, as dim as late twilight. Mies's head emerged a few meters away. "Is this it?"

As they climbed out of the water, Kai switched on his radar, which revealed the room to be a couple of hundred meters high, and an equal distance across. The ceiling was very complex, obviously composed of carbonate dripstone, sharp downward pointing stalactites intermingled with great flowing draperies. He pulled himself out of the water, dripping heavily, carefully scraped a string from the corner of his faceplate.

He sat on a knob of rock, not a stalagmite, but darker, igneous-looking. Tired, puffing a little. Time to rest, anyway. Mies walked by him, staring up at the roof, making observations.

"I don't see how we could have taken a wrong turn," Mies said. "But the presence of these stalactites suggests that this cavity is not filled during the episodes of flooding, else the carbonic acid would quickly dissolve the limestone and wash it away."

Kai looked up at the thousands of iciclelike fingers, heavy rock swords just waiting to break off and impale him. "We don't have much time left."

"On the other hand, we may have found some of the missing epochs of Pegasian life here." Mies gestured above his head. "We're probably in a stratum more than two billion years old. That rock you're sitting on, the floor of the cavern in fact, is heavily metamorphosed granite, and could well be part of the Huttonian basement complex." He carefully pointed himself in the right direction and took a seat on the knob next to Kai. Their suits bumped.

"The far wall of the chamber also appears to be limestone. There could be small solution pathways hidden among the dripstones. We'll just have to look."

"This is a damn long way to come to end up like this."

For a moment, Mies felt the urge to clasp the man's hand, but fought it down. "I know. On the other hand, I feel like . . . I've lived many dozens of lifetimes. Perhaps this is the place to call closure on it all." Lies? No, honesty for a change.

Kai said, "Strange. To me, my life always seems like the beginning of something. Hard to accept the truth."

Hard to accept the truth. Mies felt the words form, like bitter oil, in his head.

That's why you needed all those rules to show you the way. That's why you joined Indigo. It's why we're here.

Me? It was Gilman, David Gilman who . . .

So you believe you're not *David Gilman?*

Kai yawned suddenly and grinned. "I'm ready for another break. How about you?"

Mies looked at his battery indicator and said, "Well . . ."

"What difference does it make? Either we live or die. I need to catch a quick nap. Four hours?"

A sense of panic rising from little David, who'd never wanted to die, never believed he'd have to. Mies said, "Okay." And after that?

Who gives a shit?

I do. I want to live.

That's your biggest problem. Always looking for a way out. Always wanting to escape. Mies sat, silent, offended, staring out into the golden radar light and, after a while, fell asleep.

Hours had passed. Climb. Fall. Walk. Walk on.

Then the sounds. Rhythmic, tidal. Hope. Up through a submerged grotto, dark and narrow, barely large enough to accommodate the fat suits, knowing their battery power was about exhausted. Mies's about gone. A few more hours for me.

We're below sea level now, thought Kai. If this isn't it . . .

Wading through darkness, almost swimming, light suddenly appearing, as if dawn had broken somewhere, Kai pulled himself through the last little hole, feeling Mies bump against his booted feet. Amber numbers and controls spawned around his chin, ambient temperature and pressure, suitnode letting him know it understood it was still underwater. And letting him know Mies had, by extension, ninety minutes left on battery power.

Emergency batteries, then. Fuel cells popping, cooking off their energy. One more hour, with the suit powered down, more or less, acid-powered radio beacon screaming for help across the spectrum . . .

His head broke through the sloping silver undersurface of the sea, water cascading off his faceplate, silver-gray light flooding into his eyes. Long vista of a flat, slowly surging seascape. Flat water, with bits of bubbling froth here and there, little wisps of steam rising. Like the surface of some giant pot, in which some vast deity will simmer his tender pasta. . . . Not daylight. It's night now.

Mies's helmet broke the water beside him, Mies rising, head and shoulders protruding into the steamy air, face visible, eyes very large, eye looking around. Waves beaching themselves nearby. Black cliffs towering upward, toward an empty gray sky. "Well," he said, voice heavy with relief. "Well. We made it."

Kai only nodded. Nodded, knowing, for the first time in days, the other man could see his face. Made it. Going to live, after all. They turned and waded slowly up onto the ebon beach, stood together, spacesuited shoulders almost touching, stood looking at the bright-dim Pegasian sea. Finally, he said, "This is a hell of a place, isn't it?"

Only silence from Mies.

Kai turned away from the seascape then, looked up at the gray clouds, feeling almost as if he could see right through them to enormous Bellerophon and tawny B beyond. He said,

"*Mother Night,* this is *MN01* EVA-1. EVA-1 and -2. How do you copy?"

Long silence, sizzling with soft, faraway static, then a stunned voice in his earphones, Doc's voice: "My God! *Kai!?*" Somewhere in the background, a woman's voice, screaming. Ginny's voice.

Profoundly exhausted, Kai said, "We're here, Doc. Come and get us."

Excited: "All right! Crack your beacons . . ."

And then Mies, voice quiet: "Izzy? Andy?"

Doc said, "Hello, Mies. *MN01* plugged up the hole before much else could happen. They're fine. We even got the lander back up in one piece."

And Ginny: "Okay, we've got you plotted. Twenty minutes."

Kai fell to his knees in the sand, staring out across the sea. "Good enough . . ."

FIVE

Rule-sieves erupting from the darkness, volcanic, imperative . . .

Spence floated close to him in the hatchway, anger turning his face red. "Mies, I'm warning you. Just once. Stay away from her. I let you be while you were needed, but we're done for the time being, so it's time to settle this once and for all."

Mies watched all his components fragment away and recede, this bit hiding here, that bit there. Bastards. Always leaving me alone when the shit hits the fan. Don't they understand we're all . . .

No. They do not. Scientist very far away, watching from a dark corner. *Me? Not my specialty.*

Indigo eyes open, though. Watching. Waiting.

Mies blanched, backing away. "Don't worry about it, Spence. I'm not—"

"I kind of hoped you weren't coming back from Pegasus. You're a cold fish, that's for sure. What I can't figure is, just what's your game?"

"I . . . I . . ." What to say? What to do? Despair. *I don't know!* Somebody do something. Help me. He felt a certain stuffiness well up from somewhere unknown, and said, "If you please, we can finish this later. The meeting's about to begin, you know. Important stuff, not *this* bullshit."

"Bullshit, is it?" Warvai grabbed a handhold, swung himself down, balled up fist in the lead. Mies ducked as best he could, took a glancing blow off his shoulder, which brought him skidding downward, feet going up.

Panic. Helpless. Little David crying. Reiko flinching, expecting to be beaten. **Women are always beaten. That's what they're . . . for.** Scientist angry, of course, but good for nothing.

Indigo eyes suddenly flaring brilliant blue-white.

Training.

Hypnopaedia.

Rules for everything that matters.

Rules for the seduction of women.

Goddamn it, he's not trying to *fuck* me!

Scientist, amused, despite the danger: *Well, sort of . . .*

Indigo eyes: IT'S CALLED THE ANGRY HUSBAND SUBROUTINE.

Rules spooling from storage to subconscious.

Backward somersault, feet hitting bulkhead at an odd angle. Mies saw a holdbar coming at him, slipped his hand under and brought himself to a halt. Spence was in the hatchway, staring at him as though he thought it would have a physical effect.

"Let that be a warning. The others don't have to know. But you will."

Mies made himself relax. "I'm not interested in her," he said. "I never was."

Spence's face turned livid again, his mouth starting to open, but Mies turned away, turning his back, knowing he was safe.

Floating in front of the group, Rosie talked about her findings, bright ticks of light illustrating her words in the light table display. "The upshot," she said, "is that while the existing Pegasian life-forms are fascinating, worth a lifetime of study, they cannot possibly have been evolutionarily collateral, or descended from, the source of the images retrieved with the synchronoptic analysis engine."

Ginny said: "Are you willing to say, categorically, that the Frogmen did *not* come from Pegasus?"

She glanced at Mies, then said, "Yes."

We knew that. Just let it go. Our turn will come.

I see that shadow in her eyes, whenever she looks at me.

What the hell did you expect? Forget it.

And Linda. Look at Linda. Did I break her heart?

What makes you think she's got a heart? Did she think about Spence's *feelings when she was pulling her pants down for you? Just forget it. I'm sorry it makes you feel bad.*

Kai said, "So. Are we concluding the Frogmen were starfarers after all?"

Rose: "No. We're just concluding they didn't come from Pegasus."

Staring at Kai, Mies thought, Probably my only friend, just now. *Cut it out. Let's get down to business.* He said, "You're most likely right. We learned a valuable lesson down there, though. In the future, we should treat manned landings on terrestrial planets with great caution. We almost lost a lander, and it could have been worse. The mission would be severely compromised if four more of us were lost."

Ginny frowned, nodding. "We'll have to rewrite the rules a bit. Be more cautious."

Izzy laughed. "You can say that again. That was downright embarrassing."

Ginny said, "Well. We'll have all the time we need to study the Pegasian life-forms. After we finish the system-wide resource survey, we'll come back here and set up a research base. Maybe drop one lander with a bioscience team, then take *Mother Night* back out to do the mining engineering studies."

"About time," muttered Spence.

Kai said, "We'll need to start looking for the radionuclides we need before that."

This is getting out of hand, thought Mies. They're about to make a decision that—

Take it easy. I'm all set.

"I've been looking at the pictures we've taken of the other planets in both the A and B system," said Mies. "It looks like the only other place our friends could've come from is Alpha Centauri B2, which we're calling Pholos."

"Wait just a damned a minute, Mies," said Spence, face reddening. "We've done enough gallivanting around from one planet to the next, looking for these alien critters of yours. There's still no sign they came from here at all. We have a preexisting schedule in which we'll get to these worlds sooner or later, but meanwhile we'll be doing the important business of scouting resources. We should return to the outer system, checking out what's still available there. We haven't seen anything but very low-res pictures of Ixion and its moons.''

Poor Spencie. First we fuck his girlfriend and now we try to fuck up his job.

Mies stared at Spence for a second, then said, ''Pholos is slightly larger than the Earth, with a diameter of twelve thousand two hundred and seventy kilometers. It has a low density, four-point-four grams per cubic centimeter, which makes it only point-seven-one Earth masses. Best guess is that its geochemical cycle is long ended, and that it is not far into a senile epizoic phase, after a long and possibly Earthlike history. Images show some of the same types of markings found on Bellerophon and the Nephelëan moons. Water's all gone. Let's see, what else? Thin nitrogen atmosphere, exceptionally large relief between continents and former seabeds. It must've been an interesting place at one time, though in the present epoch it is clearly dead.''

Linda hesitated, then said, ''Mies, I think you're clutching at straws.''

Mies thought, Do you suppose she's still hoping . . .

Probably just a weak attempt to support Spence. She can't stand him, but he's all she's got. Forget about them.

''The paradigm said that Pegasus used to be Earthlike, too,'' said Ginny.

Mies grinned. ''And it *was*, Captain. It *was*. There's plenty of evidence that Pegasus was cooler and had a much less massive atmosphere in the past. The paradigm was right.''

''Are there any other possibilities after Pholos?'' Ginny asked.

''None,'' said Mies. ''If we don't find anything on Pholos, I'm prepared to recommend a return to the mission timeline.

Though I can't imagine where they *did* come from, if not one of the planets here."

Ginny pressed her lips together into a thin line, then seemed to decide. "A week at most, and we'll head back to the outer system. Kai, does that satisfy you?"

Kai nodded. "I guess so."

"Any other thoughts? All right, then, let's get ready."

Ginny floated, barely held by the substance of *Mother Night*'s command chair, watching the soft white face of Pegasus roll by below, wispy streaks of pale blue showing through the solid-seeming steamdecks below, jet streams disturbing the stratosphere. Good-bye to lost nightmare number one. Should we have started the datafeed back to Earth? They'll know we arrived, of course, regular radio signals able to punch across a mere four light-years . . . but, of course, not for a long time. Our wakeup call's not even as far as Proxima yet, barely out of the star system.

Thrill at the turn of phrase: *star system*. With our arrival here, with the generation of that thought, a new phase of human existence begins. We're here. It's really happened.

Amber numbers were scrolling up from around her chin, graphs forming, telling her about the ship. And a black sliver of terminator was starting to come over virtual Pegasus's horizon. We're in a retrograde orbit, meaningless for this sort of world. We'll burn over local midnight; burn our way out of A's gravity well, fall downward into the clutches of B.

Nightfall coming around the world to greet her. She glanced over at Kai, immersed in his engineering data. As if he felt her eyes on him, he glanced up, batted his pretty gray lashes, smiled.

A softness in me. Softness left over from last night. Holding onto Kai, as if trying to force him into my body, deep within my substance, put him where he can't escape, can't be lost ever again.

Memory of passion spent.

Oh, Kai. I thought I'd lost you. . . .

Kai laughing, brushing away her tears with girl-gentle fingers: I thought I'd lost me, too.

Terminator passing under them now. Ginny signaled to her controls, felt her inner ears swim as *Mother Night* rolled around her axes, nose oriented along the plus-zeta vector. Engine . . . Engine preparing to add delta-vee. She said, "All hands, twelve minutes. Secure for maneuver."

They'd be on the science deck, around the light table, hips clutched by the delicate grasp of acceleration chairs. Waiting. Waiting to watch Pegasus recede.

Nothing down there now. Nothing but night and . . . distant flicker near the dark limb, just below the line where the starry sky began. Sullen flicker, propagating toward them, fading away. A storm down there, lightning flashing above an empty landscape, blue bolt twisting down to strike some bare and rocky spire, where there's nothing left to die.

"Sixty seconds."

Over midnight now.

So many dark midnights remembered.

"Energize fuel pumps."

Something shuddered in the ship, far, far away.

"Feed reactant."

Four, three, two, one . . .

Blue-violet fire suddenly gleamed, hundreds of kilometers away, reflected off the high-albedo cloudtops of empty Pegasus, and Ginny felt herself sink back into her command chair as acceleration started to build.

Lying in the semidarkness of the cubby they'd rented for the night, Ginny had watched Jolson get undressed, watched him get undressed and listened to the fast thudding of her heart, thudding inside where only she could hear it, tried to breathe slowly and evenly, tried not to look so wide-eyed and wild. Eight years, she thought. Eight years since you let a man . . .

Foggy memory of Fathers and Brothers, Grandfathers and Cousins spasming inside her, suddenly jumping out in sharp relief, wiping away eight years on the workchicklet road, wiping out three years high in the Andes, chewing dry coca and working the mines, now five more years under the Moon, no more coca but plenty of work, work and more work to help you forget and forget . . .

Wiping away those years like *that,* while Jolson smiled and stretched, slid his shirt over his head and dropped it on the floor, flat belly and broad shoulders gleaming like tanned leather in the dim, storynet-romantic light, while he unbuckled his belt and unzipped his fly, slid his trousers down over his hips and stepped out of them.

A faint shiver, an internal tremor when she saw he wasn't wearing underwear, no more barriers between her and . . . Jolson smiling at her, standing at the foot of their rented sack, light on his feet in lovely lunar gee.

And ready to go. Ready, just like any Father or Brother, prick like a barberpole made of flesh, sticking up at a steep angle, bobbing in front of her.

Conscious of his eyes on her, smile on his face, smile in his eyes, watching me look at him. Does he think I *like* what I see? Does he think I can't keep my eyes off it, that I can't wait to rub it with my hands, put it in my mouth, have him shove it up . . .

Push that shiver away. When he touches you, you don't want to be shaking. This is Jolson. Buddy Jolson. Your best friend for the last two years. So surprised, so happy when you told him you might like . . .

Eight years. It can't go on forever, no matter what they did to me.

Ginny Vonzell, Virginia Vonzell Qing-an, wanting so desperately to be . . . normal. That was the word she bandied about, alone in the night. Normal.

Good old Buddy Jolson, reliable pal, reliable coworker, always ready with a joke, never pressuring her after an initial tame feeler. Buddy shrugging and going on to other women in their workgroup, but staying her friend even though she wouldn't . . .

Buddy Jolson nuzzling between her breasts, head under her

chin, so she could smell the slightly sweaty tang of his hair, sweat mingled with whatever cheap date-scent he was wearing, something compounded of flowers and musk, probably masking artificial pheromones.

She put her head back, trying to relax, trying to . . .

Buddy's hand between her legs, big fingers ever so delicate, palm sliding across her mons, sliding back to cup under her rear end . . .

Jaw clenched now, don't want your teeth to chatter . . .

Hard clenching in her belly as well. Oh, God. What if I don't remember how to relax enough for him to . . .

Buddy looking at her, eyes subdued.

Oh, God.

He said, "We've all been wondering, Ginny."

Oh, God.

He ran his hand over her vulva, parting her lips with a finger, obviously able to feel that . . . clenching. He said, "You're not a virgin, are you?" Disbelief on his face. No such thing as a twenty-three-year-old virgin. Not in *this* day and age. Not on *this* Moon.

She shook her head. "Not . . . exactly." Fathers and Brothers remembered, hard little pricks poking her open and sliding right inside. I could relax for them. Why not now?

"Lezzie trying to switch hit?" A bright, forced grin. "I can lick a pretty mean clit if need be." Already starting to bend his head down low.

Right. Memory of Mothers and Grandmothers. Sometimes Sisters. Older sisters, of course, but Sisters still, usually hurting you, getting even for something, even if you didn't know what. Again: "Not . . . exactly."

Good old Buddy's chin resting on her abdomen, sympathetic eyes staring in the semidarkness, looking up at her face. "You sure you want to do this? I mean . . ."

A quick nod, putting her hand down to stroke his damp hair, realizing with horror that her fingers were shaking, that he'd be able to feel them shaking and . . .

He said, "You want to talk about it?"

Talk? No, I don't want to talk about it. They make therapy programs for that.

Buddy's dark eyes looking up at her, measuring her, making sure. Then he turned his face downward, nuzzling her crotch, eyes gone away, leaving her alone to stare at the ceiling and remember. Alone. That's it. All alone. Not a man down there. Not a human being at all. Just a little machine, a high-quality masturbation device. A little machine you can . . . shut off, if need be . . .

A little machine that . . .

Soft exhalation of held breath as he started in with his tongue.

A very nice machine. A friendly machine. Machine helping her remember how to relax, if only just that. Machine a dark shadow over her hours later, opening up a space just lubricated by its third orgasm; patient machine sliding into her and doing what a man-machine must do, not so different from Fathers and Grandfathers and Brothers after all . . .

Sitting in the woman's stateroom, Doc watched Rosie's dark eyes brim with tears, moisture refusing to fall, refusing to float away, hanging there in zero gee, blinding her. Just now, he thought, the world is shattered into a thousand bright scintillae, and I'm no more than a mannequin made from vivid and colorful shadows. Pity.

Pity, for she really is a beautiful woman. Such a waste. Why do men let such women go to waste? Why do such women let men waste them?

She was finished talking for the moment, though she'd need him again in the role of father-confessor in a few minutes, when she was done going through the motions of sniffling, had wiped the tears away, blown her nose. Then she'd sit there and grin at him. Grin at him sheepishly, nose red, eyes puffy, and expect him to say something comforting.

Hard to listen to it, no matter how sympathetic I am. No matter that it's my job.

Elliptical phrases, going round and round the core problem. You thought he *loved* you, dear Rosie? And what is that? I remember how bizarre it seemed when I *was* a man, when the dichotomy existed in me as more than a memory, when it existed as more than a set of cultural and genetic habits.

Love? From a man?

Always wanting to say that to such a woman, at such a time. Dear Rosie: To a man, to any man, love is the slick wetness between your legs, the feel of your hand on his genitals, the global sense of your willingness to lie down with him. All you buy with your body is his willingness to say the words you ask for, not the reality of his feeling them.

Always wanted to say that.

Never could.

What good would it do?

She'd cry. Be angry at me. Cry. Deny. Walk away. Repeat her mistake somewhere else.

And you know. You know. Back when you were a man . . .

Rose whispered, "Oh, Doc . . ."

Coming close to him now, tears of remembrance, of regret about Mies, having him and losing him without comprehension, reduced to snuffling in her nose, an audible swallow. He put his arms around her, clasped her head in the crook between his shoulder and neck. Felt his shirt grow slightly damp, rubbed his hand on her back and felt her shiver against him.

"There, there, daughter."

Deep, internal chagrin. Did I really say that? Ninety years old and all I can think of is, *There, there, daughter?* She snuggled closer, calming down now, thoughts, most likely, settling down.

And what next, from your dear grandfather figure?

You've been through this before, this very scene, over and over again in your ninety years. What was her name? Marianne? Yes. Poor young Marianne coming to you from a broken love affair, looking for your wise counsel. Coming to your arms, wanting to be held, soothed and comforted like a child.

Did your best.

Christ.

Remember. Holding her close, going, Oh, there, there . . .

and feeling her breasts against you, the smell of her hair in your nose so sweet. Feeling that clench of awareness behind your balls, the sudden sense of *being* growing in your prick.

You nuzzled her ear. Brushed your lips against her cheek. Kissed her. Kissed her again. Whispered to her how *good* she was, how very *worthwhile*. And then you fucked her.

How many times does it have to happen to a woman before she realizes? Rosamunde Merah motionless against him now. Is she waiting for me to . . . *do* something? Well, old Doc, you've tricked us both. Now talk to her. Tell her what she wants to hear. And, after a while, tuck her alone into her sleeping hammock and go back to your own room. Something peculiar going on here. I wonder what it is?

Wry smile. Other than that spurned little Rosie picked the wrong man to come to, looking for . . . whatever it is women are looking for.

Mies's dream repeated endlessly, as though the repetition itself was a part of the dream. Two men dressed in dark blue coveralls, sitting in a little room filled with machinery, laughing. Making adjustments, watching a planetary landscape change at their whim. One cutting a broken landscape with scissors, *ka-khrump, ka-khrump,* tiny worldlets pouring forth like corpuscles. The other gouging deep craters with his thumb, row after row, a child with art clay. Suddenly the mutilated world unfurling into a rug, a flag snapping in the wind, whirling into darkness, leaving an empty starscape, him at the center of it on a pallet, looking up, searching for . . . searching for . . .

He awoke, as always, alone. Lights came up slightly, showing the familiar features of the science deck, light table, sample analysis modules. He dismissed the dream as best he could, bothered more by the feeling of inevitable repetition than the actual content. Floating in the comfort of his sleeping bag, drowsiness seeming to be imbued in the soft lining, not wanting to fall asleep again, but unable to resist . . .

Who are you? Question from nowhere.

Mies Cochrane, interstellar explorer, man of many talents and many secrets.

Who are you, really?

I told you.

You can tell yourself the truth, you know.

Mies Cochrane, savior of humankind? Carrier of the magic autoviroid. Ladies' man, intent on fucking . . .

But where is the rest of you?

The soft grumble of the engines suddenly stopped, leaving a yawning silence. Awake, without transition. Detaching the seam, crawling out, unfolding clothes, putting them on by rote. Pholos insertion complete. Time to get to work.

He took up his position next to the light table, hooked one foot into a loop, looked at the eyebubble sensor questioningly. Regaled with a hundred choices, he decided to plug right into the external photos, and . . .

Wham. He was sailing through infinite darkness, looking down on an unimaginably complex world, circle filling up his view, perilously close, frighteningly palpable. A view from high orbit, almost static.

Full Pholos, at first glance, was a yellow-and-brown world, color verging on gray in places. Clear distinction between continental and oceanic plates, even without shadows to show relative elevations. Big, big continent in the north, yellow-brown, studded with what looked like high plateaus. Oceanic crust darker, more grayish yellow, riven with great parallel slashes that, at first glance, he took to be compressional ridges. Swaths and shadings of color, windswept shapes in places, topographic in others, gave the planet the appearance of a messy artist's palette.

As their orbit progressed, the planet's terminator began to corrode away the approaching limb, darkness preceded by a startling variety of foreshortened shadows. A piece of a southern continent projected across the terminator, carrying daylight with it. Mies watched as the orb diminished in size, devoured by night. More signs of compression were visible as the preterminator region came under them. Ridges great and small giving parts of the world the appearance of a crooked gridwork.

For half an hour, Mies stared spellbound at the world, cataloging features, noting areas of interest, marking places he would have to see closer up. Of course it was impossible to characterize such a world upon such a short encounter. Pholos's land surface was many times that of the Earth.

Pholos's crescent steadily shrank behind them, southern continent still a displaced jag in the boundary between day and night. He called up an enlargement, saw that a few degrees further into the night, a little trapezoid of light had appeared, and was slowly growing. Some enormous mountaintop, greeting the sun, Mies reflected, wondering how this world had come to sustain such tremendous relief. Before he could turn away, Alpha Centauri B, blinding beacon, entered the image, fast sinking behind the planet, leaving only a thin rainbow arc behind.

A moment of intense wholeness:

This is who I am. The space behind my eyes that lights up with these numinous images; the machine that spews out explanations for them.

No. Not at all. Because . . . Indigo eyes. Waiting.

Another day, this one less than two hours long, now that they had transferred to a low Pholos orbit, barely two hundred kilometers up. The world spun below them quickly, unmuted by the thin atmosphere, its physiognomy spread out like a feast for their delectation.

Mies had come up to the command module, looking for Kai, but not finding him, had stayed, talking desultorily with Ginny about the landing to come. Talking. Talking, friendly, professional, and yet . . .

The eyes were open, watching and waiting. YOU CAN GET THIS ONE, YOU CAN, MISTER MIES. Mies feeling his nausea of anger. Scientist persona sneering: *We've got better things to do.*

CAN YOU *SMELL* HER YET, MIES? THAT DELICATE SCENT IN YOUR NOSTRILS. PHEROMONES. SHE'S FERTILE NOW, MISTER

MIES. HORMONES COURSING HER VEINS, INVADING HER BRAIN, TELLING HER TO LOOK FOR A MAN, ANY MAN.

Mies stubbornly kept his mind elsewhere, but . . . That faint tang in the air. Surely it was something from the ship's life-support system? Some irregularity in the filter cycle . . .

Indigo eyes. Laughing.

She was so calm seeming. Inviting. "Pholos looks so *dead*, hardly different from Bellerophon," she said. "I only wish we could've visited *one* living world. This whole system is beginning to feel like a graveyard."

The rule sieves churned. YES. *YES!* SAY IT! YOU *KNOW* WHAT SHE WANTS TO HEAR. SYMPATHY. *SYMPATHY'S* THE TICKET TO HER CUNT. He said, "Feeling a little homesick?"

She turned away from her instruments, gave him a sharp look. "No. That's not it. I don't feel let down, either. It's just that the mission has become so . . . muddied. I don't know what would have happened if I'd lost you all down on Pegasus. As captain, the responsibility for the choices we make devolves solely on me."

A startled blink from Indigo eyes.

Ginny said, "What do you think of the site chosen for our first landing?"

Mies thought, I don't understand how . . . He said, "Uh. I don't have enough information to make real comparison. The eyebubble seems to like it."

"That's not good enough."

"Well, let's look at it." He called up a recent image, magnified to the limits of resolution, each pseudopixel representing approximately twenty-five centimeters. "As on Bellerophon, we appear to have a region of deflation, where a thick layer of wind-deposited loess has been systematically stripped away, exposing these ancient canyons and, here, these regular wall structures, obviously artificial. The canyons certainly date from a time when there was flowing water on the planet, although after the oceans were gone."

"Your recommendation?"

Mies imagined her without her coveralls, naked, perfect lines of flesh converging between her thighs. Electric. He pulled away sharply, terrified, rule-sieves moaning around him like a ghostly wind. "Uh, um. The area constitutes a window into the distant past, billions of years ago, because recent erosion has been kept to a minimum. We've identified a number of sites so far on the seabottoms, but this one seems to be the best preserved."

"Okay. Thanks, Mies." Turning away, seeming to dismiss him.

You lose.

Eyes merely staring at them all out of the darkness.

Mies hooked himself into the current photo feed, looking down on the long, cold Pholotian night. Infrared/radar showed wire-frame topography slipping under them, temperatures ranging from one hundred and fifty to one hundred and eighty kelvins. Not much heat retained by that atmosphere . . . no greenhouse gases left at all, just nitrogen and . . .

It's a dead world.

But this is where they're from, all right.

Mies said, We've seen lots of dead worlds. Old memories. Whose? Mine? I have no memories. David Gilman's . . . Little big. Live. Dead.

Little David, crying, But I don't *want* to die.

Hush, silly. No one dies in this day and age.

Big David, amused, stirring in his dark corner. Oh, really?

SIX

Descending from low orbit, dropping toward the upper reaches of Pholos's thin atmosphere, Kai rolled *MN01* windows-down as they fell across the craggy face of the Olympos continent: vast, rolling gray mountains, starkly highlit by an unmasked sun, hard light sleeting down on hill and valley. Wearing them away, Kai thought. Wearing them away with the efficiency of . . . No. Not wind and water. Mountains down there not so rounded as the bare hills of Luna . . . and craters here and there, big ones mostly, but . . . *old.* These mountains, these craters, he thought, had been like this for perhaps eight billion years.

Beside him, Mies, in something like a stage whisper, said, "Not much evidence of any meteorological activity ever in those highlands. That says something about the history of this world."

Yes. On what was left of Earth's primordial continents, occult craters at best. On Earth, the mountains would be deep in soil, the craters buried or turned into peculiar-looking lakes. Quietly, he said, "I wonder if the biosphere got a foothold there . . . if there was a biosphere."

A chuckle from Mies. "They're here, all right. Don't worry, Kai."

They were over reddish yellow desert now, falling eastward, denser air tugging at the ship's aeroshell, making their seats

124

shiver. From one of the rear seats, an awed-sounding Izzy Feldschuh said, ''Will you look at that!'' Canyon rolling under them, like a slash in the face of the planet, a vast ragged valley very much like the one on Mars. Remember seeing Mars during your first approach? Easy to imagine the knife edge of some great planetoid slicing that gash as it roared by, ages ago, Mars lacking the will to heal thereafter. Only planets don't behave like that. Planets go splash. Planets explode.

Kai glanced over his shoulder. Izzy and Metz holding hands across the space between their seats, alike as two peas, goggling out the window as compression plasma began sheeting off the aeroshell. Memory of the argument about their both coming, Ginny finally giving in. Behind them, Spence and Lin, silent, staring, taciturn. Something godawful wrong between them. And . . . Mies was beside him, working his numbers while he looked out the window, watched the surface of Pholos grow huge and flat. Something involving him, somehow, the way the two of them glower at each other whenever he's in the room.

Are we in trouble already, over . . . personalities? Something wrong between Mies and Rosie, as well—that bruised and sullen look in her eye as the six of us prepared to embark. Eyes back out on the growing world below, hands on his controls, Kai slowed the ship, turning it with reaction jets, matching trajectory to graph, using the hull's intrinsic lift to aim them at their landing site, not so far away now.

Well. Not so surprising. People and their . . . attachments. The way Ginny feels about me despite . . . despite everything. Image of Mies, perhaps, lying atop Linda Navarro, thrusting into her, grunting his way through some crude hetero orgasm.

Right. And Spence jealous, as if his relationship with Lin had any depth at all. As if they weren't each other's default partner, because the rest of us had already formed attachments. Stupid. Another quick glance at Mies. Kai thought, I wonder . . .

Mies looked up at him, a startled look seeming to form in his eyes, furrow creasing his brow. Kai smiled, then turned back to the window, thinking, Well, well . . .

Ship hovering above a broad, gray-brown plateau now, surface wind negligible, and . . . Out there, on the bright, sunlit ground, Kai could see the black shadow of *MN01*, a tiny blob as yet, but recognizable, sitting atop a shimmering column of disturbed air, the shadow of their exhaust.

Kai rolled the ship around its axis, facing toward the edge of the plateau, and behind him, heard mirror gasps from Izzy and Metz. Mies said, "Pretty, isn't it?" The edge of the low plateau cutting off the gray-brown world like a knife edge; beyond, the rolling yellow-orange flatlands of what they'd already started to call their "dead seabottom." Pale land reaching out to a far horizon, cut by the nearby gash of a canyon, much smaller than the bigger one west around the curve of the planet, this one no more than a Grand Canyon.

And the sky. Dull blue indigo band above the horizon, like the sky of Earth's desert land near sunset, a blue sunset without clouds, sky without rain, starless black sky overhead, empty but for the searing white hole of Alpha Centauri B, as large as he had expected it, several degrees across, but not as dim, and A, a blinding flare ten degrees below it. Incongruously, one of Pholos's little moons, a tiny crescent of silver light, was slowly chugging its way toward zenith.

Kai said, "Time on target," and pulled back on the throttle, dropping them down on Pholos with a subtle crunch, lander rocking gently under them for a moment, then still.

The six of them were at the foot of *MN01*'s ramp, surveying the landing site they'd chosen. Voice laconic, Metz said, "This sure looked a lot more elaborate from orbit." A quick glance at Izzy.

Izzy shrugged. "They said to sieve for the *best* superficial site. I'm telling you, there's something about this place the AI really liked."

Walking out of the shadow of the ship, Mies planted his feet amid the rocks of the deflation armor and made a slow, careful survey of the surroundings. Something about this place . . . *Think about the AI. Rule-sieves, arrayed in a great, multidimensional tree. We're like that, you know. Kinship with the AI?*

Are we one with Mother Night's *data processing core? An assembly of many small parts, like the software packages developed from the SAE?* Many eyes blinking open. A sense of disquiet. *Look around you, comrades. The world. What difference does it make who we are?*

Behind the lander, on land rising toward the former continental shelf, a series of low cliffs stood, raising the horizon to a broken, wavering edge that almost completely hid the band of atmospheric scattering. He made a mental note to take samples at various levels along the cliff face, but his guess was that the barely discernible strata in the rock would be much alike, composed of fine dust blown off the exposed sea bottoms for millions of years.

Here and there, flanking the cliffs, were low, pyramidal structures composed of the same material. Perhaps, when the seas were gone, and the atmosphere had mostly disappeared, weather patterns had changed, simplified, and the new winds, vastly weaker, had done their best to tear down the structures built before. Here, they had done a fine job, and the ground upon which they stood was close to, if not identical with, the original shore.

In the other direction the sea floor, dropping away at a low angle, went on and on toward a distant horizon. The surface was mostly even, dark orange desert broken here and there with low, lighter colored mesas, some, especially far away, of enormous extent. Near the horizon, a long, high hill, from this vantage almost like a piece of rough twine laid at a diagonal; one of the compressional zones that he'd seen from orbit.

Long, long history here, fabulous geologic lessons to be learned. And something more.

Resting in a dark corner, letting himself be led, or driven, he listened to the seething joy of the scientist's thought, the soft rustle of data being sorted by his rules. Do I envy him? Should I envy the happiness of a tool well used? Then, whose tool am I? He bent over something that looked like a low stone wall, part of a network of such walls traced over the ground here, enclosing parcels of a hectare or so each, the whole covering maybe two square kilometers. "Odd enough for me, I guess." Voice subdued, as if buried beneath layers of intervening thought. "Almost a . . . palimpsest effect." He looked up, straight at Kai. "Probably just as well that we start with something like this."

Low stone walls, like Bellerophon's walls, eroded by the ages. And things like black lines etched on the ground. Something familiar here. I don't know what. Kai leaned down and dug with his gloved fingers at the ground, breaking through a thin crust. Underneath a layer of welded sand was fine brown dirt, crumbling into small clods in his palm.

Kai said, "You ever do the tourist thing at Pompeii?"

Sharp shock of recognition. Mies turned and looked out over the stone walls: etched lines, like a picture, like a schematic, like a city map printed on the ground, printed city not quite matching up with the rounded stumps of ancient walls. "Right."

Izzy, voice dry, said, "If you two are done being boy geniuses together, shall we break out the scanner?"

Kai made a thin grin, private-seeming, aimed straight at Izzy, and muttered, "Asshole . . ."

Izzy: "Well, if you *insist,* toots. . . ."

Mies, turning away from his vista, looked at them both, puzzled. Something going on here, invisible to me. "When you get out the scanner head, be sure to bring the particle beam generator. We're going to want to do a deep survey this time."

Izzy stayed rooted in his tableau for a moment longer, still smirking, then he said, "Right." Then, to Metz, his silent shadow, here as on Earth, "Let's go, babe. Work to be done."

Kai said, "Doc? Ginny?"

Ginny's voice, static free, punching down through the thin atmosphere: "We're all set, Kai. Whenever you're ready." Voice, now, seeming very tired.

Mies had a sudden vision. Ginny and Kai, lying together in some terrestrial bed, under gravity, a tangle of limbs and damp bed linen.

Do you wish you could be part of that scene?

Sometimes. It's . . . easy to imagine their happiness. And envy it. And realize that the vision had attracted the notice of Indigo eyes. Whispered: WE CAN'T INFECT KAI, YOU SEE. NOT EASILY, NOT TO ANY GREAT EFFECT. BUT. THROUGH HIM. A sudden, shocking image of Ginny, sprawled wide open before him, eyes no more than empty expanses of white, vulva spread wide, introitus showing, glistening with . . . Mies felt a little wrenching jar as the scientist persona swallowed him whole. Safe, he thought. I'll be safe in here. . . .

Another little while and they were set up, festooned with waveguides beside the tripod-mounted scanner head and its attachments, little dish on the ground nearby, pointing up into the sky, tracking the bright spark that was *Mother Night* for a direct radio link with the Synchronoptic Analysis Engine, which would at last be called on to do the heavy work for which it had been made.

Full scale, Kai thought. All rule-sieves open and working. If there's data here, embedded in these surfaces, we'll get it in full measure.

Mies said, "All right. Maybe aim the main scanner head sensor cluster out over the, ah, *ruins,* with a broad focus."

To the AI link, Kai muttered, "Bucket format. Coordinates six-two-four, downlink fifty-seven, rule eight." Iteration tables materialized in the air before him.

". . . and, um, maybe a secondary focus on that . . . lump over there." Pointing. "I think there's something significant . . ."

Metz, huddled beside Izzy, suddenly whined, "You gotta be more specific, Mies."

Kai said, "Latch format, node on two-eighty-one, link nine-fifty, rule seven-thirty-four under axiom twelve-delta."

Metz muttering, voice sharp, Izzy seeming to pat him gently on the back. Then Izzy said, "See? It *does* work the way we thought!"

Hooray. Kai said, "All right. Let's see what we've got. Uplink errorcheck."

From the ship, Ginny said, "Got it. Ready to roll."

Kai nodded at the master start icon and waited.

One . . . Two . . .

Mies said, "Hmh. This is taking . . ."

Kai: "Wait."

Six . . . Seven . . .

Izzy snarled, "Goddamn it, Kai, there's not enough band-width! I *told* you, back on Earth—"

"Ginny, shut down the parallel com."

"But—"

"Link yourself back in downstream."

"Well . . . Okay." Unwillingness in her voice, but . . . The graphs and tables went out briefly, came back again in the same format, now emerald green against the landscape rather than bright amber.

"Izzy?"

Long silence.

Fifteen . . . Sixteen . . .

Metz said, "Maybe if I . . ."

Twenty . . .

Izzy said, "All right. Crosslink and—"

The landscape scrolled away from their feet, turning dark blue-green, the blue band at the bottom of the black sky suddenly swelling, reaching for the zenith, subtly banded, bright blue down by the edge of the world, dark indigo overhead.

From somewhere behind them, Linda Navarro said, "Well, Jesus."

View over the edge of the plateau of a bright, deserty-looking landscape, full yellow now, brownish yellow, rather than the orange of the present day, and . . .

Mies said, "The canyon's full of water." Water, gleaming in the sun, pale, diaphanous clouds drifting overhead.

Kai said, "Izzy, where the hell's the *city*? Did we lose the fucker?"

Muttered words, then Metz whined, "Well, I don't know what happened to it, Iz. Tell him to look at the timeframer."

Kai, abashed: Should have thought of that myself, goddamn

it. He glanced at the sequencer graph. "Shit. We're about forty million years earlier than the moonbase and Bellerophon ruins."

Mies, dry-voiced, "That might do it. Why don't you—"

Spence, hushed, excited, "What the fuck is that thing?"

All around them, lush, blue-green vegetation sprawled, all of it low to the ground, moist looking, nothing like trees. And something crouched, looking at them, seeming to look at them, at any rate. Kai thought, I have to keep remembering this isn't real and I'm not here.

It stood, walking slowly across their field of view, fading in and out, motions jerky. Probably just the engine hypothesizing on how it might have moved. The sieves we just put in charge would do something like that.

Mies, voice rather amused, said, "Look there, Kai, your Frogmen *do* have dicks!"

Naked Frogman turning to stare at them again, bulging silver-blue eyes frozen, expressionless, unreadable, cylinder of green flesh the approximate size and shape of a circumcised human penis swinging limply between splayed, blotchy gray and green thighs. Kai felt a giggle welling up. "No nuts, though . . ."

Doc's voice, from the ship, "The terrestrial frogs inhabiting certain fast-flowing mountain streams of Oregon and New Zealand have evolved everted cloacas for the purpose of inseminating females in that environment, where conventional amphibian reproduction is impractical. We call them tailed frogs."

Mies: "But . . ."

Tailed. Dry memory of Latin *penis* originally meaning tail. Kai said, "We can argue convergent evolution some other time, guys." A sudden, abrupt realization: After all these centuries of speculation, now we have data to interpret, information to give our arguments substance. "I'm going to spool the timeliner forward. Try to approximate the Bellerophon era. Izzy?"

"We'll do our best, Kai."

The landscape seemed to boil suddenly, sky overhead made of shifting shadows and . . .

Izzy said, "*La voilà, la bas.*"

Walls springing up out of the ground, gleaming new walls,

tan and ocher walls, seeming to grow organically from the eroded stumps of the future now. And . . . shadows swelling from lines etched in the bare earth that underlay all the resurrected blue vegetation, things like buildings seeming to coalesce and shimmer and . . . not forming all the way. Stunted somehow, broken, as if . . . "Ruins," said Kai. Like Pompeii.

Mies said, "Nothing like trees, ever. I wouldn't have thought a people who didn't know trees would erect tall buildings."

Metz whispered, "There're big mountains here."

Izzy: "Bigger than anything Earthmen ever had."

Gleaming walls encompassing the old ruins now, buildings eroded away to mere shells, husks of whatever had been. And, beyond the ruined buildings, beyond the shining walls, the hump of rock and dirt that had been their secondary focus was welling up, image of its surface bubbling like some pale tan candy confection being cooked to hardball stage, strands pulling out and falling back in, rising, rising and . . .

Mies, quiet, but with sarcasm evident: "The pyramid conspiracy theorists are going to love this one."

Spence: "Something wrong with it. Doesn't look much like one of our pyramids."

"Too tall," said Linda.

Kai laughed. "The natural slope index is higher here. Lower gravity."

Landscape quiet all around them now, sky bright blue, shading up to that same indigo overhead. The same, or maybe a touch darker? Have to compare this to the geochemical cycle timeline. How close did they live to the death of this planet's biosphere? Just a few million years? A couple of hundred million?

On Earth, the geochemical cycle had something like six hundred million years to run. Fuck-all forever, from a humanocentric historical viewpoint.

Mies said, "Turn the focus down onto the lowlands. See if you can bring up—"

Down by the shiny little silver sea on the edge of the yellow desert, a white city suddenly sprang up, buildings clustered tightly together, bright white, like marble skyscrapers. Kai said, "Izzy, see if you can invoke the spieltier sequencer."

"Well, if you really want to play 'let's pretend' . . ."

Flicker of light from beyond the city, something lifting into the sky on a short spike of blue flame, gleaming bit of metal disappearing into the indigo blue.

Mies said, "Looks like you hit the moonbase era right on the nose."

A gusty sigh from Kai. Right. Hit it right on the nose and you can hear Mies's joy in his voice. A tingle of satisfaction in me. The joy of discovery, and pleasure in his rightness. This is as it should have been. He said, "Let's see if we can learn something we didn't know before. Izzy?"

"The spieltier's just going to guess. Look . . ."

In the distance, queues of green Frogmen were suddenly lined up beside a gateway in one of the walls, handing over something like paper money, disappearing inside.

Izzy said, "You think that's real? I guarantee you the people who wrote the spieltier sieve-complex were just writing entertainment algorithms. Why bother with it?"

But it was a compelling vignette, nonetheless. Old, old ruins, surrounded by new walls, Frogmen and Frogwomen come to show Frogchildren something of how their honored ancestors had lived. . . .

Mies said, "I concur. We can fool with this some other time. Why don't you run the laser scan on the pyramid? See what turns up."

From the ship, Doc's voice said, "Hang on, Kai. We'll have to get ready up here."

He said, "Why don't you cut the spieltier sieve out entirely? Unload it from volatile memory and use that space as an extra processing deck?"

Ginny said, "It'll take hours to reload it from the data recorder if we need it later, you know."

"Sure. But time's something we've got."

"All right," said Doc. "Go ahead."

The imaginary ancient air around the pyramid seemed to

shimmer, mixing past and present as UV lasers at various wavelengths blinked on and off in quick succession, curls of smoke jetting from the real world's rubble while the scanner head watched. Long pause as the SAE in the sky digested. Patches of air shivering here and there, blue-green veldt around them fading to pale yellow glass, then gone, leaving them to stand in a stark wasteland above which crisp trails of gray smoke dissipated.

Kai watched his graphs writhe, waiting for the engine to finish its analysis and return a compiled image, seconds stretching out, turning into minutes. Surprising, he thought, it can take this long.

Mies said, "Kai. I think—"

Izzy: "What're we going for, Metz, a world record?"

The glassy ghost of the museum city suddenly reappeared, hung suspended over the bare landscape, started to change. Sharp, clean walls fading away, old eroded walls firming up. Kai watched, delighted, as the taluslike ring of rubble around the base of the pyramid crawled up its sides, smoothing out into a clean white integument.

And, stretching across the level ground between the scanner and the pyramid, the old city of ruins was bright and new, low brown and tan buildings, streets arrayed in some kind of complex pattern . . . maybe just a simple grid, but rhombus-twisted somehow? Level streets, paved with flat tan stones, streets thronged with . . .

Curious that there are so many of them, thought Kai, gazing out over a sea of green Frogmen. And so many variants. I wonder how many actual datatracks the SAE resolved into images, how many are duplicate fill-ins, how many are blended interpolations?

"Imagine," said Mies, "what the spieltier would do with this." Not quite wonder in his voice, pleasure at what he was seeing tempered with . . .

What do I want to call it? Some carefully learned cynicism?

Linda: "Over there . . ."

Kai looked. Something. Some huge thing, creature made of

dark bronze, very much like new metal, fresh from the foundry, no time for verdigris to have set in, a shape so complex he could hardly form a gestalt impression. Four legs, two arms, like a centaur. Legs splayed, though not so far as an insect's would be. Segmented legs. Exoskeleton. Joints visible on the broad back, as if it were dressed in medieval horse armor, but made of preclassical bronze, not early-modern steel. Horns on its head. Horns like a rhinoceros, flange around the neck, like a ceratopsian dinosaur. Eyes. Christ, looking right at me, soulful eyes like a man. Bright blue eyes. Moist eyes. Dark moisture all around the eyes, darkening the exoskeleton of its face . . .

Mies: "Can you put it in motion?"

Izzy: "No. Sorry."

Metz, querulous: "Well, what the fuck does he expect?"

Kai said, "Ginny?"

She said, "Here, Kai. We're getting all of it. Pretty nice, huh?"

No sullen anger in her voice now, whatever was bothering her seeming forgotten. "Can you run this into the data recorder? We'll want to pick it apart at our leisure. I think there's nothing else for the SAE to call up here."

A pause, then Doc said, "This'll about fill up the space we allotted for SAE scans, Kai."

Izzy said, "Dickhead . . ." and Metz tittered softly.

Kai smiled. Always entertaining to see how shallow people's understanding was of their own technological surround, even while it pervaded their lives, even when their lives depended on it. "After we pick it apart, we'll run compression to weed out the factitious data streams and spool the rest into cold compression."

Ginny, voice dry, said, "Start your feed, Kai."

Kai glanced again at Izzy and Metz, then nodded to the appropriate VR control. Beyond his green graphs, knee-deep in created scenery, Mies stood stock still, staring around at his planet. What does the terrestrial planetologist think? Does he like this re-created imagery, or does he prefer the bare world, unadorned?

*   *   *

The rover was packed and set to go. Mies checked his bearings one more time, unable to see the true nature of the landscape with all the superimposed ghost images from the past. He blinked, saw the inert cliffs, desert sea bottom, life and motion gone for *so* long, once again. Nothing here now. *Nothing.*

And nobody inside, nothing inside as well.

Nobody here but us chickens.

Where are they? wondered Mies. Gone? Disquiet. How could that happen, they're part of *me*. Are we . . . alone?

Alone? No. As for them being part of you . . . well, you know, deep down, where it counts, that that's just not so.

But . . .

All of us part of him.

Who?

Are you stupid? Are you really that stupid? Mies Cochrane.

Then, where are they?

They *are part of* me. You *are inside. Safe and sound.*

I'm not sure I understand.

Probably just as well.

Grabbing a lip of the rover entry hatch, he swung himself into the vehicle, environment suit making rubbery contact with the rover seat. Kai looked over at him wordlessly, initiated door latchdown, and started up the rover's nearly silent motor. Last aboard. Everybody else safe in their seats, waiting. The car began to move, and Mies watched the flat rubble of the ruins recede. We are as impermanent as they were. Dots swept away by the merest trickle of time. And when we're gone, we're gone forever, geological stretches of time, astronomical stretches of time, devoid of us entirely.

Before them, the world had been eaten away into a wide but distinctly V-shaped canyon, not as big as the Grand Canyon, far from it, but resembling it in many respects. The far wall was broken: slashed with striations, pitted with caves, but substantially intact.

Hard to imagine how this got here in the context of standard terrestrial geology. Can't exactly call it a sea bottom, since it was never underwater, so the highland we've just quit can't be called an eroded seamount.

Continental shelf.

No, that's the gray landmass to the east, sticking up to the tropopause. No, this is strange. It's probably something that developed out of a subduction zone, full of water when this world was alive. Maybe a river flowed in from somewhere.

They got out of the rover, hatch slam in the thin air barely audible, went right up to the edge and looked down. Shadows cast by Alpha Centauri B, slowly moving toward midafternoon, filled the bottom of the canyon.

"Over there," Kai said at last. "A series of what look like broken terraces. Almost look artificial."

Mies studied the structure for a time. "They undoubtedly are. The Frogmen must have had a city down there."

"Why down . . . oh. By the water."

Down by the water. Interesting concept.

So, once upon a time, this was a low spot, full of water. A big lake, maybe not far from one of Pholos's little seas, which tended to develop in the lee of the continental shelves, in low-lying subduction zones, in what passed for deep ocean trenches.

Then what?

Well, the world got old. The core cooled off just enough. The geochemical cycle ended. The volcanoes shut down, the plate tectonics ended. In that order. So the volcanoes stopped blowing water and CO_2 into the air, and what water there was drained into the interior, where it stayed, while residual rain washed the air and made the biosphere's crucial life-support component into carbonate rocks. No more plants. No more oxygen. And pretty soon we have a reduced-pressure atmosphere composed primarily of nitrogen. No more water. No more weather. No more world. After the lake level fell, after it emptied out, what happened to the river? Did it just stop?

Sort of. Eventually. In Afghanistan, there's a mighty river called the Helmand that flows out of the Hindu Kush and down into the Iranian desert. It's a pretty big river, really. But it just flows down into the lowlands and stops. No lake. The water just evaporates, and that's that.

In front of him, Kai stooped and picked up a tiny flake of rock, turned it over and over in his gloved hands. Finally he looked up at Mies, and said, "Well. Artifact. Should we start here?"

Mies shrugged. "Why not? We've got all the time in the world."

Looking back toward the Frogmen's city by the sea, Kai noticed a thin layering of high, red dust above the horizon, a hazy line against the dark sky, and thought, When they lived, this world was only a little different. Crawling with life, but full of deserts. Sky bright with nitrogen scattering, but layered.

How obvious was it to our own ancestors that the air grew thin with altitude? Did Hannibal, born and bred in the seaside desert, watching his elephants labor over the Alpine passes on their way to Rome, think, It's just exhaustion, the work of climbing, that makes us gasp so for breath?

Or did he know? Did he know the air grows thin as you climb, implying, somewhere, an end to air? It must have been apparent to these people, who had mountains they could climb right up to black space.

Back near the rover, the others prowled the knee-high ruins of the not-quite-vanished second Frogman city, poking at this and that, peering here and there, knowing, he thought, that we'll set up the scanner and take a good look shortly. Imagine if the men and women of the First Space Age had made this jump, sometime, say, in the middle of the twenty-first century. No real knowledge of physics, stuck in the dry well of Relativity Theory, so confused by classical philosophy and its erroneous logic, that they were hardly able to reach beyond Chromodynamics to Transform Theory, much less all the way to Quantum Holotaxial logic and synchronoptic analysis.

They knew about Platonic Reality, the ancients knew about it. They just didn't have the computational tools to demonstrate that reality, the first step to accessing hyperpipes and unraveling their supposedly impossible information-carrying channels. Some people, even now, hardly believe it's real.

Mies, over there now, turning over slabs of dry brown stone, obvious bits and pieces of multibillion-year-old architecture, as if his mere eyes, his touch through the thin skin of environmental gloves, could tell him something other than . . . other than that *something* once lived and worked here. We're lucky the planet died before its people. Otherwise, the biosphere would have eaten all the evidence. And lucky as well Pholos is too small and light for a steamhouse to have formed, as on Pegasus, instead of this nice icehouse to preserve the remains, level the data, and leave it waiting for us.

"Kai?" Ginny's voice in his ears; in the others' ears as well, Spence and Lin turning and looking at him, waiting, Mies continuing to grub in the rubble, Izzy and Metz back in the lander, unshipping the scanner head and its ancillary gear.

"Here, Gin. You getting a good video feed?"

"Yes. Kai, we've just finished running a statistical array analysis on the recorded data from yesterday's scan, up at the museum city. You want a look? It's a little odd."

What else would you expect? "Sure." Tables, graphs and illustrations, little pictures marked with arrows and legends and hypertext indicators, spawned around him on the landscape. "Holy shit."

Doc's dry voice, "My words exactly."

Mies was on his feet now, looking at the empty world around him, obviously seeing the same vista. He pointed at blank air and said, "This doesn't seem to make any sense."

An iteration table in front of Kai blinked, letting him know where Mies was looking. He said, "The preliminary image-pattern parser thinks it's picking up a tertiary data set down in phantom-movement space. The SAE comprehensive controller algorithm wants us to invoke the full set of pattern-matching filters now."

A second table blinked, thumbnail image beside it enlarging, indicator beads lighting up, blinking in a pattern, marking various features of the city's theoretical construct, and Doc said, "There's some indication we should reinvoke the spieltier sieve as well."

Ginny said, "Can't do that. We just don't have a big enough power platform."

Kai grimaced. "In any case, we don't want to invoke it all at once. We'd never figure out what was real and what was an artifact. Not without computational power on the order of, say, Standard ARM's batch controller."

Mies: "So . . . what does the AI think?"

Doc said, "Well, if the analysis engine had a real being inside it, it could *tell* us what it's thinking, but . . ."

Right. Artificial intelligences don't think, they merely *know*. Kai said, "The master controller at the top of the engine's passthrough pyramid has invoked a set of rules indicating there's enough data down the hyperpipe complex to get us inside those buildings."

"People?" Spence's voice, with an undercurrent of excitement. Kai turned and saw two flimsy space helmets, clear plastic halos silhouetting two familiar faces, protruding above a crumbled and dusty wall no more than thirty centimeters high.

Linda Navarro said, "I don't think we need the scanner to get us inside. Come look."

They were standing side by side in a shallow-looking hole barely wide enough to contain the two of them and, looking down into the darkness, seeing the sloping black tunnel behind their booted feet, Kai thought, So this place sits here for billions of years, waiting for us, and then they come and walk all over it.

Not really as bad as all that; they couldn't be disturbing the interatomic bonds no matter how much they tramped and scrambled, not to mention the unreachable depths of the particle-interface superstrings themselves, orifices of the hyperpipes. But the idea . . .

Spence dropped to his knees and wriggled backward into the hole, followed by Linda, their suits' lighting systems going on as they disappeared, yellow light shining back through the orifice.

Kai shrugged, and said, "Might as well . . ." But Mies, taciturn, was already ahead of him, dropping down into the hole, sliding into the little tunnel.

Inside, the place opened up, an irregular space not quite tall enough for any of them to stand upright in, looking like the inside of a sandstone cave, something formed over the ages by the wind.

Sitting, holding his knees close to his chest, wrapped in his arms, Mies murmured, "It's hard to believe this place persisted for all this time. *Something* should have flattened it."

Kai said, "What? The planet's dead. Dead is dead. Doesn't matter if it's a million years or a billion." In any case, statistics also say objects, places, remains, all have a small but nonzero chance of surviving over any less-than-infinite timespan. "Izzy?"

Radio voice: "Where the hell are you?"

"Ginny?"

"Here, Kai."

"Vector him in, will you?"

A few seconds, then there was a shower of dirt, a scuffling from the tunnel, and Feldschuh's helmeted face appeared in the opening. "Good grief."

Imagine what he sees: the low, dark grotto, holding four crouching spacemen, the irregular wall, fallen masses of rock and dirt and . . .

"Is that a *skeleton?*"

Kai shrugged, "Maybe." Or maybe not. The dull brown splinters lying by the wall looked like bones, were strung out in some vaguely humanoid shape. But then they also looked like petrified wood, or like bits of sandstone shaped by happenstance to look like . . . well . . . to look like whatever they happened to look like.

"Shit. I'll see about getting the scanner head down here." He vanished.

Mies crawled forward, back toward the blackness, his suit lights illuminating the way, a pool of yellow spreading on the floor, washing up onto the walls just ahead of him, muttering,

"Can't hope that it goes on much . . . ." He stopped, hissed something inaudible, touched with amazement.

Kai crawled after him and looked over his shoulder.

Something that looked just a little bit like a crumbling flight of stairs, low grotto opening out, a rough thing like a natural stone pillar connecting floor to ceiling. Stalactite and stalagmite, grown to touch each other? No. Not a limestone cavern, if they have limestone here . . . they must, with life-forms so much like our own, but who knows what circumstances . . . Useless. I could speculate forever.

A trough in the middle of the grotto, shallow, with sloping walls, some kind of linear pattern at its bottom, extending the length of the chamber. Kai stood, going down the eroded phantom stairs, stood looking down at four sets of parallel lines. Lines stopping and starting, well broken up, but hardly natural looking, picked out in a dull reddish brown.

Mies, standing beside him, said, "You haven't spent much time in old terrestrial cities, have you?"

Kai looked at him, tried to peer into his face, but was defeated by the glare of the suit lights. "No. All my time on Earth was spent working for the Daiseijin. I'm more familiar with . . ." Right. Well, you couldn't call them cities, the tunnel-habitats of the outer solar system, the artificial worlds of the Oort Cloud.

Mies smiled, features shadowy behind the light, teeth showing briefly, a white flash. "If you had," he said, "you'd know a subway platform when you see one."

In the end, they had to detach the forward sensor platform from the scanner head and run it down into the tunnel on the end of long waveguides, letting it rest in Kai's lap, aimed at the putative skeleton and the wall beyond. Later, if need be, we can dig a bigger hole, he thought. Get the rest of it down here, take a scan of the . . .

Train tracks? Are they really train tracks?

The high-energy radar scan from orbit suggested a regular grid of subterranean—subpholotian?—artifacts buried under the ruins of the old city, collapsed tunnels, perhaps, maybe just water and sewer lines; suggested the possibility of tunnel openings down the cliff face, down under what had once been the surface of the sea. So they looked like frogs. Maybe they had lifestyles like frogs as well. Or maybe not. Maybe we'll find out.

A brief moment, remembering the presentation the committee had watched, regarding the new technology and ancillary science of synchronoptic analysis, of how archaeologists at Tell al-Amarna, with full pattern matching invoked, with the newly developed spieltier sieve in place, had played the scanner's view over what was left of Akhetaton and . . . So odd to see Akhetaton himself, Beloved of the Sun, looking very much like the Black North American actor who'd played him in the popular early-twenty-first century movie after all, sitting on his wicker stool, whispering softly in an early dialect of now-extinct Coptic, whispered English voice-over telling us all about his special conception, about the One Great God, whose visage was the Sun, and . . .

And playing with himself the whole time, hand inside his thin linen skirt, flabby belly folding over his narrow rope belt, fumbling with his genitals, thin erection rising and falling over and over . . .

Playing with himself while he told us all about God.

"All set," said Metz, still somewhere up on the surface.

"Ginny?"

"All set, Kai."

He nodded at the master switch and . . .

The thin, oxygenless air inside the grotto seemed to freeze solid around them, turn to fine, clear crystal, dust motes they stirred up vanishing and . . .

Kai watched his graphs scroll, and thought, All right. Let's see if we can hit this right on the money. A nod. A twitch of the nose. A glance at a set of sliders . . .

The skeleton disappeared.

Not real?

Hard to . . .

"My God . . ." whispered Mies.

Walls around them suddenly straight and clean, ceiling level, higher than it had been. Or maybe the floor was just lower? The floor itself was covered in a red-and-black pattern of clearly recognizable Penrose Tiles, Izzy muttering, "Guess they must have liked geometry, huh?"

No reason not to expect reasonably advanced math from a species that learned to make spaceships. Building spaceships makes them . . . Hell, it makes them just like us.

The far wall of the chamber was shimmering, unsteady, smoky, refusing to coalesce. As if . . . Looking at his tables, Kai said, "Ginny, it's trying to pull down the tertiary dataset. Slide in the full set of image-pattern matching filters, will you?"

"Okay."

Shimmer. Shimmer.

A swirl of pixie dust.

The image stabilized and flattened out and . . .

Long silence, all of them staring.

Finally, Mies said, "You didn't invoke the spieltier sieve, did you?"

Kai: "No." But it was . . . hard to believe this wasn't invented, conjured up from some very sparse dataset.

Izzy said, "If I had to guess, I'd say pigment particles from the original mural are still embedded in the wall's surficial dust layer. This is a real stroke of luck. If we could get the particle gun down here . . ."

Mural. All right, they were so similar to us that they had the same ability to form representational art. Too much of a coincidence? Something conjured up because *we,* not nature, wrote the rule-sieves driving our synchronoptic analysis engine? Maybe not. One of the first things a philosopher recognizes, when considering the problem of cultural relativism, is that there are things very much like pictures, like two-dimensional representational art, in nature. Shadows.

But this . . . like Western art. Like the art whose evolution began on the walls of caves in Ice Age Europe, so subtly different from the art of the East, even more different from the art of the Toltecs, the Maya, the art of cold, mechanical, tyrannical Tahuantinsuyu . . . A flat, yellow desert landscape, tilted subtly away from the viewer, not like the aerial view popular in Western art, but not the flat-on superpositions of Oriental art, either. A slightly elevated view, a real-eye perspective as if from . . .

Blotchy gray-green Frogmen, mounted on the backs of things that looked like skinny, eight-legged salamanders, red salamanders complete with flowing, feathery, branching gills. Frogs and salamanders in the desert? Making too many assumptions from my own biology. Is the SAE doing the same? Is that what pattern matching does?

But the viewpoint, quite obviously, was this same scene as if seen by yet another Frogman, an invisible Frogman, mounted on a red salamander-spider of his own. His? Her? Its? Some word we'll have to make up, when it turns out they have three sexes, or maybe eleven? View in the mural subtly distorted, bellied somehow in the middle, the part of the scene closest to the . . . narrator? Interlocutor? Maybe just call him the point of view? Bellied in the middle, compressed and . . . somehow farther away near the edges. Of course. The Frogmen's eyes were farther apart than ours. Bigger. Could they work independently, or does the fact of this mural indicate the locked stereoscopic vision of a carnivore?

Out on the desert, closer than the horizon, superimposed in front of remote, jagged, misty blue mountains, was a clot of fat, bronze-colored shapes, the shapes of . . .

Mies said, "Looks like a bunch of those things, the . . . uh. Like the thing we saw chained up in the museum city on the plateau."

Right. The things that looked like a cross between a Japanese beetle, a rhinoceros, a centaur . . . things for which his mind had already coined the term "Rhinotaurs." And now, the Rhinotaurs, obviously galloping toward the group that surrounded the mural's localized, floating point of view, eyes flashing, clawed feet kicking up dust, waved long staves over their heads. Long poles. Long . . .

Those things are spears.

And the Frogmen? Are they afraid, turning to run, steering their nice red salamander-spiders in retreat? No. Standing their ground. Waiting, each clutching a short, blunt stick in his hands. One Frogman, the one farthest from the point of view, the leader, the . . . point man? This one blotchy gray-green frog held his stick up, seeming to align it with his left eye, one end pointing in the direction of the charging Rhinotaurs.

A gun?

You could imagine the next scene, maybe imagine it just the way the artist thought you would. Fire billowing from gun muzzles, Rhinotaurs falling, flailing, screaming, dying, Frogmen triumphant. Did the Frogmen keep stuffed Rhinotaur heads on the walls of their hunting lodges? Maybe. Maybe not. You're avoiding the issue, Maeru kai Ortega. Avoiding the fact that this little world had two, count 'em, two sentient species. Species who, evidently, did not get along very well.

He said, "Spence? Linda? Why don't you go on up and start unshipping the backhoe."

With the sandstone roof slab torn away, peeled back by the arm of the backhoe and spilled, fragmented onto the adjacent hardpan desert, sunlight slanted down into the tunnel, Mies's subway tunnel, lighting up a dense swirl of dust motes, thick dust kicked up by the backhoe's teeth, lighting them up warm, buttery yellow.

Kai stood, watching Izzy and Metz reassemble the scanner head on its tripod platform, watched them reattach the particle gun and carefully realign the transponder dish. Working swiftly and silently, efficiently, like the good technicians they are, working independently, seemingly unaware of each other, yet working together. Brief memory of seeing the two of them, walking together across the desert sands of Earth, of America's red-sand Southwest, under a moonlit starry sky, Izzy and Metz, twin men, holding hands, talking softly, sighing up at the old white Moon.

Mies and Linda were down in the trough, scraping up tiny physical samples of the "track" material, muttering back and forth, arguing about twentieth-century technology, something about "third rails," while Spence stood up top, stood up in the white sunlight, looking down at them, motionless, hands clasped behind his back, face set inside his helmet, eyes expressionless dark buttons, deep in shadow, mouth like a bloodless cut.

Kai looked down at Mies and Linda and suddenly guessed what might have happened, some time in the recent past. Oh. Have I been being stupid? Sudden shallow pang, crawling somewhere inside. I guess . . . Mies and I seemed to be . . . getting to like each other? Something like that. Maybe he's just decided I'm . . . male enough to be his friend? Something like that. Too bad. Put it away now. No point in feeling . . . anything. Besides, you'd only have hurt poor Ginny's feelings. "All set?"

Izzy looked up. Muttered something to Metz, then said, "Sure. Ready to go again."

"Ginny?"

"Um. Yeah. Want to see what we can get with the same array settings?"

Kai glanced at Izzy, saw that Metz was aligning the particle beam generator with the scanner head's field of view. "For now. Mies? Lin?"

They were climbing up out of the hole, getting out of the way, stowing their samples. Kai looked down at his waist coupling, making sure all the waveguides were plugged into the correct sockets, grinned at the others. "All aboard . . ." People plugging their own cables into much simpler connectors.

When he spooled up the scanner's control panels, the datasets were still frozen at their previous settings, recorded up on the ship, waiting for him. "Okay. Let's just see what we can—" The air froze around them, the dust, which had just begun trying to settle out, vanishing as if blown away on a stiff breeze. Ceiling suddenly solid again because the SAE knew it had been there all along, knew it wasn't *really* torn to pieces and scattered across the landscape. Floor neatly tiled. Walls straight and regular, trough squared away and . . .

Mies laughed, staccato in the silence. "Looks like the AI feels the same way I do."

Kai thought, Why do people feel they have to personalize inanimate objects? Even things as mutable and complex as an AI rule-sieve are still . . . quite insensate. They know. They don't feel. Ghosts. Ghosts in the woodwork. Ghosts of dead trees. Kobolds from the Earth's natural veins of water-concentrated ore, nature spirits, inhabiting the cold dead steel of our tools.

Down in the trough, representing, he supposed, the AI's "feelings," ran long straight bands of shiny silver metal. Railroad tracks? Well. The core hears what we say, passes our speculations back into the system where the more sophisticated rules of the SAE can parse them. We said "railroad," so here are the tracks. There are supposed to be safeguards against that sort of thing, but I wonder . . .

Linda said, "Look! Another picture."

Over by one wall was a misty image of a painting, not as big as the mural upstairs, more like a poster. Kai manipulated his controls, trying to make the thing clear up. "Maybe . . ."

The particle beamer flickered, greasy smoke boiling away from the patch of wall where the picture had been, puffing up over their heads in the shadowland of the real world while the scanner's sensors twinkled, drinking up the data. Maybe . . . The image cleared, looking . . . well, looking quite real, Kai decided. Picture of Frogmen, walking down narrow roads, beside . . .

Spence said, "Hmh. Things in cages. Zoo?"

Maybe. The image of whatever was inside the cages was still quite shadowy. Some of them look bipedal, thought Kai. A prison? Almost surprising humans haven't thought of that idea. A prison with cages open to public view, so you can come in and throw peanuts to the felons, while they scoop up shit in their filthy hands and try to fling it on you like so many not-quite-extinct hominid apes.

Datasets filling up, bulking huge, scanner head turning on its altazimuthal mount, particle beam reaching out, touching first this spot, then that one. Where its lightning struck, each little puff of smoke, each little mushroom cloud, resolved into a motionless Frogman. Hypothetical Frogmen, from chemical analysis of the floor's composition, from data resting just inside the mouths of the hyperpipes.

Someday, they say, we'll be able to reach right down into Platonic Reality, rummage around, maybe reach out through other hyperpipes, up into other times, other places, other universes. Then we'll know everything there is to know. And when we know everything? Then we'll know how to change Platonic Reality itself, change the reality and, in so doing, change the nature of the shadow world we ourselves inhabit.

Now, they were looking at a motionless tableau, Frogmen caught in midstride. Look at that. Frogman, just like all the other Frogmen, dressed in tight blue shorts and floppy purple boots, holding a smaller frog by the hand, leading him along. Mother and child?

Spence said, "I thought frogs only had tadpoles."

Kai said, "Ginny?"

Her voice replied, "That's it. Unless . . ."

A shrug, looking around at the others, people mistily visible against the imaginary backdrop. Face expressionless. Wanting more, waiting for somebody else to decide. He said, "Slip in the Culture Pattern Filter. We've got computing power for that, don't we?"

She said, "More than enough."

Doc's voice said, "We'll have to talk about this later. See what we can do. It's pretty obvious we're going to need to work out some way to run the whole array at one point."

Obvious, is it? I'd say so. Kai watched the graphs change as the AI slipped this new filter into place, data entering at the top of the sieve, passing through the event handler, falling down through filter after filter, through global-include traps, coming out through the eyebubble interface and . . .

Mies said, "I wonder what we're waiting for?" He stood staring down into the subway trough, looking down at the silvery tracks, waiting, perhaps, for a magic train to appear? Nothing. Nothing there but clear air and the possibly imaginary railroad tracks.

Izzy said, "Well . . ."

Metz held up his hand suddenly, wide eyes visible through the clear plastic of his helmet.

Something. Far away, something like singing. Familiar singing. Like . . . Kai felt anger twist inside. Singing, like the frog chorus of an ancient Greek play, frogs singing, *Breckeckex-koax-koax, breckeckeckex-koax* . . .

Still standing up on the surface rim, Spence said, "Well, *shit*."

Glancing over at the picture on the wall, Kai saw that the image of the beings inside the cages had cleared up enough to be made out. Rhinotaurs, a few frogs . . .

Linda said, "What the hell is that?" Pointing.

Over on the opposite wall of the platform, beyond where the image of the train should have been, another picture had formed, picture like an icon, blotchy gray-green frogs crouching on all fours, in standard frog posture, as if about to hop, all of them looking up at . . . Strange. Indistinct image of something black and covered with long, shaggy hair, brilliant silvery eyes staring out of the mist. Many limbs. Arms and legs. Something like a top hat on its head. Like a spider character from some old children's cartoon. The spider villain from an old cartoon, spider villain smoking a cigar perhaps, symbolizing . . .

How odd, Kai thought. Its eyes seem to be looking right at me. Silver eyes burning out of an indistinct face that seemed, somehow, to combine elements of spider and lion. Leospider, the eyebubble's voice whispered in his ear, nomenclature sieve supplying a very nice term. Leospider it is. The frogs crouching on the floor in front of the Leospider icon commenced to sing as well, slowly, somehow reverently.

Hours later, Kai stood alone at the knife-edge of a sandstone cliff, looking down into the deep canyon, sunset striating the black sky overhead in gauzy, two-toned shades of red and orange, sky deep blue in the west, first magnitude stars showing, dimmer ones glimmering on the edge of vision, reddish purple in the east, where night was rising.

On the horizon, Alpha Centauri B was a fat orange ball, inordinately large now that he had a chance to really look at it, almost giving him the feeling of looking through a telescopic lens. It was bisected by a boundary layer cloud that had been glare contrasted to invisibility, so the sun looked like it'd been cut open, infinity spilling out. And Alpha Centauri A? Gone down, gone below the horizon, a fat white spark that took a lot of the ambient light with it when it set.

Too bad. I'd've liked to see the white night that . . .

Oh. Right. A will rise just before B. I'll see it anyway. Soon? No. Christ! You're *here*! Really, really here. Somewhere up there, one of those bright stars is Sol, and all of humanity but us. We ten, and the crews of the other five ships. Sixty-six people safely away before the sky falls. Well, sixty-five, remembering Sheba. Assuming no one else meets that same little programming flaw.

Which star? Elevating his head, looking up into the black sky, above the band of fading sunset light. If that's Castor and Pollux, then that one must be Capella. And a little farther? Yes. There it is.

Footsteps behind. Mies. Silent. Coming to look down into the abyss? Too bad about Mies, as well. I wonder if he enjoyed fucking Linda? Too bad.

A faint crawl of sensation between his legs. Kai smiled to himself, face hidden, perhaps, from Mies in the growing darkness, as they stood and watched the sun turn red and fall through the horizon, watched the sky fill with stars. He smiled, and thought, Now, now, little asshole . . .

Mies said, "I almost hate to go back inside the rover."

Kai thought, I'll just bet you do. Lying there in the not-quite-darkness, light from the sky outside, stars, two bright little moons, emergency lights and readouts glowing on the control console, lying in your tiny fold-down bunk, watching Izzy and Metz grapple and smooch, maybe. And feeling Spence's hard eyes on you. Feeling Linda's eyes.

Have they gotten back together? Would they be mean-spirited

enough to screw in front of us now? He grinned at the thought, and said, "I already thought about that. I hate the idea of sleeping in the rover cabin."

Another silence, then Mies said, "So?"

Kai looked at him, saw that he was still staring off into the west, watching the last sliver of B slide under, face lit up bright orange, eyes like liquid metal balls. Like the silver eyes of the thing in the picture, the Leospider, staring at me out of the far past. He said, "I was thinking of breaking out the emergency survival gear package, getting out the pressure tent and camping out under the stars." A gesture, up at a sky grown suddenly magnificent.

Mies turned to look at him, eyes invisible now in the fully evolved darkness. "That's a great idea." Something like enthusiasm in his voice. "I think I'd like to do that, too. . . ."

More silence, then Kai said, "There's only one tent."

"Uh." Mies just standing there, black form outlined against last purplish vestiges of sunset. "Is it big enough for two?"

Um. Kai felt his heartbeat quicken, and said, "Big enough for all six of us. It's a crew survival shelter."

Mies turned away, looking back into the west, head tipped back, looking up at the sky, then he said, "Well. I'd . . . If you don't mind, I'd kind of like to . . ." An unfinished gesture of some sort, motioning at the stars. "I mean, if it's all right with you . . ." Another gesture, over at the dimly white-lit windows of the rover.

Staring away now, into the fully evolved darkness, Kai thought, Well. Well, well . . .

A few moments then, alone in the night, alone aboard *Mother Night,* high in orbit around Pholos. Doc and Ginny sat together in the command module, looking out through the eyebubble interface at their new world, hips clasped in the gentle grip of the acceleration chairs.

Ginny sighed, and said, "That's it, then. The Frogmen came from here. And this star system is dead. So we stay and, most likely, no one else comes."

"Oh, they'll send another ship, I think. A shipload of scientists, most likely. Maybe even government research types. This is going to explode in the media, when our signal gets back."

She turned and looked at him, tried to gauge the feeling in his eyes. Useless. "You think there's a chance the government will try to stop the Daiseijin? Take over our bases and seize our ships?"

Silence. Then Doc grinned, very odd looking. "I don't think so. It may be ICOPOSI will whip up its own starfleet. And academic phalangists the system over will want to get out here and see this place. We'll have company, sooner or later."

Wistfully, staring down at dead brown Pholos, she said, "I wish, I really *wish,* that we'd found an empty habitable world. Think about what it would have been like."

More silence. Finally, Doc said, "Captain."

Ginny looked at him, curious at his sudden formality.

He said, "You know there are some crew problems. Centering on Mies Cochrane."

She bit her lip. Nodded.

"I'm going to conduct an investigation. Look into . . . finding a fix."

"Probably a good idea."

"Ginny, I'm going to need private, sequestered use of the processing core during downtime."

Odd request. How much processing time could such an investigation need, really? So Mies is a fucking asshole, out to fuck every asshole he gets lined up on the end of his cock. So what?

Doc said, "No oversight."

A sudden awareness of Doc's position in the Daiseijin hierarchy. What difference can that make out here? All right. We'll be alone just so long. Sooner or later, the scientists come. Or we go to join the fleet. Really, I'm not *quite* in charge. "All right. You use whatever resources you think you need. When will you make your report?"

"In a few days, at most. I'm not sure of the magnitude of the problem."

Thinking about Kai and Mies, together now on the bosom of the desert, Ginny realized she wasn't quite sure, either.

SEVEN

From the surface of Pholos, at night, the sky was a dark co-coon, breaking open down the middle to release the infinite lights of its stellar progeny. Above them, the stars of late sum-mer and early autumn were wheeling ponderously, Pholos's slow rotation almost imperceptible. Mies thought, I once spent a summer night camped on a rock ledge in the Alps, waking up after midnight to watch these selfsame summer bird constel-lations move across the sky until they set behind the Jura. This makes it feel like . . . we haven't come so far after all.

Somehow, the tent was put up, breathing around them now with a soft plastic crinkling, their suits stowed. With the tent's wan internal lighting system out, the stars flared overhead, crisply outlining the black landscape all around them, shiny bits here and there catching the ambient light, dark rocks seeming to glimmer and twinkle. Off across the rocky till, *MN01* was a dark shape against the edge of the sky, her cabin windows glowing with dim, red-orange light.

Nothing moving in there anymore. People asleep, ready for the night. This pleasant lassitude. I'm ready for sleep, too. He glanced over at Kai, was discomfited to see the man's eyes on him, a hint of liquid in the gloom.

"Well," said Kai pleasantly, "goodnight."

What do the others think, the two of us camping out here together like this, alone? Are they whispering now, snickering,

154

imagining me . . . of course they are. Kai's . . . body is no secret, his . . . Mies swallowed heavily, turned away and said, "Goodnight."

Lying there in the pitch-black night, tent circulation making a breathy noise, starlight piercing down into his eyes, Mies composed himself and tried to sleep. Closed eyelids rustled against his eyes, lashes tickling one another ever so slightly. He opened them and looked across the tent, but saw only darkness and more darkness. Images of the ghostly Frogmen played in the corners of his eyes. Damn that Metz, he was right.

Another image, probably just random optical firings. Not an image, really, but a thought. A thought dressed in dim purple and electric green shimmerings. What would happen if he reached over and put a hand on Kai's shoulder? Anxious response in the pit of his stomach. What *would* happen? Probably nothing. The man was practically wedded to Ginny. But, if that was the case, why did he have one of . . . those?

Goddamn it. He was as hard as he could ever remember being, almost bent forward with the tension of it. What would the autoviroid do, in that strange orifice? He wanted to find out. Just get up the courage . . . *Courage?* What the hell courage are we talking about? Mies screamed, oh-so-silently, to himself.

Screamed little David and big.

And the scientist persona screamed with laughter.

And Reiko-chan moaned, moaned softly, softly resigned.

And Indigo eyes said,

TICK. TOCK.
TICK. TOCK.
TICK. TOCK.
THE RULES GO IN
THE RULES GO OUT
GO IN YOUR STOMACH
AND OUT YOUR SNOUT
THEY PLANT YOU DOWN
ABOUT SIX INCHES DEEP
AND . . .
No.

For Christ's sake, no!

What are you *doing*?

Hard, hard panic.

NOW, NOW, SILLY MISTER MIES. JUST REACH OUT AND TOUCH HER. SHE WON'T MIND. SHE'S THINKING ABOUT YOU, RIGHT NOW. I CAN TELL. THINKING ABOUT YOU AND MAYBE EVEN GETTING A LITTLE WET, DOWNDEEP, DOWNDEEP.

He reached. Kai's shoulder was covered with the textured undersuit fabric, slightly damp. "Mmmph?" Kai moved, not pulling away.

Mies thought, My God, what am I doing? What if he gets angry? What if he doesn't want . . .

OH, SHE WON'T GET ANGRY, MISTER MIES. THIS IS AN EASY ONE. Any easy one. Silence. Only the breathing of the two men and the little tent. In the dark, it could have been anyone. He could feel Kai turn around in the night, seem to come into his arms.

Not feeling like a man now. Too slim. Too delicate. Too . . . lovely.

THAT'S IT, MISTER MIES.

Kai suddenly kissed him. Smooth tongue moving past his lips and . . . Mies could feel his heart flutter, as if he were about to have a heart attack, then start to pound. Oh, my God. Oh, my God.

NOW, NOW, MISTER MIES. IT'LL BE OVER IN ONLY A MO-MENT. JUST PRETEND. JUST PRETEND. JUST LIKE ALL THE OTHERS.

But he's not *like all the others.*

I *hated* doing it to all the others. I was wrong. I made a mistake. David Gilman . . . a fool! A fool! I wanted to *escape*. That's why I'm *here*!

PAY ATTENTION. FEEDBACK INCOMING. SEE? SEE THE WAY SHE RUBS AGAINST YOU? WHY, LOOK: HER LEGS ARE ALREADY SPREAD. SHE'S JUST WAITING FOR YOU TO REACH DOWN AND START RUBBING HER HOT LITTLE PUSSY. WOMEN LIKE THAT, THEY DO. EVEN WHEN THEY'RE READY, THEY LIKE

YOU TO FOOL AROUND ON THE OUTSIDE JUST A LITTLE BIT
AND . . .

Mies moved closer, reached downward, between the legs,
where he knew that he'd find . . . what? He'd seen it, that little,
perfect vulva, knew that it was there, waiting. He pulled himself
forward, raised himself a bit. Head to head, lips meeting, kissing
a mouth, spittle dribbling, tongue touching teeth and tongue.
Moment of sharp revulsion, image of Kai the . . . fingers though,
hand, letting him know what was what? Do I feel like I'm
touching a child? Remember. Remember. Revulsion fading,
scruples, cultural overlays falling before . . .

PUSH DOWN THE CLOTHING, THAT'S THE WAY IT OPENS,
LET IT OUT. Now I'm on top of . . . him. Image of men on top
of him, heavy, pressing him into the bed, unable to move. Not
now. Not me. It was never *me*. Not the *real* me. He was on
top of the man, finding the orifice between his legs.

Poking, almost afraid, but in.

Listen to the little bastard sigh.

NOT BASTARD, SILLY MISTER MIES. LISTEN TO THE LITTLE
BITCH SIGH.

Sluts. All of them sluts.

Reiko-chan crying, far away. ***Not a slut. I was forced . . .***

No one forced David Gilman to join the ranks of Indigo.
Guilt? Responsibility? Take your pick. Freedom of choice . . .

And then it was just as it should be, thrusting hips, moving
back and forth, faster and faster until he bucked and jerked,
semen fountaining out of him, orgasm dying away.

Darkness again. Nothing to say. He rolled off, back to his
pallet. No. No, God, please don't let him speak to me. Some
sound, some stirring motion, a realization that Kai was sitting
up in the darkness, probably staring at him. What is he thinking? Don't ask.

A faint whiff of sweat in the tent's confined space. A scent
of semen. Yes, only my semen. Is Kai upset that I didn't, that
he didn't get to . . .

What if he starts trying to talk to me? What will I say?

Indigo eyes nowhere to be found, just now.

You know the drill. Pull up your pants and leave. Go home. Go to bed. Get a good night's sleep. Job well done. Indigo will be proud.

Shiver. Cold sweat forming on his brow.

Don't think about it.

Hell, I may be safe at that. He's not *really* a woman, after all. Maybe *he'll* just roll over and go to sleep now, too. Mies kept his eyes shut, forcing himself to breathe slowly, deeply, feigning sleep. In a half minute, it seemed, he really *was* asleep, life displaced by unremembered dreams.

So. Breakfast and packing up, moving the rover on down to the terraced section. Exploring, barely hampered by the darkness. Poking at this and that. Taking samples. random-seeming conversation. Everybody going about their business as if . . . nothing at all had happened.

Did it? Did anything happen? For Christ's sake, all you did was fuck him. Don't make such a big thing out of it.

Then, the discovery of yet another opening, this one through the roof of some underground structure, a broad orifice, down into the darkness.

Line attached to his suit harness, Mies slipped from the edge of the opening and felt his suit tighten at armpits and belt. Even in the light gravity, the sensation was somewhat uncomfortable; as he descended into the darkness, he started to spin slightly. He looked up at the helmeted faces crowded around the opening like strange teeth. He waved, then turned his attention to the cavity below. He tightened the beam of his spotlight, until finally he could see a little oval of light wobbling far beneath. Radar showed this to be part of the long, almost immaculate floor, smooth and level. Down a little. Jerk. Further. Tiny pebbles cascaded from the opening, clicking on the plastic of his helmet. Kai had started after him.

As he approached the floor he widened out his spotlight again, illuminating a large swath of the glossy black floor. Swinging slightly, his toes shuddered in rubbery contact. Down. He unhooked his harness and fell the remaining few inches.

Radar revealed that the room in which he stood was enormous and roughly hemispherical in shape. The floor, smooth and level here, was broken in the distance by radar bright outcroppings, small cracks registering as bright dendritic rivers.

Dark down here. Dark and cool. Almost as if we were alone.

I wonder what it would be like, to be alone, alone in an entire star system, light-years from the rest of humanity. What would happen to Indigo's precious rule-sieves then?

Then maybe you'd've gotten your wish, Mister Mies. With nothing to work on, the rule-sieves would lie uninvoked forever. Maybe just pop open a bit every time you jerked off, bitching about how you were wasting the autoviroids.

I kept hoping it would happen anyway. Maybe, when we've run out of fertile females . . .

Maybe so. Then it'd be just you and me.

A feeble noise caused him to turn. Kai was down now, and two others were on their way, spiders on a web: Izzy and Metz, shepherding down the scanner head.

"Okay," Kai said as soon as he'd disengaged. "Over . . . this way." He pointed off to their right and started to walk.

"Why that way?"

"Why not? It's closest, and the radar return indicates a complex wall."

"Could be a cave-in."

But it wasn't. The wall loomed over them, light and radar readouts overlaid into an enigmatic criss-cross pattern. Mies looked closely, turned off the radar. Shelves of some sort, rising more than twenty meters. And on the shelves . . . "What are those things?"

Roughly rectangular pigeonholes, made of equal-width shelf and divider, and in the bottom two-thirds of each a mass of something, broken and compressed, black, flaky surface, showing some signs of integrity, not just ash.

Kai went up and touched one of them, brushed a wisp of flake off with a forefinger. It fluttered slowly to the floor. "Could be a library of a sort. On a magnificent scale."

"Could be a filing system for dead bugs, too." Izzy and

Metz were behind them now. Mies played his spotlight over them, watched them grimace.

The scene was becoming familiar now. Kai stood by himself, off to one side of the site where Izzy and Metz busily˙set up and adjusted the scanner head, carefully realigning its sensors from the usual rough handling they'd received, being manhandled down here. A quirk of mirth on his lips, thinking of Izzy and Metz as men. Well, they've got the right plumbing, unchanged from the way nature made them, which is more than you can say for me.

Mies somehow changed over from what he'd been . . .

Well, yes. Different from Mies-in-the-Night, you nitwit. Mies brusque now, all business, eyes empty, mouth full of science words, wandering around the huge hall with Linda Navarro at his side, a querulous Spence trailing along behind them while they collected samples. Angrily holding the coldbox while they gingerly slid one of the artifacts out of its pigeonhole and sealed it up. Books. We keep calling them *books,* without knowing what they are.

"Ginny?"

"Here, Kai." Ginny's voice cool and efficient.

Stop! You're just imagining things, trying to push her away when she's done nothing wrong. She doesn't *know*. . . . A smile to himself. Heh. Spence and Linda don't know, either. They think this is just between the two of them. Linda and Spence and poor, silly, afraid little Mies.

Are we getting into a godawful mess?

Should I be talking to Doc about this?

But the space between his legs felt very nice indeed. It's been a long time since I was anything but Ginny's little man. I'd almost forgotten just *why* I made the change, so long ago . . .

He said, "How far can you power down?" Not theoretically. I know that from reading the ship's engineering specs. Put her to sleep and we can burn 98% of the main reactor's output on the SAE, free up more than 70% of the external processing space of analytical storage spillover . . .

How much can we *really* set free?

What can we *do?*

She said, "We figure eighty-four percent. Any more than that and there's a risk, a very slight risk, but real, that we'll redline the batteries and not be able to relight the engines."

Eight-four percent. "Did you reRAM the spieltier sieve?"

"Yes, but . . ."

Doc's voice said, "We think you should run without it for the time being. See how much you can get on raw processing power and pattern-matching filters alone."

Stay *away* from that ole debil spieltier, if you value your data, eh? Imagining the way they said it worked, when they told him about its risks. You take the data, say a scrap of lace doily, maybe a centimeter from here, a square millimeter from there. Let the analytical engine guess what was next to the pieces you had. Then you pretend what it thinks up is real. Let it guess the next bit and the next. Let it keep on guessing, iteration after iteration, until you've got a complete doily in your hands. How likely is it the square meter of lace you're holding is the real lace from which those two little scraps descended?

Why the hell do you think the programmers called it their *playtoy,* you asshole? Being silly, of course. *Spieltier* was just an old German word for a child's stuffed animal.

He said, "I concur. I think we all do. We can uplink the complete data platform and run a first-order analysis. When that's done, the dataset captured and bottled, we can invoke further sieves and see what they come up with."

Izzy said, "We're all set here, Kai."

"Okay."

Mies, Linda, and Spence were starting back across the floor toward them, stumbling over uneven black rock, Mies walking slower than the other two, falling farther and farther behind, sample case tucked under one arm, eyes on the floor.

Distracted, thought Kai. By me? Or do I flatter myself?

Mies stopped in the middle of the floor, seeming to look at his feet.

Spence, looking back, said, "What the fuck . . ."

Mies was just standing there, seeming oblivious to the passage of time.

Kai said, "Mies?" Putting dry irony in his voice, but also a touch of . . . warmth. Just a hint of what I want him to know I'm feeling. "Mies, whenever you're ready?"

Mies stooped and put his sample case down, bent close to the floor, seemed to brush at the black dirt with his gloves.

"What is it, Mies?"

Nothing.

Kai sighed and jerked his waveguides out of their sockets, tossed the thick, braided cable on the floor, and walked over to where Mies was kneeling. "What have you found?" The others were coming over now, too.

Mies looked up and smiled weakly, seeming to look into Kai's eyes for the first time since they'd left the pressure tent. "I . . . don't know." Pointing at the dirt.

Kai kneeled, leaned down close. Long and thin, like the rotten carcass of a long-dead snake that scavengers had failed to eat. He reached out and prodded it with his gloved fingertip, saw a fresh gleam, as of clear glass, and recoiled, with a sharp intake of breath.

Ginny said, "What is it, Kai? We can't quite see . . ."

He smiled at Mies, waited for him to smile back, however tentatively, and said, "If I didn't know better, I'd say it was a piece of old waveguide cable."

Silence, then Doc said, "You mean, like a datalink?"

Kai nodded, not thinking about whether the eyebubble node would relay it to the people up in the ship. He turned and looked over his shoulder. "Iz? Why don't you guys drag the scanner head over here."

Metz stamped one small foot on the rock, kicking up a few tiny dirt clods, and said, "Damn it, Izzy, we just got the fucking sensors *aligned*!"

Kai shrugged and said, "It's what you boys are here for."

Izzy stared at him for a second, then said, "Well. Fuck you." But they turned away and walked back to the scanner, started uncoupling the screwjacks from the ground and folding up the tripod's legs.

Finally, they were set up again, this time for a local site scan, sensors angled down at what looked like a dozen centimeters of dirty black rope, particle beam generator on its little boom arm, off to one side, aimed independently of the sensor cluster now, and Kai said, "Ready on the ship?"

Doc's voice said, "We're all set, Kai." Sounding weary, the way he sometimes did. *I haven't had a talk with Doc since before the three of us last made love. Sharp memory of that last night aboard the ship, he and Doc giving Ginny a good going over. Only two days ago? Seems like a lot longer. I hope he's all right. . . .*

Familiar VR controls and reporting instruments scrolling out of the air all around him, telling him all was right with the world, *God secure in his Heaven and all that . . . old imagery. What the hell is it I'm thinking of? Lights, camera . . .* He said, "Roll 'em. . . ."

Izzy muttered, "What—" but the eyebubble core understood and passed his instructions on to the SAE master controller.

Nothing.

Metz said, "You know, the damned thing's several billion years old, Izzy. I'm not so sure we'll get all that much out of a fossil magnetic field."

Izzy said, "Well, maybe not. Even if there're plenty of old field lines tangled up with the superstring loops, they've been going round and round for a long time. And who knows how much information flowed through that waveguide when it was alive? Might just be one hell of a tangle in there. Nothing *we've* got the balls to unravel."

Alive, thought Kai. *Interesting term.*

Ginny's voice said, "SAE says it just received an exchange-acknowledge from the sensor head, Kai."

He nodded slowly, watching the graphs form up. "I see that. Doc, I think you can start the uplink spool now."

"Right."

A flat white square formed in the air before them, seemed to take on depth, building into a featureless white cube. Not quite featureless. Like there's white smoke in there, almost but not filling the damned thing.

Metz said, "Shit, Izzy."

"I guess you were right, bud. Nice try, Kai, but we better—"

All of the graphs around him suddenly started to grow taller, starting to inflate with data, and Kai said, "Metz?"

Voice suddenly tense, alert, perpetual whine vanished: "Hang on, Kai. I think it's—"

Ginny's voice said, "We're getting a very heavy dataflow, Kai. The spool's filling right up."

"What's the pattern-matcher say?"

Doc: "Not a goddamned thing. Not a peep from the little bastard."

Ginny: "That's it, Kai. The spool is full. What now?"

Nothing. Kai stood staring at the white cube for a long minute, then said, "Metz?" A slight edge to his voice, an implied demand. This is your job, Orang Metzalar Ho, boy wonder.

"Well. Well, I . . ."

Izzy said, "Hey, no one ever ran the thing on billion-year-old artifacts before."

Mies, muttering, as if to himself: "Closer to four billion."

Doc's voice said, "Kai, the analysis AI has unilaterally initiated global filtering. It's adding on everything we haven't got locked out."

"Is it trying to slip in the spieltier array?"

Ginny: "Can't. We've got that sequestered."

Probably a good idea: "Has it issued a request to the system?"

Izzy said, "So far as I know, the SAE can't ask for anything marked as sequestered."

"Well . . ."

And Metz, voice surprisingly loud: "Well, look at that! We've got a priority override request in the system. See that little flag, Kai?"

Izzy, voice dry and ironic, said, "Well, those *wascally* pwogwammers . . ."

Spence, out of nowhere, voice angry, "Will you shut the fuck up, asshole, we need to—"

Mies said, "Let him be, Spence."

A moment of silence, then Spence said, "*Fuck* you, dickhead."

Ginny: "Kai? It's your call."

He stood still for another long moment, staring at the swirling white cube. "All we've got now is raw data we can't process. Pull all the blocks. Let it have the spieltier array and anything else the general analysis sieves ask for."

Spence, still angry: "So? All we'll have then is make-believe—"

Doc said, "If we let it have whatever it wants, it may shut down the ship's core and steal its processing space."

Good point. Kai said, "Ginny, you know how to start a trickle bleed off the main drive reactor plenum?"

Silence, then, "Um, no. Sounds like the kind of thing they tried to keep us from learning in pilot school."

Kai grinned. "Engineering school's a little different."

Spence said, "What the hell are you trying to do, Kai, get us all fucking killed?"

Mies turned suddenly, and said, "Goddamn it, Spence, I told you to shut up."

Stunned silence. Mies and Spence facing each other, Mies's mouth set in a strange-looking grimace, Spence gaping with astonishment. Beyond them, Linda was standing still, eyes closed, seeming to sway.

Kai said, "Heh. That's a pretty good little testicle display, guys, but it's got nothing to do with our jobs. Ginny?"

Very dry, almost amused: "Here, Kai."

"Look in my core files under *skunkpussy*. There's a routine there called glass-alpha-one. It'll set things up more or less right. Let the eyebubble core monitor it, so it can call a quit option if it does the task wrong."

"Got it."

"When it's finished, pull the blocks and turn the SAE loose."

"Okay. And if—"

Right. "Yeah. If the VR display in the control room goes out, punch the emergency override switch, do a shutdown of the SAE via interrupt line hexAFF9AE, then start the manual power-up procedure. Even if the core's reactor system has gone out, the bleed off the main engine will allow you to relight it."

Spence whispered, "Jesus fucking Christ, Kai . . ."

And Mies said, "I thought his middle name started with H . . ."

In the background, Kai could hear Izzy and Metz giggling and wondered just where Mies had found a sense of humor. Not to mention the will to treat Spence like that.

Dry thought: Well, hell. If he was willing to fuck the guy's girlfriend . . . And, of course, the sudden image of an unexpected Mies Cochrane, coming to him, silent in the night.

Ginny said, "All done, Kai. It left the gyros on, so attitude control is stable, and the VR monitoring system, but pretty much everything else is gone."

Metz: "She'll have needed to maintain the orbit-to-ground link and probably has safeguards to keep the core linked up."

Kai thought, *She?* And then, *Probably?*

Nothing. White cube just sitting there, insides swirling slowly, like clear sugar syrup discoloring cold milk. Izzy said, "Hell, maybe it's not going to—"

The white cube vanished and the entire underground chamber seemed to twist away from them, as if flipping through some other dimension. When it stabilized, everything was sharp and smooth, details clear, like . . .

Like, Kai though, it's new, like we're . . . here.

Walls lined with pigeonholes, pigeonholes full of the little black prisms whose crumbling, ashlike descendants they'd named "books," though without good reason. White light, the light of a noonday sun spilling down on them out of . . .

Kai looked up and saw blue sky above them, visible through the triangular latticework of an old-fashioned fullerdome, like a gigantic skylight. He thought, I wonder just how the hell it managed to turn to rock over the last few billion years. "Ginny?"

"Still here, Kai."

"Is the spieltier invoked now?"

"No. It's just loaded its regular filters into processing space it took from the eyebubble."

"How much?" asked Spence.

"Maybe ninety percent. It took everything it could without shutting down the interface."

More details filling in the space around them. A milky-white cube again, this time mounted on a pedestal, surrounded by things like tiki torches, tall, spindly black things, burning with a smokeless blue flame. And Frogmen, of course, dozens of Frogmen; Frogmen in tight black jockey shorts and low, floppy black boots, walking in a circle around the white cube, singing away in their froggy voice, a familiar Greek chorus, straight from . . .

Oh, thought Kai. I remember now. Sophocles.

Or is it a Gilbert and Sullivan number?

Izzy said, "Kai? We think the waveguide was hooked to the white thing."

"Some kind of computer?"

Metz: "Don't know."

Linda, long silent, said, "What's that?"

Mies: "Looks like a dead Rhinotaur. Hard to tell."

A big pile of dead meat, with four or five bloody frogs clustered around it, sawing away with long pink knives. Butchers?

Doc's voice said, "It's starting in on the main dataset from the waveguide now. *Mother Night*'s available processing space is exhausted. Unless it shuts us down . . ."

In which case, we shut it down, and that's that. The white cube swirled, seemed to shimmer and grow clear. Images inside. Some kind of swampy scene, full of meaty blue-gray vegetation, something like a raft, or maybe a very low-draught canoe, two blotchy, gray-green frogs inside, frogs dressed in white jockey shorts and low, floppy white boots, poling themselves along.

Mies said, "So. Maybe some kind of 3V?"

Kai nodded. "Maybe. Not a very advanced model, though. Mid-twenty-first century, at best."

Mies said, "No one's accusing them of building starships, Kai. Not anymore."

Doc said, "SAE just tried to load the spieltier, then stopped. Not enough space. It's issued a must-answer inquiry, asking for permission to unload the eyebubble core from memory. The core's trying to block it, telling us not to proceed with the operation."

In the background, Metz whispered, "Iz, the core thinks it'll be dead, if we let that happen."

Izzy said, "What're you talking about? The core doesn't think it's alive."

Metz: "I know, but—"

Kai said, "Tell it to let go."

Long silence, then Ginny said, "We had to issue a parity-checked password. It went through its shutdown and unload procedures a lot more slowly than the manuals say."

Metz said, "See, Izzy? *See?* We used to see this phenomenon back when—"

Doc said, "It's loading the spieltier array into the eyebubble core's vacated opspace now."

Spence said, "Here we fucking go, boys and girls. Playtime."

On the surface of the cube, odd, inscribed-looking blue-green shapes were blinking on. Above one, English words started mounting themselves:

Probable ideograph.

Saga? Story? Epic? Play? Tale? Lesson? . . .

The list went on for several hundred words, piling up in the air over their heads, little orange diamonds marking the highest probability interpretations. Something midway between "epic" and "divine truth."

Next to two more glyphs it put: "Possible phonetic representations."

Of what? *Breckeckeckex-koax?*

Spence said, "Aw, how the fuck can it pretend to be reading

Frogman symbols? We just haven't pulled that much fucking data out of the ground yet. This is thin-air bullshit!''

Metz said, ''You know, Iz, there's a funny pattern-match on the graphs now.''

''What do you mean?''

''See here? It's like the same dataset was piped through that waveguide over and over again for a long damned time. The same data, reinforcing itself, for maybe a hundred thousand years? Something like that.''

Izzy said, ''Hmh. Weird.''

Odd, irregular, multilobed symbols were starting to fill the air under the dome now, crowding each other like so many bright alien butterflies. Symbols spilling into the sky, thought Kai. Like, what? Like a data dump of some kind. He opened his lips to speak, but the white cube, still displaying its two little Frogmen, suddenly exploded into their eyes.

Suspended in gray-white fog, Kai said, ''Well. This is nice.''

Mies said, ''Reminds me of what happens when your eye-bubble link fails in the middle of a VR movie.''

Izzy said, ''This might be a good point for us to remember that the spieltier array *was* developed from the underpinnings of commercial VR movie-generating software packages.''

Spence said, ''See? I told you so.''

Nothing. Kai said, ''Ginny?'' Nothing.

Metz: ''Maybe the link with the ship is down.'' Worry apparent in his voice. Maybe this wasn't such a good idea after all?

Kai said, ''Then how would the SAE be able to maintain this illusion?''

Izzy: ''Um, maybe that's why it's just . . . static?''

Mies, suddenly sounding upset: ''Could we get stuck like this?''

Metz giggled, and said, ''Dork.''

Mies, annoyed, ''What—''

Kai said, ''All you have to do is unplug your waveguide, Mies. It isn't *real*.''

''Oh. Right.'' Definitely abashed.

A soft voice whispered, "Pattern matching complete. Invoke download."

Silence, then Izzy said, "Um, anyone we know?"

Metz said, "It's probably just repurposing the eyebubble's voice generator."

Makes sense to me. Kai said, "Software link ID."

The voice whispered, "Analysis engine to spieltier software downlink inverter."

Good enough. He said, "Download channel open."

The voice whispered, "Acknowledged."

Spence said, "Hey, wait. What if—"

Æghôl the Sarpùd—

NB: Æghôl's family identified with the Sarpùd, a small, flatland carnivore—

—as was the custom in those days—

XB: Phonological representations of *[breckeckeckex-koax-koax]* words produced through direct-substitution array synthesis of the written language remnant record in the waveguide relic. Actual *[breckeckeckex-koax-koax]* speech sounds hypothesized from visual records/data insufficient for actual re-creation.

—poled his side of the leafboat, feeling the long strong muscles of his legs and back flex comfortably, taking up the slack of his much weaker arms, which mainly served to hold the pole in place.

Beside him? Ah, good comrade Éna Re-horiq—

NB: Re-horiq is an obsolete word for one of the tools used to make flint implements, usually a round piece of granite used to drive a bone chisel onto the flaking edge of the flint.

XB: Hammerstone.

—wielding his pole as well.

Under the blazing suns, their skins dried by the winds of this alien place, they poled and poled, watching the high place of the Darkdemons, the breathdevils, loom far above them.

Vista of endless mountains. Mountains like the mountains of Farhome rising up and up, clouds wreathing their summits, long penons of snow blowing in the high altitude winds.

Æghôl sang: Remember, beloved comrade, when we climbed those familiar heights together, in the days when our legs were short and weak? Adventures together. Lessons well learned.

Éna remembered, and sang of the breathless heights, of the blue-black sky, of looking down on the whole world.

Sometimes, Æghôl would forget just how it had looked-felt-tasted. In those times, Éna was his trusted memory. Éna could forget what they'd done, could forget how a task was done, could forget so much. But he always remembered what they'd seen.

The two of them had been paired out of the egg for just that reason, nursemaids reading the pattern of their spots and placing them together in the same little crêche.

Now, though, many years gone by, many adventures experienced, many lives lost and regained, limbs torn off, regrown, pains endured, making them grow strong . . .

Æghôl sang the darkdemons song, while Éna extemporized bits of the lost breath chorus. We will learn now. All those old stories. Old songs. Priests telling us that no one can go to the darkdemons Heaven. No one can go there and breathe-live-sing-see.

No one has ever returned, of the many who've tried.

The gods eat them.

Éna sang a brief memory of Hulliq and Séllâb, old friends, dear friends, friends going out on the Truthseekers' Road once again. This time. This time. No greater deed to do. Go look upon the face of God. Know, once and for all, and tell all men, just what happens in the world where the dead are said to dwell.

Ten years. No word. Great Hápáqq circling the world ten times. Little Hápáqq making a fifth of a Greatyear's journey. Time enough for two lost friends to voyage across the flatland to Darkhome, climb her ramparts, and return. Twice time enough.

You see? the priests sang, voices triumphant and bitter. No

one returns from the land of the dead, whether they die and sink to the bottom of the sea, or whether they ascend to Heaven, and go directly to God's belly.

The Mountains of Heaven towered above them now. Blue ramparts beyond the mountains, towering into the sky, become empty silver peaks, shining in the sun.

There, they sang together, words piling on words, just so. There.

XB: Voids in the dataset appear intentional.

Æghôl and Éna, standing in a mountain pass, a narrow passage through the Mountains of Heaven, looking up at those same blue ramparts, blue ramparts looking taller than ever. No breath in their lungs to sing now. Hardly breath enough to walk.

Like those days, those long ago days, when we climbed the ramparts above Home. You climb, air cold and thin, like obsidian chips in your throat. No songs. Then, too weak to walk, you crawl, while your skin blisters and swells.

Éna, a breathy whisper of a song: Though we won great honor, we almost died, crawling back down to where the sky is blue again.

Æghôl: This is the route that the others took. We've seen their footsteps. If we find their bones, at least we'll know no furry black godlings came down to eat them.

Éna: We find their bones, only if we're stronger than they. If. If. If . . .

<intentional void?>

Æghôl lying on his cold belly in the snow, snowflakes blowing on a fierce, cold wind, under a black sky filled to overflowing with impossibly frozen stars. Æghôl lying, silent, helpless, while the godling took poor screaming Éna in his huge, clawed hands, turned him over and over, silver eyes gleaming in the night.

Poor Éna babbling childhood prayers, drawing breath for a last, saving song, failing, failing, crying out . . .

The godling held him close, maw opening on bright silver fangs, fangs sinking into poor Éna's side, blue-gray blood starting out on his skin, freezing there.

The godling seemed to suck gently.

You could hear its soft voice, a pulsating, deep throb: Mmmmmm . . .

Silver eyes gleaming with something like joy.

Mmmmmm . . .

Æghôl watched Éna grow smaller and smaller, until he was nothing much more than a blotchy, blue-gray hide, flapping in the frozen wind.

The godling, larger now, fatter, radiating fantastic heat, put Éna's husk aside, advanced on poor, poor Æghôl, foolish truth-seeker. Æghôl feeling those hot silver eyes on him, imagining those hot silver fangs in his side, imagining himself growing smaller, the world growing dimmer . . .

The godling held a stone, an impossibly smooth stone, silver like its eyes, silver like its fangs, in one of its black-clawed hands. Reached out, *snick, snick, snick, snick,* each little sound, sharp, abrupt, accompanied by a splinter of hard pain, as the godling cut off Æghôl's long green fingers, one by one, until all eight were taken.

Mmmmmm-hm-hm-hmmm . . .

Black-furred godling disappearing into the storm, Æghôl passing out with the cold fingers of the wind still on him . . .

<void>

Æghôl kneeling in the temple now, back home, alone, after ten long years. Holding up the scar-tissue paws that he had now in place of once-dexterous hands. Holding up his paws and telling the priests of how he'd waited and waited for them to begin to grow again. But the god had them, had kept them, and because the spirit of his fingers, you see, was with the god. . . .

The priests smiled to each other, knowing how this tale would affect their followers. It's true, you see? We told you it was true . . .

And when Æghôl the Sarpùd had finished with his tale, the priests held him still on the Dark Altar before all the Multitudes of Home, and slit his throat with their dull black knives of sacred volcanic glass, and bled him dry the way gods always bleed men dry, chanting, in the deepest, darkest voices they could muster, Mmmmmm-hm-hm-hmmmm . . .

A lesson very well learned.

The gray fog shattered like shards of smoked glass, leaving the six of them standing together in the dimly lit underground chamber, blinking and staring at each other.

Spence said, "What the fuck . . ."

Static in their earphones, then Ginny's voice said, "Kai? Anyone on the surface? Do you read?"

A sound something like panic in her voice. Kai said, "Here, Gin. You all right?"

"Just barely!" Relief strongly evident now. "Kai, it shut us down and wouldn't let us back in! What the hell was happening down there?"

He looked at Mies, then at Izzy and Metz, watched them all shrug and look at each other. "Not sure. Um, what happened up there?"

Doc's voice: "It put us out of the loop about half an hour ago, left us locked in here with only the engineering storage systems active. We had to break out the paper manuals from the control room safe and go through a manual reboot of the core system. If you hadn't had us set up the engine bleed—"

Kai said, "Hmh. Weird." Metz's words, said so short a time ago. A technician's words for any what-the-fuck situation. "What's the dataspool look like?"

Silence. Then Ginny said, "Mostly erased and handed back to the eyebubble core. The SAE is maintaining a small synopsis file."

"Well. I wish you two could have seen the whole thing, but . . . Take a look at the synopsis and we'll talk about it later." He paused, then grimaced, and said, "Oh, yeah. Restore the system lockouts. And unload the spieltier from RAM again."

Ginny said, "Good idea . . ."

"Mies? You ready for the next site?"

"Sure. Let me secure the waveguide sample in a coldbox. No sense just leaving it here."

Spence suddenly shouted: "Are you people out of your fucking minds? You'd risk the ship again for some kind of software-induced fantasy?"

Metz, beginning to unship the scanner head, tittered and said, "Jeez, Spence, he *told* them to unlink the spieltier filter. Let's just go get some more data."

And Izzy said, "Me, I thought the whole business was pretty cool."

Cool, thought Kai. Right. That's the word I was looking for. He glanced at Mies and was pleased to see him smiling again.

Standing in the shadow of a crag, light from Alpha Centauri B blocked out, light from A cutting a cool gray swath through the top and right side of the shadow, Kai stood looking at the eroded white salt flat, layer on layer, concentric outlines, showing where the little brine sea had gotten smaller and smaller, season after season, stood looking at the broken buildings of the fallen village, thought of the Frogmen watching their world come to an end.

We saw how it began, up there, saw in their museum city, saw it through the allegorical veil of their religious story. And this is how it ended. A few little froggies wasting away by the shores of a black salt sea, while the sky grew dark overhead.

Maybe they prayed to their furry black godlings, Bring back the water, freshen the air.

This is probably why they developed a technological civilization, probably why they went to space, why they set up bases on Bellerophon, why they set their ships down on the crushing surface of Pegasus, two-gees to their zero-point-seven-seven. Three gravities to them.

I wonder what went wrong?

Why did they fail where we did not?

Or have we succeeded? Just because ten men and women stand by this for now farthest shore, just because other ships are on their way to farther stars . . . What if darkness falls before the fleet can leave? What if the ten thousand die, along with all of humanity? What could we ten do then? What could the other little groups of eleven do, landed on their possibly habitable worlds? We know the words of the fable, but, seven men and three women . . .

He smiled, and thought. Six men? For Christ's sake. Changeling me. Izzy and Metz. Doc with no dick. Sad, sulking Andy. Spence and Mies. It's probably a good thing we have the wherewithal to practice technogenic . . .

Ginny. Linda. Rosie.

Hm. Maybe not.

Let's visualize the ten of us, supported by our technologies for centuries, until we go mad and kill each other. Remember Pitcairn's Island? They didn't expect us to survive and reproduce like Adam and Eve. Hiraoka knew it wouldn't be viable. Otherwise, he'd've sent healthier specimens, instead of us smartasses.

Izzy said, "All set, Kai. What the hell are you grinning about?"

"Nothing. Mies, get your ass out of the fucking way! How the hell many samples of salt flat do you need?"

Mies looked at him, frowning, pieces of samplekit in his hands. "I don't know. There're some very interesting organics here. Probably chemical fossils of the sealife. Rosie will want to . . ."

A puzzled-hurt look on his face. A hurt little boy look? Small wave of warmth washing through Kai. And a further visualization of the sleep time to come. Will we camp out under the stars again? No. We'll camp out under the afternoon sun this time and . . .

Remembered sensation of Mies's prick sliding into him, of Mies whispering pleasure as he pushed and pushed. Wonder how he'd like . . .

Kai frowned, watching the man pack up his samples and trudge toward where his waveguide connector was waiting. No, not Mies. A sigh. Well, pretty soon we'll hop back up to *Mother Night*. Ginny, now. Ginny will surely want . . .

That was nice to think about, too. "Gin?"

"Here, Kai. Ready."

Graphs spooling up, landscape shimmering and . . .

Black water so still before them, a broad white lake under a dull, cloudless blue sky, surface flat, rather oily looking. Something bobbing out there. A piece of wood. No. No woody plants ever part of the Pholotian ecology. Something, anyway, floating rather high.

Mies said, "I guess the specific gravity of this water must have been up around one-point-seven."

And, beyond the flat water of the salt lake, the town. A dim collection of low, rounded domes, surrounded by some kind of fog. Real? Some unknown phenomenon analogous to terrestrial habitation fog? Or just an artifact of the SAE process? Kai studied his graphs and thought, Artifact, almost certainly.

Linda said, "Look!" Pointing, to the open area of the dead sea bottom beyond the little town.

A cloud of dusty smoke, a bright spark of blue flame rising, blue flame flickering gently, pushing a winged white vehicle toward the dusty blue sky.

Mies said, "Well. They still had space travel, at least."

Kai said, "As near as I can make out, this scenario is at least seventy thousand years after the colonies on Bellerophon. If we ever get these people's history unraveled, we'll surely have food for thought."

Izzy, voice quiet, said, "When you think of what we've got here, an entire civilization, as complex as anything that ever existed on Earth, persisting for close to a hundred thousand years . . ."

"Longer than that," said Doc. "Some of the polar artifacts we've seen on the radar scan look a lot damned younger than these."

Kai watched the rocket dwindle in the ersatz sky, watched the vignette flicker and recycle. Well. Flat lake. Little city. Rocket lifting off . . . He said, "I guess that's all we're going to get without invoking some higher-order filtering structure."

Spence said, "Goddamn it, Kai . . ."

Mies said, "I don't think this site's worth the trouble. Let's move on."

Kai watched the vignette cycle a third time, admiring the vehicle's clean blue exhaust. Probably a very good design. Probably they had a long time to work out the bugs. He said, "I agree. Anyway, once we get back up to the ship, we can take the time to play around with improvements to the software. Let's go."

Kai stood once again on top of the cliff, looking down into the chasm, where the last Frogmen had apparently lived and died. Now, with the two suns high overhead, the canyon seemed washed out and colorless, the red, yellow, and orange striations of its walls pastel, almost indistinguishable, more or less the color . . . Well, the color of rock.

Behind him, the plastic survival tent flexed in the gentle wind, soft crumpling sound of its not-quite-stiff material coming through the thin plastic of his helmet. *I could take the helmet off, we don't really need these suits at 400 millibars surface pressure. Take the helmet off, put on an oxygen mask, feel the winds of alien Pholos in my hair . . .*

Right. And feel the UV roast my skin. Hot out here, too, dry, dead surface of Pholos baking in something like 1.31 times the surface illuminance of Earth. The surface temperature, displayed on a neat little graph, was just under 320 kelvins right now. *Enough to toast my little nuts, if they were still hanging out in the wind.* Looking back at the tent, he could see a shadow moving inside; Mies, getting ready for bed. *Getting ready for me? I can't tell.* Well, at least he agreed to sleep out here with me again, instead of back in the lander with the others. *Probably still trying to stay away from Spence and Linda.*

But . . .

I saw him watching me, while we ate dinner. He thinks of me as a woman now. When a man thinks of me as a woman, his eyes go . . . elsewhere. Avoid my face. Look at my crotch, measure the shape of my hips. You see them, imagining them-

selves with me splayed out naked, imagining my pussy, like I was a *thing* on a pornnet spoolie.

Soft thrill between his legs. I like it when they do that.

Remember trying to tell Ginny about that? Pissed off at me, mouth set in a sullen frown. Goddamn it, Kai, if you were a *real* woman, you wouldn't . . .

But I'm not a woman, Ginny. I'm a man with a woman's body, doing the things men always dream of doing when they dream of having women's bodies. That's the difference, all right. Men never dream of *being* women. They just dream of having themselves as women, of imagining themselves as the men they'd please, if only they could direct the actions of women.

And, oh God, when the dream becomes real . . .

Exhilaration. Freedom. Adulthood. Kai was floating in a long, gritty-walled gray corridor, somewhere deep inside Vesta, when the final-exam grades from Murphy-Bauman Higher Technical Institute scrolled up into his eyes, when a soft voice whispered, "Congratulations, Engineering-Technician First Class Maeru kai Ortega . . ." And, of course, under the list of solid exam grades, was his graduation rank, thirty-second out of 970, with an old-fashioned cumulative GPA of 3.71.

Well. EmBee wasn't the best engineering school in the solar system, not with schools like CalTech and Oxford still pumping out endless PhD theoretical research engineers, but it *was* the second best school off-Earth, after Mars's Argyre Technicum.

And that GPA will get me a berth on a decent space crew. Which will break my last link with Titan . . .

And, of course, with his parents. Image of their angry faces fading right away to nothing and gone. A feeling of sadness building up. When did it happen that my parents and I started hating each other? No particular time. No specific event. It just . . . happened. That's all.

The long gray corridor opened up into a spherical space about a dozen meters across, a lit-up space full of people drifting in slow arcs, caroming this way and that, Vesta's low-gee almost like zero gee, but not quite. You could tell which ones were the people from high-gee worlds, men and women from Earth and Venus slamming through the air on almost-straight trajectories, Martians and Selenites more delicate, not quite so muscular in their movements . . .

Low-gee folk like me knowing just how to move. Oh, maybe not me. Titan's gravity is almost a fifth of Luna's. Asteroid people best of all. Folk from the tiny out moons of Jupiter and Saturn, people from deep in the outer system, Kuiper Belt colonists, workers back from years in the Oort Cloud . . .

People of the Black Sky.

A sudden thrill to realize that, in no more than a year's time, he'd be out there as well, away from the sun, away from all the worlds of humanity. And, most especially, away from Titan. Away from all the conchy old farts in all the old colonies.

The arc he'd launched himself on came to an end, Kai drifting down feather-light to a set of handholds by an open round hatchway, bright light spilling out, eyebubble programs detecting his presence, reaching into his eyes and ears.

"Georgetown Bar and Grill, here. Georgetown Bar and Grill. If you don't already know, don't come in . . ."

Heavyset, sleepy-eyed looking man looking out at him from a workstation just inside the door. Sleepy eyes not recognizing him, just waiting for him to enter or bounce away to somewhere else.

Eyebubble-generated image forming on his retina, the slim, azure outline of a . . . well, maybe a dancing girl. At least, the featureless figure was dancing. Dancing with a lot of suggestive hip movement.

Kai hanging by the doorway, swinging from the tips of his fingers, dithering the seconds away while the fat man watched with increasing interest. As if he knows what's going on. Well, maybe he does.

Tâsqeau and Jemima talking about it back in the dorm barracks. This place and that. Whispering, really, about . . . *those* people. And you knew what they meant. My God, they'd whisper. What could it be *like*?

Kai remembered laughing. Like us? No agreement in their
eyes. Not like *us*. Tâsqeau and Jemima both shared his bed,
usually one at a time, sometimes together. Delicious memory
of that night a few weeks back, the three of them rocking in
delicate unison, whispering to each other in real-time, not wanting netconnect for something like this, whispering timing cues,
then Kai spasming in Jemima while Tasqueau spasmed in him
while Jemima crooned her own soft pleasure, moisture soaking
out on Kai's thin thighs . . .

No. Not like us.

He looked the fat man in the eye, then swung in through
the door.

The fat man lifted a hand, and said, "Two-ceu cover."

Kai looked into the scanner's eye and started to assent, then
hesitated. There was an amused smirk on the fat man's face.
"Don't worry, little boy. As far as the eyebubble core is concerned, you're in a peepshow flickerbar. Nice, wholesome entertainment for the horny young."

A quick, nervous nod at the scanner, then an equally nervous
glance back at the gatekeeper, who smiled, eyes still ironic. The
man said, "No, we don't tell that to slummers. We let them
think there'll be a record for the police to see."

Police. No, it's not illegal. But when the police need
someone . . . *safe* to roust . . . He said, "But . . . how can
you . . ."

A little laugh from the fat man. "I can tell."

Kai gaped, quickly brought his face under control.

Another laugh: "No, it's not that obvious, but . . . *I* can tell,
you see."

Do I? Do I see?

The fat man said, "Go on in. Enjoy yourself." And an interested look, eyes examining his young man's body. "Tell me
later what you think of . . . us."

Us? A quick, circumspect examination of the fat man. Is *he*
one? Doesn't . . . look like one. . . .

The fat man was smiling at him, clearly quite amused, amusement pushing him away, pushing him on into the hazy reddish light of the Georgetown Bar and Grill.

Circular space. Dim red light. Diaphanous haze. Tables clinging to the walls. Blue-glowing model Earth spinning in the center. Look closely at these people, heart pounding hard in your chest. Yes. It could be. Most of them very slim, very young looking. Like boys in early adolescence. Or slim young girls. Most of them with short-cropped, feathery-textured hair, hair lying flat against shapely skulls, faces wan, pale, devoid of obvious racial characteristics. Hair sometimes light brown, sometimes straw-blond, sometimes pale gray, eyes usually matching hair.

Matched sets of slim, young boy-girls, holding hands in the dim light, sitting together, nuzzling each other, eyes mostly turned, though, toward the stage on the other side of the spinning Earth.

Spinning Earth, Kai realized, that strategically blocked any view of the stage until you'd committed yourself by coming all the way into the room. Neatly done. Because Astraean State Law says if you voluntarily look at something, your personal standards no longer apply. You've accepted the standard of the presenter and can file no damage suit, no matter what the sight or experience does to your precious, delicate little immortal soul. . . .

Kai drifting around the room, seeing people notice him. I look very different, very out of place here, don't I. And rather nervous, too, I bet. . . .

Stopping by an empty table, holding himself still in the air by a hand on the back of one attached stool, holding himself up against Vesta's weak gravity by the muscles of his wrist, ignoring the stares, the smiles, the titters, the faint motion of slim boy-girls nudging each other and nodding in his direction, Kai looked at the stage.

Dancers dancing, whirling above a dance floor made of little glass lily pads, little platforms somehow suspended in thin air . . .

Engineering voice in his head suddenly whispering out different plausible scenarios, ways you could so easily work that little trick in Vesta-class low gee . . .

But . . . the dancers!

Forget about the engineering tricks. Look at the dancers.

Not boy-girls at all, it seemed. Slim, naked young girls. Very young, apparently, though they were incongruously tall. Young girls without a smudge of pubic hair. Without the pudendal darkening that let you know they were merely shaven, or had had their hair tattooed right off.

Young girls without breasts, dancing and dancing, whirling into the air, passing close by each other from time to time, pausing in midair for a kiss.

All right, so it's just strange-looking girls, doing a silly dance. And, in a minute, we'll see them go lickety-split, and all these slim little lezzies will get all excited and jerk each other off and . . .

No. You know it's not that.

You've heard all the stories.

One of the slim little girls did a slow starfish tumble, and Kai felt his breath grow very shallow indeed as he watched a shiny-wet snake slide out between the lips of her girly-girl vulva. Suddenly, she was a slim little boy. Slim little hairless boy with a shiny-wet erection, spinning in a starfish tumble toward that other slim little girl, spinning by her, other girl suddenly a wetprick boy, wet penises sliding over each other for just a second, like crossed swords of flesh . . .

My God.

Kai, holding his breath, watching, hardly aware he wasn't the only one in the room, but conscious of his swiftly grown erection. Kai, watching the dancers dance, watching them slowly, oh-so-slowly, begin to make love with each other, to each other, first one, then the other, offering and accepting penetration . . .

Kai, after the dance was over, aware that he'd had an orgasm, aware that things were wet inside his pants. Kai, after the dance, aware that just about every eye in the room was on him now. Waiting to see what he'd do . . . Kai turning away, flushing with embarrassment, fleeing out past the fat man at the gate, running away to his school barracks and shower, hoping to get cleaned up and . . .

Kai lying alone in his bed at night, having told first Jemima, then Tâsqeau, that he just wasn't in the mood, maybe tomorrow . . .

Kai lying alone in his bed, wondering just what it would be like to make love with a being that could be both Tâsqeau and Jemima at once. Visions of that lovemaking, simple at first, then ever so much more complicated, as the notion raised itself: what would it be like, then, to be . . . one of *them*?

EIGHT

Back aboard *Mother Night,* the ten of them sat around the science deck's light table. I feel, thought Mies, like everyone's eyes are on me.

Maybe they are . . . then again, it is a mark of adolescence that you feel everyone is watching you, that you are somehow special, that your every act is performed for an invisible audience.

Is that what you think? That I'm immature, an adolescent?

At one end of the light table, Ginny sat in a zero-gee chair, rounded hips gently gripped by its sensitive arms, holding her in place while she stared over steepled fingers down into the display's depths, where the surface of Pholos rolled by.

Orbital velocity, thought the scientist, *5.9 kilometers per second.* Every now and again, a bright bead would appear on the surface, AI marking the places where the ship's radar and optical scans had detected what it parsed to be ruins.

My God, she's pretty. Really pretty. Better looking than most of the women I've known, out of all the hundreds. Hundreds that I've . . . A brief image then of Captain Vonzell, naked before him. Not floating in zero-gee darkness, no. Not aboard *Mother Night* at all. We're on Earth, he realized. One full, natural gravity. Ginny stripping for me. For some reason, slipping out of her shorts first. Standing there in panties and blouse. Then slipping out of the panties, lovely hips exposed, rounded curve of buttock, furred slit of vulva.

Rule-sieves opening. IN THE HISTORICALLY DOMINANT, OCCIDENTAL-DERIVED CULTURE OF EARTH, WOMEN ARE TAUGHT TO VIEW THEIR BREASTS AS THE PRIMARY REPOSITORY OF THEIR SEXUALITY.

You have to wonder how that happened. I mean, we don't fuck their tits. . . .

Ginny slipping out of her blouse now, hard breasts of a muscular and fit woman bouncing and surging in high gee, nipples already erect, pleasing indeed to the . . . rules. Quite . . . *piquant,* thought Mies, imagining himself bending down, bending down to surround one of those fine, crinkled nipples with his lips, touch it with the moist tip of his tongue. Aware, suddenly, of an erection forming, down in his pants, uncomfortably doubled up, penis caught, somehow, in his own pubic hair. God. Good thing I'm sitting down. No one will notice. Give this thing time to go away. . . .

Ugly laughter from the scientist persona: *You see? Isn't that what a teenaged boy does? Looks at the pretty teacher instead of paying attention to the algebra lesson. Gets a fierce little hard-on. And then frets that everyone will notice. I can hear little David, metamorphosing to big David, even now: Snap out of it, Davy! In just a few minutes, you've got to get up and walk out of here. Western Civ is only ten minutes away! Oh, God! Oh, God! What if I* can't *control myself? What if I come in my pants and it soaks through? Everyone will see the wet spot and then they'll* know! *What will I do?*

Somewhere, down deep, the two Davys seemed very angry indeed.

And Ginny was saying, ". . . then I think we're all agreed on the tentative content of our first major report. First, that this star system is superannuated, something we should have taken into account, despite the astronomical indications. Given that we *knew* Alpha Centauri was in excess of eight billion years old, it was very unlikely that any terrestrial planet with an active geochemical cycle would survive."

Rosie said, "Maybe so, but no one could have predicted for sure. Not enough data. I mean, given the possibility of a Gaean feedback effect, it was entirely reasonable to suppose, even after the cessation of the geochemical cycle, that an active and mature biosphere would prolong the planet's habitable phase.''

Kai said, ''Now we know different. That's something to factor into the Daiseijin's master equation.''

But too late. All the explorer ships are already on their way. There won't be time to send out a second fleet.

Mies sat silent, watching Ginny's face. Look. The glisten of her eyes, so fine and intelligent. So full of . . . depth. Watch her lips move as she talks. You can see the white of her teeth. The pink tip of her tongue. Imagine what those lips and tongue and teeth . . .

Ginny said, ''Second, we are agreed that there are at least one and possibly two sentient species, now extinct, native to this system, who have left an extensive network of ruins and artifacts, most of them in excess of three billion years old, on all the major bodies we have visited. We anticipate there will be such artifacts throughout the star system and further speculate that a more extensive network of ruins existed in the system's Oort Cloud, prior to its disruption by Proxima.''

Spence said, ''You have to wonder where it's gone. The Proxima transit event is contemporaneous with Alpha Centauri's passage by Sol. It's not out of the question that a percentage of the artifacts are actually going to pass through our own system.''

No craters on Atalanta, no disruption of the Oort. My God. Maybe they had used it up. I should have realized . . .

Watching Ginny talk, Mies found himself imagining that he was already inside her, thrusting, thrusting, autoviroids getting themselves ready. The sensations . . . a thousand remembered fucks? Or do I imagine she feels the way Kai did, subtly different from a . . . real woman?

Ginny said, ''Third, our preliminary investigations reveal that the presence of a technological civilization in this star system, persisting quite possibly over geological ages, has depleted the major and minor bodies, other than gas giants, of their readily available resources.'' She looked up from the light table.

"Meaning, of course, that there's no viable colony site here. The fleet is not to come."

Mies felt himself start to ejaculate, rising tide of inevitability, a cramping nausea in his bowels, making him squint, making the light in the room seem to grow painfully bright.

Jaws clenched. Pubococcygeus muscle clenched. Maybe we can stop it.

Fat chance.

Holding. Holding.

Uh.

Prick hopping around down inside his pants, semen spilling into his underwear, going all over. Is anyone watching? Are they looking at me?

They've got better things to think about than what's going on in your pants.

Rosie, though . . . looking straight at him, eyes dark and unreadable. She said, "The presence of actual life-forms here, on Pegasus, at least, as well as a wealth of fossils, will prove important for the future decision-making processes of the various committees. We've suddenly got a much larger database. When the other explorer ships arrive at their destinations . . ."

Kai said, "We should probably consider beaming our signal at the other target stars, as well as back to Earth. We can time the transmissions to coincide with the expected arrivals."

Izzy said, "We're not really set up for that kind of thing. We'd probably have to build a special transmitter from the spare parts store, and then do something to get their attention."

Metz said, "Not necessarily. The AIs are coded to watch for astronomical manifestations of that sort."

Sick and empty now, Mies felt cooling semen start to work its way around in his pubic hair. In a few minutes, it *would* be soaking through the front of his pants. Then . . . He made the chair let him go and stood, the others' eyes on him now for certain. He said, "I'm sorry. I've *really* got to take a shit. I'll be back in a few minutes. Go ahead without me."

Silence. A bizarre little snicker from Metz.

Mies turned away, closing out their prying eyes, got out into the axial corridor and pulled himself aft, toward the centrifuge deck. Down the ladder. Ten empty coffins. One full one, control panel covered with red and amber lights. No one here. Good.

He closed himself into the little washroom and started peeling out of his shorts, odor of semen suddenly filling his nostrils. Stood flat-footed, looking at himself, naked from the waist down, in the little mirror over the faux-stainless steel plastic basin. After a moment, he began to sob, watching the face in the mirror, not his face, eyes empty, full of tears, tears running down his cheeks, cascading off the sides of his chin and falling to the floor.

Hanging in her sleeping bag, clutching its netting with crooked fingers, Ginny stared out into the dim almost-darkness of her cabin, seeing it somehow as a featureless empty room and wished, for the hundredth time in as many minutes, for the surface gravity of a substantial terrestrial world. The way I feel right now, she thought, grim, depressed, flattened out, it would be appropriate. I could lie here, naked on my bed, legs spread like an abandoned wanton in some old film, one arm thrown across my eyes, tears streaming back across cheekbones, falling into my ears . . .

That brought a little smile. There was a song about that. Where was I? On Venus maybe? The bartender in the off duty miner's bar who fancied himself a historian of labor culture. All those old ridiculous songs about men who worked shitty jobs and the women who betrayed them because they weren't rich. Yes, I could lie here, thinking about the way he greeted me with a peck on the cheek, a surreptitious glance at Mies, who was studiously avoiding most people's eyes, especially poor Rosie's . . .

And that business with Lin and Spence. For Christ's sake. How has it gotten to be such a mess? We did all right back on Earth, working our way through years of training, forming pairs where they weren't already formed, and we've only been *here* a little while. Is it the distance that matters? The knowledge that we *can't* go out and prowl the sexual underbrush of human society until we find a new partner? Is that why everyone is suddenly fucking up?

A renewed image of herself then, the woman abandoned by her lover, lover gone off to some new woman's body . . . Image of Kai then, lying under Mies. My boyfriend's left me for another man? Old jokes, fossil memes inhabiting our culture. Renewed image of herself sprawled on a wide white bed under full Earth gravity, legs spread, arm across her eyes, crying and . . . beginning to feel that old, familiar desperation. Her lover with another, herself with no one and no one to turn to. Slim hand reaching down across smooth belly to cup her vulva in a warm palm, feeling its heat, fingers seeking out . . .

And the anger afterward. The bitterness. You masturbate alone, and then you cry, because . . .

The eyebubble blinked a phantom light in her eyes, letting her know it knew she was awake. Her standard query, rule set up long ago: If it's sleep time and I'm awake, check to see if I'm pretending to be asleep. All it would take would be not acknowledging the summons, but . . . I know it's stupid to lie here and sulk. I know I can't be a man for Kai, no matter how hard I try, and I haven't really tried, won't try, can't try, but . . . A hard fact: Mies will not be a woman for him, at need.

She stirred and looked at the sensor pack over the door, her gaze enough to let the core know she was awake and willing to be disturbed. And a soft voice whispered in her ear: "Ginny?"

A cold surge of annoyance. For Christ's sake. "What is it, Mies?"

"I'd like to talk to you, Ginny. Can I come in?"

A cooling breeze of dismay. What does the bastard want to do, come in and gloat, see me hanging here naked with my hands on my crotch, fingers prepared to take Kai's plunge for him? I . . . Feelings, resigned feelings, collapsing. Useless. It's not like I can run away or anything.

Inner voice disagreeing. Run to Doc's arms. He'll stroke your back and tell you, Oh, there, there, don't cry, Ginny, and eat your pussy for you, if that's what it takes. . . .

"All right. Come in."

The door opened and closed, eyebubble core having understood what was about to happen, a shadowy form bobbing through and hanging in the gloom. "Are you all right, Ginny? It's dark in here. . . ."

Asshole bastard. She said, "I'm trying to sleep. Do you need a light?" Sensitive to my own words. Overanalyzing. He'll hear me say, *trying to sleep,* and picture me here crying my eyes out, sleepless over the loss of Kai and . . . She glanced at the sensor pack until it called up a set of simple room controls, eyed the slider until the room lights came up a bit, nodded the controls away. "That better?"

Mies, face flat, affectless, eyes so very still, staring at her.

What is he seeing? Me, hanging here in an open net, sleeping bag open now, brown body hanging in the light, gleaming with a little perspiration maybe. Looking at me . . .

Not looking at my face. No. Staring at my tits now, eyes maybe drawn to my nipples. Looking lower down now, at my crotch. Remember talking to Kai about this, Kai laughing at her naïveté about men's interests in women's parts.

No, everyone's not the same, Ginny. But we're . . . similar enough. You can look at the stuff in the pornnet topics and see how limited our variation is. So what's Mies looking at now? A swatch of black pubic hair, nothing else visible at the moment. Kai telling me about the surge of feeling men experience, seeing a woman, flat on her back, as if seen from the foot of a bed, legs spread, knees apart and bent, feet pressed together.

Looking at such a picture with him, by way of example, and thinking, Oh. It looks like she's . . . ready. Nothing like that here now, Mies. Go back to your own room. Because now you know Kai can look like that. "What the hell did you want, Mies? Just to come in here and see me bareass?"

He seemed to flush, jerked his eyes away, looking at her face at last. "Uh. Sorry. It's just . . ." A weak gesture, down at her body.

Yes. It's *just.* Goddamn you. A malicious smile. "All right, Mies, you've seen my titties. Now can I go back to sleep?"

Frown forming on his face, proper anger in his eyes, but . . .
He said, "I'm sorry you're mad at me, Ginny. Truly sorry."

A long silence, while she wondered what to say and could
think of nothing.

Mies said, "I'm really sorry about Kai, Ginny. I didn't mean
for it to happen. You . . . I mean, it just happened. You know."

Ginny felt sullen anger well up, that old phrase, *you know.*
It just fucking *happened.* . . . What the hell is wrong with his
face? Mies's eyes as empty as the painted plastic eyes of a
cheap doll, muscles of his face . . . not quite working, not
enough movement for that, but . . . no, not twitching. Tension
there. Some kind of conflict . . .

Mies bobbed forward, fingers reaching out to clutch the netting of her bag, hand not far from her own, eyes looking into
her eyes, still so empty and strange and . . . A sudden blossoming of incredible earnestness. Mies said, "I'm sorry it happened, Ginny. I can see you're here alone. Alone and . . ."
Eyes flickering downward at her naked body, taking in breasts
and a presumably foreshortened view of her sparse pubic hair.

Ginny felt herself shiver suddenly, something mighty odd
about . . .

Mies said, "All alone with yourself. No one to help you . . .
sleep." And he reached out, put his hand on one of her breasts.

Feeling his fingers surround her nipple, Ginny felt a long
moment of almost hypnotic paralysis, mind supplying a series
of images: Mies's fingers palpating her nipple, nipple crinkling
up erect, warm wet forming between her legs, Mies kissing her,
soft tongue invading her mouth and . . .

She let go off the net with one hand, stiff-armed him in the
chest, watched him sail away, eyes wide, rebound off the far
wall with a grunt, arms flailing, steadying himself. She muttered, "What the *fuck* . . ." and glanced at the sensor pack.
The eyebubble was watching this. Judging with its rule-sieves.
At some point . . . all it would take is one shout and . . . no.
You're the captain. You've got to handle this. . . .

Mies coming back toward her, eyes shining, fumbling with
the front of his coverall. Fumbling, getting his fly open, hand

clutching his own erect penis. As Ginny listened, stunned, he said, "Please, Ginny. I want to help you. I didn't mean for you to be left all alone. Let me . . ."

Babbling. He's babbling. What the hell is going on? When he grabbed the netting again, reaching out for her, she put her hand in the middle of his chest, ready to shove again, and said, "Mies, I'm telling you no! Now get the fuck out of my room!"

Eyes looming in front of her, mouth open, breath coming in short gasps. "Please, Ginny. I love you, too. I love *both* of you."

Shit. Asshole. She said, "Mies, that was an order. Now go!" She gave him a push, watched him drift backwards to the door, where he hung, staring at her and . . . Hand pumping up and down on his prick now. Well, she thought, this will be stupid. So he'll jerk off in front of me and then go away, satisfied he's done his bit? Something is dreadfully wrong here. Doc's going to have to deal with this, somehow. Not me.

By the door, Mies suddenly moaned, "Oh, poor Ginny . . ." Let go of his penis, which swung stiffly back and forth, clutched the door frame, got his legs under him, launched himself hard across the room. Ginny met him with a fist in the face, felt his nose jam against the small bones of her hand, a little splinter of pain . . .

Mies tumbling end over end away from her, opening up like a starfish, arms and legs spread, thin mist of black blood from his face and . . .

Little white blobs flying from the end of his penis, flying in all directions as he tumbled and . . .

Mies curling himself into a little ball, caroming off a wall, reaching out, grabbing the edge of her dresser module, stopping himself, looking away, toward the door, up at the sensor pack, then back over his shoulder at her. Eyes wide. Mouth open, a dark hole in his pale face. Eyes full of obvious fear. Mouth working. Lips forming words. My God. Oh my God . . .

The two of them just staring at one another.

Then Mies turned, pushed himself at the door, which opened quickly, not quite quickly enough, Mies's shoulder bouncing off the edge of the door as he went through. You could hear him mutter, hear him thump off the opposite wall before the door closed.

Ginny sat silent, watching bits of clotting blood, little islands of floating semen, drift around the room on the air currents, one by one making their way to the air intake to be sucked into the filter.

She thought, Why don't I understand what just happened here?

Maybe because he just tried to rape you? Because he just tried to rape you, and you've tried, for a long goddamned time, not to think ever again about being raped.

Drums then, drumming against the Antarctic night.

Drums and pain.

And long years of . . . fixing yourself.

Think about that first.

Then go on to the other thing.

She looked up at the sensor pack, the blind eye of the eye-bubble core, and thought, Why the hell weren't you looking after me, *Mother Night*? Vision of the ship sulking, core angry because we . . . let it die, made it go through the pain of resurrection. No. Not a real person. Not a being. Just a collection of rules. The ship watched us fight, and maybe some rule-sieve decided we were . . . just playing. Just making love.

Sometimes, it's hard to know the difference between sex and rape, making love and . . . all those other things human beings do to . . . with . . . for . . .

Oh, not really each other.

For ourselves alone.

She felt the tears trying to seep out from under her eyelids, started the internal process of suppressing them. Because, she thought, what's the point?

By the light of a single, dim bedside baridium lamp, a sleepy thirty-four-year-old Virginia Vonzell Qing-an watched young Paris get undressed in the heavy, too-warm air of a residential cubby somewhere under Ishtar Terra, somewhere under the

Maxwell Mountains, somewhere under the Venusian arctic. Hot and clammy in here. Air too goddamned still. Sweat sitting motionless on my skin, inviting a bacterial bloom . . .

Paris was young and slim, a smooth Nordic boy with an almost featureless chest. Hair on his head such a pale shade of blond it sometimes seemed almost white, armpits and crotch just the same, accented by glacial blue eyes, blue-ice eyes now watching her watch him strip for action. Narrow-waisted Paris, slim-hipped Paris, Paris who made her think of snake-hipped lovers . . .

Who was it who called them snake-hipped lovers? That old twentieth-century Chinese writer, the one named after a fictional Venusian king. The one who liked to whine about discrimination while simultaneously gloating about the riches of success. She was the one who talked about snake-hipped lovers while bemoaning the failure of marriage bliss to survive all her hard-won successes.

Imagine. Money and freedom and orgasms by the thousand, at your beck and call, whenever you bothered to lie down for a summoned man. . . .

Still, it was an apt turn of phrase. Maybe the long dead Venusian king would have liked Paris now as well, swaying his slim white hips in the dim red-orange light, meaty tentacle of a grown-man's prick oscillating with his sway, meatiness belying the image of boy . . .

Paris kneeled at the foot of the bed, kneeled between her legs, and regarded her with shadowed eyes. Finally, he reached out and took one foot in his soft, warm hand, massaging her toes gently, and said, "So, this is it, Ginny? One last time and, *adios*?"

Looking at his soft smile, feeling his hand on her, Ginny couldn't even muster a nod. Paris ran a smooth hand up her muscular calf, fingers kneading ridges of work-induced muscle, stroked the inside of her thigh and waited. Finally, she said, "I wish I could take you with me." But, do I? Or is this just something we say? It does feel like time to move on, more or less, though the liquid tingle inside says otherwise.

Smile from young Paris broadening, Paris leaning forward, cupping her mons under his palm, running soft fingers through sparse, wiry black hair. "I should probably say the same to you, Ginny, but . . ." A little shrug. "The Black Sky Country's no place for me. No place for me even if I loved you true . . ."

A little pang deep inside her then. *Even if . . .* But then, you knew that. Young Paris no more than a sort of bought-and-paid-for companion from day one. Just the pretense of love, for someone who wants to stave off loneliness. By Monday, he'll have a new lover. Another lonely woman, perhaps, or some dark man with shadows behind his eyes.

Paris said, "Good-byes should be special, Ginny. Tell me what to do." Eyes on her face, waiting.

My God. Long silence. So. After all these years, I still can't ask. Can't tell even this . . . creature what it is that I want. A part of me somewhere that halts the flow of speech, that cringes still at the admission of desire, as if it were, somehow, a shameful thing. Shameful, perhaps, because desire was the driver of the Mothers and Fathers? Mothers and Fathers who . . .

Paris smiled, asking for her, interpreting for her, deciding for her, putting his hands on the inside of her thighs, pushing her legs apart, sprawling gracefully between them, sprawling gracefully despite the crushing weight of Venus's high gee, gravity that had left Ginny exhausted day and night for weeks and months after arrival.

Years spent on Luna and Mars and out in the Kuiper Belt shifting the balance of my muscular development from legs and hips and back to shoulders and chest and thighs. It was a good decision to come here; a good, balanced decision.

Still, in the morning you'll board the shuttle and ascend above yellow clouds to orbit under a wide and starry sky once again. Rise to orbit, board the highliner and fly away, fly on out to the infinite deep of the Black Sky Country. There'll be precious little gravity, out among the Oort bodies. And, just now, there was young Paris between her legs, grazing peacefully on the grasslands of her vulva, calling forth slick, albuminous moisture whether she paid attention or not. Young Paris, determined to tell her good-bye.

In a little while, he'll judge me ready, will climb the bean-stalk of my body and kiss me on the lips with his tangy breath, breath full of my own demanding pheromones, insert himself just *so,* combine thrusting with a circular rocking motion so few men ever master, pubis bone beneath his soft skin like an impertinent thumb, forcing me higher, whether I want to go or not . . .

If he knew how far his talents extended, he'd charge more than just room and board and sex and fun. Ginny smiled at the dim ceiling and thought, I'll miss him, I suppose. But only a little bit.

Doc floated alone in the central atrium of the living quarters deck, where the axial corridor widened a bit. Mostly lockers here. Things bolted to the walls here and there. Hatches between hanging equipment. Hallways to people's rooms. Hatchway to the wardroom, to the head complex and zero-gee showers. As always, thinking about these things, he automatically thought, We should have had the sense to put the shower facilities on the centrifuge deck. It'd be so nice . . . Thought suppressed. Useless.

Ginny's voice on the intercom: Could you come to my room? We need to talk.

Upset. Very upset.

Christ. I've got a bad feeling about this. He glanced up at the eyebubble sensor and muttered, "Gin?"

She was in her sleeping bag when the hatch whispered open, but it was quite clear that she hadn't been sleeping. Her eyes seemed open hard, dark irises fixed on him as he pulled himself inside. She unfastened the netting and threw it apart, floated up where she could reach him, grabbed at him, encircling his mid-riff with her arms, and squeezed him in a bear hug. "Oh, Doc. It's been a long day."

Just something to say, he realized. Something to say until she figures out how to . . . he waited, holding her tight until it seemed his arms would give out. This was slightly out of the ordinary, but not terribly so. Perhaps she just was lonely, now that Kai . . . Finally, he let go, and she dropped away, turning a few degrees, looking elsewhere. "I think we've got a real problem developing. Mies was here."

He laughed, bitter irony crystallizing the sound. "Yes, Mies. I wanted to talk to you about him. I would've been here first thing after breakfast. So, Ginny, what did Mies do while he was here to bother you so much?"

"He sort of tried to rape me. He was so *strange*. Completely out of control, muttering *non sequiturs*." Her voice was steady, hardly revealing the enormous strain.

Sort of? Looking at her. Looking for telltale signs. "You just . . . let him into your cabin?" Look at her knuckles. No, Mies would not be prepared to cope with her.

"Yes . . . yes. I was feeling . . . moody . . . myself, I'm afraid. I didn't bother to dress."

Something she's not telling me. "Are you all right?"

"Yes. I can handle it. There was no real damage done."

"Do you want to . . . do anything? About Mies."

She glared at him, biting her lower lip. It was a second before she answered. "No, of course not."

She's so aware of the delicate thread by which her authority hangs. He said, "Well. I've been studying Mies's behavior myself, Gin, and I don't like what I'm finding. His personality's been . . . deteriorating ever since we got here, in ways that fall nowhere near any of the appropriate axes. This latest incident is all the more disturbing; there seems to be a pattern to what's happening to him, but it looks all the more like some kind of . . . personality disorder than any normal psychosis."

Things starting to fall into place. The curious shape of Mies's files. But I can't tell her that. Something *mighty* odd about Mies. He said, "It may be that Mies Cochrane has never been the man we thought he was."

A curious look in her eyes. "What do you mean? I know the selection committee should have detected—" Stopping short. Looking away.

You can say it, Ginny. The selection committee should have understood he was a problem. And *I* was in charge of the selection committee, though behind the scenes. *You* knew I selected myself, and disapproved. Said nothing because you thought it would mean I'd go ahead and make sure you and Kai stayed together. He said, "I think Mies may have a hypnopaedic personality overlay."

Startled look in her eyes. "What?" Voice bewildered.

He said, "Hypnopaedic personalities decay over time. That could be what's happening now."

"That . . . seems far-fetched. I mean, *why?*"

Doc shrugged. "Maybe just to make the crew. People cheat on examinations all the time. That's how we all get past the educational system's academic phalange, how we get admitted to the ranks of the priesthood. Mies may simply have had himself made into a better scientist."

Troubled look. "Then who is . . . *was* he?"

"That's what I'd like to find out."

Curiosity in her eyes.

He said, "I'd like to make extensive, unsupervised use of the AI core. Tonight, while everyone's asleep. I need for you not to interfere. You or Kai."

Anger in her eyes, blocking out her curiosity, deafening her to what he'd just said, distracting her from being alerted. "I imagine Kai's busy."

"You think . . ." Yes. Yes, Mies *would* likely flee to Kai after . . . He said, "I'm sorry, Ginny. I'll give you a full report, a *private* report, in the morning." A long silence, then, "Did Mies ejaculate?"

Ginny looked at him for a moment. "Yes," she said, "all over the place."

Doc bobbed over to the main air-circulation grating, squinted at the coarse metal weave. Sure enough, here and there little droplets of semen could be found. He said, "This will be helpful."

Despair in her voice, Ginny said, "Help yourself."

*   *   *

Floating in the middle of his room, light drawn down until the corners were full of shadows, Kai watched Mies hang in his netting, asleep, moving fitfully, but obviously asleep, one hand still clutching the pair of cotton underpants they'd used to stop the flow of blood from his nose. Image of the door whispering him awake, Please, Kai, let me in . . . Mies's voice, odd somehow, choked, whispering through the eyebubble interface, door opening and . . .

My God, Mies! Letting him in, turning to the sensor pack, about to call Doc, Mies's hand suddenly on his arm, No, please . . . I need to . . . I need your help. I need to talk, Kai. . . .

Talk?

Looking down at Mies, then, dark blood smeared across his face, fingers pinching the bridge of his nose as he breathed through his mouth, eyes desperate and . . . Looking at me. Familiar eyes. Eyes looking at . . . Looking at what? A lover? Or just a friend? Memory of deciding that *friend* might just be good enough, for now, of making a decision, thinking of what to do, rummaging in his underwear drawer, separating silken girl-panties from the rougher cotton ones that were for when you felt more like a man and . . .

Even then, thinking just how silly that was, having mood-related underpants. Maybe I'm outgrowing this? But putting the thought aside for later, turning to help Mies . . . and noticing, from one corner of your consciousness, that his fly was open. What? Did he suddenly have a nasal aneurysm while taking a leak? Hmh. You do know better than that. Well, Mies with the bleeding nose and exposed crotch. Have another little fight with Rosie, did you? Eyebrows arched, grin on face, but . . .

Mies's frightened eyes looking at you over the already red-stained underpants. Muffled voice: No, ah . . . And the story tumbling out.

Kai then, in cold shock, hardly able to believe what he was hearing. Tried to, um, *rape* Captain Virginia Vonzell Qing-an, of the Daiseijin starship *Mother Night,* here, right here, in low orbit around Pholos, Alpha Centauri B-2, home of the Frogmen, home of the Rhinotaurs, home of the . . . Image of a religious icon: Leospiders.

But . . . *why?*

Oh, I don't know, Kai, I . . .

Mies floating in the netting of Kai's zero-gee bed, starting to cry, making his nosebleed worse instead of better. And Kai holding him close, stroking his back, telling him it would be all right, sleep now little Mies, and we'll straighten things out in the morning. Straighten things out, fix up this little misunderstanding, and get on back down to Pholos, get on with our work, you see . . .

Christ. I wanted to push his head back, kiss away his tears, rub my face in his blood, and fuck him happy again. Fuck him, like I was the man and he was the woman. Old, old parts of me still alive. Parts no surgery can alter. Immaterial parts, cultural parts, hormonal parts. . . .

And, feeling Mies's well-formed man-body against him, those other hormones starting up, from implants and altered glands, secret place between his legs relaxing, growing moist, getting ready. Yes, dear little sweet Kai, you can rub yourself against him, little frotteuse, rub him conscious of you, rub his thigh with the curve of your pubis bone until his own hormones awaken.

Nothing so wrong with a man that a woman's pheromone-sweet breath in his face won't . . .

Soft words from Mies, holding him close: Lost. Dear God. Falling apart . . .

Mies closing his eyes, suddenly freezing motionless, holding still like that for a long moment, then just as suddenly relaxing, one deep breath, then another . . .

Asleep?

How could he suddenly fall asleep like that?

But . . . familiar, all the same. Mies falling asleep the way a terrified child falls asleep, the way a child escapes into sleep. Holding him close then, letting his own feelings subside. What now? Call Doc? A long, hard look at the sensor pack over the door. Call Doc? No. If . . . if whatever *really* happened was big, bad, important, they'd already be here, getting me, bring me in on . . . whatever it was.

How likely is it that Mies has imagined this? How likely is it he's just . . . feeling guilty?

No. I'll hold him now, and we'll both sleep. Time enough, in the morning, to straighten things out. God. He feels so warm and nice. . . .

They don't put you to sleep anymore.

Kai, age twenty-one, Kai now a fully emancipated adult by the laws of SaturnCorp, by the superseding laws of the Solar Alliance, lying on his back in a small, cold room, small room gleaming with hard white plastic and mirror-bright metal; Kai lying there naked, waiting for them to begin.

The right decision.

Or not?

Just now, I should be boarding the Standard ARM packet for Neptune. Just now I should be anticipating my training time, first in the Standard ARM finishing school at Chronopolis, on Triton, then on Nereïd. Then . . . Then on out, on out to the deep, black sky.

Memory of a night spent with Count Maxilon, lead harmonist of the famed *Maxilon Ineas* tempaxsie combo. . . .

Fucking him so sweetly in his little girly slit, then bending over before him, letting him take me in the time-honored way of the most manly of men. . . .

Count Maxilon's throaty girl-voice whispering, You'll love it, Kai, sweet Kai, when we are . . . just the same . . . just the . . .

Count Maxilon, voice stilled by passion, gasping, gasping and heaving inside him, one, two, three, done . . .

Now, the machine, machine-guide, the eyebubble-living machine, hovering over him. Waiting. Waiting. His heart pounding in abject, anticipatory dread. Tendrils reaching out, touching the warm spots over his veins. A faint pinprick, here, there, everywhere . . .

A hard scald of nausea as the biots flowed in, hot, oily,

invisible little machines flooding him through and through and . . .

Snicker-snack.

Machine hand reaching down like lightning in the clouds of orange-banded Jupiter, machine hand reaching down and snatching his manhood away, cold air on his insides making him gasp, making him turn his head and, wide-eyed, follow the bloody lump of his cock and balls, familiar cock and tender little balls plunking down in a little white dish, other little machines scurrying in to make their changes and recede and . . .

A sudden, horrid crackle, a billion-trillion bee stings all over as his manly hair follicles died from the inside out.

A secondary tingling, not quite so harsh, under his scalp, and he was conscious of his head hair dropping away, falling to the floor like a cloud of blond feathers.

Worms, then. Worms in his head.

Feathery gray hair growing out like old-time movie magic.

A sudden popping in his eyes, like ripples spreading across little pools of mineral oil. I can hardly wait to look in the mirror and see . . . eyes of a different color. Face of a different man . . .

Man?

No man.

Machine hand bringing back what had been his cock and balls, nothing dangly up there now, machine hand at his crotch. Flicker-flash of a fleshwelder lighting the ceiling tile pale blue as it put his skin back on and . . .

Hot, *hot* scald in his veins as the biots gathered and rushed back to their entry points, crushed together, rush hour in his heart, gathered and swarmed and were gone. Tendrils receding. Machines receding. Leaving him alone, suddenly exhausted.

Done.

Word like a single dull drumbeat at the center of his soul.

Gone Maeru kai Ortega the boy.

Gone Maeru kai Ortega the incipient man.

In his place, Maeru kai Ortega the . . .

No pronoun. No word. *Androgyne* sounds so . . . clinical.

Kai reached down with a trembling hand and felt his own hairless little slit, felt dry, smooth, hairless skin, felt his heart trip-hammer in his chest, and thought, So. This *will* take some getting used to, after all. . . .

Doc floated, almost motionless, rigid in the air of his stateroom, stretched out straight, ankles locked around each other, arms wrapped around his chest, head tipped downward, chin almost resting on his breastbone.

Not quite motionless. Some drift. The far wall of the room was moving slowly, transiting behind the array of open windows the eyebubble placed in his eyes, windows like bright, square holes out of the real world, into some other dimension.

Imaginary windows. Windows the AI core has placed in my eyes.

Windows with words. Windows with images of Mies Cochrane. Past and present, some hints of the future. Pictures in my eyes. Words, voices in my ears . . .

I lived before this technology was born. It still seems, somehow, sometimes, strange to me, eerie and new and impossible, though I've used it for decades, grown familiar and comfortable and arrogant in its use. AI core and eyebubble interface. The perfect amanuensis. The perfect information slave.

In front of them all now, the window holding the results of the ICOPOSI psychotropic analysis software's run on MIES-dot-ALL-at-MNcore. All right. So I've been stupid. So I should have done this before. Forget about that. Focus on this, Doctor Matel.

So, the psychotrope believes Mies's records are falsified. Prepped and transferred from outside the system. Which implies a pretty damned good command of network-extraction protocols. And Mies himself shows no evidence of being such a good hacker. Hack job possibly done with expertise not less than that of Orang Metzalar Ho. But not using Metz's known programming style.

Well. Records indicate there are at least three thousand such programmers living in the solar system. Ninety-four of them employed by the Daiseijin. Six of them, in fact, outside the solar system entirely. One of them right here: Metz, with his datamatcher, Isador Feldschuh.

All right. At need, I'll call on them.

Kai? Yes, Kai could probably do something like this, though less adroitly than Metz. No connection. No correlation. This was not an inside job.

Psychotrope studies all the files we've made of Mister Cochrane, since he came to us. Psychotrope suggests the possibility of a hypnopaedic overlay, now in decay. Psychotrope finds no evidence, however, that such a coherent overlay exists. Psychotrope suggests Mies Cochrane consists of five to seven distinct personalities, working in unison, sometimes in conflict.

A traumatized child.

An anesthetized young man, hardly a conscious personality at all, more of a shadow, or fragment of a previous overlay.

A young woman, fragmentary, surfacing rarely, showing some evidence of being a multiple rape victim, or possibly an abused prostitute.

Evidence of a construct-overlay master personality, following the main paradigms of hypnopaedic personality transfer/generation. But not in full control, as if the overlay process had been mismanaged.

Strong evidence of a scientific data manager overlay. This one is the most like a classic hypnopaedia session, most likely done with commercial educational software.

All right, that's five. The other one or two?

Some evidence of an external personality, possible formed as a result of the vector sum of the five internal personalities.

And there is, as well, some evidence that Mies contains a God Conscience Module.

The sort of thing we used to see being inserted by religious cults, back in the eighties and nineties?

Correct. A data management process outlawed by ICOPOSI.

Shit. Diagnosis?

Classic: Multiple Personality Disorder in Terminal Fugue.

Modern: Unrenormalized Secret Agent Syndrome.

Doc curled slowly into a ball, moment arms pulled in now,

so that he started to rotate a little faster. Secret agent syndrome. God *damn* it, why didn't I do this sooner? Cold hand on his heart. If the Daiseijin has been infiltrated by some agency other than ICOPOSI, we've got a . . . big problem. Why the hell didn't I do this back on Earth? Why didn't I do this to every prospective crew member?

Stupid.

Goddamn it, stop wasting your time on recriminations, Doctor Matel. Get to work.

And do what?

You know what.

All right, where is he now?

He glanced over at his eyebubble control analogues, blinked away the file windows on Mies, started to lock them down . . . no, leave the system open. You're going to want to put your . . . new data in here as well. Run the software on it. Study it at your leisure. Because you know what you're about to do.

Excitement building.

Just like the good old days.

He let the AI scan the ship, set it to looking for him, not bothering to watch the quick succession of images it showed. Ah. So. Mies. Cuddled in the arms of his lady love. You're a Goddamned *fool,* Maeru kai Ortega. But no more a fool than I. All right. Do it.

He unballed himself, blinking away the interface. Kicked against the nearest wall, arrowed out through the suddenly open door. Get the hardware. Get to the . . . research site. Get busy. You'll have a couple of hours, at least.

Locked in Mies's room, Doc thought, it smells funny in here. People's quarters always have a faint, characteristic smell, no matter how clean they are, short of sterilizing the environment on an almost daily basis. But this is . . . stronger than usual. As if Mies were giving off a uniquely powerful effluvium, with his exhalations and farts, his shedding hair and epidermis.

Probably to the good. Give the synchronoptic analysis engine something to work on. A quick glance. He had the scanner head platform clamped to the top of the dresser; no particle beamer, just the scanner head. Don't want to blow the place up or electrocute myself. Drawers pulled open, door locked . . .

Two hours. No more. Then I've got to get out of here.

All sorts of crap in his drawers. Stuff from other parts of his life? Hard to tell. No sense in pawing through it. Even a disintegrating spy will have some caution left.

He called up the SAE software and started loading modules into his personal software space. Not really a lot of space in there. I'll have to be very selective. Wish I could wake up Izzy and Metz and have them give me a hand. I'm not really trained for this sort of thing.

There. That'll have to do.

I wonder if Metz will realize I've been playing with his toys. Probably.

Well. This won't stay secret for very long. If it's what I think, we'll have to . . . do something.

I wonder who they are?

Probably, some other government bureau. UNBI. Industrial Espionage Counterintelligence Organization. One of those. Hell, maybe even the Division of Interplanetary Vehicles Registration. Those bastards could be mighty damned interfering, for a simple licensing bureau. Remember how mad Ras used to get at the size of the bribes he had to spread on Diver officials?

Bloodsuckers, one and all.

All right.

Run the bastard.

Scanner head suddenly nodding and twisting, pale green light glimmering on the walls of the room. Up down, back and forth, graphs and tables and charts spooling up out of the air.

Face of a small boy.

Big, moist-looking eyes.

Dry-looking, uncombed brown hair.

Label: David Gilman.

So who the fuck is David Gilman? At least now I have a real name. Wonder how he picked Mies Cochrane? The label was joined by scrolling information windows. Born here, parents, sister. Possible sexual involvement with sister at an early age.

Well, that'll do for a victimizing trauma.

Other windows opening, data starting to spool into his files. Images, words. This and that. Fragments, really. But it's clear I could get the whole story if I had the full use of the SAE software. Imagine what the spieltier could do, unleashed on this stuff. All the data fresh, lying in the mouths of the hyperpipes, just waiting to be picked up.

Hell, they've had fourteen years to play with this software, back on Earth. By now the place is probably a madhouse. Unless, of course, ICOPOSI, in its infinite wisdom, has seen fit to suppress this technology. Given what I'm seeing here, that's a high probability.

Well. Nine years from now, after the signals have had time to make their round trip, I'll probably find out. David Gilman growing up. Becoming a high-class programmer, though nothing like the quality of Izzy, much less Metz. Going to work on the Human Matrix project.

Well. Jesus Fucking Christ. I remember when ICOPOSI suppressed that one, not wanting anyone to be able to look too far into the future, because of the negative effect it would have on free market competition practices. Just trying to keep some silly ass from fucking up the stock exchanges.

The images suddenly froze in place, bright bead message from his own file controller blinking in the air. POSSIBLE CORRELATION.

A glass window hanging in front of him, adult version of David Gilman looking out at him, scruffy, barely out of adolescence, eyes weak and confused, full of . . . some remote loss or another. Never mind, it'll be in the files when you're done. What correlation?

This adult David Gilman, looking a lot like the lost little boy, looked nothing at all like Mies Cochrane. Not surprising. The other trauma spies face is frequent changes of body conformation. And I know how hard *that* is to live with. . . .

David Gilman, silent in his window. Seeming to look

through. Look right into my eyes. The image said, "Indigo? I don't understand, Seesy. How can we sterilize the entire human race without someone finding out?"

What?

Doc locked his hands behind his head, staring at the motionless face of the boy/man in the window. All right. Continue. Let's see what we can find out.

Indigo. Nothing in my personal memory. Have to scan my open files later and see if we knew anything at all about something called Indigo. Deep blue. Not quite black. Interesting name.

Well. ICOPOSI's not perfect, not all-seeing. Far from all-powerful. Be interesting to see if we even knew the name. . . .

Now Kai floated in Ginny's room, floated in midair, more or less stabilized, drifting a little bit to one side, watching her hang in the netting of her sleeping bag. She looks lovely like that, he thought. Dark brown woman with plain white underwear setting off her skin, white underpants just suggesting the outline of her vulva. White bra holding her breasts in place, making her look like an image of a woman, rather than the reality.

He said, "I don't know what made him do it, Gin. I'm glad he didn't hurt you."

Ginny staring at him, that little furrow between her eyebrows. She's angry with me. And who would blame her? Have I betrayed her? Did I ever give her my word that I wouldn't . . . Silly. Looking for excuses. Just say you're sorry. Start the work of repairing our relationship. We're going to be together for a long damned time. . . .

He said, "You know, Ginny, I didn't mean for it to come out this way. It's just that I . . . well. You know about my needs."

The visible flash of anger in her eye. Christ. I . . .

She laughed suddenly. Laughed and said, "I always did relate to you as woman to man, Kai. Not hard to figure out. You look like a girl. Sometimes you even act like a girl. But you're not a girl."

He reached behind him, shoved against the wall, floated over to her, hand catching in the sleep netting. "Oh, Ginny, I'm so *sorry* I—"

She said, "When the time comes to talk, you talk like a man."

Anger building up in him now, a desire to let his own eyes flash and retort, Whoever said I *wasn't* a man? But he reached out instead and touched her on the arm, lips somehow locked shut, chains of words erased from his mind. Somewhere in here, somewhere the words still exist, but something else has . . . taken control.

Voice soft, she said, "I can see it in your eyes, Kai. You think we're going to fuck now, and everything will be all right between us again."

Isn't that the way it works? No. That isn't the way it works. You know that. You know what's going to have to happen now, don't you Kai? Does it make you feel bad? Well, maybe a little. Why is that? You know damned well Mies is still back in your room, sleeping like a sweet baby, waiting for you to come and kiss him awake. . . .

He shook his head slowly and said, "Maybe not. Maybe I . . . understand just a little bit. I really am sorry all this happened." Well. Maybe just a little bit. Can you understand that, Ginny?

Nothing much in her eyes.

Okay. She's read what she thinks is the truth, and that's that.

He said, "We're all here, Gin. No one's going away. We'll get things straightened out by and by."

That cold stare, not softening . . . Finally, she said, "I've already spoken to Doc. We'll see."

Yes, we will. After a while, Kai turned and left the room, went back to his own.

No use sitting here, fuming all by myself. The little bastard. The fucking little bastard. And, Ginny thought, I can't even really blame him. I knew. I *knew* something like this would have to happen one day. Knew it every time we settled into bed, every time I'd run my fingers over a little girl's crotch, coaxing out the secret man within. Old, old damn echoes . . .

So, on up to the control room, where no one ever went except her and Kai. Is Kai up here now? No. Just an empty room, windows out into the black sky, yellow Pholos rolling below, uninhabited just now; Pholos waiting for their investigations to resume.

God. Our pathetic brawls and crawly little fuckings seem so . . . absurd in the face of . . . Eyes on the empty world below. In the face of *this*. Why can't we just do our jobs and be . . . all right with each other? The job matters, Pholos matters, the secrets of the Frogmen matter, not the silly things we do with our damned plumbing!

Still, wistful, wishing that he'd come on up here ahead of her to be alone with his male thoughts, whatever the hell they were, if anything. We could be rolling in the air right now, making love, forgiving each other . . .

Each other.

Raw anger.

What would *he* have to forgive?

I haven't done anything wrong.

After a while, she turned away from the planet, unsettled, angry, and went back through the ship. People mostly asleep. Doc in the biolab, up to something, still playing with Mies's spilled semen, no doubt. You have to wonder why, but he's not saying, not ready to say anything yet.

Izzy and Metz in the wardroom, eating a meal on the little table by the big picture window, heads near each other, whispering as they watch Pholos's landscape fly by underneath. Anxious to get back down? Stab of envy. Twin men. Perfect for each other. Perfect together.

Linda and Rosie sitting together in the lounge, talking, falling silent, looking up, expressions odd and guarded, when she came to float in the door. No Spence. Well, the door to his room is shut and . . .

Hell, that'd be the perfect next act to this farce: Rosie and

Linda start a nice little lesbian relationship, having lost Mies to Kai, leaving Spence out in the cold. Who would he . . .

Sudden iciness inside her. Will asshole Spence be the next rapist to loom outside my chamber door? She imagined herself killing him. Spence's dead, bloated face gaping with astonishment as she towed his carcass to the airlock and spaced him.

Ha. Spacing spent Spence, Spence spewing spuke as he sploated off in space . . .

She grimaced and went on, down through the tunnel to the centrifuge deck. Haven't been here lately. We're not doing the exercises we should, relying on the biots to keep us in gravitational trim. Row of eleven coffins, ten of them empty. One . . .

Bald man with a fringe of red hair, a pointy red beard, sitting on the floor by that one occupied coffin. Man looking up from his reading spool, looking at her through whatever imagery the eyebubble was displaying for him.

"Uh. Hello, Captain."

Captain? This is something we should have fixed long ago. She walked up the curve of the floor and stood looking down at him. "Hi, Andy. Visiting with Sheba?"

A sigh. A nod. "Sort of."

"You want me to open her up, let you take a look?" She was gruesome, but . . .

A quick headshake. "No. I've got . . . memories are better."

But, looking at her dead, you'll know it's real. And if you know it's real, you might come back to us all the sooner. She said, "How are you feeling? You doing okay?"

A somber look, then a shrug. "Sure. I mean . . . Hell, Ginny, I know what's going on with me. Sorry I have to be like this. I'm not letting my work slip, am I?" A pleading look in his eyes now.

You are, poor Andy, but . . . She said, "No. You're doing fine. But I want to know how you feel." How you feel. Man on the spot before a woman's penetrating eyes? That's the way it always looks but . . . well, I'm not a man. I don't know what's really going on in their heads. Only what they tell me, which, near as I can tell, is always a lie.

He said, "Just a little lonely, Gin. You know. I really loved her. Seems like we were together forever, and now . . ." A glance at the coffin.

Shit. Now he's said it and I feel like a jerk. Softly: "I'm sorry, Andy. I didn't mean to . . ."

He glanced up at her, briefly at her eyes, and tried a little smile, maybe made up for her benefit, maybe not. "Don't be, Gin. It's all right." Looking away again, seeming distracted. By Sheba's lost memory? By his memories of lost Sheba?

Into the silence, Ginny's inner voice, dry, ironic, bitter: He's not looking at your face, you know. And he's not looking at some memory of his dead wife. Look where his eyes are aimed. That's right, Virginia Vonzell Qing-an. The little bastard's got his eyes pasted on your crotch. He's sitting there, looking at the outline of your hips under the cloth, the vague outlines suggesting the shape of your vulva, and he's imagining . . .

The idea surfaced out of nowhere, planted its hooks in her conscious mind, made her smile angrily. That's right. No man ever born . . . She reached up and started unzipping her coveralls, Andy looking up at the sound, astonishment widening his eyes.

"Captain?"

Captain. Hah. Off with the shoes and coverall. Off with the bra and little white scrap of panties, the whole mess kicked into a scrambled pile of discarded cloth while Andy watched her strip, wordless, gaping, somehow paralyzed. When she was naked, she stepped close to him, crouching slightly, putting her knees on his shoulders, smiling down at him, her vulva maybe ten centimeters from the tip of his nose.

"Come on, Andy."

Andy looking right at her crotch now, face very pale, seeming to hold his breath and . . . A glance up at her face, a confused smile, a shaky laugh. He said, "I guess . . . Well. I guess . . ."

She grinned, felt her face stretch around a smile that was half pleasure and half rage. "I guess so, huh?" Here you go, Andy Mezov. Time to get better. No, that's not it. Here you

go, Maeru kai Ortega, you little shit. Here's a nice kick in the
balls, wherever the hell you're hiding them.

No, that's not it.

Here you go, Virginia Vonzell Qing-an. Here you go.

Andy's mouth, breath moist and warm, on her vulva, tongue
already reaching out to her through a thin curtain of crisp,
curly hair.

Is that it?

Maybe so.

Who knows?

Not me, that's for sure. . . .

The two of them were floating loose in her room, Doc going
one way, very slowly, movement just barely perceptible, Ginny
going the other, equally slowly, as if they were alone in space,
two bodies in orbit around one another. Inane thoughts intruded,
Ginny thinking, And if we were alone in the universe, that's
just what would happen. . . .

Doc's bland hazel eyes bore into her. "Do you understand
what I just told you, Captain?" Demanding eyes. Officious
words. Captain. Calling me *captain*.

"I . . ." Inane thoughts trying to pull her away, so no understanding could form. Something in me doesn't *want* to understand. "How could you know these things about Mies, Doc? I
mean, this business about some kind of revolutionary terrorist
group, this bullshit about something called *Indigo,* working to
undermine human fertility and bring down civilization? It's
like . . . something out of a holonet drama." A holonet drama
written by a Daiseijin sympathizer: Look! All of you! If we
don't go to the stars, *this* is what we face . . .

A frown forming on his empty face, eyes looking away from
her momentarily. As if trying to decide about . . . something.
What? Finally, he said, "I've been stealing time on the computational tables to . . . investigate things. People. Last night I . . .
used the SAE."

Pale inner pang, the possibility of what that might mean and . . .
"Stealing SAE time? *Stealing* it, Doc?" Another distinct possi-

bility: something is terribly wrong here. Might some of that have to do with a . . . derangement? Doc? Are you all right? She stared at him for a long moment, trying to hold onto his eyes: "How could you steal time on the SAE? The core has sieves that would . . . make it report any anomalies. Besides which . . ." Yes, the SAE consumes enormous power, guzzles down our computer time so much that . . . "Doc, I'd *know* if the ship were drifting on gyrostabilization alone, if the RCS were shut down."

Eyes serious, somehow as empty as Mies's. "Would you?"

"Well . . ."

He smiled, and said, "Ginny, I've got access to the system master code key."

A sudden shallowing of breath. "You . . . mean the code key Kai and I share? For emergencies."

A little headshake, hardly disturbing the vector of his float across the room. "No, Captain. I've got my own code key."

"What are you talking about?"

"There's a second master code key into the system. Mine."

Well. So much for being captain of the Daiseijin starship *Mother Night*. Anger starting up, deep inside. Betrayal. She said, "So the central committee decided to invoke its own rules after all. And great leader Erasmus Hiraoka's life-long buddy, Founding Father Ernesto Matel . . . By *God* . . ." Voice rising, roughening with rage.

A small grin, a secretive grin. "Committee had nothing to do with it. Nor silly old Ras."

Well. "You're telling me this for a reason."

A nod. "As far as the central planning committee of the Daiseijin and Erasmus Hiraoka knows, you are master of the ship; you and Kai have two halves of the only system master code key ever forged and that's that. They don't know I've got one, specially created for me, a key that can override everything."

"But . . ." Goddamn it. Bitter anger still rising. "But *why* . . ."

"Ginny, I'm an agent of ICOPOSI."

Short, sharp shock, like ice in her veins. Fuck. "Doc? Um."

Look into those eyes. There's not a person in the world who can't go mad, be in desperate need of biochemical adjustment, can't have his or her head fill with all sorts of crazy power fantasies and . . . "Doc, weren't you one of the founding members of the Daiseijin? Didn't you go to *school* with Doctor Hiraoka?"

He smiled, as if remembering. "Ras and I used to go out together to pillow-geisha houses. We used to watch each other screw fancy ladies and cheap whores and make silly jokes while we watched. It was a fun time."

Distracted now. Maybe forgetting . . .

He said, "Ras was a genius. He was always a genius. Always first in school, first in line for scholarships. Me, I was just an ordinary joe." A serious look, a convincing look, eyes on her eyes again. "Ginny, I was recruited right before my école graduation. I went to college on a police scholarship."

Nothing. Nothing to say.

He said, "When they put me aboard, by the act of hiring me as a spy, ICOPOSI was making a decision not to suppress the Daiseijin. There are . . . elements in the bureaucracy that support interstellar colonization, after all. They're not as big as the status quo control elements, but they're there. Big enough to prevent the Daiseijin's suppression. Big enough to push through a destructive devices license for the Daiseijin." A grin at the apparent look in her eye. "The particle beam catapult, Ginny. How did you think we got a license for a generator big enough to vaporize a fair-sized asteroid? Excellent bribery skills?"

Well. "Why are you here?" Why aren't you back on Earth, being high and mighty?

Voice quiet: "I'm here because I wanted to be here. And because I had the power to stick myself at the head of the line."

Another betrayal. So much for merit. "Does Doctor Hiraoka know?"

A shrug. "Probably. He's not stupid."

Which changes everything? No. That's the way things always were. It just changes my . . . view of things. "So . . . what . . ."

Too many questions.

"Mies?" He sighed, shook his head. "The work's important, Ginny. Too important to let go. And Mies is what we have. I don't know exactly what's going on, not yet, and I've got to find out. I thought it was time I brought you in on things."

Bitter twist, deep inside. "Well. Thanks."

Floating opposite her, hanging in the air like a parade balloon, Doc beamed at her, and smiled.

NINE

Flat land below them now, low, rolling desert country reaching out to Pholos's blue-sky horizon, dark sky overhead, and Kai, hands on the controls, could feel *MN01*'s engines rumbling away, somewhere down below. Over there, on the flat white ground, was, once again, a shadow of the lander, now a double shadow: flat, black shadow where Alpha Centauri B's light was blocked, dim, faint blue-gray shadow from the remote spark of A. Underneath each shadow, you could see the shimmering outlines of disturbed air, twin columns converging as they neared the ground.

Behind him, Izzy and Metz whispered to each other, commenting about the surface, the landscape. Also back there, Andy Mezov, surprisingly brightened, surprisingly restored to life. Almost as if . . . as if Sheba lives again, somewhere, somehow. He'd been humming to himself as he'd helped load equipment and supplies aboard the lander.

In the other rear seat, Rosamunde Merah. Mies's abandoned Rosie. Looking at them both, dark-eyed, cold. Taking her seat beside Andy without a word. Beside him, in the flight engineer's seat, watching his imaginary instruments diligently, Mies seemed stiff. Taut with some inner tension.

Kai banked the ship, letting it drift across the white ground of the salt flat, watching clouds of dry white dust rise, gypsumlike, and whirl around, drifting lower, drifting toward the remains of the old city. I wonder whose idea this was, this crew rotation? Doc? Maybe he thinks Spence and Linda need some private time together?

Or Ginny, getting even with Mies? Not her style. Not really. But here we are. And that's a surprise, too. Did Ginny tell no one? Maybe. Maybe not. Something in Doc's eyes, as well. Something's going on that I don't know about. Maybe I can guess, though. What we're doing here is important. More important than this . . . bullshit. Typical human bullshit. You'd think we'd outgrow it. But no one ever does.

He stopped the drift when they were near enough to the ruins, if you could dignify the pathetic blotches by calling them ruins, close enough they wouldn't have to unship the lander, but not so close they'd blow salt all over the place. Hovering, looking around. "I guess this is good enough."

A glance at Mies, who nodded impassively, then he brought the ship down, deck falling out from under them like the floor of an elevator, salt whipping around outside, splashing away from the cold-gas exhaust of the electric turbines. The ship grounded, surface crunching under them, rocked back and forth, settled, and was still.

"Well." A bright look around. "Here we are, gang!"

Andy stood, rubbing his hands together. "Let's get out there and take a look!" Turning away, he headed for the spacesuit locker.

And Kai thought, What an odd look he just gave me. Hmh. He turned back to the control panel and started safing his systems.

Mies stepped down onto the hardpan surface, tiny crunch of salt crystals underfoot. Things getting too complicated. His relationships with these people starting to mirror the disorder inside his head. No longer his imagination. Everyone genuinely was staring at him now. Rosie and Kai were the two big offenders. Rosie looking for an explanation for the great wrong that had been done to her?

Jesus. Listen to yourself.

Me? I'm not making all these thoughts!

Jeering: *Then who is?*

Well . . . right. Sometimes I forget.

Kind of melodramatic, that Rosie bit about "the great wrong that had been done to her."

And Kai, in waiting mode, looking at him also, more curious than anything, as if expecting . . . what? He knows. He knows.

Well, you told *him.*

Not that. I mean . . .

Asshole. You know what you did. Now put it away and let's get to work.

He looked around, analyzing. Wisps of halo up there, like bright nebulae around the suns. Must be some dust in suspension. Blue band a little thicker, too. The atmospheric pressure here would have been higher then, too.

And the world, flat and pale as a white pine tabletop. Here, near the center of the Pholotian sea bottom, the playa went on and on, ad infinitum, to the featureless horizon. Maybe once upon a time, this had been the location of a great salt marsh, hundreds of times larger than anything on Earth, the dying gasp of Pholos's hydrosphere. Not enough topography to make much of a sea here; from here on in the water just got shallower and saltier. Salts precipitating out once the concentration got too high, just like in the cut-off Pleistocene Mediterranean, brine killing even the hardiest aquatic life. Here, the water never came back.

Over there, Kai and Andy were already setting up the scanner head, hovering over some flattened shapes of colored sand protruding from the ground, showing only a few centimeters of relief. Kai noticed him looking and waved, then he was back at work, concentrating, lithe, thin muscularity showing even through the loose-fitting suit.

What does he think of me? How can he not guess?

Just because your thoughts seem like the whole world doesn't mean they are visible to anyone else.

Rosie came to stand next to him, also scanning the distant

horizon, hand atavistically raised to shade her eyes from the bright suns. No hard feelings?

She said, "If the organics in the salt samples from the trench are any indication, life must have had a hard time adapting here. With desalinization, the Frogmen could probably supply themselves with enough freshwater to support a small population, I suppose."

Doing her job? Good. I'll do mine. "You're forgetting the ice from the outer system. Think of Atalanta—"

Kai: "Icebergs from space, just like in the old stories. Not so far-fetched, though we never had to do it."

On the other hand, the ice out there was full of impurities too, some of them deadly. It seems unlikely that'd be the answer.

Rosie turned to face him, standing so that he was on one side of her, the others beyond her back, her face hidden from everyone but . . . *me. From everyone but me.* Cold, stark terror crawling somewhere below his belly.

Big David Gilman awoke suddenly, and whispered, Somehow, we *always* get caught . . . should've stayed home, found a hiding place in the crowds. Mies could see her nod, off center, motioning to one of her VR controls. Which one? Oh, God. Private link.

Anger in her eyes. Bitter. Biting. She said, "I wondered. I wondered what was taking you away. Now I know." A glance, letting him know she meant Kai, bending to his labor. "At least that explains your . . . impotence."

Look at her: flat smile, eyes calm. She's satisfied with that as an excuse. Grabbing at straws, that one seems to have been strong enough for her to recover her pride.

Voice thick, she said, "So what is it, Mies. You just like doing an *andy?* That get you worked up? Or do you wish you could go home and get an operation of your own?"

Good. No reason to disabuse her of the idea, though it rankled somewhere inside him. I want, thought Mies, for people to . . . like me.

You want them to admire you, respect you, be mystified by your . . . cachet. But like *you? Bullshit.* Mies felt his anger boil up and subside. To Rosie, he said, "I'm sorry that it had to work out the way it did."

She turned away, began to pull out her sampling apparatus. End of that problem? But there are so many more where that came from. Maybe you've got a friend here, more than a friend. Maybe he can . . . help.

Showtime now. Yes, that's right, blather on about this and that; mask your confusion with big, dead words. Walk around, gesturing like you know what you're doing, point at this, point at that.

Hardly any reason for going on, is there?

Why do you make me do it, anyway?

What difference does it make to you? What are you after?

And why, for heaven's sake, don't you fucking give up and stop the playacting?

Look at their faces. Peek out, see how they're reacting to you. Hey, even Rosie acts like you're real. Ask a question; Okay, good response. Good boy, Andy, that was correct. Am I here, talking to you? Answer now, I want the truth.

You think there's somewhere you can escape to?

Who said that?

There's nothing for it but to keep on. There's no alternative. Keep us alive, keep us . . . alive.

Oh, God help me. The dream. The memory . . .

Loaded down with thoughts of the short and perilous nature of existence, David slowly walked across Blackfriars Bridge pedestrian walkway. The late-seeming May sunset was in progress over the old city behind him, clean air sweeping the last remaining rain clouds away, leaving a sky the color of ripening lemon. Below him, the dark river surged.

Loneliness. Hopelessness. The words of depression. Maybe I should go down to the psych ward, check myself in. They can fix anything, these days, with their powerful hypnopaedia machines. Use a combination of drugs and VR interface to feed in the elements of a new personality, drugs shredding the old, bad bits, hypnotic sleep-learning device supplanting the old with the new.

They say it wears off. . . .

But, to be whole, be new, be fresh, *happy* . . . to walk the world with innocence renewed. Wouldn't that be worth it, if only for just a little while?

A chill breeze hit him like a pillow, ruffling his hair, sinking in along the open places in his clothing. Smell of pretzels. Open bridge is a bad place to be. He began to walk again. It was getting dark, the four smokestacks of the Bankside Industrial Museum reflecting the last traces of the yellow west.

Trudging. He liked the concept. Not walking. Trudging through Southwark.

The address his sister had given him was a large, brick townhouse on the corner of a small intersection. He stood before the tall white door examining the ornate inlaid design on the knocker, pausing, afraid to touch the interface. He seemed to apprehend the vastness of the universe for just a second, knowing that, despite its size and seeming importance, it was really nothing, too.

He touched the icon with a fingertip.

Seesy opened the door a little, stuck her head out. "Davy. Hi. Come on in."

She led him to a large, well-furnished living room, inset lighting here and there, night pushing in through a large, bay window nook.

"Where's the party?"

"That's next week. Oh, don't look confused, Davy. This is the right date. Have you had any supper yet? I've got some chipotle and croissants. Would you like a hotcola?"

Seesy sat him down on the luxurious, deep sofa and disappeared into the small kitchen, returning in a moment with a tray, which she put on the low table in front of him. Quickly she poured out two thermals of the hot brown liquid, rich-smelling steam blossoming, inverting on itself. He took a croissant and began to pull it apart, stuffing a piece in his mouth.

"Davy, I won't beat around the bush. When we met the other

day I could see that you haven't been able to pull yourself out of the funk you were in when you were a teenager. I doubt that the inheritance will make much of a difference. You always had enough money in the old days."

He nodded, slightly confused. "I . . . suppose I am in a bit of a state. Dah and Mummy dying didn't help."

Hard look. "Don't give me that crap. You've always been a fuckup, I've known that since we were toddlers."

Fuckup. Well, I guess that's as good a way to describe it as any.

"I've got a proposition for you." Sitting on the corner of the table, turned toward him, close enough that he could reach out and caress a knee. He raised his eyes to hers, noticed the same blank, hard look that she had when she tapped the bubble, eyes slightly liquid, highlights glistening. "A way you may be able to avoid being a fuckup for the rest of your life."

He felt a little scald of anger. Fuckup? How dare you say something like that to . . . then a larger scald of defeat. Fuckup? Yes, that's the word I try to avoid using. Sure, my part in the programming lab at Human Matrix was big, but . . . meaningless. I did it because it was . . . default behavior. Easy.

Nonetheless, his words came out freighted with sarcasm. "So. What's this *proposition*? You got some new job lead for me? Now that Human Matrix is shutting down . . ."

And goddamn them for that. We were *onto* something. I just don't understand why they suddenly closed up shop and put us all in the unemployment lines.

Seesy's eyes on him, dark with . . . something? Anger? No. More like pity. God, I hate it when people pity me.

She said, "Not exactly."

"Then exactly what?"

She said, "Davy, you remember when Kermit Ballinger joined Parenteral Dream?"

"Sure." Kermit, as much a fuckup as anyone could want to be, had finally flipped out and joined some crazy religion that believed your soul inhabited the parenchyma binding your intestines in place. He snickered. "That was the funniest thing I ever heard of."

She smiled. "I thought so too. But you remember what happened?"

He shrugged. "He went off somewhere to be indoctrinated. Injected with their illegal biots. Came back and opened up a storefront church to make more converts. I stopped paying attention around then."

"Davy, why do you suppose Kermit was so happy, after that?"

"Um. Because he imagined he'd found some overarching purpose, some meaning for his life." I always envy people like that. People who can believe a lie until it makes them happy. I wish . . .

Seesy said, "Davy, I'd like to tell you about something called *Indigo*."

Look at the shine in her eyes. Oh, Christ, that's *all* I need, for my sister to have flipped out and joined some damned cult religion. "Mmh." Noncommittal. Maybe it will be all right. "Deep blue."

She smiled again. "Almost black."

A silence between them then, and Davy watched her make some kind of decision. Probably dreaming about our new life together, believe with all our hearts that God resides in the lining of our descending colon or something . . .

Strange, hungry look on her face. "I've found the Answer, Davy."

You could hear the capitalization in her voice. Dear God. Well, no sense letting this go on. Profound disappointment. And bitterness, too. Now I'll be all alone in the world. All alone. He said, "I'm sorry, Seesy. I need for my answers to be real. Not some . . . some . . ." He gestured uselessly.

And she laughed. Laughed and rolled her eyes back. Reached out and touched him on the forearm while she laughed. He thought, Her touch still has the power to thrill me. I wish . . .

She said, "Davy, I'm going to tell you just a little bit about Indigo. You tell me, then, whether you want to hear more. I'm taking a chance. But I *know,* when you hear what I've got to say . . .''

He sighed. She's my sister. For God's sake . . . he said, ''All right. I'm listening.''

And she said, ''Davy, in less than one hundred years, the absolute carrying capacity of the solar system will have been reached.''

He blinked. All right. Surprised? Lots of people know. Hell . . . ''I didn't know you followed the early Human Matrix research reports.'' Before whoever it was stepped in and imposed secrecy. Industrial espionage, they said. A great deal of value here. Got to protect our proprietary interests.

She said, ''Oh, people have known. For a while. A lot longer than you businessman prophets.''

Sure. Ever since Thomas Malthus. But one technological revolution after another kept pushing back the end, shoving it over time's horizon until we came to *expect* . . .

She said, ''In less than one hundred years the absolute limits of technological evolution will be reached. In less than one hundred years, we will reach the limit of derivable scientific knowledge.''

He nodded. We figured that out. At the cusp, beyond which no mere program can look, new scientific research requires the deployment of energies and data processing algorithms larger than the total output content of the solar system.

Looking into his eyes, she said, ''In less than one hundred years, humanity experiences the classic closed-system extinction event.'' She moved her hand, with index finger extended, up a logarithmic curve, then dropped it vertically.

Bacteria in a jar full of nutrients. Nothing but nutrients. No predators. No nothing. Just bacteria and nutrients. The population of immortal bacteria grows until all the resources are consumed. Then, in a single generation, the population crashes.

Crashes to zero.

He whispered, ''Just before they shut us down, we discovered that all possible futures lead right through that cusp. There seemed to be nothing on the other side. In most scenarios, not only do humans go extinct, so does everything else. In a few very improbable scenarios, some life survives on Earth, but then the geochemical cycle ends and that's that.''

Seesy said, ''All possible futures but two.''

He nodded again. ''Sort of. We concluded, however, that humanity could not deploy the resources necessary for interstellar colonization. Not in time to bleed down the population to less than one percent of its present value, at any rate.''

She said, ''An immoral solution, even if it could be made to work. All we'd do is make more closed systems, each of which would swell and die. The very idea . . .''

Davy thought, We called it the Human Plague Scenario. Immoral. Right.

Seesy said, ''And the other solution?''

Right. That one. He shrugged. ''One of the research teams calculated that if we murdered not less than ninety-five percent of the current population, *without* wrecking any planets or moons in the process, the way you would, say, by using high-energy solar masers, the remnant would gain a thousand years or so in which to come up with a more permanent solution.'' He smiled wryly. ''We couldn't think of a quick enough method. In all our scenarios, people caught on and put a stop to the slaughter before enough were killed.''

She nodded, eyes dark and somber. ''Did you work through the vectored sterilization scenario?''

''Of course. The notion of a stable population of sterile immortals . . . Hell, in most scenarios, we *cause* the crash. And, of course, people would never *agree* to . . .''

Because, you see, people, genetic-mandate driven, are selfish.

If it happens, after I'm dead . . . they think.

We just keep *forgetting* we're all going to live forever. It's too new, and it happened too subtly, too unexpectedly, too slowly. People just kept living longer and longer. Half the people now alive, fully expected to die long ere since . . .

Seesy said, ''*If* people know.''

''Um.'' There is that.

Seesy said, "Davy, you have to decide now if you want to hear about Indigo. If I tell you, then you have to have a hypnopaedic implant."

Startled. Implant? "You mean, go down to the hospital and . . ." And what?

She shook her head. "Not at the hospital. Not a legal psych."

You heard about these things. Hypnopaedic implants could make you whoever you wanted to be. Quite illegal, of course. A restricted-access technology.

He said, "So. You seem to have gotten yourself in pretty deep, Seesy. What if I listen to your story, then refuse?"

She said, "Then, some time in the next few hours, you'll have an accident."

As simple as that. Davy felt his heart pound hard suddenly. Accident. Like Mummy and Dah? No. They could not possibly have . . . He thought about walking across the bridge. About the color of the sky. About the notion of going on down to the psych ward and checking himself in. Having himself . . . fixed. That's the word I want. *Fixed*. Fixed, so I'm not a fuckup anymore.

He said, "All right."

And then she told him about Indigo. And told him about the autoviroid plague.

Standing here, out under the two bright suns, Kai thought, You can hardly believe it was ever real, that they ever lived at all. Stretching away from the humped sand ridges and etched-in colorshapes of the "ruins," the white salt desert seemed to stretch away to infinity, becoming almost like glass, or water, as it got near the horizon, landscape tipping imperceptibly down, so grazing-incidence light from the sky reflected up into his eyes, turning the ground silver-blue.

So this dark spot over here was a palace. These brown lines were the city walls. Over there? We don't know. A place where thousands of rocket ships lifted off, touched down, the old city spaceport from long, long ago?

Superficial readings on the soil and artifacts tell us this place was, when it existed, very much younger than the other artifacts we looked at. The city by the sea. The ruins on the moon, on Bellerophon and Pegasus, out on cold Atalanta. Hundreds of millions of years . . .

Imagine a world like that. Imagine a civilization that's existed for geological ages. Imagine a world and a people who've made no progress in all that time. Something wrong with the Frogmen? Something wrong with them as beings, as a culture, that's not wrong with us? *We* make progress, after all. But then, they did, too, once upon a time.

Is this what awaits humanity, when progress ends, when we . . . give it all up?

Disturbing thought. But they never made it to the stars, so far as we can tell. And here we are. Over by the scanner head, Izzy looked up, and said, "All set, Kai."

"Ginny?"

Her voice, soft in his ears: "We're ready, Kai. Proceed when you want to."

Something in her voice. Something communicating itself to me. He glanced over at Andy, standing quietly with Rosie, the two of them putting away sample kits, recording sample sites on the eyebubble interface. Andy suddenly stopping, looking up at him, looking away again.

Hell with it.

"Let's go." Familiar tables and controls scrolling out of the air. Maybe this will be the one on which we run a first-pass test of the new link-locks. Maybe not. In any case, I'll have to do more work, get Metz to put in more programming time before we'll be ready to run the spieltier again.

The white salt flat turned to glassy water and the sky seemed to lighten and turn green. Izzy said, "Well, that's interesting. I wonder what happened."

Looking at his graphs, Kai said, "Some change in atmospheric composition. Surface pressure's way down from where it was during the Froggy Space Age, about halfway down to its present value." And the nearby city? Reconstructing itself, familiar Frogman architecture rising out of the level sand.

Mies said, "Similar, but not quite the same. More like what they had in their earlier civilization, the chalcolithic museum city . . ."

City walls. Defensive towers. What were they afraid of?

Andy said, "Anybody see any signs of a spaceport?"

There was nothing visible outside the city wall, except for a low quay of some sort, sticking out into the brackish water of the flat, shallow sea. Not far from the main gate. So much for that.

Mies said, "Let's bring it closer."

The city seemed to slide toward them across the flat landscape. Now, they could see Frogmen moving about on the wharf, unloading big, heavy-looking bags from a small ship. Small, wooden ship, Kai thought. At least, something that looks like wood. Dried reeds, maybe? A quick look around showed no reeds growing anywhere nearby. That's okay, without advanced filtering, if they left no trace for the scanner to pick up, the SAE wouldn't show them. Too much interpolation.

Mies said, "Very odd. A sailing ship. And yet many signs of advanced technology . . ."

Each of the Frogmen, laboring under a heavy load, wore some kind of face mask, black leather over the lower face, goggles over the eyes, hoses reaching down to a square, waist-mounted apparatus.

Rosie, standing closer to Andy now, said, "Not very advanced. That looks like an archaic rebreather unit. Lithium hydroxide gas scrubbers, maybe a pressure regulator. We've had things like that for centuries."

When Kai glanced at Mies, he could see the man staring at the woman, face expressionless, seen through the occluding plastic of his helmet. He said, "And I guess these folks have had them for about four hundred million years."

Izzy said, "Take a look up at that tower, will you? The window."

Kai looked and could see a flat glass window, Frogmen visible within, moving around, indistinct. "I guess they've got the buildings pressure-sealed, huh? I wonder why they didn't just go ahead and put up a dome?''

"That's not what I'm talking about. Look at the reflection.''

Something reflected in the window, some movement out on the desert beside the seashore. Kai turned and looked. Nothing. Empty desert and flat black sea stretching out to the horizon under a sallow green sky. "Let's tighten the focus a bit . . .''

Metz muttered to himself, fooling with something on the scanner head, and the window popped out of its socket, expanded, came to float in the air before them. They could still see through the window into the room beyond, see the Frogmen gathering at the glass, see them gesticulating, pointing . . .

As if reacting to . . . us.

But we're not really here.

Andy said, "What do you make of it?''

Things, big black things, far out on the white desert beside the black sea, things coming closer, raising a cloud of white salt dust.

Voice hushed, Mies said, "It's the Rhinotaurs.''

A lot of them. Hundreds, maybe thousands. Not enough to call a horde, but . . .

Kai said, "Well. I guess they must have gotten out of the zoo at last.'' Deep inside the room, you could see odd-looking furniture behind the staring Frogmen. Old equipment, some of it looking like electronics, all of it looking, somehow, eroded. Corroded. Just . . . old.

Rosie said, "That's a very nice picture of one of your Leospiders mounted on the back wall.''

Black, with featureless silver eyes, long silver fangs, no backdrop in the painting, Leospider watching the Frogmen out of cold white mist, like the mist of a mountain storm.

Ginny's voice said, "That's all we can get, Kai. You want to try anything else?''

All sorts of things, but . . . "No. Let's just move on to the next site.''

Aboard *Mother Night,* down on the science deck, Ginny sat beside the light table, where the current surface worksite was displayed, the flattened out ruins of the old city rather diagrammatic, the only real-looking object the shiny silver-gray model of *MN01*. That and the tiny figures of spacesuited men and women.

Across from her, Doc gestured at two of them: Andy and Rosie. "You set that up?"

Staring at them, Ginny felt an uncomfortable squirming inside. What was I planning for him? Did I think I was going to put Andy permanently in my bed, have him take Kai's place? They're not at all the same. . . . She shrugged, frowning. "No. I . . . I guess I just thought they both needed to get out and about."

Doc's eyes on her, a sort of smile on his lips. I suppose, she thought, he knows everything. With access to the SAE, as well as access to a system master key for the ship's eyebubble core, he probably knows more about me than I do. She said, "And speaking of out and about, where're Linda and Spence?"

The smile broadened. "Not to make light of their interest in these momentous exercises, but I think they retired to Spence's quarters for a quick hump or two."

Hmh. "Back together already?"

Doc grinned. "Why not? Kai pretty much made it clear he's taken Mies away from her. Even if she really wanted him, which I doubt."

Sitting here, then. Staring at him. Is the lying bastard laughing at me, behind that bland old face, those transparent eyes? Just now, Doc looked like some kind of mannequin, stitched together out of fine, used suede, face soft and supple and meaningless.

What the hell am I going to do?

Am I going to do anything?

A terrorist. A government spy. Lovers quarrels. My boyfriend off being someone else's girlfriend. How much more ridiculous is this going to get?

Doc said, "I'm going to power down the RCS now and run up the SAE, using my own filter sequence. I'll be careful not to interfere with the new sieves Kai, Izzy, and Metz are building. And I'll let you know shortly what the score is."

The score. The real truth about Mies. Who, what, when, where. I was glad as hell to find out *I'm* not sterile. Poor Rosie. She said, "Is Kai in any danger?"

"Well. I don't know. There's no sign Mies is a killer, if that's what you mean."

"I meant . . ."

Doc shrugged. "I don't think sexual contact with Mies can make him sterile, if that's what you mean. He's not really a woman, after all. I'll know more after tonight."

"When?"

"I'll have the answers we'll need by morning."

Answers. Morning.

And then what will we do?

Do I have to decide, because I'm captain? Or does Doc outrank me? She watched him turn and launch himself across the room, toward the biolab module hatch, closing the door behind him. Well. Time will tell. It always does.

She waved off the light table display, waved it back on with a real-time orbital view of Pholos, and sat there, watching the world spin, yellow with dust, gray with mountains, white with flat salt plains. Somewhere down there . . .

I wonder. I wonder if I'd like to watch them do it. I wonder if that'd make him like me again. I wonder if I could get him back. Why the hell do I feel like I've done something wrong, something to drive him away into the arms of another?

Feeling the tears start to well up, she felt angry and more than a little stupid. It's been a long time, she thought, since I felt quite *this* stupid.

Walking from her dorm hut to the community shower, dressed in a white terrycloth robe, thick red towel draped over one arm, Ginny stopped and looked upward, up through Peridot's featureless, almost invisibly transparent plastic dome, at the things in Triton's flat black sky, black sky like a nonexistent backdrop over a rubble of chaotic, gray-white-pink landscape, sky beyond the low, irregular horizon.

Dim, blue Neptune was pretty today, white stratus sheeting across much of the northern hemisphere, clouds gathering density as they had for the past several weeks. The dark bloom of a southern hemisphere storm was nowhere to be seen. Maybe just on the backside, maybe gone. It had been dwindling for weeks, slowly changing from the huge indigo oval it'd been on the day she'd landed here to last night's tiny blue-black dot.

Pretty. I liked having it there. A familiar marker.

And the sun, of course, a fat spark on the horizon opposite Neptune. A couple of pale white dots that were probably other moons, though to this day she couldn't keep the names of the little ones other than Nereïd in memory.

The ship that had been orbiting up there, freighter/transport coming in from Pluto, she'd heard, was gone already. It'd been a big ship, looking impossibly close as it swung slowly along no more than fifty klicks up, a heterogeneous collection of girder towers and big, round, white fuel tanks . . .

Away from the dome's glare, she'd be seeing an assortment of first and second magnitude stars, even in full daylight. After nightfall . . .

Ah, blue Neptune suddenly popping out in brilliant glory. And the sky spangled by the light of a hundred billion suns. What if I live long enough? What if the great discoveries are made before . . . something happens to me? What if I get to go? No sense wondering. You live a dangerous enough, interesting enough life, and something *will* happen to you. They say a cautious woman could live a thousand years, what with modern medicine, but . . .

Right. Image of some other Ginny, some *careful* Ginny, leading a cautious life, down deep under the Antarctic snow, managing the Family's estates, keeping its machines in sturdy repair. And living on and on, prancing and chanting barefoot on the warm hypocaust floor, squatting over all the little boys and girls as they came of age, one by one . . .

Brief memory of a fire flaring bright white on a cold black

night. Brief memory of a news story on the net a few days later. Accidental fire. No one hurt. No one missing . . . Bemused rage. No. What the Family does isn't illegal. Were it that, I could just have called the police. But . . . community values, of course. You wouldn't want it broadcast around, whatever the neighbors might suspect or even know. . . .

Long gone, of course. Pain from twenty years ago.

She finished the walk to the shower building, went inside, into steamy air, stood for a moment inside the door, letting her eyes adjust, letting her body adjust. Familiar shapes in the mist, clouds of water vapor swirling round and round, big drops and little, bouncing high in Triton's very low gee.

Ginny shrugged out of her robe, hung it on a peg, put the towel on top of it, walked forward into the mist, stood under a showerhead, standing still, eyes closed, letting the water sluice like thin oil over her shoulders, run greasily down her belly and back.

Nice. Nice and warm.

Over on the other end of the room were cold showers, most of the people congregating there, imagining that the icy needle spray was just what they needed to wake right up. Wake up the "natural" way, they said, because Standard ARM discourages the use of drugs among its employees.

Bullshit. Opening her eyes now and looking at them down there, listening to them yip as they pirouetted under their cold nozzles. Bullshit. A cup of strong red tea, that's all I need. Fabled British Army tea, leaves boiled right in with the water, sediment in your cup, tea staining the milk reddish brown . . .

Another shape in the mist, closer to her, someone else who likes the water warm. Closer look. It was a tall, skinny girl, pale white skin, short gray hair. No tits at all, just little pink nipples like a boy. No pubic hair. Closer look still. No, this can not be a nine year old girl. Face odd. Like a . . . prepubescent adult? Not anybody I've seen around here. Maybe just came in with yesterday's ship.

The girl stepped forward, seeming to smile, making her feel a moment of embarrassment. Not supposed to stare at other people's crotches in the public shower. Jesus. But the girl put out her wet hand, and said, "Maeru kai Ortega. Titan. Flight Engineer."

Ginny took the hand and felt an unexpected strength in the long, slim fingers as she looked into those odd gray eyes, realizing the eyes, the hair, the girl's whole conformity had to be . . . ersatz at best. "Virginia Vonzell Qing-an. Earth. Command Pilot." They were saying their assigned roles, of course, telling what they'd been trained for, it being unlikely that anyone you met in Peridot had ever been out before, other than the instructors.

The girl said, "Got your assignment yet?"

Ginny nodded. "Yesterday. ARM Prospector XQ1450."

Gray eyes brightening. "Hey! Me, too! We're shipmates."

Ginny suddenly inspecting the girl's body more closely, emotions very cool, looking down at those little nipples, that hairless slit of a vulva, realizing, yes, it was ersatz, that . . . Christ. I've drawn an andy for a flight engineer. A tiny feeling of something like revulsion? Somewhere, way down deep? How could anyone . . . *choose* to do this to themselves?

The girl was smiling still, and . . . she? He? It, perhaps? said, "That's right, Ms. Vonzell. Captain. Ask me again in private, I'll even show you . . ."

Looking back into pale, lustrous gray eyes, seeing only goodwill, Ginny felt a slight pang of something like shame. She said, "Sorry, I . . . It's just . . . well. Impossible not to be curious, uh, Ms. Ortega."

The wet hand was out again, the pretty little mouth set in a broad, ironic grin. "It's Mr. Ortega. But . . . everybody calls me Kai."

Ginny felt herself blush as she took the hand again, gripping it tightly. "Ginny." A moment of looking at each other, both of them, perhaps, a bit flustered, Ginny suddenly feeling . . . She put the feelings away suddenly, as suddenly as they'd come on, surprising her, making her feel just a bit . . . queasy. Tried to smile. Smile gamely. And said, "Come on. Let's go find out who we've drawn for navanalysis, com/con, and mining engineer.''

When they walked back to where they'd left their robes and towels, Ginny walked behind this . . . odd person. This Kai, and found herself watching her . . . his? Astonishing. Watched those slim buttocks wriggle and wondered at the feelings in herself.

Darkness falling again at last, the protracted end of the long Pholotian day, Kai stood still inside the pressure tent they'd set up on the slightly elevated landscape beyond the dead city. Hardly that. The memory of a dead city. Kai stood looking out through the slightly cloudy plastic of the little survival dome, which would have been a tight squeeze for six people but was pleasantly spacious for two.

The low, mounded rubble of the unknown fortress town, destroyed, perhaps, all those billions of years ago, by vengeful Rhinotaurs? Remember the impassive faces of the Frogmen behind the window. No way of knowing what they thought. No way of even guessing without invoking the spieltier software. And no way of knowing, then, if you've invoked an accurate guess.

Soft sigh. But there's nothing else to be done. The data's too old, has grown too sparse. There's almost nothing left for us to do here but sift the endless sand for microflecks of almost nothing. Which is what the real archaeologists will do, when they come.

Will they?

Will they follow us here?

Or will the discoveries at Alpha Centauri, the discoveries on uninhabitable Bellerophon and uninhabitable Pegasus and uninhabitable Pholos be just too trivial? Think of it. Think of their reaction. Life! Life on other worlds! At last!

Think of the network buzz.

Maybe. Maybe now the government will get up off its ass and put the money into . . .

Into what?

What do I want them to do?

What do I think is possible?

And, of course, there was no way of telling what the other starships will find. Alpha Centauri wasn't the likeliest of targets, being a double star, though the separation between the suns was more than enough to give us stable orbits inside two ecospheres. What about Tau Ceti? What will *Bokonon* find, when she arrives there? Eleven-plus light-years. Somewhere they sleep in the dark between the stars, no more than halfway to their destination.

Committee arguments clearly remembered. We wanted so badly for them to target an explorer ship for Delta Pavonis, soliton star almost exactly like the sun, but . . . Eighteen light-years. A sixty-year one-way voyage. Another eighteen years for the first signal to return.

Erasmus Hiraoka nodding slowly, smiling almost to himself. Yes. The best of all possible targets, but . . . in eighty years, there may be no more humanity. We can't wait that long. Maybe someday, from one of the star colonies, our children or grandchildren can launch such an expedition?

And Doc, chuckling softly, people looking at him from around the little conference room. Our children? He'd said. No. We ourselves will one day make the voyage of discovery, for we will still live on. If we are careful.

Bright stars were out now, in the perpetually dark sky up around the zenith, as the light grew ruddy and dim, Alpha Centauri B setting, carrying A with it. If we are careful. Humans are never careful. We've had too many lifetimes expecting to die. Death so completely inevitable that it raised life's value to infinity while rendering it worthless.

He looked down, wondering if it was time to put on the tent's illumination. Mies was sitting off to one side, still dressed in his undersuit coverall, sitting, looking out through the tent wall, toward the part of the horizon where the suns were going down, arms clasped around his bent legs, chin resting on his knees. Beyond him, over by the edge of the salt flat, *MN01* was a tiny, flattened silver-gray cone, windows lit up from within. You could see a shadow there, maybe another one, people moving around.

Look at him. As if he were all alone now. What happened to the . . . passion he showed only two days ago? "Mies?" Nothing. Mies still staring at the sunset. Well . . .

He walked over and interposed himself between the man and his worldview. Still nothing. Like I'm transparent. Like I'm not even here. How odd his face looks in this light. As if it keeps changing, changing from one expression to another, though he's not moving a muscle. Like he's changing from one person to another, inside, an assortment of variegated people trying the body on, checking its fit, getting ready to . . .

What?

What the hell am I saying to myself?

"Mies." A flicker in the eyes, then, but no direct response. All right. Looking at me now. Kai smiled, put his hand to his coverall collar, slowly slipped the zipper down its track, stood there with the flaps hanging open, smooth chest exposed in the dim light.

What does he see now? A young boy? A girl? A grown woman with poor mammary development. But looking at me, all the same. Watching me. Waiting for something. He shrugged his shoulders out of the garment, stood there with it draped around his hips. How about this, Mies? Do you like this? It's a pretty sight, isn't it? There are men and women who'd pay for an image like this and call it art.

And, of course, many more men, especially men, but even quite a few women, who'd pay for the image and call it a masturbation aid. Which is it to you, Mies? Beady eyes staring at me here as the red light faded to a dim spectral twilight, the suns long gone, stars flaming, bright white overhead.

All right, Mister Cochrane. Kai toed the heels of his soft bootliners, kicking them off, then let the coverall fall down around his ankles. How about this?

Mies's eyes were moving now, away from his face, away from the little boy chest with its little pink nipples, lingering on the flat belly and abdomen, distinct hipbones outlined under soft white skin. And, of course . . .

What do you see when you look at that place between my legs now, Mies? A woman? An object of sexual desire? A helpless child, waiting for your exploitation? A perverse creation with the power to drive you mad? What do you see?

He stepped out of the coveralls, leaving them crumpled on the plastic floor, turned away from Mies momentarily, imagining his rounded white buttocks glimmering in the dim light, glimmering, invited . . . turned back, completing a full, graceful pirouette. What now, Mister . . .

Mies's eyes, somehow cold upon him. Not the passionate Mies at all, not the friendly Mies, not friend Mies, not . . .

Kai stood still for a moment, facing the man, biting his lip softly. How do I get through this? No man is as troubled as this Mies facing me now. Men are simple creatures, easily distracted from almost any problem. I know this to be true.

Remote being grinning like a gargoyle in the back of his consciousness. Of course you do, silly. Being such a simpleton yourself . . .

Kai ran his hands down the soft skin of his belly, holding them just so, thumbs turned in, fingers pointing down the length of his thighs, hands making a picture frame for his vulva. Come on, Mies. This is how men want women to behave. React, goddamn you. I'm waiting.

He pressed in with his hands, flattening the soft skin of his mons, labia spreading open so Mies could see the structures within. So long as I let nothing extrude, it's hot, glistening female tissue you'll see here, Mies. Come to me. Touch. Taste.

Use me, goddamn it. . . .

Mies, voice flat and empty, said, "I'm sorry, Kai. I'm just not . . ."

Well, shit. Kai grinned, thinking, There's not a man born . . . He stepped closer to Mies, hips swaying, brought his belly close to Mies's face, thrusting his genitals forward, being careful not to let his penis emerge. The doctors had done a good job down there, implanting his skin with altered apocrine glands that output a perspiration loaded with dense hormones. Hormones not *quite* under his conscious control, but with neural feedback mechanisms that . . .

Just now, he thought. Just now I must smell, to some midnight creature buried in the depths of his brain, like a fertile woman, like a woman who's just ovulated, who's ripe for . . .

Mies's face twisted, eyes gleaming strangely, and he put up one hand, planted it in the middle of Kai's belly, gave him a hard shove. Kai stumbled back, propelled by muscles still adapted for high-gee life, stumbled in Pholos surface gravity, ten times what he'd grown up with on Titan, stumbled, fell over backwards.

Long silence. Nothing but the sound of quick breathing. The two of them alone together.

What am I waiting for?

Hell, I'm waiting for the bastard to apologize, come over and kiss me, stick his face in my crotch and make amends. Jesus.

Kai sat up, mouth open to speak angrily, tell Mies . . .

Mies was on his feet, tense, staring. Fists doubled up.

Oh, for Christ's sake. Kai stood up, reeling heavily, getting his balance, getting used to Pholos again, the same way he had to every time he stood up. "Goddamn it, Mies." Walking closer to him, trying to look into those shadowed eyes. What is he thinking? "What's wrong? I—"

"Look. I'm just not in the mood."

Kai thought, What the fuck is *not in the mood*? Women are not in the mood. Men are only momentarily distracted. He put his hand on Mies's shoulder, looking earnestly into his face, and said, "Come on, Mies. This is just—"

Mies's eyes widened, staring through him, and . . .

Kai thought, Odd. He looks . . . what? Afraid? Afraid of me? I don't . . .

Mies's hand came up, swung around, bounced off his temple, pain jolting through, sensation strong that his brain was sloshing back and forth, soft tissue bounding off bone as he fell. Fell and rolled quickly away, rolled to his feet, old reflexes taking over, adrenaline and testosterone mixing in his blood, igniting with a bright blue hypergolic flame.

Mies advancing across the room, eyes gleaming empty in the starlight.

Kai crouched, settling his feet on the supple plastic floor, trying to get his knees braced so they wouldn't buckle, memory of a hundred barroom brawls welling up, of any number of surprised bullies caught off guard. No. No he won't be realizing how fit your arms can get, fighting inertia in low to zero gee all these years.

Mies looming over him now, arms raised, fists clenched, some kind of rage hissing between his lips.

Kai popped him a good one, right in the nose.

Mies now, staggering back, eyes bright with astonishment, flooding with pain, blood starting forth like a black stain on his shadowed upper lip from a nose that had hardly begun to heal from Ginny's almost identical blow.

Kai said, "You little shit . . ."

Staring at the sky, staring, trying to be the external world, clean, beautiful ruddy light across the precise slash of the horizon. Warmth on his lip and chin changing to wet coolness, blood evaporating in the dry atmosphere of the tent. Mies's mind worked like a little mechanical carousel, identities coming around, bobbing up, swinging away. He looked over his shoulder at punisher Kai, just sitting there on his pallet, no expression on his face, rubbing the palm of one hand with his thumb.

Christ. I never imagined that I would end up . . . in this place. Kai, I didn't mean to . . . but I don't need to set loose the ravening Indigo eyes, don't need to wonder who, or what, you are for the hundredth time. There are enough contradictions echoing through my little, little soul now. There's not enough room for you and your silly genitalia.

Why is everyone so quiet now? Where are all the voices? Where the hell are you when I *need* you? Nothing. No one. A sensation as of a cold wind, blowing right through his head. Dull, ominous, moaning wind. Image of him standing in Ginny's room, completely out of control. It's got to end. I've got to do something.

Look at him over there. As sullen and closed off from me as any woman. He just wants his fake cunt filled, wants the pleasure of having even a minimal amount of control over me. Mies. When I picked the name I had no idea what it really meant. I thought *I* would have control. How wrong I was. How fucking unforgivably wrong can you be?

Night coming.

He looked again at the man in the corner, scrunched forward, elbows on thighs. This time their eyes met. Kai looking sad, perhaps penitent. My God. Out here with these people. He's my only hope. I have to, at least, try . . . Silence, for a moment. Now . . .

"Kai?" The name sounded strange in his mouth. "I'm . . . very sorry, about what happened. I didn't mean to . . . hurt your feelings." Nose still partially clogged, giving the whole thing a ridiculous nasality.

Kai shrugged. "I'm sorry, too. If I'd known . . ."

Genuine sympathy? Maybe, he needs something from me. Barter system, quid pro quo, you scratch my back . . . "Come here. Sit next to me, please? I have something that I have . . ." Fuck it. Choking up, nasal mucus starting to run. "I need you to help me."

Kai came halfway across the tent, skin burning red in the last light of B. He needs it to be physical. I need . . .

Tears streaming down my face. From relief?

Kai slowly held out his hand. Ready to pull back. Mies took it, felt the heat of it. Shake hands now, that's what you're taught. "I'm not who—or what—you think I am, Kai. And I'm falling apart."

Strange look on his face. Not revulsion, something else. "What is it you need from me?"

Pulling him to me, grappling with him as if he were a woman, or I were Reiko once more. "Oh, please. No. Just listen to me for a little while. But stay here."

Kai put his arm around him, under the armpits, a firm but light touch. "I'm listening."

Kai, yes, I do believe you can see me, if only through your fucked-up little groin. Maybe I can trust you, even, just a little.

And then the story, tumbling out, word after word after word. And no one inside trying to stop him. It's all fallen apart now. All decayed. No one wants to take responsibility for what's happened. For what we did. Because responsibility equals guilt.

And we're afraid of guilt.

Seesy and childhood. Confused young manhood. I couldn't *do* it, you see. It was *always* too hard. Everything was too hard for me. Dead parents, like a prop kicked out from under my world. Human Matrix and the possible end of the world, kicked under the rug. Then Seesy again. Then *Indigo*. Two birds with one stone, you see. Three birds. I loved my sister. I loved her. You understand?

Kai was still listening. Gray eyes as empty as glass.

What the hell. Go on. Get it over with.

Indigo. First the hypnopaedic session in which my loyalty was bound to the organization. To the Plan. To the salvation of humanity. Ultimately, you see, my loyalty was bound to humanity itself. I wanted to . . . save us. Save us all.

I see.

Yes. Go on. Get it over with.

The autoviroid plague. Transmitted so easily from man to woman. Who cares about men's fertility? A woman, after all, has only so many eggs. So many easy targets. And genetic mandates will keep them fucking and fucking until we've caught them all. All but the moral few. Those few from which some future humanity, some *better* humanity, will spring. . . .

I see.

Go on. Get it over with.

A simple story. Going forth. Going forth, so eagerly, to fuck the women and make them barren. I was . . . eager to begin.

I'm sure you were.

Eager. But . . . I still couldn't do it.

No?

Nothing had changed. Not really. I was still . . . me. Still a fuckup, you see.

A gun doesn't *really* make you brave, does it?

No. Not really.

So?

So they sent me back for another hypnopaedic implant. Seems this problem's fairly common among the sort of men who join Indigo.

Kai's gray eyes, judgmental eyes, seemed unsurprised.

Ran a rule-sieve into my head. Rules, you see, for the . . . seduction of women. Then they sent me forth to . . . be fruitful and multiply.

Gray eyes.

Just staring now.

Oh, my God.

"Kai, you have to help me. You know about what happened with Ginny. I'm . . . just . . . not . . . working right. I can't go on like this for very much longer."

Kai looked sad. "So. Rosie. Lin . . . Me?"

"I don't think it can work that way. I'm . . . I'm not sure."

"And you wanted . . . Ginny, too."

"The Indigo rule-sieve. Not me."

A wonderful excuse. Tell him that. Tell him!

Kai reached out and touched his cheek, wiping away moisture. "Mies, I'll help you if I can."

Kai stood still in the black night, listening to the soft crinkle of his environmental suit inflating, little amber VR readouts flickering on, telling him all was well, blinking off, looking down at the dim form of sleeping Mies Cochrane. Twitching. Twitching gently in his sleep, like a dreaming dog.

Sudden, brief memory of watching a dog sleep. Not used to pets. Few of them out there in the gulf between the worlds. Then, mostly parakeets and gerbils and lab rats. Sheba's dog, brought from Mars, hardly able to walk around on Earth at first, lying on the carpet before their radiant heater, sleeping, dwarf black lab dreaming. Legs running, making running motions, at

least, though it lay on its side. Faint yipping sounds, a whine
shaped to be something like a bark. Running. Running. Jumping. Teeth exposed. Jaws working, throat clenching convulsively, imagined swallowing, dream of a meal, hot blood, warm
satisfaction . . . I remember laughing at the time. Do dogs ever
dream that they're getting laid? Little red penises popping out
of furry sheaths, hips thrusting, semen jetting . . .

Mies, there watching with me, staring, eyes empty, remote,
cold fish Mies Cochrane. And Sheba laughing, arm around
Andy's waist: I'm just glad poor Gus never dreams he's taking
a shit. She was sorry to leave the dog behind. Dead by now?
Maybe. The medical treatments that keep us alive can keep
them alive, too, but few people bother, ownership of dogs and
cats a declining practice, even on antiquarian Earth.

And Mies now, whining softly in his sleep. What does *he*
dream? If there was light, would I see an erection poking at
the side of his sleeping bag? Would I take off this suit and try
to crawl inside? He watched Mies squirm in his sleep, and
thought, No. No, I would not.

Memory of Mies crying in his arms. Memory of Mies babbling out the details of his life, this . . . strange, horrible confession. My God. David Gilman? Who the hell is David Gilman?
Indigo, ICOPOSI, autoviroids, universal human sterilization . . .
My God, what if he'd managed to rape Ginny? And what
about . . .

I really ought to get over to the lander, talk to the others.
Izzy and Metz? Andy? Rosie . . . Oh, my God. Rosie. Get
outside, at least, patch through to the ship, see if I can talk
to . . . would Doc be the right one to talk to? I don't know.

He slipped into the airlock, zipped the inner door, let the air
whisper away, zipped open the outer, stepped out onto the flat
surface of Pholos. Across the plain, *MN01* was dark now, a
small shape barely sticking above the far horizon, a tiny outline
against the starry sky. It looks more . . . real like this. Like a
starry night out on the deserts of Arizona. I feel almost as if I
could get out of the suit, feel a warm breeze washing over my

face. I *liked* being on Earth, being in a natural environment at last. It was like nothing I ever dreamed. Nothing. Wonderful.

Other dark shadows.

Kai stiffened, peering into the night, about to call up the suit's optics and . . .

What the hell. There's nothing here. Nothing. Everyone who ever lived here, every *thing,* has been dead, gone, extinct, since the days when life on Earth was nothing more than invisible specks in a nutrient sea. When the Frogmen were here, the Rhinotaurs, worshiping their Leospider gods, our ancestors had yet to invent the concept of the cell membrane.

Shadows, outlined against the sky, bipeds in crinkled, not-quite-transparent spacesuits, walking together, holding hands, looking up at the stars. Kai called up the lander's eyebubble node and IDed the figures, expecting to see Izzy and Metz.

No.

Well.

Not Izzy and Metz after all.

Andy Mezov and Rosamunde Merah, arms around each other under a black sky sleeted with cold, bright stars, watching a tiny crescent moon drift through the heavens. He thought of them making love, then, a fleeting image of man and woman in coupled embrace. Imagined jetting semen and welcoming womb. Then thought of Mies's . . . no. Thought of David Gilman's slinking autoviroids. He turned away, glancing in the direction of the eyebubble sensor, thought of linking to the ship, of waking up Doc and Ginny, of . . .

He shook his head slowly in the darkness, turned away from the starry sky, and started walking back toward the pressure tent, where Mies Cochrane, whoever he was, still slept and dreamed.

TEN

With the biolab hatch door closed and the lights down low, Doc sat in front of the photomultiplier microscope's 3-D display and watched age-old events unfold. An ancient technology, he thought. Late twenty-first century, at best, but adequate. And quiet.

Up on the screen, Ginny's fertile egg was a pale, glassy ball of cool blue light, organelles and nuclear material dimly visible as shadows within. Orb of life, waiting patiently to make a being out of nothingness, out of raw materials, out of pure spirit force. . . .

He grinned, shaking his head slowly. Old, old memories. Memories of a young man with his ear down on a young woman's smooth, rounded belly. Listening to sounds from within, medical training making him catalog all the little gurgles and chirps, but . . .

I remember. Remember thinking, the life force inside is my life forces as well as hers. *Our* baby. Our child. Memory of Giannetta as a child, dark eyed, wild-haired, running, shouting, playing with other children. Somewhere, back on Earth, she was a woman in her seventies; a woman with children and grandchildren, perhaps even great-grandchildren by now. . . .

Fading smile of remembered happiness. Giannetta's offspring's offspring were part of the . . . problem. Yes, indeed. All of the problem.

But I remember lying with my face on my wife's belly, listening to our child stir . . . and being tempted. Sliding my face down to the base of her stomach's curve, nuzzling her genitals, thinking how appropriate the term seemed just then, listening to her giggle as I . . .

Up on the screen, sperm cells from Mies's semen gathered round the egg, egg separated from the others he'd extracted from nitrogen storage, the just-in-case storage in the ship's research lockers, little oblong heads pressing into the egg's cell membrane, flagella whipping, spinning, powered by almost-depleted battery packs at their collars.

There. Enzyme leaking out, head of one cell suddenly plunging in. The surface of the egg seemed to shimmer, cell membrane changing texture, and . . . the other sperm cells were excluded, tail of the winner dropping away, cell wall closing behind it. In due course, rapid due course, the genetic matrix would break free of its container and . . .

Doc nudged the egg out of the horde of still-flailing sperm cells, back into the compound that held its brethren and sestrin, watched the dying sperm mill aimlessly, left behind.

Sure never thought of it that way, when I'd be fucking some woman or another, feeling the slick-rough surface of her vagina slide on me, feel myself suddenly grow larger and harder, my head swim, my spine tingle suddenly and . . . Never thought about the fate of the sperm as you felt them go, breath stopping, mind clenching shut, excluding the world. Well, if this were happening inside Ginny, the egg would be lying in the narrow confines of her fallopian tubes, just a few centimeters from the ovary and . . .

Inside the egg, you could see the shadows moving. He kicked up the gain, switched to wavelengths where the cell membrane was more transparent, probed gently with a very low-energy radar. There. Spindles forming, DNA strands pairing off, linking up, arraying themselves, codons counting off one by one, devising a new and more or less unique human being.

Unique in the tiny details, if nothing else. Unique in the ''junk code'' that lay between the few percentage points of

DNA that defined a full creature. As he watched, the strands did their job, and the cell began to divide, beginning the long task that would ultimately build a baby. Nothing. Nothing out of the ordinary. Two. Four. Eight. Sixteen. Thirty-two . . .

On impulse, he kicked up the gain until the blob of cells was huge, focused on the nucleus of one and watched for another little while. Nothing. Matrices doing their jobs. He let the focus wander, watching the organelles do their own breeding dance, watched the mitochondria, parasites living inside all animal cells, all that made multicellular life possible, divide and divide, maternal DNA spitting and redoubling and . . . Individual co-dons, individual molecules in the junk sequences switching in and out, trading places, neutral molecular evolution in action and . . .

Nothing? Maybe so. Neutral. Neutral evolution. Just the clock ticking away and . . . Yes. Yes, that's where *I'd* hide . . . whatever it is. He let the focus drift on over to the cell wall, watching the cell prepare to divide, wasp-waist pinching in, cell membrane slicing open, responding to inner enzymes, wounds in separate daughter cells now starting to ooze closed as new enzymes instructed them to . . .

He suddenly kicked the gain higher still and watched the cell membranes form, molecular strands created out of the proto-plasm, attaching themselves, an occasional bit getting away, falling out into the world-medium that mimicked Ginny's in-sides, lost. Think about that for a minute, Doctor Matel. Think you can do it. You've been . . . *thinking* for a long time, haven't you?

He let the focus drift after one of the lost strands, watched it twist and turn, bubble and hiss as it died, disintegrated and died and . . . Hmh. Interesting. As it died, tiny motes fell away, disappearing in the murk. Hmh. He kicked up the gain yet again and followed one of the motes. Falling. Tumbling, falling. Molecules rolling around each other. It twitched. Twitched. Started to bend double. Straighten out. Bend double. Straighten out. Moving now, corkscrewing away from the blastula, follow-ing a widening circle.

A little like a search pattern. Mapping out the walls of the chamber. Seeking. Seeking. Doc sat, stunned, and thought, What utter fucking brilliance.

After a while, the little molecular machine, narrowing its careful search, found the structure that mimicked Ginny's ovary. Found an egg. Slid through the huge pores of its cell wall. Found the nucleus. Slid through the nuclear membrane. Found a neatly folded double helix of DNA. Disappeared, like a bit of dissolving sugar, into a stretch of junk-code.

Staring at the innocent image in the 3-D monitor, Doc thought, How clever. Like a virus's virus. I wonder . . . He compared the stretch of DNA codons to its reference scan from the ship's records. No difference. Of course not. We simply do not maintain databases at that level of detail. Why? Because the submolecular construction of the DNA codons is invariant down to the chaotic attractor level. We've known that for two hundred years. If we kept such records, they'd be meaningless.

What utter fucking brilliance. I'd like to meet the man or men who thought up this one. Well, now . . . When he dropped the infected egg into a milling swarm of Kai's sperm, all went well. One sperm poked its head in. Contributed its datapacket and . . . nothing. No cell division. In fact, he realized, this thing is just . . . hell. Just a single-celled organism now.

He tried the rest of the eggs in the ovary, one by one, realized that, somehow, they'd all been infected, were all . . . changelings. Call them changelings. Infected by the single intruder? No, most likely there were a thousand, thousand other motes, whose courses I did not track.

He got another egg out of cold storage, gave it to the sperm cells, watched the act of penetration, watched the blastula begin to form. All right. That settles it. Jesus, what a thought! You see, my dear fertile woman, the *next* baby you try to have will be the last. . . .

He sat back again, sighed with frustration, and wondered if there was any way that an infected woman could pass the cellular machinery on to her subsequent male partners. Well. They'd have to be awfully fucking clever to manage *that*. But it's not out of the question. And another thing. Would Mies, screwing Kai up his manufactured cunt, be able to pass on . . . Unlikely, but . . . I guess, when we get them back aboard, we'll find out. He sighed again, nudged himself out of the seat's gentle grasp, floating toward the biolab's hatch. All right, Ginny, show and tell time.

A second, a minute, hours, and Doc said, "There you have it. Not pleasant, I'm afraid, to have this happen in our midst. Linda, I don't know what to say to you. I'm sorry."

Spence turned away from the luminous image on the light table, stomach knotting, fist clenched. Sperm carrying . . . sterility. It made a kind of perverse sense. Emotion hitting now. Linda. This is going to change everything. For the worse. He glanced at her, hanging over the table like a ghost being exorcised, bewilderment and fear on her face. Doc and Ginny looking at her with concern. Well, it happened to her, not me. She needs me to comfort her. Take her hand, massage the nape of her neck, that's what she likes.

Image of every corny sit-mance projected across his mind. Whitebread model actress taking her husband aside, afraid to tell him the good news, afraid he'll be upset. Honey, I'm . . . Pausing. Why afraid? I never understood that as a kid, never understood that in real life, that pregnancy was far from a happy thing. Especially for the man. Oh Christ, he thinks, There goes *my* life. Now I'm really stuck. Unless I can talk her into getting rid of the damned . . .

Honey, I'm . . . sterile. Different sort of ring to it. Hollow. Hey, no problem. Doesn't mean the end of the world. Maybe it does, to her. Not in real life. Never in real life. In the real world, we've got the technology to reverse . . . oh. But not here. Not now, anyway. Thoughts running away. Inane, yammering and yammering and . . . well, the egg and sperm samples in cold storage can be thawed and . . . oh. Of course. He said it was possible that the . . . viroids? . . . that they might be hiding in her somatic cells as well and . . . oh, shit.

Time has stopped. Look at them. I could run down and get

a soda, come back and they wouldn't have noticed I was gone. Can't let her think that I don't care. He held out a hand, put in softly on the curve of her forearm. Just a touch, meant to reassure. Why doesn't she say anything? "Linda, maybe we should . . ."

Shaking her head, pushing his hand away. Most definitely not looking at him.

Ginny said, "We might be able to reverse the effect, with the lab supplies and computers, maybe with a little research and . . ." Low, calming voice. Women know how to handle these things.

Doc said, "And with a little information from Mister Cochrane." Cold. Flat. Empty. Hollow.

Linda looked at him, eyes shadowed. "The fleet might still come, mightn't it?"

Ginny, looking at Doc now, said, "We . . . don't know. Maybe."

Telling a lie. Trying to make her feel . . . Okay. For now. But *I* know this system is useless to the Daiseijin. Maybe they can send a shipload of scientists, and send us some . . . or, hell. Maybe we can just go home. Home.

Spence said, "What will be done about Cochrane?" Roast the bastard? This was, after all, his dream, too. Little Spences spreading out through space, carrying his genetic material, colonizing and exploiting the galaxy. Generations of them, one built on the other. Persisting, as Hiraoka would say. Not now.

Ginny frowned, made an inconclusive gesture. "That hasn't been . . . decided. He's needed during this phase of the exploration."

Little catch in Linda's throat. Eyes opening wider, looking up. "I wanted to . . ." Everyone hanging on the little girl voice. Never did like scenes. Wonder if I can get her back to the room. . . . He reached for her wrist. "Come on, let's go."

She forcefully swung her arm up, twisting and shaking his hand off. "Let go of me . . ." Hissed in a hard whisper.

Uh-oh.

Tears were collecting in her suddenly reddening eyes, small

globules caught on her eyelashes. Scary stare at Ginny. "This is not just going to be forgotten, is it? Ginny? There has to be a law against . . . this." Eyes staring at nothing. Hand over her mouth, retching? "Oh my God."

Ginny: "You'd better calm down. Mies will be . . . dealt with."

Spence could see her anger. Of course. The piece of shit is down on Pholos right now, screwing Kai.

Linda had lost her foothold and was drifting upward, slightly bent over. "I wanted to . . . I can't believe it." Sentence punctuated with sobs. "I feel so dirty." She balled up her fist as if to strike, then let it go limp. "Ginny, I feel like I've been raped. But this is worse than rape, a thousand times worse. You can't just let him get away with it. Can you understand?"

Ginny's face looked almost as distraught as Linda's. She muttered a low, "I understand. I do. Now you'd better take a sedative and go to bed. Spence, can you take care of her now?"

Yes. If she'll let me.

Holding her, enfolded in his arms, thin nightdress soft against his skin, lights dimmed, just sailing along. And, later: Sleeping now. Artificial sleep. This has changed her, I know it. Changed *us*. Why did she have to sleep with him? What in God's name made her go with that cold fish scientist?

She got what was coming to her.

No, that's not right.

Why can't I feel anything but dread?

Christ. *I'm* not sterile. . . .

Kai sat back, letting Pholos's still heavy-seeming gravity wedge him into the acceleration chair, staring out across the salt flats to the world's dark horizon. Nighttime here and now. Many hours of night still to come, but we'll be flying into day, northward into daylight. It's summertime just now in Pholos's northern hemisphere. Eternal day above the arctic circle.

He ran through the lander's checklists silently, watching datasets scroll up out of thin air at his beckoning nod. Everything's right with *MN01* and all's right with the world. . . . He glanced over at Mies, realized that the man was paying no attention to his duties, staring away at empty space, out at the dark world, at the starry sky above, his swollen nose a ruddy knob in the middle of his face.

All right. I can fly the damned thing by myself. Who the fuck cares? You do. You do, Maeru kai Ortega. You wanted him in you again, loving you again, not crying on your shoulder. Not confessing . . . My God. Not confessing all that. More confused imagery. More thoughts of, What am I going to *do*?

One more of Erasmus Hiraoka's famous dicta: When all else fails, do nothing. A lot of people imagine that means, Leave well enough alone. But it doesn't. No. It says, When *all* else fails. When you've done your best, then, only then, stand back and let the sky fall down. He grimaced, wishing the sensation of longing that had settled between his legs would go away. Damn it. Last night I dreamed I was fucking him. Bending him over in front of me and . . .

He put his hands on the manual controls and willed the little ship into the sky, seat rumbling under him, sparkle of light falling on the ground, lighting up the blowing salt as they rose. No fire. Just the friction-induced glow of our turbine exhaust. The ship went up, rolling around its short axis, windows turning to face east, starting its long suborbital arc up to the north pole, while Kai and Mies, Izzy and sleepy-eyed Metz, Rosie and Andy, holding hands in the space between their chairs, sat transfixed and watched the double sunrise, first B, then brilliant A, then bright blue sky rising up to swaddle the edge of the world.

Sometimes, it's like I'm all alone in here again. . . . Scientist's voice like a ghost's whisper, like the moan of some faraway wind, carrying with it the scent of storms to come, the sort of wind a child imagines into something like a human voice: *You are alone. You've always been alone. None of us real. Not even you. Only . . . him.* Only him. Only Gilman. David Gilman was real. The rest of us . . .

Mies craned his neck, looking out the big window, watching as they continued up the broad, gray valley, moving up onto the continental shelf. On either side, the pointed horns of glacier-carved mountains were sharply defined, highlighted against the black sky. Horizon that looked like it had been bitten off by some crooked-toothed carnivore, jagged ridges broken with indentations. Deep-cut glacial valleys feeding down into the immense, U-shaped basin below them. And in that basin, the peculiarly shaped, clearly outspreading topography characteristic of glacial flow. The bedrock here was overlain with the lighter-colored broken rock transported here by the glacier, meandering walls of boulders marking the edge of the glacier as it retreated back up the valley.

Up there, somewhere, if the orbital analysis was correct, is what's left of the glacier, a comparatively tiny bit of pristine ice from the days, aeons ago, when Pholos was wet enough to have snowfall. Hmmm. I can still do this. Surprised that I can reintegrate so well with the viewpoint of the scientist personality. That's the only benefit left to me, that I can look out at *this* with his eyes, see the beauty in this desolation and understand why it is this way.

You could've just studied.

In the pilot seat, Kai was clearly enjoying the vista, fully distracted from the revelations and reconciliation of last night. Maybe that's why he's so trustworthy, in a way. He *really* appreciates that there's a difference between the external world and his internal emotions. So hard to do when the world is so . . . inhospitable.

God. The confession of his secret had come, and yet, things remained the same, at least on the surface. Well, I can . . . prolong that feeling. "Look down there, to the left, just at the base of that terrace. The thing that looks like a giant snake; it's called an esker. That means that at least this part of the main glacier melted quite rapidly."

Kai grinned over at him. "We don't have any terrain exactly like this on Titan. But there are places where the hard water ice is carved by solid flowing wax. The mountains that result are almost as impressive as these in places."

The valley was broadening even more, mountain chains

slowly shrinking as they drew farther away. Blue was becoming visible in the deepest bites, almost as if it had gotten caught in the interstices like some kind of webbing.

"What else can you tell from the lie of the land here?" Kai asked.

Mies studied the terrain for a long moment. "Looks like from this point on, there was a very slow, steady retreat of the glacier. I would say, from here on up, the glacier was subject to an extremely cold, arid climate. No melting, but no more snow, either. Only slow, slow sublimation, lasting for millions of years."

Hardly any voices in my head at all, at times like this. It's almost like we're . . . one whole person again. *Sometimes, we are.* Mies sighed, another inner wind, wind of a self-pitying lost soul, self-consciously self-pitying. I guess I'd like that. The notion that, one day, somehow, some way . . . the incredible notion that I'll be whole again.

"There's the head of the valley," Izzy said. "Looks like a giant dug it out with his hand."

Andy was pointing. "Can you see them, over to the right there? A real city, not like the sea bottom."

Sure enough, tiny spires surrounded by a cluster of little white hemispheres, easily visible now.

Metz's slow drawl: "This'll be very interesting."

"Get ready," said Kai, "we're going to land."

Suddenly distracted. Image of falling the remaining kilometer to the ground. Flailing, shouts becoming whispers in the thin air. Sickening colloidal sound when I hit. Then, nothing. Almost a blessing. How will I face death, when it comes? Down deep, you really don't believe it *will* come, do you? I'll look old Death in the eye, and say, Just as I supposed. Nothing *is* anything, and this proves it. Will that give me any comfort?

MN01 landed amidst the glacial till with a satisfying little noise, like biting into dry cereal. Over there, curled up in the recess of the gray, double-lit mountain, a cat-shape, dark, covered with a scaly covering of broken rock, the old glacier, or what was left of it, under its coating of ablation crust. Beside it, wonder of wonders, a comic-book city of domes and little pyramids, white as snow, from this distance as clean and sharp as if they had been built the day before. Mies began to undo his restraining belt. Lots to do before I have to face that moment, I hope.

The sunlight at the pole, Kai thought, has a peculiarly watery look to it. Thin white light slanting down out of the black sky, blue-gray light a rim around the horizon, light slanting down from two suns—a thin smile, maybe call it a sun and a half . . . a sun and a tenth?—illuminating the interior of the blue-ice glacier, illuminating the area where Mies had cut away the reddish surface crust, ancient . . . things inside, things still no more than shadows. He turned back to the little cluster of sealed domes, bubbles of white plastic cowering in the shadow of the old glacier, to where Izzy and Metz were assembling the scanner head. "Ginny?"

Doc's voice said, "Monitoring the software load, Kai. We're about ready."

"How's it doing?"

"It sure as hell is a lot smaller now. I can't imagine how you guys managed—"

"Easier than you'd think. The team who put this together on Earth, five, maybe six programmers, working with a big rack of AI code generators, had to follow old-fashioned object-oriented programming protocols, build the pieces separately and weld them all together later."

"So?"

"You know Izzy and Metz used to be toolmakers?"

"Sure. That's why they're here."

"Well, they ran what modern programmers call a bugshit express algorithm on the source code. What it does is mathematically folds all the code objects into a single eka-object that can dynamically simulate various aspects of the original source code at runtime."

A moment of silence, then, "I don't see how that's possible."

Kai smiled to himself. "It's sort of a distant descendant of the early relative-addressing schemes, in the context of Gödelization.''

More silence. "Oh. Um. Wouldn't that . . . slow things down?''

''No. Compact code is faster code.''

''Oh.'' You could hear, in his voice, that the concept had no meaning for him.

Ginny's voice said, ''That's it, Kai. Spieltier's in active RAM, occupying around four percent of the processing platform.''

''Good enough.'' Kai looked back over at the glacier, where Mies's torch flashed, bright light reflecting off the surface of the glacier, bouncing around inside. ''Might as well get started.''

''Full array?''

''No. We'll start off just like before, and work our way in as we sort out the data. I think Iz and Metz are right about the spieltier. We need to know what's real, how much data we actually *have* before we start playing around with detailed pattern matching.''

Izzy said, ''So, now that we've *fixed* it, you don't trust the software anymore? Fuckhead.''

''Come on, guys. Let's just see what we've got.''

''What about them?'' A gesture at where Mies, Andy, and Rosie continued to work.

''They can watch later, if they want. Let's do it.'' Kai nodded at the helmet sensor, then from control to control as each materialized in its proper place. The scanner head turned on its mount, regarding the cluster of ancient buildings with a somehow almost supercilious stare, funneling data to the microwave link and on up to the analysis engine in the sky.

Izzy said, ''Well. Nothing new here.''

''Give it a minute.''

The landscape around them seemed to smear and blur, sky darkening, then growing lighter, rugged hills seeming to breathe and flex underfoot, though there was, of course, no actual motion. The domes turned misty, seemed to fade, then firmed up again.

Metz said, "Oh, look. The glacier."

Vast, towering over them, bright blue-white, reddish photo-dissociational crust gone with the years. And the landscape around them, gray rocks sharper and better defined, less eroded, were suddenly covered with a thin limning of white frost as the sky climbed upward, black overhead lightening to purple.

Doc's voice said, "So what're we looking at here, two, maybe three hundred million years after the Frogman Space Age?"

Kai checked his graphs, and said, "Something like that. Hard to tell. This habitat was here, essentially unchanging, for a very long time. In the tens of millions of years, at least, maybe a lot longer. That tends to muddy the timescape a bit, though it does give depth to the datascan itself."

Ginny said, "Hard to imagine. They had the technology to colonize Pegasus, back when it was a habitable world, but they didn't."

Metz said, "It wasn't *really* habitable to them."

Doc: "They could've adapted to the gee-problem. We're talking about evolutionary timescales here."

Kai thought, True. From the time of the ruins on Bellerophon, to the time when this site was . . . functional, we're talking a time frame comparable to the Mesozoic. Time enough for the dinosaurs to rise and fall. "Hard to know what happened to them, really. With the technology they had, there's no reason why they couldn't have colonized their whole star system, built a large-scale deep-space economy like the one we have, then gone on out to the stars."

I'm still imagining them colonizing Archaeozoic Earth, Kai thought. Despite the fact that I *know,* I can't quite get it through my head that Sol and Alpha Centauri were *nowhere* near each other, three billion years ago.

Ginny said, "It's like their culture somehow . . . fossilized."

Kai stood looking at the domes for a while longer. No sign of movement outside. No lights in the windows. "I don't think we can pin down the inhabited phase from here, with these sieves."

Doc said, "You think we can find out, at this site, exactly when the Frogmen went extinct? And why?"

Kai thought, Good question. And, of course, the unstated question: If the Frogmen could survive the death of their planet's geochemical cycle, if they could survive the quick collapse of the biosphere that should inevitably follow, could survive in their little technological cocoons, for, what? *hundreds* of millions of years? Why aren't they here now to greet us?

Metz, voice very soft, said, "You know, I keep thinking when we cut through the wall, they'll just . . . be there."

Me, too. What a goddamned shame, to come all this way, only to find out that we've missed them. "Particle beam ready?"

Izzy said, "Just a deep scan, or—"

Kai: "No. Let's go through the wall."

Metz: "You better run the auxiliary power lead back to the rover's reactor, Iz."

Kai waited, looking away from the silent, motionless domes, back toward the glacier. Inside its white mass, you could see the shrunken remains of the modern glacier, like a glimmering shadow seen across vast, empty time, Mies's torch flickering within.

"All set."

Kai nodded to the appropriate control and watched. One long, brilliant blue flicker-flash, error bars forming inside graphs, columns of numbers weaving in and out. "Looks like . . . hell, I don't know."

Izzy: "We won't make much sense of this. This fucking wall's been sitting here in the wind for more than four billion years. The data's layered so deep we'll never get it back. Not without some kind of interpolation."

I know. I know. "Go on in."

"Right."

The particle beam flared, brilliant yellow-red, sparks cascading off the wall, thick red line of fire causing the cold, thin air to fluoresce and shimmer and . . .

Bam.

A big, ragged-edged square burst from the side of the dome, dust puffing out behind it, fell flat on the ground, slid a short distance toward them, stopped, rocking gently, was still. Kai flinched, and Izzy said, "Odd. Still pressurized a bit."

Odd, indeed. Pretty damned good engineering that could contain air for all that time. "Maybe just an ongoing problem with outgassing. Look at the composition."

Izzy said, "Plenty of styrene vapor, all right. Wouldn't that have been bad for them?"

"Bad for us, anyway. No, probably just built up after they . . ." Right. After they were gone. "What've we got?"

Ginny's voice said, "The scanner's radar echo shows there's nothing inside. Looks like they moved away and took their furniture with them."

"Moved away to *where?*" Izzy demanded. "I mean, what was the *point?*"

Good question. Why bother moving from one habitat to another? Consolidation, perhaps, as the population fell and fell over the eons? Kai said, "You know, it's not inconceivable, once the population got low enough, that they just took all their portable goods, loaded them aboard whatever ships they still had flying, and abandoned this star system." Found somewhere else to live. "They could still be around somewhere. On the other side of the galaxy, maybe."

Romantic notion, but a fat lot of good that does us. Or them.

Doc said, "How would they maintain an industrial base big enough to manage that, with their world dead and their population collapsed?"

"Well, the domes were built to last. Maybe, by this time, they had a big stockpile of old ships, equally durable. No reason for them to make a *fast* transit. I mean, just because *we're* so damned impatient doesn't mean Froggy generation ships weren't . . ." Yeah. Right. And any other fairy stories you want to make up.

Ginny said, "Iterate the data, Kai. Might as well see what we *do* have."

"Sure."

The scanner head nodded slowly, peering deep into the gloom, up and down, back and forth. Metz, querulous, whispered, "What a mess."

Then Izzy: "Here it comes . . ."

The dead air inside the little dome suddenly sparkled, a hash of pixie-dust motes, shimmered, shimmered . . . The air went glassy for a second, then filled up with frozen, overlapping ghost images, like an Escher puzzle of interlocking frogs and toads.

Metz said, "Shit. Look at that."

Kai said, "I guess we should've expected something like this. After a few hundred million years, the hyperpipe channels would be choked with data. It doesn't *really* ever go down the drain to Platonic Reality or anything. . . ."

Izzy sighed, turning away, flapping his arms against the sides of his suit in exasperation, a short, sharp snap of sound, muffled by the thin air. "We're not going to get anywhere this way."

Kai stood staring at the shiny eyes of all the dead Frogmen, eyes superimposed on eyes, hundreds of eyes, thousands, millions, an impossible number of eyes, all seeming to look right at him. Waiting. Waiting for me to . . . do something. Something to recall them from the grave. He said, "No. I guess not."

Doc said, "So what're you going to do? Fold up and go somewhere else? What about the things stuck in the glacier?"

Over there, the torch was out now, Mies and Andy crawling inside the hole they'd cut. Going in to retrieve some dead fish or another? What good will that do? Rosie was standing outside by herself, motionless, seeming to stare up at the sky.

Kai said, "No. Ginny? Go ahead and put in a comp call to the spieltier revision. Let's see what it's willing to, um, invent."

"Okay."

Scanner head nodding and dipping, pointing this way and that as the rule-sieves conferred, told it where to look, while every now and then, the particle beam flashed briefly, evoking a puff of pale, hot vapor that curled and dissipated in the watery polar light. The air inside the dome hardened again, and . . .

Interlocking ghosts gone.

Dome suddenly lighting up, shell transparent, bits and pieces of this and that appearing, one thing at a time. Furniture? Maybe. Things like couches and chairs. Things like electronic consoles. Refrigerators? Stoves? Things that stood in their stead, at any rate.

Frogmen. Frogwomen. Frogchildren.

We still don't know which is which, Kai thought. We assume the little ones are the kiddies, because we think they were a lot like us, remembering what the spieltier told us about old Æghôl and Éna, but . . . Blotchy, near-identical gray-green-brown frogs, walking erect, on their hind legs, bulging, expressionless eyes darting this way and that . . .

Doc said, "Interesting how they don't seem to have evolved physically, once they reached their technological plateau. I mean, a few hundred million years . . ."

Ginny said, "Still wearing the same clothes, too. Tropical underpants, floppy suede boots."

Izzy said, "And old-fashioned rebreather masks for going outside."

Must have been pretty fucking cold, going outside in the arctic night, air temperature down to the point where . . . Kai said, "That hoarfrost on the rocks is carbon dioxide, isn't it?"

Doc: "Seems to be. This was the end stage, with a polar cold trap similar to the one on Mars."

Little froggies, Frogmen and Frogwomen, big ones and little ones, conducting some kind of ceremony inside the dome. Two adult-sized frogs stripped naked, strapped to low tables, Kai noting with interest that these frogs lacked the prominent cloacal eversion of the others. It almost looks like they've got nothing you mistake for genitals, or organs of elimination. Terrestrial frogs? Don't know. Not many frogs on Titan. Didn't think to look between the legs of the ones in the park . . .

Other frogs gathering round them now, rubbing against them, rubbing their faces on other frog faces, stripping off their jockey shorts, keeping their boots on, everted cloacas swinging between their legs, glistening in the bright artificial light, seeming to drip . . .

Kai watched with fascination as one of the everted frogs crouched over a strapped down victim, rubbing its cloaca on the eversionless frog's belly, leaving slick, shiny trails behind, trails like the one's the park's population of slugs would sometimes leave on the trunks of the white birch trees.

Ginny's voice, very dry, very cold: "Well. I guess we know which ones are the males, now."

Doc said, "Well. Not necessarily."

Izzy laughed. "Don't be so damned ingenuous, Doc."

"Well . . ."

Kai said, "Just between us boys, rapists are always men." Looking at this scene, I can imagine the tied-down frogs are women, or, rump up, maybe even men. I can imagine myself . . .

Ginny said, "Men are always so naïve about these things. Even when they pretend they're not men anymore."

Metz said, "Look. Up in the sky . . ."

Kai looked, suppressing human cultural intrusions. Well. Of course. Something very much like one of *Mother Night*'s landers, dense violet fire boiling underneath it as it slowed, as it dropped to the frozen, frosty ground, not far from the cluster of little domes. He said, "At least that proves they still had spaceships."

Izzy, voice crisp: "Proves nothing. The spieltier *thinks* they still had ships, that's all."

Kai thought, I *want* them to have ships. I want them to have gotten away. I want so desperately for them to have lived on, to be waiting for us, somewhere, somewhen. The ship settled in a cloud of cold dust, sat canted against the landscape between the glacier and the domes, waiting. Waiting and . . . As they watched, a pocket panel door slid open, long ramp extruding from the side of the ship, tongue of metal extending to the ground beneath the opening.

Izzy said, "Well. I'll be damned."

Standing in the open door, looking down at the domes, seeming to look down at the little group of humans clustered around the nodding scanner head, stood two of the furry black beings, the ones christened Leospiders.

Doc said, "Maybe . . . I don't know. More religious interpolation. Like that business in the mountains."

Kai said, "Looks real to me." But it isn't. The software's just dreaming this.

Ginny said, "There're plenty of contemporary human religions, evolved over the past two centuries, that focus on beings who come down from the sky. Flying saucer cults. Not so different from the cargo cults of the twentieth century."

The two Leospiders were walking down the ramp now, carrying some kind of metal box between them, walking across the intervening space between their grounded spacecraft and the nearest dome. Inside the dome, the Frogmen had finished their task, the two tied-down females lying wet-bellied on the tables, the others, presumptive males, quickly toweling off their cloacas, redonning their shorts, gathering round the inner airlock door, waiting.

Kai said, "You notice the Leospiders don't seem to need breathing gear?"

Doc said, "Neither did the ones in the old story, the ones up in the mountains."

"In any case," said Ginny, "you'd expect gods to be superhuman . . . uh, superfrogman?"

The Leospiders were cycling through the lock now, seeming unperturbed by the change in air pressure and humidity. When they entered, the Frogmen backed away, seeming nervous, the two tied to the table rolling their eyes, trying to look at the Leospiders, at each other, the other frogs.

Especially the little ones, thought Kai. Their children?

The Leospiders put down their metal box, flipped up its lid, backed away, gestured. The group of Frogmen came forward, started taking out bits and pieces of . . .

Metz said, "Looks like old solid-state electronic gear. Is that a portable computer? There was a big collection of them, spanning the first third of the twenty-first century, at Clavius Museum of History and Technology."

Frogmen carrying the . . . shall we call them gifts? What's going on here? thought Kai. In any case, carrying things off into another room, leaving the box empty, coming back empty-handed and . . . The Frogmen, big and little, seemed to array themselves around the outside wall of the little room, to stand motionless, looking at the tied-down females, watching, waiting. The Leospiders shut the lid of their box, shoved it over to the airlock door, turned and walked over to the table. Table or altar? What am I seeing here?

Thin, shrill piping sound, the first sound the spieltier had seen fit to offer them, from one of the Frogwomen on the table. Thin, reedy piping from one of the Frogkiddies, big Frogman hand suddenly clamping over the little one's face, silencing it. The Leospiders came and stood over the two females, seeming to admire them, seeming to . . . look at them, with those empty, reflective silver eyes. Seeming, Kai thought. How much is me, how much the spieltier, and how much real?

"Oh, hell," said Izzy.

Leospider leaning forward, silver claws on blotchy Frog-woman skin. Frogwoman jerking as silver fangs went in, Frog-woman shivering and shivering. Second Leospider leaning forward, jaws and claws flashing in bright artificial light. Another Frogchild piping, really no more than a soft mew, a tiny squeak, abruptly cut off. You could see the Frogwomen's eyes glaze over. See them start to grow smaller and softer. See their skins start to wrinkle as they emptied.

Doc's voice, very soft, "First they rape them. Then they sacrifice them to the gods." A moment of silence, while the Frogwomen shuddered and the Leospiders grew plump and the Frogchildren watched, then, "I wouldn't have expected our first contact to be with nonhumans so very much like us."

Frogwomen now just empty gray-green bladders, draped over their bones, lying dead on the tabletop. Leospiders bowing low to the Frogmen, low to the Frogchildren, fangs put away, narrow black tongues flicking out, licking their lips. One of the Frogchildren seemed to shrink against the wall, the others seemed unmoved.

Metz whispered, "In what human religion do the actual gods come down from heaven in a spaceship to consume the sacrifice?"

Doc said, "Well, the Aztecs . . ."

"Anyway," said Izzy, "they're not really human, so we don't know much about the nature of their symbolism. Besides, the spieltier . . ."

Outside, the engines of the Leospider spaceship lit off, blue-violet fire driving them up in the sky, while, inside the dome, the Frogmen turned away, turned away from the empty corpses, as if they'd ceased to exist, went into the other room, and started looking at their new toys.

Walking alone, following a pressure ridge across the top of the glacier, Kai looked up into the deep black polar sky, where the brighter stars were plainly visible, the suns, scraping low above the southern horizon, not generating enough glare to wash them away. There's almost a red color, red-violet maybe, a subtle hue lying over the blackness. Or behind it. Didn't look that way in the Frogmen's day. I wonder if they would have liked the way it looks now?

Maybe liked it the way I liked the look of the black sky, the dark between the stars, out in the Oort? Those days are beginning to seem like a long time ago. And it sure as hell is far away.

Standing on the edge of a crusty, frozen cliff, Kai could look back down to the surface, to the cluster of ruined domes, like so many bubbles made of pale dust. *MN01* sat beside them, drowned in shadows, orangish light shining through the forward windows of the rover control room, petals flat open on the ground.

Somewhere to go, tomorrow? Maybe not around here. So much else to be seen. So many other places on this big planet. Pholos is a whole world. I keep forgetting that. Easy to forget a planet's more than just a *place*. Too used to the little worlds of the Oort, pieces of rock and ice hanging in space, hanging in the middle of nowhere, one house-sized rock to every cubic AU. Emptiness profound. When I got to Earth, I'd forgotten Titan. Forgotten what it was like to live on a world. I kept thinking of Earth as just one more place. Kept being surprised when it turned out to be a world *composed* of places. Many, many places.

Down there now, inside the lander, Mies would be having his dinner, would be mulling over all the discussions they'd had.

What *if* the Leospiders were real? Real beings, not the mythological demons we've been assuming. Those radar echoes from the highlands. Well. Tomorrow. Tomorrow we'll see. Maybe we *should* go there next. Imagine what it must be like, up on Olympos . . .

The sky up there will be blacker still. Black like the sky of deep space. God, I loved the dark sky. The sky of eternal night. It was a sky in which a lost soul like me could hide. Really hide.

Sometimes, I wonder why I left. I wonder what I'm doing . . . here.

In the long ago and far away, Kai floated in the warm, machine-oil-scented air of Ginny's quarters aboard *ARMP-XQ1450,* listening to the slow whisper of her breathing, looking out through the cabin's ten-centimeter porthole at a sky full of stars. Stars every which way you look, even if you look back toward the Sun. . . .

A *bright* star, to be sure, but from over five thousand AU out, still only a star among stars. . . .

And this place is hardly the Black Sky Country we talk about when we romanticize the lightless dark between the stars. Hardly lightless at all, this landscape of a hundred billion suns . . .

Happy to be here . . .

Floating now above Ginny, breathing in the subdued musk of her scent, breathing in the warmth of her presence while he looked out at the stars. I really ought to go down to the head, get cleaned up. Stavros is on watch. Maybe he'd like a game of checkers and . . .

Wry grin. Yes. Maybe he'd like a crack at me, too. Thin grin. A crack at my crack. Yes, I can tell he would . . .

Poor Ginny. She'd be so jealous if she knew. And she'd feel

bad, too. Wants me to be a man so badly, wishes she'd met me before I . . . Like some old-time man imagining his little lesbian friend would come round, if only she'd bother to sit still while a *real* man threw a few fucks into her.

Image of Stavros holding her close, his hot breath blowing in his ear as he shoved on into her. Image of how it would feel as that short fat prick of his . . .

Odder grin still. Listen to me. Inside my head, thinking about being fucked by a man, I turn into *she*. And then I think about sticking my dick in poor Ginny, think of myself pumping merrily away, think of myself shooting off in her nice little snatch, and I'm *he* again right and true . . .

Goddamn. How the *hell* did I get so confused? Just lucky, I guess. He turned and took a look at the sensor, waited for an instant while the eyebubble core sieved his habits and brought up his offduty menu. A meaningful look at the right item and he was parsing the netsqueal menu, paging through seemingly random news items. Eyebubble knows what I like, has gotten real used to me already . . .

Though they'd only been on their way out for a mere 347 days. Hmh. Bullshit. Rioting in Antarctica. Starving in Taiwan. Hurricanes in Yucatan. Bullshit. This thing, though . . . Society of the Great Sky People dedicate their new power generation facility, laser transmission facility at 0.1 AU to generate so-and-so many terawatts for inner system use, selling at the approved governmental rate, proceeds to be used to fund the society's studies on interstellar colonization . . . Well. How nice.

A quick look through the accompanying imagery, mostly of the society's leaders, some of the new facility under construction, Kai's eyes drawn to the details of beloved machinery . . . Just a standard powerplant and transmitter, of course, and . . . Eyes riveted to a detail or two. A very unusual maser station. That is a particle beam head. Big Oort freighter over there. And what would they be doing with a magnetic sail loop? Only use for those sorts of things was pushing deadweight cargoes back in from the cloud and . . . Mouth suddenly dry.

Kai glanced down at sleeping Ginny and thought about what

they'd been talking about, between fuck and sleep. Talking about how, if they lived long enough, they might one day, themselves, head out, not to the dark between the stars, but to the stars themselves. Another look at the hardware floating in low-solar orbit. And then he started paging down into the ship's database, freshly updated, less than a year ago, when they'd lifted out of Neptune's orbit. The Daiseijin, you see, busy lo these last twenty-five years or so . . . My God. Look at that. Down in the database, there was, in fact, an e-mail address.

ELEVEN

Ginny felt a surge of anger and eyed Doc's pleasant, nondescript face once more, searching. For what? We've known each other for a long damn time, but I know so little about him, really. Image of him suckling at her breast, Kai in the background for the moment, watching as the two of them spun away together. Feeling the warm roughness of the ceiling bulkhead against her back, bouncing slowly off, damp skin adhering slightly, peeling away like sunburn. Everything irrelevant, except for the pulsing of his mouth on her, the slow manipulation of his fingers on her vulva. Just the way she liked it. Where did he learn that technique?

Easy, when it's all lies. How obvious I must be to someone who is so much in . . . control. Reach down to reciprocate, but nothing there. No way to take away any of that control. In control now, damn him.

The corners of his thin lips turned up a bit, a kind of smile. "I can see that the repercussions of Mies's . . . condition are not going to let us just proceed with the mission. His presence is too disruptive, on a number of fronts."

You can say that again. Thinking about the hatred in Linda's eyes. If we don't do something, she might. Not to mention Rosie, who doesn't even know yet.

Not thinking about Kai. No.

"And it's not as if he is making much of a contribution

anymore," Doc said. "He has no more expertise in archaeology than Kai, or me, for that matter."

Ginny nodded reluctantly. "True. The SAE's doing all the work."

"Consider that his planetology knowledge is just an implant, Gin. There's no way to know how reliable his conclusions are."

"He must've done well back on Earth, to get picked."

"Is that so?"

Ironic. Yes, quite right, the selection process seems more flawed every time I come back to it. Image of wise old Hiraoka giving them benediction. The mission should have worked better. Considering its importance, in the scheme of things.

"Okay. I'll concede that we need to do something. But what? We just don't have the manpower to keep watch over him every minute. And *Mother Night* didn't come equipped with a brig."

"Ginny, you're not thinking. There are plenty of options. Easy ones. We could just put him back in his coffin. Or we could space him. Either one would be sufficient to get him out of the way with little fuss."

"Space him . . ." Well, that would certainly serve him right. Brutal, but . . . Kai.

Quiet realization. Doc's giving me the latitude to decide. "Is there a way that he could be . . . repaired?"

"As an autoviroid vector, certainly. Easy enough to restructure his body so that wouldn't be a problem."

She winced. "You mean castrate him."

Doc nodded. "Yes. As far as fixing his personality disorder, though, that would be very difficult. How difficult depends on how fucked up he is inside, how much of his original personality is intact."

"Is it worth trying?"

"You're the captain. I'd say the benefits are limited."

I need Kai most of all. How will he feel when he knows about his dirty little boyfriend? He'll want to take the humane solution of course. Anything else, well . . . "Let's try. They'll need to come back for resupply shortly. Then we'll act."

*   *   *

Floating in her hammock, floating alone in her room now, Ginny watched out an ersatz window, watched bright Pholos rolling by below. Always the same. Always those same meaningless features. I'd be glad for a Martian-style dust storm to blow up, cover the whole world in a dense shawl of opaque yellow fuzz. Imagine that. Clouds of dust boiling up over the dead sea bottoms. Growing, coalescing, gathering force, rising up to fill the empty sky, until the continents would seem whole again, would seem real, mountainous gray landscapes separated by long stretches of soft yellow ocean.

All right. Let it go. Let yourself look at it. You feel like you . . . what? Do I feel like I failed, somehow? It was my job to make sure everything went all right with this expedition. I was supposed to keep everybody straight and on course, because we'd be so far, so very, very far from home.

Not my fault. I didn't pick this crew. I didn't make Mies be a terrorist. David Gilman? Who the fuck is David Gilman? I didn't make Ernesto Matel turn out to be a government spy. I didn't pick the crew. I was picked with it. Picked by Erasmus Hiraoka and his cronies, who . . . Yes. Look at it that way. And who are Hiraoka's cronies? Men and women from the original founding committee, the steering committee now. Among whom we find, most prominently, the name of Doctor Ernesto Matel. A soft whisper of anger inside.

Well. Now that I've decided what to . . . No. Now that *he's* decided what I'll do . . . So the surface team will be back aboard tomorrow. So we . . . arrest Mr. Gilman and lock him up. Then what? Space the bastard? Image of Mies, bug-eyed with terror, struggling and screaming. Tied up, most likely. Tied up in a neat, spacesuitless bundle, bound hand and foot, hog-tied as they say, begging maybe, pleading with us, not to . . .

Will he cry when we lay him in the airlock? Will Mies's eyes fill with tears as we rest him against the cold, cold door? Will he call out to us in a panic-stricken voice as we seal him in? Will we hear his muffled screams for mercy as we lay our hands on the controls, as we . . . Hell, no. As *I*, goddamn it, as *I* put my thumb against the emergency hatch-blow switch, as I lift its cover seal and take hold of the switch, as I . . .

We'll hear, *thump-WOOSH!* Deep pitched, eerie. And, if we're looking through the little window, if we've got the courage, we'll see the door spring open on black space, see the hog-tied little bundle of Mies Cochrane, whoever you are, go tumbling away, end over end, superimposed against the bright landscape of Pholos, sliding by down below.

Oh, Christ.

Remember, back in the Oort, when we had to get Dinny Morrison's corpse out of his ruptured suit? Frozen eyes popping, staring, eyes disfigured by little frozen bubbles. Skin covered with what looked like a petechial rash. Blood in his nose. Blood in his ears. Blood and shit in his underpants.

Tomorrow, then, we'll sit in judgment, then, the nine of us, in judgment of the tenth. I wonder how Sheba would vote, were she alive? I wonder if he fucked her, back on Earth? Did Sheba die because Mies's autoviroids interfered with the suspension machinery? No one's thought of that yet. Certainly not Doc, or he would have said so. If I bring this up, if we look into it and find out that it's so . . . Well. Will I have the nerve to look through the little window as I throw the switch? Will I have the guts to stand there, cold eyed, and see him die?

Maybe. Maybe I can talk Doc into just giving him a little shot. Then we can dump Mies's dead body overboard. Fucking cop-out. That makes Doc the killer. If you're not willing to kill him yourself, Ginny-girl, then you'd better see to it he doesn't die.

Remember kitchen duty, when you were a kid? Mothers and Sisters and Fathers and Brothers laughing as they set you to strangling little cornish hens, set you to cutting their little throats lengthwise and draining their blood into a pan. Can't eat them if you're not willing to kill them yourself, Ginny-girl. Want to be a vegetarian, Ginny-girl? Vegetarians are victims, Ginny-girl. Come here, little Ginny-girl and bend over the sink. I'll fuck you, Ginny-girl, while you kill the little chickens,

Ginny-girl. Teach you how it feels to be a victim, help you make your little choice . . .

Sudden darkness, cold darkness, wind howling softly round you, flash of white light against the white landscape, thermite bomb going *thump-hiss* . . . No. Not a past you want to visit. Not hardly. If you want to visit the past, go someplace more . . .

God. Sometimes, I wish we'd stayed out in the Oort. Out where it's safe. Why the hell did we come in? Why are we *here,* Kai and I? Because we wanted to help Hiraoka save humanity? No. Some will survive the coming crash. Little bands on Earth, on other worlds, even technologicals, out in the Oort, far, far away. Some of those survivors, the Oort groups, perhaps, will one day spread between the stars, hopping from world to little lost world. Someday, their descendants will come here. Someday. But not now . . .

The view outside, from within a standard-issue Standard ARM low-kay, zero-gee EVA worksuit, was stupendous. If you looked hard, focused right off the end of your nose, Ginny realized, you could just barely see a hint of internal reflection. When the light from the ship caught it just right, you would sometimes catch a glimpse of your own eyes, staring back at you out of the depths of black space from just a few centimeters away.

Splendid view. Not that that excused the cheapness of the suits . . . Life's cheap. Police-quality hardsuits are expensive. So sayeth the pezcounters of Standard ARM Accounting. But the view. *XQ1450,* floating a couple of klicks away, was a small, dark bundle of fuel tanks and sparkling blue engine muzzles, life-support canisters and pressurized spaces, all held together by a spiderwork of black girders. Like a dark ghost, her wan worklights barely detracting from the brilliant spangling of stardust beyond, the framework of the sky.

Other superimpositions. Kai floating beside her, almost like a shadow, and Stavros beyond him, both men looking as if naked against space, the pale shine of their transparent glassite suits like bubbles of air trapped against their skins. Transparent to a narrow spectrum of visible light. Opaque like a porthole pane, to everything else.

Just as well. Cosmic ray flux density out here beyond the heliopause is fierce. Not like being down Jupiter's gravity well or anything, but . . .

Slight pang, seeing hairy brown Neanderthal Stavros, half Anatolian Greek, half God-knows-what, reach out to touch Kai, floating close to Kai, keeping their trajectories covalent. All right. Forget it. You can't give him everything he wants. You know that. Gives you the willies when he asks you to stick a finger up . . .

All right. But knowing is not feeling.

Still a few klicks off, but slowly getting bigger, the coal-black lump the ephemeris called Xmass-221z was an irregular shape, a hole in the sea of stars. Sea of stars that seemed so close now. As if you could just reach right out and . . .

Ginny was conscious of her arm stretched out in the darkness, reaching toward the brilliant, silver-gold clotted ribbon of the Milky Way. And, suddenly, the sky receded in all directions, leaving her suspended in a vast hollow of nothing-at-all, leaving her with a faint, nagging swirl of vertigo.

Nowhere to fall. Ends of the universe equidistant in all directions.

But the hard wanting was still there, superseding the faint uterine longing that cramped, ever so slightly, whenever she stopped to think about Kai. To think about . . . to remember . . .

Stars so very far away . . .

Oh, all those childhood dreams. Time in between chores, between interminable adult fuckings. Time spent spinning the accessible portions of the net, far beyond a world in which you chopped ice and washed floors and listened to ideological teachings and pulled your pants down so someone older and stronger could . . .

Remember the day when you found that old serial, spooled into the net by some anonymous spinner before you were born? *Twenty-Third Century,* it was called. A tale of the faraway year

2240, when a group of men and women, cold, clear men and women, seemingly sexless men and women, men and women like a . . . like a band of brothers, worked in secret on a remote moon of Uranus, a moon no one had discovered for some reason. Band of men and women developing, in secret, away from governmental suppression, away from corporate greed, the magic hyperdrive, the secret of FTL travel . . .

Band of men and women boarding their crude starship *Excelsior,* making the trip to Alpha Centauri in a horrific twelve weeks, finding . . .

Ginny looked up and to the left, found Centaurus in her sky, followed its form to brilliant white Alpha. Yes. Still there. Still so very far away. No hyperdrive. No *Excelsior* flying like a magic carpet to the strange double planet Karaharan-Vae, where the solution to all the world's problems waited.

Will we never go?

XQ1450 could get there. Fill her cargo spaces with fuel. Fire the engines to exhaustion. It'd only take forty years or so. Wry smile. Of course, the crew would be dead for the last thirty-six of those years. And, of course, no way to slow down, but . . . No. I'll still be out here, working for Standard ARM, drawing my pay, looking forward to a time when I can buy a hunk of rock somewhere back in the system and retire and . . . Hell. Retire to what? What's left, after work? Marriage and children with Kai?

A quick look at him, floating beside Stavros. Well. At least he can't get pregnant himself. Not yet, anyway. Who knows what technological advances are waiting over time's horizon? But I won't be going to the stars. Not unless . . .

Kai's voice whispered in her ear: "Okay. I did it."

Nervous tremor in her belly. "You're *sure* the recorders aren't listening."

"Positive. I know what I'm doing, Gin."

"And they won't notice we're off line?" If we get caught, if we get caught . . .

"We're not off line, just filtered. Breathing noises. Real-time telemetry . . ."

"Stavros?"

A short laugh. A nervous laugh. "Stop being a scaredy-cat. I looped him out. He won't notice a thing."

"What if he sees your lips moving?"

Giggle. "Jesus, Ginny! I'll keep my head turned away, all right?"

Puff of released breath, followed by a pang. What would the core make of that? What if . . . Shit. Shit. She said, "All right. Tell me."

"It's real, Ginny. Daiseijin was founded just a few years after Erasmus Hiraoka released his *Malthus Revisited* datamatrix . . ."

"I know that one. It was part of the religious tractate used by my family." Cutting that off then. Memory of surfing the matrix data, studying Hiraoka's claims about a coming twenty-third-century doom, doom seeming to rule out, forever, the flight of starship *Excelsior* . . .

Not so bad, as a root cause for a survivalist family, but then there was that other thing, Benjaminh Belleau's *Pygmychimp Goddess* datamatrix, with its suggestion that the future sexual well-being of humans lay in their early introduction to sexuality, its condemnation of the "lonely masturbation orgasm," linked to all sorts of absurd primatology studies over the last few hundred years . . .

Memory of an older Brother fucking her, snickering as he screwed slowly away, making her recite the reference section of *Pygmychimp,* one reference per thrust. . . . Cold shiver. Attention snatched back from the past.

Kai was saying, "They've faked everything up, as near as I can tell. Just for the public, though. The government has to know what they're up to. That petawatt power station they've bought is collimatable to the point where it would have to be licensed as a weapon of mass destruction, subject to government inspection and control."

"So what the hell are they up to, then?"

"Well . . ." A reluctant sigh. "They've been building their membership for more than fifteen years. Putting together a lot of wealth. Most of the members are what's called passive investors. Pay their dues and get a newsletter in exchange.''

"Like a SIG."

"Well, the Daiseijin is posing as a SIG."

"But . . .''

Kai said, "Daiseijin dues are in the form of a tithe, Ginny. A damned big tithe. Every member puts eighty percent of their annual earnings in the pot. No exceptions, no minimum, no maximum.''

Soft sigh of amazement, the pretense of a whistle, Ginny still conscious of her breathing forwarded to the core. Kai had probably thought of all this, was damping down irregularities in the data, but . . .

Kai said, "Since January 1, 2200, when they incorporated, Daiseijin has collected over fifteen billion ceus."

Fifteen billion. In an economic context in which a fully equipped Class D Oort freighter like little-old *XQ* cost sixty-seven million ceus, in which the 30,000-ceu a year salary of a freighter pilot was considered princely.

Kai said, "They just dropped eight billion on the petawatt station. Its income potential is one billion a year for its thirty-year service life.''

"So? Eight years from now they'll starting getting a tidy addition to their income?''

"I don't think that's it." Long silence, then: "I did some calculations last night. You fire a petawatt beam through that little magsail and you'd be able to accelerate a fully-loaded Class A Oort freighter to something over ten percent of lightspeed. You'd be able to brake when you got there using the ship's engines and, maybe, a lightsail . . .''

"A . . . one-way trip."

"Right."

Heart thumping slowly away in the silence between the stars. People live a long time, nowadays. Live a long time, but they're lockstepped into the old patterns of human culture. Used to thinking of seventy years as "a lifetime."

Think about this Hiraoka character. He's, what? Sixty years

old now? Something like that. Once upon a not-so-long-ago time, a man of sixty would be thinking about the grave. People still don't plan for the centuries to come, but . . . "What do you think?"

"I don't know. I think we ought to find out."

"Standard ARM's not going to let you—"

"We're due to stop for refueling at Sandow Station in thirty-three days. I'll send a packet from there. Ask them to leave a squealdrop we can pick up when we swing back through in March . . ."

And Sandow Station belongs to ZeeCorp Entertainment, which won't be monitoring our mail, so long as we pay our bills in good order.

She said, "You really think they're building a starship, Kai?"

Silence, then: "If it was me, I'd be building a starship."

"To what end? Just for the glory of it?"

"I don't know. Maybe they figure they can get the government off its ass if they show the way."

"Fat chance."

"Yeah. Maybe they think, if they show there's money to be made, the corporations will come running."

"Fat chance."

Another silence, then Kai said, "There's one other possibility." A pause, a nervous sigh. "Think about how many Class A freighters you could buy with the money they've got, with the ongoing tithe, with the income from the power station."

Ginny shrugged to herself, did the arithmetic, and said, "What? Maybe a couple of hundred? That's a big merchant fleet, all right, but what's Standard got? A thousand ships? Fifteen hundred? No competition."

Kai said, "Ginny, what if they wanted to send all ten thousand Daiseijin members on that one-way trip?"

Ginny's turn to be silent, silent and thinking about . . . "Holy shit."

"Yeah."

Ahead of them, Xmass-221z had grown huge, blotting out half the stars, demanding their attention.

*   *   *

MN01 was crossing the dark sky now, drifting laterally, rising at a shallow angle above the yellow desert, engines rumbling softly. Mies sat relaxed in the flight engineer's seat, looking up the enormous vertical wall of spectral gray rock. Down here, the granite was weathered, lined with channels and protruding seams of more resistant rock. Standard mountain stuff. But up there, more than fifty kilometers away, the nature of the rock changed, losing its rugged character, gradually forming into closely aligned vertical columns, smooth enough to catch the wan light of A in precise linear highlights.

In a way, it almost looks like the prow of some colossal ship.

A sitting up there, far brighter than a star had any right to be, moving slowly across the remote blackness of space, toward eclipse behind the distant cliff top. No atmospheric scattering, he thought, but the way those columns appear to converge gives a clear sense of scale. He had known intellectually that Pholos's continents were elevated, but . . . No idea any natural object could be this impressive. "Look at it!"

Kai nodded. "Olympos is extremely appropriate. Home of the Gods."

"The Himalayas have nothing on this," said Metz, awe in his voice.

Izzy: "Maybe the wall on Miranda."

"Scarp," said Mies. "*Verona Rupes.*" Silence. Don't Andy or Rosie want to add any commentary? No. Look at them, arms entwined, whispering to one another. Human nature strikes again. Forget about them.

Indigo eyes, opening briefly, then closing again.

No rules-sieves there. Good old evolutionary biology in action.

Kai said. "Just how did this scarp develop on a world like this?"

"Complicated. The Pholotian continents are hard to explain. Lower density planet, but the crust isn't thick like you might expect. Less gravity, that helps. We'll have to rethink—"

"So you don't know," said Andy. "It doesn't hurt to admit it."

People look at you. And, in their superiority, the secure secrecy of their minds, they think they know you.

Soft breath of voice from Reiko-chan: **They always knew me. Men's eyes. Seeing. Knowing.**

Little David: Grown-up eyes. Penetrating. Seeing.

No one ever knew. All people do is imagine they know.

MN01 continued to rise, cliff top growing, edge dropping out of the sky at a steady rate. The atmosphere was thinning quickly, halving every five kilometers or so. Must have been pretty thin up here even in the days of the Leospiders. Suddenly, B slid out, washing their eyes in light, dimming the cliff face by contrast. Still midday, more or less, after all these hours.

Days just as long back then. What must the weather have been like? A giant obstacle like this protruding out of a real troposphere must have disrupted global air circulation big time, blocking jet streams completely. Maybe the analogy should be ocean currents controlled by the continents of Earth. Did they have their own separate weather patterns up here, or was it essentially weatherless? Depends on the temperature profile, more than anything else. If little B could heat the surface of the continents, get air to rise, there'd *have* to be condensation and weather.

I just don't have any model for this.

The lander suddenly leveled out. Kai said, "Coming over the top." Another world: long, low plain of rock rising slowly to craggy foothills, spiky mountains beyond etched in brilliant light. A world of stark beauty, shadows and dark rock, beyond the ability of the suns to lighten.

Going for a landing, already. Kai wants to stand at the edge and look out over the world. And so do I. A little fold of rock, sitting in lemony sunlight, so close to the precipice that he felt a gust of acrophobia. Wanted to say, Are you sure?

Insulting to him. Just keep your peace. He knows what he's doing.

Slipping downward then, jet of air raising wisps of rock dust, long shadow reaching off into the abyss. Down with a thump this time. Must be pretty well consolidated out there.

They got out, then, everyone moving a little faster than normal, fire lit by the magnificence of that view. Watch the shadow come to meet your foot, there. Crowding down to the edge, careful not to make a fatal misstep. Mies hung back for a moment. Almost feeling good, almost feeling whole. He took a breath, then another, of clean, sweet, spacesuit air.

Standing at the edge of the abyss, Kai listened to the silence and wished for the wind. It would seem so . . . right. Wind sighing over the empty gray landscape of high Olympos, desolate black sky hanging over us, empty but for the two suns, the little crescent moons, the . . . If you looked closely, you could see glimmers here and there, high in the sky, away from the bright landscape below, the brilliant yellow-orange blanket of Pholos, stretching away to a far, curved horizon. First magnitude stars. If it were just a little dimmer out there, we could see them.

He stole a glance, back toward the dark gray mountains, massif towering above the rolling black hills of the continent. Yes. There. And there. Little white dots of light, wan and brave against the stygian sky. Which one is that? Regulus, maybe? Doesn't matter.

Down below, the lowlands stretched out before them, like a strangely colored ocean. An ocean, Kai decided, of molten orange sherbet. This is a really beautiful world. I could live here forever. Yes, I could. He glanced at the man beside him, Mies's face, visible through the stiff plastic of his faceplate, impassive, staring at the same lovely landscape. Empty eyed, perhaps.

Eyes, at least, no more than a wet glimmer, crowded by the shadows of his face, reflecting the lowlands of Pholos in miniature, much the same as it was reflected, dimly visible, in the downward curve of his space helmet. Too much reflection there. Got to renew the optical coating on the suits when we get back up to the ship. ''Mies?''

Nothing. Eyes motionless, looking down on the world from on high.

"Mies, I'd like you to talk to me."

Another moment of nothing, then Mies turned. Turned and looked at him, eyes, seeing him, just as empty and unresponsive as they'd been when fixed on inanimate nature. Goddamn you, Mies.

Mies said, "And say what?"

Good question. If I were a real woman, I'd know. Know like magic. Real women have all the words in the world. But I'm not a real woman, I . . . Hell. He said, "I'm sorry I hit you, Mies. I was afraid you were going to hurt me."

Mies stared at him for a second, just stared, then turned away and resumed looking down at the dead sea bottom. After a while, he put his hand up, brought it to the front of his faceplate, stopped with his gloved fingers a few centimeters away, as if about to touch the tip of his nose.

Still hurts, does it?

Finally, Kai heard a pale ghost of a sigh in his earphones. Mies said, "I *was* going to hurt you, Kai. I think I was going to kill you."

Kai felt the hard pang rise up his chest, felt a lump form and subside in his throat. Kill me? I . . . He said, "But . . . why?"

More silence, the landscape still in front of them, the silence profound. Kai thought, It really would help if there was a little wind. Something to make this seem . . . real. I feel like we're suspended in VR nothingness, locked up in some empty theater whose sound system has failed, leaving us to the mercy of its anechoic walls.

Hell. Am I just wishing for theme music, then? Fool.

Mies looked at him again, really seemed to look at him this time, eyes dark wells of . . . something. Empathy, maybe? Am I seeing some kind of real feeling now? Have I called him back from wherever he'd gone?

Mies said, "I don't know, Kai. I really don't know."

And, thought Kai, I'm man enough to understand that. All the swirl of feelings, feelings that we know mean nothing, coming and going in our heads, while our thoughts follow a divergent track, compartmentalized, kept safe from our feelings. We do. Do and die. Without knowing why.

He put out his hand, put it on the man's suited forearm, squeezing gently, and said, "It's all right. Nothing bad happened. I'm . . . Hell, Mies. I'm glad you . . . told me about *Indigo*."

Dark eyes regarding him now, distant again, perhaps. "I'm not. I should have kept my fucking mouth shut." A quick glance, back toward the pile of ruins, to where Izzy and Metz, Rosie and Andy, were unloading hardware from the lander.

Kai said, "The others are going to find out sooner or later, Mies. We've got to talk about this. Figure out what we want to . . . do."

"Do?" Mies's eyes were on the sky now, his face seeming drained, exhausted, seeming . . .

Kai thought, He looks afraid. So. Do I ask him, now, something stupid? Do you love me, Mies Cochrane? Is that what I want to ask him? A hard look at the face, face struggling now to become impassive again. No. I'm not a real woman, no matter how hard I try to pretend I am. I don't care if he loves me, if Ginny loves me, if anyone loves me. I'm just a man, caught in the usual little trap that lies between friendship and sex.

Finally, he said, "Well. We can talk about it later, if you like. Right now . . . I guess we better get back and get on with the work. It's what we're here for."

Mies looked down at him again, and Kai thought he caught a glimmer of a smile. Mies said, "Yeah. It is, isn't it? I keep forgetting." And with that, his face went hard and cold again, eyes alert and intelligent.

Kai shivered inside his warm, protective spacesuit and followed him back toward the lander.

As the six of them prowled the ancient ruins, Kai thought, Like something out of a dream, out of an old Victorian gothic fantasy. Somewhere among the shadows, there should be a tapestry of spiderwebs, the gleam of watching eyes. But there were only old walls, hard, black, plastic walls, walls with a subtle, pebbled texture, covered by a fine patina of gleaming gray dust. Incongruous imagery. But the dust did resemble the patina of a statue, brown bronze turned dark green, as if the gray sheen were a result of chemical changes in the surface itself, rather than a superimposed layer.

Old buildings, then, subtly shaped, surfaces all curved, no hard lines. Very different from the squared-off buildings of the Frogman chalcolithic, not so different from the last buildings of the Frogmen's Final Age. But you can see, you can see even now, with no more evidence than your own eyes, that these buildings are not the product of Frogman hands. Conjure up then, that now familiar image of a black-furred being, all silver eyes and silver claws and sucking silver fangs.

Metz's voice said, "These are *remarkably* well preserved, Iz. We'll get a lot with the SAE, even if we don't invoke the spieltier."

Standing close to a wall, Kai reached out and touched the surface. Smooth and soft, hardly any dust at all. A little bit like touching velvet, despite the intervening substance of the glove. And so . . . eroded looking. You can see, here, the effects of a long, long rain of micrometeorites, the etching force of the stardust's infinite fall.

Izzy said, "This stuff's a lot younger than the ruins down in the lowlands. Maybe six, seven hundred million years younger than the city by the glacier, up at the pole."

Andy: "But it's still more than three *billion* years old! I don't see how it could *possibly* have survived intact all that time. I mean, the weathering alone . . ."

Kai turned and looked at him. Andy and Rosie holding hands. Beyond them, Mies, standing quite still, seeming to watch them. Or maybe just looking past them, looking at all the wonderful old Leospider buildings. He felt the first surges of a warm, supple pleasure, of imagining how nice it must have felt, for Andy and Rosie, to have found each other so soon, to have so quickly erased . . .

Clutching fear, looking at silent, staring Mies. Rosie must

be . . . infected. Now Andy . . . God. Does it work that way?
I don't know.

And Mies said, "What weather?" Arm raised in a slow gesture at the black sky. "It hasn't rained up here in a long damned
time. Certainly since before the era during which these buildings
were erected."

True. Iterative modeling showed that the peculiar shape of the
continental slopes, the Devil's Tower-like fluted sides, erosional
processes more prominent at the base than the summit, indicated
that the continents of Pholos had always protruded above the
tropopause, had been exposed to stratospheric conditions since
the era of planetary formation ended and the Juvenile Terrestrial
Phase had begun.

He said, "It's still interesting that they lasted, Mies." Mies
looking at him now, eyes alert, interested. Ah, scientist Mies. I
see you in there. Another part of you so attractive to me. Rational man. Lovely, rational man.

Izzy said, "I'm not sure I understand *how* they did, Kai. I
mean, impacting microfines and solar-wind erosion's been more
than enough to round off the mountains of the Moon."

Mies said, "There's enough air to intercept most of that.
Besides, architectural structural materials are usually much
harder than your typical basalts."

Kai nodded, reaching out to feel the surface of the wall again.
"True. Of course, granite would wear away, too, just like the
granite up there," he said with a gesture at the low, rolling
hills that lay between the ruins and the first range of towering
mountains. "And the materials we usually build with in deep
space, the various steels and plastics, would simply *evaporate*
over time."

Andy said, "Well, maybe glass—"

Metz laughed, "Supercooled fluid. It'd just flow over the
years and soak into the ground. This's got to be some kind of
very rigid ceramic."

Kai: "Most likely. Anyhow, you could take some of our very
advanced technostructures . . . maybe take a sapphire matrix

engine bell and leave it out on the surface of the Moon. It'd still be there, probably still functional, three billion years later.''

Mies: ''So you think this is still the product of a technology no more advanced than our own?'' Unstated: This is the work of a civilization which had, by then, persisted for more than a billion years, for more than the duration of the entire Phanerozoic. A billion years ago, life on Earth consisted of no more than large heaps of gunk.

Kai smiled. ''Well. I didn't say that, did I? Let's get the scanner head set up and find out.''

Time hardly seemed to pass before Kai was looking at his graphs and tables and imagiform controls, watching the scanner head atop its tripod go through its setting-up exercises, Izzy and Metz fidgeting with their widgets, getting everything just right.

Ginny's cool voice buzzed in his ears: ''All right, we've got everything set up in processor space. You want—''

''No. Leave the spieltier sieves off-line for now. We'll . . . just see what we've got. It'll give us a good idea of what lies in store. An easy way to judge how much is real and how much is software artifact.''

''All right.''

Her voice is so flat, almost affectless, Kai thought. A little bit . . . Pulse of unpleasant realization: A little bit like Mies's voice. Similarities? Of course there are similarities. People choose friends and lovers with similar characteristics. Even . . . even normal people do that. And I've got the two so very *thoroughly* mixed up in my life.

She'll be angry with me, yes she will, even though she knew it'd happen someday . . . even though she knew it'd happened in the past, tacit knowledge, to be sure, but knowledge nonetheless. Sometimes, I must have come to her smelling of other men. Mies, just now, was no more than a shadow nearby, standing unobtrusively behind Andy and Rosie.

Keeping his own counsel, that's for sure. He said, ''Everybody ready?'' Silence. ''Okay, let's do it.'' And a nod to the appropriate control.

Time reversed its arrow, the stars shifting in their courses, and they returned to the past. *A* past, at least, thought Kai. Platonic Reality holds all possible futures and all possible pasts. It's *that* which we access with the synchronoptic analysis engine, what we manipulate with the mathematical tools of quantum holotaxial dynamics, not some *real* past, some real past whose data is recorded only on the structure of the present.

Old fantasies. Old ideas. Time is a dimension, they imagined. A dimension, like any spatial dimension. A place where you've been. Perhaps, a place to which you can return and . . . My God, the buildings look so shiny now.

Mies said, "Fair evidence that there was erosional wear, though we knew already there'd be some micrometeoroid gardening up here in the highlands."

Fair evidence.

Rosie said, "Look at that, will you?" Pointing.

Beyond the glistening, windowless, lightless, motionless, meaningless buildings, lay a pile of rubble. In our time, Kai realized, no more than a mound of solidly sintered dirt. Here . . . the ruin of a Leospider spacecraft, just like the one that had come to the sealed arctic city, come to deliver electronic artifacts and empty the blood of victims. The ruin of a spacecraft allowed to fall into disrepair and die.

Izzy said, "So much for the notion that they built enduring artifacts."

Kai said, "The spaceships must have been very old, even then. This one must have been sitting here, unused, for tens, or even hundreds of millions of years, in the era we're looking at."

Andy: "Why would they stop flying them? I mean . . ."

Mies laughed, a low, humorless sound. "Nowhere to go, my friend. By this time, the Frogmen must surely have followed the Rhinotaurs into extinction."

Rosie said, "So. What did they do for . . . for their *victims,* then?"

Victims? Interesting. Kai said, "What did they do before the Frogmen came? Remember Æghôl and Éna." He sighed, nodded to the appropriate control, and blinked away the past. "All right. So they shut the door and locked it forever. Let's go inside and see how they spent their days.''

"And years. And millennia," said Izzy.

"Eons . . ." said Mies.

Metz said, "Wouldn't it be a fuck of a thing if they're in there now, waiting for us?"

Izzy: "Christ, Metz. Waiting for the bogeyman to go *boo,* are we?"

Standing back, standing beside Mies, Kai watched as Andy and Izzy set up the particle beamer, connected it to the lander's reactor system and . . . Light flashing, sparks cascading as they started to cut through the wall, line of dim, glowing material appearing as the thing worked its way slowly upward and . . .

Izzy muttered a curse and said, "Goddamn not getting through. This stuff is fucking hard."

Metz tittered, "Well, what'd you expect?"

Kai smiled. "Probably carrying away all the heat we can throw into it, reradiating as soon as it's clear of the phase-transition zone."

A brilliant plume of incandescent gas suddenly started blowing out of the bottom of the cut, extinguishing the glow of the material, playing like a beam of transparent smoke over the legs of the particle beamer's tripod, and, excitement coloring her voice, Rosie said, "Still pressurized! Let me get a sampler . . ."

Mies said, "Probably not too much in the way of biologicals surviving the trip through the particle beam. . . ."

Kai: "Might not be much left after three billion years, anyway. . . ."

"Life still survived in the caverns of Pegasus. Why not here?"

True.

As they watched, the plume slowed and the thin line of light went on, extending itself vertically. It turned a corner and cut a meter or so across, started down toward the ground, cutting the shape of a ragged door in red-orange light, got to the bottom, started back across.

Metz suddenly said, "I hope they won't be too mad at us for cutting a hole in their house."

Shit. Funny. Wall falling down. Us coming up to look inside. And out pops a hairy little black furball, all silver eyes and fangs and claws, gun in one hand, little badge in another. So! Interstellar vandals.

Silent *bang.* Something like misty smoke puffed out around the door shape, and the piece of wall jumped out, fell to the ground, slid to a rocking stop beside the beamer tripod, and Andy said, "Glad we thought to set this up on an offset."

Kai had a sudden image of Andy and Izzy lying under the wall fragment, crushed, but Izzy, stepping forward and toeing the thing, setting it to rocking lightly, said, "Can't weigh much more than a kilogram or so. This must be good stuff." In fact, the wall had been no more than a centimeter thick and . . .

Through the hole in the wall was a lightless interior, nothing but darkness, no details picked out by daylight falling in. Just a patch of shiny black floor, that was all.

Andy said, "Well, guys. What're we waiting for?"

Waiting for them to come out and invite us in?

Rosie put on her suit lights and stepped up to the opening, illuminating the interior. Acute disappointment: "Well. Nobody here." A sigh. "Jeez, I guess I really *was* expecting . . ."

Poor Rosie, Rosamunde Merah, biologist, hoping for life when we got to Alpha Centauri, excited by the finds on Atalanta, on Bellerophon, by *real* alien life, relict in the caverns of Pegasus. Here's a whole alien ecology for you, Rosie, complete with not less than *three* sentient species. Only it's gone. We missed it. Them.

Kai walked into the room, looking around. Black shapes by the walls, things like furniture. What sort of a chair would you need, if you were a little furry round thing with four arms, two legs, and a stubby little tail? The thing over by the wall was, more or less, a three-legged stool.

Kai walked over and reached down, reached out his finger

to touch the leatherlike upholstery and . . . "Oops." The three-legged stool came apart, long, flat splinters making a slow-motion fall, a sprawling cascade to the floor.

Like . . . I-ching sticks, thought Kai. Telling our fortune?

Standing in the middle of the room, Mies looked down at his feet, watching dust motes rise to sparkle in his suit lights. "Looks like they didn't keep up with their vacuuming, in the end."

And when was that? How long ago did they leave?

Izzy said, "This place looks deliberately abandoned to me. Unless they lived *very* ascetic lives."

Metz: "And how the hell would we judge what was ascetic to a Leospider?"

Kai said, "All right. Let's get our samples collected, then set up the scanner head. There's bound to be something."

When the SAE came on, the empty room filled up with imaginary light. Light, Kai thought, is what chokes the hyperpipe's throats, pervades the topologically infinite space of Platonic Reality, washing away contrasts, creating the illusion of chaos. Photons falling, ultimately, everywhere we can see, can reach . . .

Walls around them firming up, bit by bit taking on the image of reality, of the way they'd looked in the long ago time of whatever past this scanner head was accessing, scanner head bouncing up and down, nodding and dipping, gathering data . . .

The room suddenly filled up with myriad shapes, ruined furniture leaping back to life first, missing furniture extruding from the floors, falling out of the walls, as the SAE culled stored images from superficial surfaces and brought them back to life.

A chair, a table, something like a lamp. A rack of shelves beside the chair, filled with shadows that might be books. Hard to know. Hard for the analyzer's rule-sieves to know. It can extract the bookcase from the wall's surface, but it can't derive the books themselves from the derived surface of the bookshelves. Limits. Everywhere we look, there are limits.

Rosie said, "This thing over in the corner that looks a little bit like a hammock in a frame . . . its bed?"

Watching an oval ruglike thing uncoil into existence on the floor beside the hammock, Kai said, "Somebody's bedroom, that's for sure. Comfortable, too."

Metz said, "This looks a little bit like my old room on the Moon." A soft sigh. "I loved that little room, with its view out onto the surface. . . ."

Izzy snorted. "Trust you, my dear, to spend half your income on a dinky little surface room, while I got ten times the cubic for a quarter of the price, ten levels down."

"Fucking tunnel rat."

Kai thought, Now, now, boys . . . No windows in here. I wonder what that says about the Leospiders' original lifestyle, back when the world was new? Did they live in tunnels under the ground? Why aren't they living in tunnels in the "now" we're looking at here? I wonder. Not really much room in this cluster of buildings. Could this have been just . . . an outpost?

He blinked away the empty past, the static image of some Leospider's long-lost bedroom, and said, "Okay. Let's move on to the next room. Assuming that thing over there is a door."

Izzy: "And assuming we can get it open."

Metz patted the beamer head and said, "I think the big power cable will reach in here all right."

Kai walked over to the door and took the handle in one hand. Something odd. He tugged and felt resistance. Most likely welded solid, metals and whatnot flowing into each other, melting together over the ages. On one side of the axis, there was a handle, like the handle of an old-fashioned screen door, a shorter rod on the other side, sticking out at an angle from the first, maybe 130 degrees. "Looks like it was maybe for two-handed use."

Rosie said, "Well, the Leospiders . . ."

Conjure that image again. Four arms, two legs. Beady silver eyes. He put both hands on the thing. "Yeah." Subtle *wrongness* under his hands. "Feels like it was made for two, ah . . . two *left* hands."

Image of the Leospiders, with their skinny, hairy black arms. The upper arms, off the ventral surface of the shoulders, had smaller hands, with claws like slivers of chromium-plated steel, on the ends of shorter arms. Shorter than the big, muscular ape-arms mounted on their shoulders' lateral surfaces, arms ending in fat cartoon fingers with claws like straight-razor blades . . .

Mies said, "Give it a twist."

"Which way?"

No way of knowing. Will it break off, if I pull the wrong way? What difference does it make? He took his hands away. Hmh. Nothing like finger knurls, just smooth metal. Knobs on the end offset counterclockwise. Hmh. How tall was a Leospider? A little more than one meter. So this thing was about at shoulder height for them. Meaning they'd lean down, holding it in their left hands and pull . . . *this* way . . .

Andy said, "For chrissakes, Kai . . ."

He grasped the levers and leaned and . . .

Felt the soft clunk of sliding bolts through his hands. The door swung silently open, exposing darkness beyond. Kai looked back at the others and smiled. "They seemed to have built things to last at this stage of their civilization."

Metz snickered and said, "By this time, I guess they had a clue that maybe they needed to."

Mies: "By this time, they must have had some established notion about not wasting resources."

Remember. Remember those stripped ice-moons. Remember the things they did on Pegasus and Bellerophon. Remember . . .

"Why d'you suppose it was only the Frogmen we saw in space? It's clear the Leospiders were . . ." What were they? "The source of the technology, maybe?"

"Only one way to find out."

Kai pulled the door the rest of the way open and said, "Notice the hinges?"

Rosie, standing beside him, said, "Like a spacecraft hull hatch."

Andy: "Like they were expecting the occasional odd blowout."

Mies, close behind them, said, "Things happen."

Kai stepped through the door, light from his suit flooding up onto walls and ceiling, filling the room with long shadows, shadows cast by the piles of rubbish that heaped the floor here and there. "I guess they didn't take everything, after all."

Izzy stepped up to a nondescript pile of pieces and prodded them with a booted foot, watched bits of black, metallic ash flake away and crumble. "Three billion years. You know, if they'd built things just a *little* bit better . . ."

"I guess," said Mies, "they weren't expecting us."

Rosie said, "I wonder why not? Did they think they had the answer to Fermi's Paradox?"

You stand under the empty black sky, stand on Earth, looking up at the heavens of night, you float among the fixed stars, out in the Oort, and you wonder, you really wonder, thought Kai, just what the hell's keeping them. "The fact that there were three intelligent species on Pholos ought to have made them assume the skies were full of minds like their own."

Mies: "Maybe not. There're plenty of people in the world who don't seem to believe there're minds behind other people's eyes, despite the evidence of their own existence."

Startled, Kai thought, a little *cogito ergo sum* in there, Mr. Gilman? What do *you* believe? Nothing? Something? Why won't you say? Mies just staring at the rubble on the floor of the room, eyes shiny marbles embedded in his face. He said, "Let's get set up. If there's data here, we might as well take a look at it."

This time, when the room filled with misty *zeitsenschein*, it filled as well with things and beings, all motionless, pristine, crystallized out of thin air and swirls of dust. Kai felt his breath catch in his throat, waiting for the exclamations, the comments of the others, but heard nothing.

Walls now covered with smooth, dark plastic. Not black, no, but almost black. Dark brown, perhaps? Very dark brown. We still know nothing about what spectrum may be visible to those silver eyes. Eyes unlike our own, thought Kai. Eyes unlike the lowland, blue-sky, surface-living eyes of the Frogmen and the Rhinotaurs.

Six little furballs sitting around the room, sitting perched on six three-legged stools, before six consoles of instruments. Like air traffic controllers. Like bored spacemen monitoring the approach traffic to some little asteroid base or another, maybe way out in the Oort, or in the Kuiper Belt, perhaps. Back in the Piazzi, they'd be busier than this. . . .

One furball leaning forward, silver eyes on a pane of glass that must be a viewscreen, small hands of his gracile ventral arms resting on some kind of keyboard—the image was a bit blurred there, so you couldn't really make out the keys themselves—robust lateral arms hanging by its sides, hands palm-down on the floor, fingers splayed, silver claws extended.

"Doc? Ginny? What've we got in real-time terms?"

Doc's voice said, "It's a little hard to tell. There's a fair amount of data spooled onto the timebind reel, but the AI has made no attempt to do anything with it."

Ginny: "I don't think there's enough there to produce anything . . . real."

"Dump it down the sorter."

The scene before them burst into activity of sorts, the screens in front of those empty silver eyes filling with a fuzz of static, the hands of the one motile Leospider blurring with his keys. Nothing, thought Kai. A loop of no more than a fraction of a second.

"Well . . ."

"Goddamn it," said Mies, "just invoke the spieltier and get it over with!"

A moment of silence, watching the static roll and swirl, then Kai said, "Concur. Do it."

Doc: "Done."

So we let this shit loose on ourselves again, not knowing if it's real or fancied. If I could go back, if the radio link were days, even months, instead of years approaching a decade, I'd call home, make them roll those programmers' asses to the microphone and fucking *explain* just what they had in mind. . . .

The room wasn't changed, not much, only a detail or two here, pictures on the walls and . . .

Andy said, "All the pictures are of Frogmen. No Leospiders. No Rhinotaurs."

Rosie said, "Memories of a lost love."

Mies: "Memories of a lost dinner? I don't think so."

Izzy said, "Well, the Frogmen must have been extinct, by this time, for longer than they and the Leospiders coexisted and knew about each other."

Metz said, "Maybe they preserved the Frogmen, too, just like they preserved themselves."

The fragments are starting to fit together, thought Kai. Horrific image. Somewhere, somewhere in this late, airless, Leospider world, were there Frogmen still, living in cages, naked like animals, bred like animals, living out their short, miserable lives, like chickens in a meat factory, but, unlike chickens, knowing, horribly knowing, what was to come?

Image of Frogmen shivering, crying, waiting for the fangs.

Hell. Maybe chickens know, too. What if they do? Do I care?

Chicken lore: They come with the dawn, put an end to your song. Cut off your head, let you run around dead . . .

Mies said, "This is . . . some kind of library, I think. Look at what's on the screens."

Spieltier software thinks it is, anyway. Something like that. Screens full of complex images, images of . . . the air over the TV screen, antique flat screen like something from the dawn of the Third Millennium, started to fill with symbols and words.

Izzy said, "I guess the AI thinks it can do the same thing here that it did down in the Frogman city."

Right. Software fancies it can pull the wool over our eyes and magic Leospider words out of thin air. Well . . . the particle beamer started to flash delicately, coils of gray smoke rising here and there around the room, scanner head drinking them down and spooling them up to the software packages aboard *Mother Night*.

Look around now. Do what Mies told you. Look at the screens. What the hell is going on there? Images. Symbols. Leospider typing on his keyboard. Doing what? Taking notes? What for? How did they busy themselves, over all eternity? Why did they stay *here*?

No answer, of course. Not yet. Maybe never.

One of the screens suddenly flared, bright blue-violet-white, exploded to fill the room, exploded into their eyes.

One day <the spieltier whispered> Vermilion-the-historian-of-long-lost-chert-flakes prowled by the edge of the world.

<Visual image> Leospider of lustrous black fur, rainbows shining in his hair, sexually alluring semimale <you could see the sucking organ on his thorax if you looked closely, peeking through the hair> walking slowly, bipedally, alert, full of life, along a bare, gray cliffside.

Vermilion plying his trade. Leospider bending, examining the chert flakes, measuring them, taking notes on his powercomp, filling the spools with trackless immensities of data.

Vermilion whispering to himself: Words a thrum that vibrated his lovely throatpouch.

<Because you are a quondam female, this tape prescribed just for you, you feel a longing in your breast, longing to grapple with Vermilion, feel his sucking organ on your breeder nipple, feel him draw forth your substance.>

Vermilion bending to touch this chert and that one, meaningless black flakes to you. But the tape lets you know *he* knows, this expert who's measured cherts for a thousand years and more. This one made by the frost, you see. This one made by the random footfall of some animal or another. This one here, rubble from some Leospider toolmaker a million years dead, from the days when all we knew was the working of stone.

<Imagine your substance flowing into him, tides of lovely light reeling through your brain. Imagine him carrying it away to his quasimale lover, sharing your substance, the two of them processing it, finding a macrofemme, impregnating her, macrofemme wandering away with the seed of your child and theirs.

Maybe the macrofemme will search *you* out, every quondam's dream and . . .>

This chert here, Vermilion's charming thoughts exposed, exposed for you alone, so sweet, so . . . knowing.

This chert here, so different from any I've known before. Mmmm-hmmmm . . . throat pouch thrumming, an unnatural touch of hunger, as if he were sitting down to sup at the throat of some farm-bred blood animal or another.

<How odd, you feel, though in the real world you know the truth about this strange mix of sex-hunger and food hunger. But how *very* odd you feel, just now, in chert-Vermilion's long-ago discovery time.>

Vermilion holding the stone blade to his lips, black flint sliding along silver fangs, lovely, shivery grating sound. That *smell* . . .

Vermilion standing, transfixed, at the edge of the world.

<View downward, from the heights, sky dark indigo overhead, landscape bright down below, the upper surface of pale, diaphanous white clouds, heavier clouds on the low mountains, snow down there, though few bother going down to the fetid depths below, to the wet heat of the lowlands, which sprawl pale green and bright yellow, rolling all the way to the banded blue sky of the horizon.>

<Jump cut, most likely intended by the production team?>

Vermilion-the-historian-of-long-lost-chert-flakes prowling through the hot, suffocating winds of a lowland blizzard, following his nose. Following, following, delicious stone blade tucked away in a pouch with his specimens, his tools, his powercomp.

Why am I down here? His throat pouch thrums, thrilling you, Vermilion speaking his thoughts aloud for your benefit, and, ah, how you feel your breeder nipple swell as you hear him speak. Vermilion asks himself, Have I gone mad? The delicacy of his thoughts, his self-awareness, so appealing . . .

<Leospider standing still in the snowstorm. Standing still in the snowstorm.>

What could these things be?

Two forms lying almost still in the heaped white snow.

Animals, of course. Lowland animals. There are plenty of highland animals, most covered with fur like the Leospiders themselves. These things. Bare. Radiating heat like they were bottomless wells of energy. Lowland animals, freezing to death in the heat of the storm. Lowland animals . . .

Frogman opening its weird, bulging, watery eyes, staring at him. Vermilion smelling a Frogman smell. Pang of hunger stabbing into you, just as its stabs into him, that irresistible smell in your nostrils.

Vermilion taking up the little Frogman, listening to it bleat, tongue now sensing the heat of its veins. Fangs probing through soft, incredibly soft gray-green skin . . . *pop*. Flow of blood as you suck.

Explosion of light in your soul.

Explosion, like an explosion of sexual pleasure.

But . . .

Better. Oh, so *very* much better . . .

Mmmmmm-hm-hm-hmmmmmmm . . .

Blue-violet light swirling then, scene of a mountain snowstorm swept away, whirling down the drain, back into the flat screen. Room returned to its previous aspect, six little furballs sitting in front of screens and . . .

Mies said, "Look at that one. The one in front of the . . . story we just . . ."

Furball sprawled in her chair, just now. *Her?* Well, that's how the spieltier saw it. Quondam female sitting in front of a black screen, robust arms fallen to the floor, gracile arms curled in her lap. There was a thing like a black nipple protruding from her chest hair, dribbling some grayish fluid . . .

Izzy said, "All right. So the Leospiders had something like pornography."

Kai said, "Maybe it was just a cooking lesson."

Rosie, voice dry, said, "Doesn't look like a cooking lesson to me."

Quondam female reviving at her console, looking down at the mess she'd made on herself. Doesn't seem too concerned, though, not looking at any of the others or anything. She got up, blanking out the screen with a gesture, walked across the room, stooped . . .

A hatch opened in the floor, pale neutral light spilling up from below, the quondam female stepping down, disappearing, hatch closing over her head. The floor where the hatch had been seemed smooth again, no sign of the door. Kai said, "Hell. Mark that." Door outlined in red on the floor. "Let's get out of harness and see if it was real." Leospider world suddenly collapsing in on itself, beings and machines once more piles of dark rubbish.

Eventually, when the possibly historical door's locus was a ragged hole in the floor, ragged-edged glow fading, the six of them stood looking down into the darkness. Interesting, thought Kai. So the floor's no thicker than the walls, suspended, flat and level, over a void. All right. We could build things like this as well, especially in this gee. Waste of time, though. Build floors out of cheap, abundant stuff like rock.

"So," said Mies, breath puffing out, inflating his cheeks. He looked up, away from the hole in the floor, looked right at Kai. "Is this where she went, or was that a software fantasy?"

Andy said, "Yeah. Could be nothing more than foundation stone down there."

"Or a kilometer-deep pit," said Metz.

Kai shrugged. "What difference does it make? Easy enough to find out." He tightened the focus of his helmet light, shining its beam down through swirling airborne dust . . . must be very fine dust, floating on the currents of a thirty millibar atmosphere . . . shined it down through the dust, illuminating a flat patch of floor.

Mies said, "I guess those things are the stairwell pediment."

Rosie: "How would the spieltier have guessed there were stairs under the floor?"

"It didn't," said Izzy. "If you replay the loop, you'll see she just went down the hatch. We never saw what was below. Spieltier didn't know."

"Still," said Metz, "it *looked* like she was going down a flight of stairs. You know . . . down, stop, down, stop, down . . . the movement of her head."

Right. Left to its own devices, the spieltier would just figure that, when you went down, you went down steep steps, a ladder, something. So what're we looking at, really? The pediment of a chute? Not a fireman's pole. The SAE probably would've detected that. "I wonder what her name was."

Mies, quizzical: "You think she was real?"

"Well, the symbol of someone real, a whole class of some-ones. The, uh, idealized *quondam female* who was the target audience for the Leospiders' flip side to Æghôl and Éna."

"Maybe."

Rosie said, "We can stand here and guess until the fleet shows up. Let's go down. It's only a few meters."

Kai watched her teeter on the edge of the hole, watched her step off into space, drift downward . . . Despite a few years on Earth, my visit to Mars, I *still* have this sense that she's acceler-ating under power, driven by thrusters. *Falling* . . . when you fall, it's gentle, slow, .07 gee or less. A fall is only dangerous when it's a long way, and only then when you're wearing an unpowered suit or . . .

Brief memory, crawling across a deck that throbbed under-foot, rocket engines rumbling through the structure somewhere far away. Where? When? I remember. When the eyebubble core of old *XQ,* old ship, old information systems crudely upgraded by Standard ARM on the cheap, failed under acceleration, when *somebody* had to get down below, get to the main waveguide trunk.

I remember, in extremis, my surprise at the raw thunder of Ginny's footfalls as she jumped from her chair and *ran* from the control room. All I could do was crawl along the floor in her wake, while Stavros, Nereïd born and bred, could merely lie there and whisper, flattened, helpless under .8 gee.

Hardly more than we experience here and now. He stepped off the ledge and fell, years of space experience brushing aside one small, queasy moment, landed on the balls of his feet, crouching, looking around.

Already beside him, Mies said, "Imagine what the spieltier will do with this."

"I . . . hardly think we'll need to invoke it."

Darkness receding in all directions, the lights from their spacesuits barely able to penetrate the gloom, to light up a hangarlike cavern, cavern cluttered with . . . things.

Metz, voice high and breathy, said, "Like new, Izzy! They look brand *new*!"

Over here, beyond the edge of the stone platform on which they stood, standing like soldiers in a row, were small, conical towers, each a couple of dozen meters tall. Windows in the nose, thought Kai. Just like the Leospider spacecraft we saw in the arctic scene.

"What's that thing beyond them?" asked Rosie. "The big cube shape."

One side open, in its maw, what looked like a half-finished spacecraft.

"I don't understand," said Andy. "If they were still *building* spaceships . . ."

Beyond the black-box spaceship factory, another black box, small mountain of cindery boulders beside it, clutched in the embrace of four mechanical arms. Arms, Kai realized, very much like the four arms of a Leospider. Now, what did this one build? Ground cars. Airplanes? Did the Leospiders use airplanes? Why would they bother? Even when there was still enough air up here to . . .

Mies, walking beyond the boxy shapes, brought his helmet light to its tightest focus, shining it away into the distance. "This place goes on for kilometers. I guess that deeper shadow is a far wall. There're things like tunnel mouths in the floor, all over the place."

I guess, thought Kai, suddenly feeling overwhelmed, that they did live underground, after all.

Metz: "Izzy. Kai. Come look at this."

The thing next to him was . . . what? A ghostly outline

shape? A bell shape made out of glass so fine and clear, so nonreflective, so optically perfect, that it was almost invisible, not just in the gloom, but in the full glare of their suit lighting systems.

Kai reached out and felt it. Hard. Not glass, of course, we know that. He tapped the thing with one fingertip, then reached out with his other hand and felt, through the material of his suit glove, the delicate vibration go on and on.

"So . . ." said Izzy, "you're the techie. . . ."

Kai su, teknon? He shrugged, and said, "An engine, of course. You can see the shape of the combustion chamber, expansion bell optimized for vacuum thrust. Up here, the outlines of a hot-bleed-cycle pumping system, used to pressurize the fuel injectors. . . ."

Lovely, lovely machine, orders of magnitude better than our sapphire-matrix nuclear engines. Inside those black boxes, the remains of vacuoles. Vacuoles that once built these machines and more, with a nanotech possibly, *quite* possibly, better than our own. I wonder. I wonder if the little biots remain. I wonder if the black boxes still function. Can we coax them to build us one more Leospider spaceship?

A small frown. No, probably not, silly Maeru kai Ortega. The nanobiots' programming was far, far more delicate than the mere *things* they built, built to last. Cosmic radiation will have erased their instruction sets long, long ago.

Izzy said, "So, should I start setting up the scanner head, Kai?"

Mies put his hand on Kai's arm, looking at him intently. "Maybe not."

"But . . ."

Kai stood still, luxuriating in the thrill of Mies's touch, at the same time wondering just how he'd gotten to be such a fool. Really . . . How badly did I ever want to become a silly girl? My God. He smiled, made sure he was smiling at Mies, and said, "I don't think so, Iz."

Mies let him go, and said, "I think we've proven, beyond the shadow of any conceivable doubt, that the Rhinotaurs and

Frogmen and Leospiders came from Pholos, that this system was the site of a civilization as grand as anything we ever imagined. A civilization that persisted for something like one billion years." One billion, to our own paltry few thousand.

Kai said, "I guess we have to conclude this is important enough that we will now set aside, permanently, *Mother Night*'s original exploration program."

Rosie: "But the Daiseijin—"

Mies said, "There are no longer any habitable planets in this star system, Rosie. The fleet won't be coming."

Sudden, hard words crystallizing inside. The fleet will not be coming. Yes. Yes, I knew that. Knew it already. But, saying it again, I . . .

Andy, horror in his voice: "Not coming? But, with the chromobraking shield ruined, we're *trapped* here."

Trapped. Not going home. And if the fleet doesn't come, then Sheba Zvi is dead forever. "I'm sorry, Andy. Yes, we're stuck here. And we've got a damned big job to do, all by ourselves."

Izzy, voice soft, said, "Oh, I don't know, Kai. They might want to send another ship or two, diverted from the main fleet. Send a handful of *real* scientists, maybe."

Real scientists. Real. Unlike us. Why the hell are we here? I try not to wonder anymore. A glance at Mies. Somewhere, back up the line, there is a flawed filter, whose sieve picked a wrong crew, indeed.

Mies said, "It'll be all right. Until that day comes, we've got work to do."

Kai nodded, putting away all his fears. "We might as well do it right, then. Let's forget the spieltier for now, and the SAE along with it. We've got conventional instruments up on the ship. We can . . . take samples up, do a preliminary workup. Decide what to bring down, set up a research camp here, and begin digging in."

Metz said, "And what about us? What about the synchronoptic analysis engine?"

Kai shrugged. "Time enough for that when we've found out

all there is to find out by conventional means. At least, it'll give us a better base on which to interpret, ultimately, whatever else the scanner can dig up.''

"Including," said Mies, "our friend the spieltier sieve."

Long day. Long, long day. Mies closed the coldbox and latched it tight, then strapped it into its place in the cargo hold. Business of the day done, time to go . . . home. Unwillingly. I don't want to leave. Don't want to have to deal with Ginny. Or Doc, for that matter. If it could only be me and Kai, exploring this planet forever.

Me.

A slight, startling shock.

You know. You *know* who's talking, Mister Mies.

Implants decay. They always decay. What's left after the artificials die? Is it me? How would I know? Memories still in place, of course. Not just the natural memories that made up whatever was left of David Gilman, lost child grown up into a lost adult. The rest of it still there. Bits of personal and scientist and fuck-me girl . . . because I went places as them and . . . did things. *Things.* Cold shudder. Things.

We won't lose it all, he said. When the hypnopaedic pathways decay, they'll leave behind memories of their own. You'll . . . remember having remembered.

I'm becoming someone new. Wholly new. I . . . like that. Across the way, the ruins still standing, black and hard and permanent. Waiting since the dominant form of life was the bacterium. Still waiting.

"Mies, get over here." Andy's voice. "We need some help stowing this stuff." Getting a bit peremptory, aren't we, Andy? Nothing like a girlfriend to buck up your confidence, give you the will to dominate others.

Kai and Andy had pulled out the entire complement of electronic gear and were repacking it slowly and carefully, making sure every piece was securely fastened in its holder.

Kai looked up at him as he approached. "We don't want to have this stuff rattling around during the launch."

So, mindless work. Not his particular cup of tea, but working side by side with Kai was different, somehow. His pleasure at getting something done right, no matter how trivial, was contagious. He took a seat on the hatch door next to the man.

"When we come back I want to run a scan on some of the more resistant rocks around here. I'm still having difficulty picturing the external world during the period of the Leospider habitation."

Kai looked up from his task for a moment. "Easy enough to do. What don't you understand?"

"Well, as far as the meteorology of ancient Pholos, I don't understand much. It's easy enough to just picture this planet as a terrestrial analog, not worry about the differences. But look. If the Leospiders were living up here back then, it implies a lot of things that I just can't explain. Even in the warmest, wettest climate allowable, it would be cold up here. Very, very cold. And dry."

"Could have been inhospitable even for them," said Andy. "They were living underground, after all, in pressurized habitats."

Kai: "But there's a lot of evidence they lived up here in the distant past, too, before their technology developed."

Rosie, from inside: "Think of that fur. They were clearly warm-blooded, which makes them very adaptable."

"A simple answer," said Mies, "would be to suppose that they evolved in the lower portions of the continents, not far from sea level, and moved higher as their technologies allowed them to. But that supposition produces other questions, like why."

My words. Words all starting to make sense. Becoming *my* words. Mies felt himself flush with pleasure. My God. I'm becoming a real, live boy. A little self-directed mirth. Yes, you even have that in you. Kai's going to like a man who . . . when did I start thinking about him that way?

I can't *infect* him after all.

Were those Indigo eyes opening on the dark? I can't tell. I can't tell anymore.

The Indigo seduction rule-sieve came first. It is the least integrated. When it decays, it will decay first and . . . more completely than the others.

The others? Me. *Me,* for God's sake.

Kai said, "Okay, that's it. Let's get this bucket off the ground."

The others, waiting in orbit. But we're coming back. Coming back. Kai and I. I feel happy. Frightening. What if this feeling goes away? What will I do then?

When the ride to orbit was over, Mies sat in his seat, staring out the forward windows at *Mother Night.* Unchanged. The ship is unchanged, hanging against dark and starry space above yellow and gray Pholos. Why was I expecting it to be different?

The ship grew larger as Kai carefully closed the distance between them, seeming to rotate as they came around toward the forward end, drove in toward the docking adaptor at the neck, ship foreshortening, glistening blue muzzles of the nuclear engines turning away, becoming occluded by the rounded bulk of the fuel tanks.

Computers doing the driving really, Kai just managing their task.

I expected it to be different, because *I* am different. A sudden thrill. Tonight. Tonight I'll tell him and . . . Shadows suddenly filled the window as they swept in under the command module's chin. Then a soft shudder, the cessation of forward movement.

Kai said, "Contact." Lights on the control panel. A gentle shiver. "Hard dock. Pressure equalization." A remote hiss filling the cabin. "Welcome home."

Home? Is that what this is? Mies commanded the chair to let him go, floated up above the control console, turned to glance at Kai and . . . Looking at me. That light in his eyes. My God, he *knows!*

How could he know? You're just imagining things. Stop fantasizing.

But he knows. I swear he knows.

In a few minutes, they had the connecting hatch open, were floating back into the bright light of the ship, all the others going first. Izzy and Metz, bumping together, griping about the trip, saying how glad they'd be to get back to their little rooms and the showers and decent shipboard meals and . . .

Andy and Rosie, floating through the door, hand in hand.

Happy. I'm happy for them. My God, I'm sorry, Rosie. How can I make things up to you? Cold cramp in his stomach. The autoviroids. God. They'll have to be told.

Indigo eyes, hardly more than a flash against the darkness now, like heat lightning far beyond the horizon.

Kai floated out the door then, momentarily blocking his view through into the docking adaptor's central node. He's facing Ginny now. What will she see? Does she know? Of course she knows! Remember what happened the last time we came up.

Not me. I swear it was not me! How can I tell them? What story can I . . .

You goddamned fool! Just tell them the truth!

Filled with fresh determination, Mies pulled himself through the hatchway, almost eager. That's it, he thought. Confess. Confess it all now. Right now. Ask for their help. My God, these people are your friends. *Surely* they'll help, they'll find a way to . . .

Kai. Kai will help. Kai has always helped. He'll . . .

Doc's voice boomed: "David Liam Gilman. You are under arrest."

Doc and Ginny, anchored across the node from the lander's docking hatch. David Gilman? A momentary surge of bafflement. What's that thing in his hand?

Doc said, "Put your hands on top of your head."

It's a policeman's pistol. Gas propellant. A variety of loads. Drugs. Solid. Explosives.

Agony. Mies thought, Oh God. Don't leave me now. *Please . . .*

Ginny snarled, "*Now,* Mies!"

Indigo eyes opening, full of rules and suggestions, urging him to act. QUICK! QUICK NOW! BACK INTO THE LANDER! YOU KNOW HOW TO FLY IT! YOU CAN *ESCAPE,* IF ONLY YOU *ACT!*

Wailing. Wailing. Little David: No, don't *hurt* me, Dah! I'll be good! Please! *Please!*

Reiko-chan, sobbing. **I was dead. You told me I was dead . . .**

Big David, dry, laconic: Well, of course. I'm a fuckup. I've *always* been a fuckup. Just what the hell did you *expect?* Assholes.

From the forward hatch, Kai shouted, "What the hell is going on here?"

Slowly, very slowly, Mies let go of the hatch frame and laced his fingers together on top of his head. Sweating, he thought. My head is sweating. All the others now, frozen. Frozen in place. Not the people in the node. No. The people in his head. Useless. All of them useless. Big David is right. Just fuckups, every one of us. A band of goddamned useless fuckups.

Ginny turned and looked at Kai. "I've got some things to tell you," she said. "Things you're not going to want to hear."

Kai floated silently for a moment, then turned and looked at Mies.

See? See the sorrow in his eyes? That's what you just lost.

Exhaustion suddenly flooding his voice, Kai said, "Well. I already know about the autoviroids, Ginny."

Doc's gun wavered for a moment, as if, possessed by a will of its own, it wanted to turn on Kai. "Maybe," he said, "you'd like to explain?"

Kai nodded slowly. "Sure."

Floating in his quarters aboard *Mother Night,* Kai hung in the familiar nongrip of zero-gee, keeping himself steady with an occasional touch against wall, ceiling, or floor, hardly conscious of the practiced movements that kept him in one place, staring out through the porthole, not bothering with any senseless VR displacement. Good to look down on a real world, look down on Pholos of the wonders, Pholos where . . .

My God, what will happen now? It's all come apart, come to pieces in our hands. . . . What should I do? What's Mies feeling now, locked away in his makeshift prison? Mind reeling, reaching this way and that, grasping at straws, erecting straw men and tearing them down, thinking, thinking . . . no conclusions. You should've known, Maeru kai Ortega, that it would come to this, come to something like this, when he told you, told you . . .

But all the memories were of that single, unexpected night, in the survival tent, out under the dark sky of a lost world. Mies suddenly upon you, just the way you wanted him to be, just the way you imagined . . . Jesus. You fool. You silly little fool.

I cultivate, in myself, not being a woman, so much as being a woman I imagine must exist, somewhere, crafted from all the allegories, all the images, all the fantasies of Woman. I cultivate the icon, not the thing itself, because the thing itself is beyond my reach. I . . . Fool. What good does this do? The time for childish fantasies is past. *Think!* But no thoughts would come. Only the empty rolling vistas of Pholos, bright and dark, rolling from day into night and back again every couple of hours.

Finally, the door hissed open behind him. Hissed open, then hissed shut again, having admitted someone, no doubt. Kai found himself unable to turn and look. Unwilling to turn, just continuing to stare out the window at the bright world. Such lovely yellow-orange deserts . . .

There was a hand on his shoulder, pulling him away, and Ginny's voice said, "Kai."

Strange. I've gotten so used to her being just a disembodied voice on the ship-to-shore radio link, in just these very few days. Is she no longer real? A ghost? A . . .

She turned him around, anchored to the overhead by one hand, one leg stiff against the floor, the other arm rotating him in space and pulling him erect, so that their reference vertical occupied the same frame. "Kai." Earnest look, but still rather . . . cool? She said, "I'm sorry it had to happen like this. Believe me—"

"I believe you, Gin. It's certainly not your fault." But then, whose fault is it?

Pained look in her eyes, a furrowing of her smooth, dark brow. Wondering the same thing? She said, "You should have told me."

"Told you what?" Be ingenuous, then, hold false naïveté in front of you like a shield.

"Told me that he . . . that you . . ." Stuttering, then, looking away.

Am I the cause of this much misery for her? My God. He pulled her in, reeling himself against her chest, since she was the anchored one, holding her in his arms, snuggling into the side of her neck. Tried to think of what to say next. Came up with nothing.

She pushed him away, held him at arm's length, seeming to peer into his eyes. As if, he thought, suddenly bitter, eyes are not capable of lying. What do women see when they look into men's eyes? Why don't I know?

She said, "I guess . . . I guess I'm not angry at you, Kai."

Why not? You should be.

Ginny just floating there, bobbing gently in the air between floor and ceiling, anchored by foot and hand, seeming to stare at me. Questioning. Questioning. What the hell is she trying to get out of me? If she'd just *tell* me what to say, I'd fucking *say* it. I'd . . .

She said, "Why are you angry at *me,* Kai? Because of Mies?"

Startled. Angry? Am I angry at her? I guess so. Starting to talk myself into anger, at any rate. . . .

She said, "This isn't about us, Kai. I've known all along that I couldn't be . . . everything to you. I knew about Stavros, about . . . all the others. Most of them, at least. I . . ."

A flush on her cheeks now, but not looking away. What is this all about? Is it mainly about my sleeping with Mies? Isn't that irrelevant in the face of . . .

She said, "It's easy to see why you were attracted to him, Kai. He was perfect for you, chopped into so many little pieces like that, first this man, then that, none of them so complete as to be a threat. Each piece representing something that you wanted.''

Kai feeling nettled, then, subjected to her analysis. Who let *you* in on the big secret of what it's like to be a man? Even *my* sort of man.

She shook her head and said, ''I'm sorry I said that, Kai. Sorry if I'm offending you. But . . . I know what it's like. I'm all in pieces, too, just like you, just like Mies. And drawn, like magic, to people in smaller pieces still.''

Another little smudge of anger darkening his thoughts. Am *I* then in littler pieces than you? Is that how you feel, Ginny?

She said, ''That's what Andy was all about for me. I just felt so damned sorry for him.''

Tiny clench of adrenaline, released deep within. *Andy?*

She smiled a quirky smile, half amused, half upset. ''You didn't know?''

Andy . . . Hard realization. ''Oh, my God, Ginny. The autoviroids.''

She shrugged. ''I didn't know. You didn't tell me.''

A gusty sigh. It had to have happened before Andy came down to the surface. It's not my fault. Not my fault. ''I didn't know yet, when . . .''

''But, when you did know, you didn't say anything to Rosie.''

Pang of memory. No. But I remember wondering if I should. He said, ''She'd already been sleeping with Mies. It didn't matter. Besides, are we even sure it can be transmitted from female to male?''

''That was an early question people had during the retrovirus plague back at the turn of the millennium. It's called excuse-seeking behavior, Kai. Very commonplace.''

Pinning you down, Maeru kai Ortega. At some point, you're just going to have to admit . . .

She put her hand to the collar of her coverall, seized the zipper tag and pulled it all the way down, cloth splitting apart to reveal dark breasts, flat stomach, small patch of sparse black hair. She looked into his face, frowning, and said, "Don't worry, Kai. I really don't think I'm infected."

Christ. As if . . . Despite himself, he said, "Did you have Doc test you?"

Anger in her eyes then. "No."

The two of them floated in the dim light, staring at each other, wordless. Finally, Ginny shrugged out of her coverall, so the cloth bunched around her waist, releasing her grip on ceiling and floor, and said, "Don't turn me away, Kai. You're really all I've got . . ."

A long moment in which he could contemplate the agony on her face, in her eyes. Am I reading her better now, or has she just made it so obvious that even a male mind can . . . He watched her pull up her legs, start struggling out of the coverall, slowly tumbling backward in the air. As he gazed at the vista of her buttocks, Kai felt his hormones surge, unbidden, far, far beyond the reach of his conscious will, and said, "There was never a possibility that I would."

TWELVE

Ultimately, for lack of a proper facility, a dedicated . . . court-room, they did their deed in *Mother Night*'s wardroom, gathered round the table where, so the original designer supposed, they would be having communal meals. Adventurers together. Comradeship. Hearty camaraderie. Heroes of the spaceways. Explorers embarked on the bosom of the infinite deep.

Floating by the big recreational window, bay window made of almost invisible material, Pholos a yellow curve against black night beyond, Kai suppressed bitter thoughts, ridiculing thoughts. Designers not responsible for us turning out to be assholes. People always assholes. Everywhere you turn. Out to take things from one another. Give as little as possible back. All the wonderful old theories of reciprocal altruism. The social compact. Bullshit. Little mice, that's all we are. Stealing each other's kibble.

Eight people, floating at various angles, hanging onto things, sitting in chairs. Anger and disbelief on faces. All the words spilled now. All the confessions made. No one knows what to do. I don't know what to do. Eyes on Mies now. Mies? Can't get used to any other name. I never knew anyone named David Gilman. Look at him sitting there. Nothing at all in his eyes. Face frozen. Every now and again, the eyes will flicker. An involuntary blink. A movement to left or right as he processes a thought. Looks up, eyes darting toward his eyebrows as he processes a visual image.

God. All the theories agree we're just elaborate robot computers within, legions of bit players, sometimes working in concert, sometimes in conflict. Each part doing its bit to the best of its ability. Well. Good old Mies is evidence of what it's like. I wonder . . . Oh, hell, Kai, you're liable to find out! Closeted with Doc and Ginny before this sham of a kangaroo-court trial. Their earnest eyes upon him. No, no, no, I will not do it.

Ginny's eyes full of surprising compassion. We've got to do something. What if the . . . crew votes to put him out the airlock door?

Kai looking at her, momentarily surprised. Then angry. You're not going to do something like that, Ginny. I know you. He's just going to wind up back in his coffin. You'll put him in cold storage until . . .

Doc's voice gentle: Until when, Kai?

Right. You *know* that, even though we keep trying to put the best complexion on things. Fleet's not coming here. And *Mother Night*'s really in no condition to go elsewhere. Not even home. We keep lying to ourselves. Telling fairy stories about a slow transit home. Or to the colony, wherever it winds up.

Bullshit. We are staying right here. For good. For however long *forever* means in the context of practical immortality. Right. Think about that one. We nine, with Sheba's corpse, whatever we decide about Mies Cochrane, are going to be hanging around here for a while.

Until something happens to us. Misadventure? Decades. Centuries. Millennia. When the navy found Pitcairn's Island, a mere generation later, there was only one old English mutineer left alive.

If we're lucky, the Daiseijin may spare a couple of scientific ships, or the government may come, and, in due course, we'll move on that way. But, most likely not. The colony will be founded elsewhere. The Ten Thousand will go to their happy hunting ground in the sky. And we'll rot, right here, for as long as it takes.

A brief fantasy: The others all dying off, one by one. And here sits Maeru kai Ortega, all alone, living aboard his starship, keeping the systems in good working order. Visiting the empty worlds. Over and over. Until one day . . .

What *could* happen? A ship comes visiting from the successful, populous, logical colony of the Daiseijin? Or the evolved and no longer human Oortlings come wandering on in from the deep, deep dark? No. More likely the Earth dies and the colony fails and here I sit, the last . . . man. What then?

A million years go by. Dead old Alpha Centauri wanders away from charnelhouse Sol. Light-years becoming light-centuries becoming light-millennia. I sit here and watch the stars go by, as my raft of empty worlds carries me around the curve of the galactic lens.

Maybe one day a ship comes. A ship much like *Mother Night*. A crew of . . . *others* is aboard her. What they find here will surprise them very much. Food for thought, they tell each other. And try to see that the same thing does not happen to them. Fanciful hogwash.

Doc said, "That's it, then. Don't you have anything else to say for yourself, Mister Gilman?"

A tiny shrug, barely a motion at all. Finally, he looked up and said, "I wish you wouldn't call me that. David Gilman, as near as I can tell, is dead."

Doc smiled faintly. "I've had an implant or two in my time, Mies. I have some idea what you've been through."

Mies looking at the old man curiously. Some sympathy between them? No. No sympathy in Ernesto Matel for anyone. Master Agent of ICOPOSI, Mister Government Spy. Anger sizzling somewhere. No one, thought Kai, enjoys discovering they've been deceived.

Ginny said, "There's one thing I'd like to know, before we discuss our course of action."

Kai thought, Pretense. Still maintaining the pretense that *we're* going to talk things over. That *we're* going to decide. As if she and Doc didn't work this out between them and make all the necessary decisions, including who the executioner will be, while the rest of us were still down on the planet.

Ginny said, "Mies, did you fuck Sheba Zvi while we were still back on Earth?"

Cold, crystalline tension in the air. Lin and Spence across the room, floating in the air. Looking at each other. Linda's eyes full of pain. Spence looking sorry. Who in that relationship was fucked by whom?

And, sitting in adjacent chairs, just across the wardroom table from Mies, Andy, and Rosie. Rosie another subject of Cochrane's implanted will. And Andy? Growing very tense indeed, just now.

Mies looked up, eyes suddenly alive with . . . something. Turning, looking straight at Andy Mezov. "Yes. I did. A couple of times. She was . . . nice."

Kai blinked once, twice, looking out on a cold and grainy gray world. Watched Andy take his hand out of Rosie's. Watched him shrug out of his chair, watched him float above the table.

Ginny's voice, alarmed, "Andy?"

Rosie: *"No."*

Kai watched Andy's booted foot kick against the back of his chair, and thought, For a groundhog, he seems to have done a good job of adapting to zero gee. And look at Spence. Look at his eyes gleam. And Linda. Willing Andy through the air. Do it. Do it for us all.

Kai balled himself up, put his feet against the windowpane, and punched hard with his heels.

Ginny: *"Andy!"*

Mies not moving. Head recoiling, whipping back and then forward again as Andy landed on him. Not defending himself. Eyes empty. Oh, so empty. Poor Mister Mies. Andy's hands on his throat. Fingers and thumbs digging in. Mies's face growing dark, taking on a blackish hue. Eyes popping out.

Little sounds, coming out of nowhere. Gurgling rasp as Mies is choked. As he struggles to breathe against his will. Breathe around the fingers somehow. A little whine-growl. Andy. Rage. Revenge. Killing. Killing. Sheba Zvi's spoiled carcass probably filling his eyes, along with Mies's contorted features.

Look. Mies's tongue is sticking out now.

Others in the air. Milling uselessly. Doc. Even Ginny. Unable to act. Because, they know, they *know,* that this is what he truly deserves. Die, Mies Cochrane. Meet your maker. Whoever the hell he was.

Kai landed on Andy's back, driving him down onto Mies, grappled with swift, sure, practiced arms and legs. Curled around them like a ball. Put his feet on the arms of Mies's chair. Put one arm under Andy's chin, around his throat. Looped the other under an armpit, back up over the shoulder, around the back of Andy's head.

Deep breath now.

Hold it.

Tension.

Twist.

Pull.

Throw.

Andy Mezov came off Mies, arms and legs flailing, voice a high-pitched gagging yip. Flipped out from between Kai and Mies. Sailed over Kai's shoulder. Kai let him go and watched him tumble, end over end, a complex twisting whirl, really, to the far end of the room. Carom off a set of lockers. Hollow, crumpling boom. Bounce to a corner. Bounce away. Struggle in the air. Get his feet aimed at the nearest solid surface. Hard kick . . .

Kai, admiring: Jesus, he's really good at this. Who would've thought? Well, as a practitioner of Physical Culture, fitness an article of religious faith . . .

Somewhere under and behind him, Mies's breathing was a weird, two-toned whistle. Gasp. Wheeze. Gasp. Wheeze. Throat probably still collapsed. He'll need medical attention right away . . .

Kai met Andy head on, put his head down between his shoulders, and butted the man away. Christ. Seeing stars now. Little bright sparks coming in from the edges of his vision field, fading as they crossed into the fovea's focus. Crouching. Putting his hands on the chair legs, getting ready to leap.

Suddenly, Izzy and Metz were in the right place and ready, the two of them pouncing on Andy, a coordinated zero-gee ballet. Getting hold of him, the three of them tumbling away. Izzy and Metz stopping him from regaining control. Then Spence, adding his bulk to the mix, Kai shouting, "Careful! Don't hurt him!"

Milling. Milling. People breathing. Angry words. Arguing. Settling down. Kai floating in the air beside Mies now, watching Doc massage a throat covered with banded red finger marks. Listening to the calming whistle of Mies's breathing.

Doc said, "You were lucky. If he'd crushed your throat, I'm not sure I would have been willing to . . ."

Life suddenly flaming in Mies's eyes, voice a furious whisper: "*Really?* Why don't you just finish the job, then? Go ahead." Tipping his chin up, exposing livid bruises. "*Bastard. You're as much part of the problem as me.*"

Doc nodded and smiled. "Bits of the program still alive in there? Good. It'll make what comes next easier for all of us."

Rosamunde Merah said, "What *does* come next?"

Kai, feeling the anger well up again, as the adrenaline of combat faded away to a simmer: "You all might as well know the truth. Doc and Ginny have decided we'll use the synchronoptic analysis engine to . . . evaluate Mies's implants." Mies's eyes on him now, beady, surprised perhaps. "Then we'll use the eyebubble core to . . . interfere with his programming."

Silence.

Most of them don't know what it means.

And then Metz said, "God almighty."

More silence.

Then Izzy, sounding ill, said, "Doc, I'm not willing to participate in an amateur mindweave."

Kai said, "I can't do it alone, Iz. You and Metz will have to help."

Doc said, "If you don't, our best option may be to put him out the airlock door."

Not really, thought Kai. They'll kill him with an injection, if it comes to that. Doc would be willing to do it. But . . . the drama and horror of imagining him . . . killed. That's a good psychological tool to use on the rest of us.

Metz said, "Mies is right. You *are* part of the problem. Kai?"

"I don't know." He squirmed uncomfortably, turning in the air, floating back over to the window. Down there, Pholos was waiting for them all. Christ. Why did it have to happen this way? It could have been so much *fun*. He turned and looked at Mies. Eyes back to being obsidian chips again. Won't tell us what *he* wants. Maybe he doesn't know.

Ginny said, "I'd like to take a vote."

Rosie, sounding exhausted: "Why bother? You've decided what to do. *Captain*."

"Still . . ."

A growl from Andy, sitting now between Izzy and Metz. Sitting where they could grab him, if need be. "Mies, did Sheba die because of . . . what you did?"

Mies sat staring at him, eyes flickering. As if listening to some inner voice. Which is probably what *is* happening, Kai realized. Mies said, "I don't think so, Andy. But I don't know."

Linda whispered, "Then I can't go back into suspended animation. I can't go home."

Spence, full of fury: "Just space this piece of shit and get it over with!"

Ginny said, "It's not as simple as that. We . . . don't have redundancy on this crew."

Rosie, voice faint: "I think we can probably scrape by without a planetologist."

Linda: "A fake planetologist, at that."

Kai thought, They want him dead. They all want him dead. There's a tiny ghost of Princess Kriemhild in every woman's heart.

Doc said, "Well, that was the one good thing about all this. My investigation implies that the planetologist part of Mies consists of a superficial behavior algorithm patched to an indexed download of the University of Arizona Planetary Science Library. He knows all there is to know."

Kai thought, I can end this. He said, "You know what we need to do, don't you Metz?"

The man frowned, eyes far away. Far inside. "I think so. We can't *erase* his implants, or change them in any way. The eyebubble interface works through the sensorium. It's not magic, no matter how magical it seems to the untutored. All we can do is . . . overlay."

Kai said, "We can amend his psychiatric jump table. The parts we want gone will still be in there. But they won't be able to act anymore." A quick look at Mies. Eyes bright. Flakes of bright glass. Bright with horror?   .

Yes, he probably understands what I just said. Oh, Christ, I'm sorry Mies. . . .

Mies, all in fragments, all apart now, all alone now . . .

Lash of anger. *Stop feeling sorry for yourself!*

I thought, I really thought, that things were coming together, that we were going to be . . . whole again one day. That we . . .

Mies, left to his own devices, made a hard, dry swallow. Throat still sore. Very sore, a kind of a dull ache, unfamiliar. That was . . . close. Too close.

Little David, whining from an infinite distance: Not so unfamiliar. You remember.

Yes. Yes, I do. Sore throat the kind of sore throat you used to get when you wanted to cry, needed to cry, but couldn't.

He sat bolt upright in the zero-gee chair, feeling almost welded in place to the flexible material. The chair's restraints were wrapped around his forearms, locked securely, holding him in place, making it difficult even to flex. He gave it a few hard tugs, as powerful as he could manage, and then gave up.

Not strong enough. He looked around the small room, felt himself panicking slightly, physical heart speeding up. Caught. Trapped. Things at an end. Breath coming in little pants. Take it easy, now. Time to run away. To disappear. Just hold still and no one will notice the fear. Little David? Is that you? No. It's everyone.

Maybe it's just as well.

Chorus of indignation. This is *you* we're talking about. You must go on. There's no alternative. Jesus Christ. Are they . . . are they . . . going to . . . Can't say it. Can't even *think* . . . that they might . . .

Indigo eyes open wide, expressionless. Empty.

How did I get so fucked up? Seesy called me that, so long ago. But her solution was worse. Better to still be in hiding. Now there are so many me's I don't . . . A tiny quirk of anger, owner unidentified. Not me's. Just because they're in my head. Leading to: there is no me at all anymore, if there ever was. Just a set of masks, some chosen, some imposed. You can put on a mask, but the mask isn't you.

That's what they say. But everyone hides behind their own personal mask, peering out through the little eyeholes, waiting for others to slip up, show the disfigurement behind theirs.

All I ever wanted was to be happy. Is that too much to ask? I wanted to take off my masks and show the little, cringing David to the world. But there was too much wrong inside. Fear. Anger. Strange lust. That wasn't the problem, though, it never was really, even at the worst. I let the masks be me. Why? Because it was . . . easier. Because anything else was too much work.

Silly. Confession-mode now. That's what you do when they've got you. Apologize. Pretend you're sorry. Put on another mask. And if that doesn't work, whine and plead and whimper and grovel. Confession is easy. Living is hard.

So what do we do now?

Mies felt his guts freeze solid when the door slid open, the three shadows floated in bearing their cargo of . . . Oh, God. The scanner head. Kai, Izzy, and Metz, bearing the scanner head for the synchronoptic analysis engine. Hypnopaedia hardware. I recognize . . . I remember . . .

Come here. Come here now. Come here to . . . He felt his intestines cramp, way down deep, down deep. Pang of shame. *This is . . . the last of it for all of us. Don't spoil our final moments by shitting your pants, Mister Mies.*

Mies flared with white hot rage. Don't you understand? Don't you *understand*? They're here to *kill* us!

Little David suddenly crying.

Big David looking up from his long reverie, bewildered. Kill . . . me? But . . . why?

And Reiko-chan: **Thank God. Thank all the gods. Time to go.**

Mies felt the panic build and surge, until it felt like everything in the world. Suddenly, unexpectedly, he opened dry, quaking lips, and said, "Kai? I'm sorry about all of it. And . . . I trust you."

There. There. That's it.

Kai hung in midair, looking down at Mies, feeling the words resonate in his heart. A sharp pang of regret. Of fear. A surge of adrenaline. But . . . Mies just sitting there. Looking up. Something in his eyes. Pleading? No. Trying to see into me, see something he can latch onto. "You little bastard."

Little. Little. You could see a momentary flicker of something else in Mies's eyes now. Puzzlement. Rule-sieve not getting its desired result. Hmmm. A bit of an adjustment needed to this one, Dr. Frankenstein . . .

Earnestness now. Mies said, "I really meant it, Kai, whether you want to believe me or not. I'm sorry what's happened has . . . blinded you to what good there is in me."

Kai reached down and took hold of one chair arm, not far from Mies's wrist, watching a spark of hope ignite in the man's eyes. Reached out with the other hand and took hold of his chin, watched his eyes flicker back and forth. Not looking at me. Suddenly doesn't want to look into my eyes. Looking for a way out now. He said, "In just a few minutes, Mies, I'll *know*."

Mies's eyes froze, held still, looking at nothing, for a long moment, then Kai saw the horror blossom. That's right, Mister Mies. Think about it. Mies was suddenly staring into his eyes, his own eyes very bright, squinting against the light. Lips working slowly. Trying to form words.

Just, "*Please,* Kai . . . "

Kai turned away, releasing the man's face, releasing his grip on the chair, pushing away, turning in the air, headed for the corner where Izzy and Metz had finished setting up the scanner head and clamping it to a corner of the bunk.

Unpleasant looks on their faces as well. Hard anger from Izzy, who feels he's forced to participate in an . . . execution. Metz, though, the smarter, more enigmatic member of a highly effective partnership. Interested in what's going on. Maybe looking forward to seeing this, helping it take place.

He floated beside them, one hand on the scanner head, looking back at Mies. Mies in shadow now, despite the diffuse, sourceless illumination of his sleeping quarters. His final resting place? I can see that's how he feels. That he's about to die. And the shadow on his face is the shadow of the executioner's axe.

Mies Cochrane, just now, in the position of the endless line of condemned criminals who've preceded him into the infinite dark. Sitting there, in the deathhouse, chair like an electric chair, like the chair to which they strapped men and women in ancient gas chambers. Mies sitting there, waiting to hear the master switch clunk home, or hear the pellets splash into the acid, hear them sizzle and steam, watch as the vapor rises round his sorry ass, bowels suddenly liquid with fear and . . .

Izzy muttered, "Christ, Kai, let's just do it."

Terror jumping into Mies's eyes. No. No. Wait. Take as long as you want, fellows . . .

No need to plug in a bundle of waveguides now. No powerful transceiver to allow communication between the scanner head and the SAE central processing unit aboard *Mother Night*. No need for anything but . . . he glanced at the sensor in the corner of the room, saw Mies's panicky eyes follow his motion, lock onto the thing as if it were the instrument of his destruction.

He nodded. Watched tables and graphs and empty charts scroll up around him out of the air.

The scanner head nodded once, slowly, and Mies's head jerked around, staring at it. Face pale. Beads of sweat popping out on his brow. Swallowing convulsively. Oh, very melodramatic, Mies. Who the hell do you think you're fooling now?

But, deep inside, that pang of sympathy continued to well up. This is a terrible thing I'm doing. As terrible as the thing he did. As terrible as the thing that was done to him. Got to make this come out all right. Somehow.

Scanner head tipping back and forth, nodding up and down, faint green illumination showing the shipboard air was not completely free of dust. The technician in Kai seemed to make a mental note. We've *got* to spend some time fine-tuning the life-support system. This ship was warranty-rated to last a century or so, by manufacturers who expected it to be stuck out in the Oort for a long damned time. Five-nines reliability's no longer enough. It may have to last thousands of years . . .

Graphs and tables filling up now, as the synchronoptic analysis engine parsed the data it was pulling from Mies's physical substance, the history it was reading from his quantum mechanical substructure. Reaching. Reaching down deep. Deep into his soul?

By God. Men don't have souls.

Metz, looking at his own displays, whispered, "Look at that. *Cool.*"

I wonder how Metz views himself? Programmers and systems analysts tend toward mechanistic theories of self. After a while it becomes . . . obvious just what we are. All of us.

Shadows forming in the room, filling the space between Mies and the machine. Can he see? No. We gave him no feedback on this. Just torture. Nothing but torture, that's what we thought. Be kinder to . . .

But, now, he sits in a room in front of a humming machine and three staring, motionless executioners, people whose eyes see something his cannot. And he waits. And waits. For the end to come.

The room suddenly flooded with blue-black shadows. Flooded with things like ghosts. Flooded . . .

One.

The small boy. Label, David Gilman. Little David. Not really all that little. A boy of many ages. A toddler, barely remembered. A big boy, at the cusp of puberty. Shadows of all the boys in between. David Gilman as a confection of many memories. Of many fragments.

Two.

A grown man. A young man, really, mostly in his teens and twenties. Shadows clustered toward the earlier end of the spectrum. Interesting, thought Kai, looking over his graphs and tables. As if he grew up physically, but continued to regard himself as . . . *thirteen?* Something like that.

A woman's voice whispered, Fuckup. You've been a fuckup all your life, David. . . .

Three.

Indigo eyes opening out of the shadows. No form. No features. Just eyes.

"Holy shit," muttered Izzy, "will you look at that?"

Metz said, "This is great. That's his metaphor for the rule-sieve stack associated with his first implant."

Kai said, "As near as I can tell, it's not a custom implant at all. There's no structured superficial personality. No behaviors."

Voice dry and angry, Izzy said, "I know what it is. Goddamn it, Metz, they imbued him with a slightly modified version of the old Social Cocksman sieve. One of those things asshole teenagers used to use to get themselves girlfriends, back before hypnopaedia was properly regulated."

Metz: "You mean the one about *How to Make Love to a Woman?*"

Izzy: "Yeah. One of those."

Mies's voice, like a terrified moan: "It didn't need to be special. I just needed to know how to get them to fuck me . . ."

Four.

A young woman, tall, thin Japanese girl, really, in her late twenties, perhaps. Dressed all in clingy, washed silk. Looking at them. Face empty.

Izzy said, "Hmh. I'll be damned."

Label: Harada Reiko. Reiko-chan. Nice girl. Nice girl. Nice little kitten. Climb into daddy's lap and purr while I pet you. Reiko-chan slithering out of her silky gown, letting it slither to the floor. Naked girl. Pretty naked girl. Small, solid little tits.

Flat belly. Small black patch of Asiatic pubic hair. Just what the doctor ordered.

Kai watched, revolted, as the girl reached down, slid her index finger two knuckles deep in her vagina. Pulled it out, glistening, popped it in her mouth. Sucked it gently. Smiled engagingly.

Izzy cursed, and said, "What the hell's the point of *this*?"

Metz said, "Look at the physical structure phase diagrams."

Despite all the pheromone generators, despite the shape, Reiko-chan, like Maeru kai Ortega, was still male inside. And keyed. Keyed to standard male pheromonic cues, so she . . . he . . . Hell. Cued to orgasm simultaneously with a rutting male.

Autoviroids cutting loose, just after the male's semen exited his now safely pH-neutralized urethra. Slinking right up the old waterspout. . . .

Clever.

Demonic.

I want to go back home now and kill them all.

Five.

Mies Cochrane standing there, a fully mature man, smiling, dignified. Image staring right at Kai. *Hello there, Engineer-san. Do you know my name?*

You're the scientist, aren't you?

That's right.

Why've you got a personality, when the other rule-sieve does not?

Do I? Look closely.

Mies suddenly divided in two.

One Mies suddenly colder, more pompous. Full of his own knowledge.

The other one . . .

Voice quiet, warm: Hello Kai. I guess you see after all.

Metz said, "I think the Mies personae we're looking at are a vector sum. Probably autogenerated during the decay process."

Izzy said, "Christ. Look there."

Behind the five, now six, Mies-imagos, a clustering of shadows, vague shapes gathering on a darkling plain. Filling up the

world to infinite depth. Who can they be? That one there. Is
that the fabled Seesy, the devil-sister who led him here? And
that one. Maeru kai Ortega? How can that be? Everyone we
meet. Everyone we ever know, or think we know, comes to
reside within us.

Forever.

Kai sighed softly. Not just five Mieses. Hundreds of Mieses.
Thousands of Mieses. All vying for control. "All right," he
said. "Time to . . . rip these Mieses to pieces. . . . "

Clamped in his chair, Mies let out a short, chopped off, high-
pitched scream.

Helpless. Random jiggles of consciousness. Here I am. No,
over here. Whoops, no, that must be someone else. I'm, well,
I'm . . .

Indigo Eyes sloshing around, squinting, bloating. Rule number one is, always remember to take your vitamins. Glaucoma
taking me, internal pressure rising. No! No! No! Stop this right
now. I . . . don't feel well at all.

The conflicting lines of thought grow wilder, each individual
personality flopping like a crab thrust into boiling water.

Scientist persona analyzing, analyzing, wheels slipping,
applying imaginary statistics to hold away the night. Erecting a
little crib around myself, erecting stars in the dark firmament,
then cataloging each star, gauging its brightness, inventing faux
constellations. Then, monotonously, naming names, attaching a
little bright label to each one in turn. Busy, yes. Busy.

Little David bawling. Mummy, Dah, don't . . . Don't *punish*
me. Why don't you like me? Why am I not good enough? Please.
I'll be good. I promise. Honest. Come and save me, now. Or else.

Big David saying, I didn't do anything. This isn't my fault. All
the problems are caused by life being a piece of shit. It is, isn't
it? It'll be a relief to get this over with, to get away, to admit
finally and once and for all that I am nothing. No one. Even if I
don't really want to do it. Do I have to?

Reiko-chan thinking, **If only I could do my tricks, these
little men wouldn't have a chance. Why didn't I strike when**

I could? Oh Andy, Kai, look at this luscious body, come, come fuck me. I'm so horny. You know it'll feel good, go ahead, I want you to. I want *you*. Come here, please, let me pull your hand down between my legs. You'll be happy, I promise.

And finally, Indigo Eyes, calling for more prey. Looking, looking for someone, no one here, though. Simple repetition. LOOK FOR SOMEONE. NO ONE HERE. LOOK FOR SOMEONE. NO ONE HERE.

Something happening. Something very . . . deep. I can feel the changes, inside. Who am I? This is who you are. Remember. Remember. This is who you will be.

How does this feel? Tinkertoy memes like strands of DNA coming apart, with funny, liquid pops, the sound of lips sucking open. *Pop pop pop.*

Then emptiness. Silent. Anechoic. Emptiness so vast that the farthest edges were nonsense. A universe without the big bang to cause it to come into existence. Nowhere.

What are we? Not people. What are we? Not things. What are we? Not anything. Look down at yourselves. What do you see? Nothing. We see nothing. Good.

Pop. Pop. Pop.

What does consciousness feel like?

It feels very much like this.

That's the correct answer.

It's the only answer.

Slowly, a flowering within the desolation, like an instant photograph developing.

Is anybody in here?

A memory to play.

Harada Reiko leaned up against the ashcrete wall, still warm from the long August afternoon now over. Across Kita Aoyama a giant LPD crystal display window was blossoming with light, throwing illumination on the hurrying people, showing images of naked men and women in quick-cut motion, flickering in and out of existence so quickly that they were almost subliminal.

She took a big gulp of Japanese porter from the cooler in her small purse and let her eyes roam up and down the street. Tokyo. This red light district might just as well have been in Kansas City, Missouri

There. Indigo eyes open on night.

David Gilman, crushed under a thousand tons of cotton candy, moaned, moaned softly, Oh, God. Oh, please. No more. No more.

Little David so very frightened. Images of Seesy, naked. Images from dreams. No. No. Don't do that to me . . .

Older boys and grown men always stronger. Always afraid that they'd . . .

Eyes raised to the tall buildings a few blocks away, most lit in entertaining patterns, some changing color gradually. The fluorescent blue-green sky was vacant and featureless. *Snap.* Momentary reunification, so shocking, so . . .

I shouldn't be here. This is dangerous.

YOU LIKE IT.

Sounding like the voice of his sister.

No. It's grotesque. It makes me sick. This is the last time.

Okay. Just this one time more.

She hiked her leather miniskirt up a few inches, leaned harder against the wall, shifted some weight to the balls of her feet. Ready for a long wait. Got to get to sleep before midnight, though. I can't be late for the reorganization meeting tomorrow, and I have to look fresh and alert.

Awful. I'm an idiot to do this.

STOP IT. YOU KNOW YOU ENJOY IT.

You enjoy it. I have no choice.

Inside, the great hunger bit at her. Wetness soaking into her panties, cunt throbbing subtly. She felt the penis hidden in her vagina like a hidden weapon. And, of course, that's what it is. *Crackle.* Coming apart again.

Reiko-chan, soothing inner woman: **Just relax, David. This is a lot easier, isn't it. They come after you. Attracted by you. What's a good analogy? Venus's-flytrap? Ant lion? You**

just have to wait, and it all happens, almost as if you didn't have any say in the matter.

Dangerous. I could be hurt.

It's the way you always wanted it. Spontaneous. Happening *to* you.

Little David: Leave me *alone*.

Carried along. Carried along, like trash in a stream.

It hadn't been that difficult to adapt at first, though the insistent little whore in her head was given to begging until she gave in. Different kind of rule-sieve, maybe more advanced. Sometimes it feels like it is me, in my soul, not on my shoulder. It doesn't have to persuade me, because it doesn't have to.

Memories of all the many nights, all the men. Crushed under them, pinned to mattress and floors and even the cold ground, being hurt, losing any sense of control. Doing good work, though there was no way to know whether this method of propagation worked every time. Best guess was around seventeen percent. Not very good, really, and the risk was there to be contemplated. She remembered the stubby near dwarf swerving into a dark alleyway, pulling out his knife, chattering in some sort of broken Japanese. "No pay. You give." The fear almost interfered with the ability to ejaculate. Fortunately, the man thrust into her for almost fifteen minutes, and she relaxed enough to do the deed. Afterward, she had vomited in the smelly doorway of an old shop, crying and crying.

Car pulling over, new model wheeler. Better go look. Dark Japanese man with handsome features, neat bowl haircut, smooth shaven. The window slid down. "You got a place?"

YES, YES. THIS IS THE ONE. YOU WON'T BE DISAPPOINTED THIS TIME. I PROMISE.

"No. But you have plenty of room in your car. I'm *very* flexible. And I know a place we can park."

Furtive glances around. Afraid I'll mug *him*. "How much?"

"You pay what you think it's worth." Smiling, as though I trusted the bastard.

Thinking. "No. How much?"

Okay, we'll play it your way. "Two hundred."

"Get in."

It's not too late to—

Slipping into the front seat, soft sound of leather on leather, swinging her feet in, careful not to knock her shoes off. "Get into the traffic, I'll tell you where to go."

"Mmmp." Grunting to himself, not even looking at me now. The kind who prefers an impersonal little hump, probably embarrassed in advance as to how quickly he'll come.

I'd better be ready. She slipped a hand under her dress, bringing it up, sticking three fingers up her cunt to where the cock was growing hard. Give it a good couple of strokes, just in case. "I don't do head."

"Mmmp."

No sense in saying anything personal to him. Image of me holding my fingers up to his nose, wafting the smell in his direction. Might scare him away. But what I want to do is get it over with, grit my teeth and just do it.

"Here it is. Pull in that little alleyway." Car swaying, coming to a stop. Bright sky coming in, throwing enough light to see pretty well. She pulled her panties down around her ankles, left them there with her shoes. "Come here, big man." Open to him. A couple of more strokes on the cock, lifting one leg up onto the seat, sliding her butt toward him a tad. He folded in the steering wheel and began to undo his pants, fumbling with the zipper. *Pop.*

Reiko: **Stupid fucker. Nervous as a cat. They're all the same.**

David: I can still get out.

Reiko: **You'll enjoy yourself. I promise.**

Finally, his pants and underwear were stripped down, and he began to reach for her.

There it is. Hard enough.

Revulsion.

Ecstasy.

On me, heavy. Pushing me back by the shoulder, head folded up against the door.

In his control. Subservient. His little whore.

All right. He's in. Wriggle into a better position, I don't want to break my neck.

Okay, this is perfect. Slow strokes, regularly spaced, building in speed.

Beginning to cry. He's not even looking at my face.

NO, DON'T STRUGGLE, JUST RELAX, IT'LL BE OVER SOON. COME ON, YOU'LL ENJOY YOUR ORGASM, I KNOW YOU WILL.

Sick. Can't move. I want to get away so badly.

He's speeding up. Here it comes. Go. Scream a little, he'll enjoy that.

No. No-ooh. Scald of nausea. Horrid little twist of pleasure and . . . inside his belly, shooting semen at the same moment as the man. Perfect.

"Get out."

Dirty. Used. Again.

"Get out."

"What about—?"

"Out."

Oh. I'm crying.

Get out.

Quiet. Awful quiet in here now, Kai thought. Nothing much left of him at all. Memories pouring out, flooding out into our real world, like a ruptured dam, small leak growing to a hole, water surging through the hole, enlarging it, ripping it wider and wider, until the whole facade comes tumbling down.

The room, the whole of *Mother Night,* the entire universe was gone now, displaced by VR images, by the SAE's interpretation of Mies's inner self, his many selves, overlaid by scrolling charts and tables, Mies reduced to a complex of data and little more.

He's always felt so alone in the world. We all feel alone. All of us. Always. Why did it seem so much worse, so much more frightening, to David Gilman? Why did it . . . leach his will? Why did it paralyze him? I'll never know.

Some are born strong.

And some are born weak.

That's all.

Fix him now. Doesn't matter what you're feeling. You started this job. Now you've got to finish it. An ache inside. Regret. Get out? Let Izzy and Metz finish? They'd be angry, but they'd come up with something. There'd be some kind of Mies, some functional planetologist or another, left over when they were done.

I want him to be more than that.

Some image of Mies that formed within me, down on Pholos? Just my imagination? Maybe. But I want it to be real. Selfish? How can I know? All right. The fix then. Just do your damned job. *The materials.* All right. There's nothing we can do about the legions in outer memory. Remembered voices. Remembered faces. But we can give the new Mies some way of dealing with them. Give him some way of dealing with what the voices say to him. A conscience? Is that what I'm trying to give him? Arrogance in me. I can't give a man a flawless conscience. I don't have one myself. Wouldn't know one if I saw one.

Just make up some rules.

Ways of dealing with people.

A sudden, horrible impulse to reach back, into history and culture, spool out the rules of religion, the ethic of the virtuous pagans. Do unto others . . . Why do I feel it's unfair to make him thus? Perhaps, because those rule-sieves were imposed on me, from without, as a child. Imposed on me, and I resented it.

Image of his own parents floating up.

I hated them, because they controlled me. Didn't even give me a name of my own. Mr. Maeru's son. Ms. Ortega's boy. *Kai* no more than the Greek word for *and.* Somewhere, down in that crowd of remembered faces and voices are David Gilman's parents. What did he call them? Mummy and Dah. Dead, by misadventure, long before he could detach from them. Before he, maturity delayed by their extended social foolishness, could grow up on his own.

Rubin's Law: *Kill your parents.*

But if they're already dead, how can you kill them?

Opportunity lost. Stolen.

Kai posted markers in the Mies file, letting Izzy and Metz know which parts of Gilman's memories to wire over. Install jumpers here and here. Leave the memory of the parents, but render them powerless. And Seesy, as well. Yes. Good thought. Get rid of her.

A tiny voice, somewhere, calling out. You can't do this to him! Immoral. Evil. These memories are *his*. Who are you to destroy them? Memories are all that give us our sense of self. We are who we were. . . .

Imposing order on chaos now.

Rather, think: We are who we can be. The past is gone. Our memories no more than stories we make up to fill the void left by the passage of *now* into *then*. Just stories, there to be edited.

All right. Done with memory, per se. Now.

Little David. Nothing to bother with there. You could go in and rewrite those memories. Maybe make them more satisfying. Go back and create a twelve-year-old David Gilman who *did* fuck his sister. Form a little story about the two of them rutting by the seashore one fine, sunny summer day . . .

No. Leave him be. And big David, as well. That's who he *was*. He has to know what he was, and remember what he did, for whatever emerges next to be able to understand just *why* we—

Indigo eyes snapping open.

Fury. Fury now.

A perverted version of the sustain-algorithm that helped ward off hypnopaedic decay as long as possible. Kai felt his own anger well up. The bastards. Evil men and women who would treat a human being thus. Make him no more than a tool . . .

Calmly, he reached out for his own tools, hypnopaedic instructions pouring in through physical Mies's eyes and ears, jumpers in place, bypassing the Indigo rule-sieve entirely and . . .

A soft giggle escaping from Mies's lips.

Crack.

Indigo eyes frozen, colorless, transparent, empty.

Eyes of glass.

Kai planted markers around Reiko-chan, watched her go flat and dimensionless, become, more or less, like a painted image. Like a story told in words. Something a person would have to invest effort in before they could truly understand. Let him remember her. Remember, that's all.

An expression of gratitude frozen into Harada Reiko's painted eyes. **Gone,** the eyes said. **That's all I ever wanted to be.** Pain no more.

Very good. Very clever indeed. But what about me? You can't do away with me. I'm the one you originally intended to bring: Mies the Planetologist. But there was doubt in the pompous voice. *Can't do without* me . . . *momentary unease* . . . can *you?*

Fear.

Fear from Mies, waiting to die. Afraid to die. Afraid to resume nonexistence, but he knows he doesn't belong here. Knows now he was never real, not even as a hypnopaedic implant. Mies Cochrane nothing more than a by-blow.

Swiftly, Kai added markers to Mies's internal jump table, scientist persona too startled to protest, then gone without a trace, Mies Cochrane wired directly to the planetology rule-sieve. Mies crying out, astonished, then: I . . . I'll miss him.

He's not really gone you know. Just wired out of the circuit. Helpless. He can watch, can see what you do. Can admire the knowledge base as it grows. But . . .

Fading. Fading. Without reinforcement, he'll wither away soon.

Kai made a lateral connection between personal Mies-plus and the still sleeping reality of David Gilman. Felt awareness surge. He'll awaken. Awaken finally, as the others drift off to sleep.

Metz said, "It won't hold, you know."

Izzy: "This kind of crude construct never does. It'll decay faster than any single implant; decay just as chaotically as the mess Indigo's programmers made."

Kai nodded. "I know. A few months. A year at best. But what emerges then will be the real David Gilman, back from

hibernation, colored by the things he's seen and done . . ."
And, he thought, colored by his relationship with me. I'll do
my best, David, to make you whole again. Dread. Dread at
what is yet to come. I wish there were some way I could stop
it from happening, but . . .

"Sleep," he said, and watched Mies's eyes fall shut.

Sleep. And when you awaken . . .

Dreamtime.

In the great darkness, the stars begin to go out, one by one.
Don't do this to me.

Little dinghy out of control, meandering aimlessly among the
giant swells, barely afloat, water swirling around their feet. In
the distance, lights of the greater ship winking off as it plunged
silently below the surface.

All of us here. No preferred self. None of us at the rudder.

An enormous wave came sweeping by, outrigger currents
spinning the dinghy like a compass needle. More water around
their feet, dinghy almost foundering.

Oh God, please don't let us go under.

God, smooth-shaven and handsome, dressed in a neat, white
lab smock, looked down at them, night sky parting around his
shoulders like a curtain. Watching them. Waiting. Then reaching
down, and with the barest touch of his luminous finger . . .

Capsized. Cold water drenching us, pulling at us, our flailings
making insignificant splashes. Lifeboat gone. Kick legs, wave
hands, keep our heads above the implacable dark waves. Must.
Stay. Afloat.

There goes Harada Reiko, slim arm protruding from the water
like a sea serpent, three fingers outstretched in a crude girl-
scout salute.

Gray-black water lapping those big, shiny eyeballs, surging
over them, pushing them down. Waterline behind the big dark
pupils. Getting waterlogged.

What'll happen when we're all gone? How will I, I mean,
who . . . ?

Scientist holding his breath, big, red, puffed-out cheeks, eyes squinted, hair tousled by the waves into a little pixie curl. There he goes.

Going under, one by one. All the little Mieses and Davids. Heads disappearing, leaving only dark, flowing water.

Black roller takes me under. A moment of wild turmoil, panic-induced motion, lungs bursting with pain. Then nothing.

Nothing but the empty sea.

The empty sea of dreams.

As the blue-green light of the fleshwelder flickered on the opposite wall, Ginny thought, Why am I watching this?

Mies, sedated, was fastened down like a frog on a dissection plate on the biolab's operating table, stripped naked, machines on pantograph arms hovering over his midsection, sparkling with potent energies as they did their work, eyebubble sensors bending low to their task, Doc floating in the air in the background of the scene, a dark shadow superimposed against the far wall.

Doing his job.

Though which job, I'm not sure I . . .

Mies's genitals suddenly swung away on the end of one robot arm, a gobbet of wet red meat, completely unrecognizable as anything that might once have belonged to a human male.

Turned . . . inside out.

She felt her stomach surge, then settle down. Quickly glanced up at Kai.

Motionless. Silent. Eyes wide. Visage stern.

Just watching.

Keeping things inside.

As the robot arm slid the little wad of red meat into a container, Doc said, "I'll run a complete analysis on these tissues, for my report to the authorities on Earth. Then I'll destroy them."

Still looking at Kai, watching his emotionless face. Once they're gone . . . Oh God, do I think this is winning him back?

Doc said, "Now, I want you both to understand something. I do not know how they programmed Mies's body to manufacture autoviroids, so I don't dare use back-cloning regeneration to make him . . . whole again. We can't risk it.''

Kai said, ''We're not going home again. Do you think we're going to breed here?''

Ginny said, ''Linda's volunteered for an experiment, Kai. Doc's going to remove her ovaries and fallopian tubes and start her on an old-fashioned course of hormone replacement therapy. Then he's going to fertilize one of Linda's frozen base-reference ova with some of Spence's base-reference semen.''

Kai was staring at her, face still empty, eyes reflecting the sparkles and sparks from the operating table as the welders closed Mies up. ''Is Spence . . . infected?''

Doc said, ''Yes. It seems he had intercourse with Linda less than forty-eight hours after Mies, and the autoviroids got into him.''

''So. What're you going to . . . ''

''Simple sterilization. We've established that the autoviroids can get through barrier contraception, but we think they'll be trapped by vasectomy.''

Ginny said, ''Andy, Izzy, and Metz are clean, Kai. The only one we haven't checked is you.''

Doc laughed. ''And me, of course.'' He swung the hardware away from Mies and pulled apart his legs, poking at freshly welded red flesh, inspecting a urethral opening, surrounded by the semicircle of pubic hair. ''My, my, we're almost twins now.''

Kai said, ''So, what next? You going to make him bald, too?''

Doc's face twisted into a grimace. ''If he wants.''

Ginny said, ''Rosie is infected.''

''She going to have her ovaries out, too?''

''No. She and Andy . . .''

Doc said, ''I think Andy expects, one day, he'll get Sheba back.''

Kai floated over to the table, looking down at sleeping Mies. What is he thinking, I wonder? He said, ''She could surrogate Sheba's eggs.''

Ginny felt a startled pang. *Rosie already said that to me. It's what she wants. But she wants Andy to think of it on his own. Kai's face so very still. Just watching Mies sleep. Oh, hell. I* have *lost you, haven't I?*

And after all we've been through. Together. Oh, my God, Kai . . .

Awakening on Earth was, in some ways, a familiar experience. *All those Antarctic years, spinning back to the infinite depths of infancy, depths which had no beginning, only a clearly seen end, those later years under the Andes, different and better years . . .*

Ginny stretched, feeling wrinkled sheets under her bare back, looking up at an empty, white-painted ceiling, and thought, *Better because, though the work was so very much harder than any old Antarctic family chores, you always awoke just the way you fell asleep.*

Never woke to the feeling of someone's fingers invading your crotch. . . .

Funny. After a while, I got so I could immediately recognize who was on me by what their fingers were doing to my pussy. Grandpa Sammy always liked to stick his fingers inside, worming his middle finger in bit by bit, no matter how dry I was. Brother Jacques always started out rubbing my clit. Sister Jannine . . .

One brief memory of Jannine's soft, soft whisper, Jannine always talking just to herself, Jannine's fingers bypassing her crotch, going for her tight little asshole . . .

She turned away from the memory.

Funny, all right.

Hear me laughing?

Funny, loose wetness in her groin right now, tacky memory of the previous night's labor of love with Kai. *Getting better at it, now that the medwork to increase the density of his muscle fibers has taken hold. Kai getting stronger, endurance building fast.*

Memory of Kai on top of her in the night, finally, like a

man, like any man, gasping and sweating as he heaved away on top of her, holding still, so still, as his prick jerked and twitched and spewed inside her.

I was so relieved he was finally able to do it, I forgot about myself. Kai's place beside her in the bed empty. Yellow sunshine falling through the slit between the curtains, making a long, narrow, warm patch on the rumpled sheets where he'd been. Sound of the shower hissing in the background. Going to work? No. Not today.

Hard for them to make ends meet, tithing eighty percent each to the Daiseijin, trying to live on less than half a single income. Good thing we've got marketable skills. My 14,500 ceus as a netjock, his 22,000 as an engineering technician . . .

Reversing our old positions, down on the ground. Standard ARM paid its junior command pilots 20,000 ceus, new flight engineers only 16,000.

A very good thing, those jobs. Hard enough to make it on 14,600 ceus between us. Try to imagine if we were accountants or some such, pulling down maybe 8,000 apiece, then handing over all but 1600 to the Great Star People.

Make or break, today, we've promised ourselves that. Today, we go in for our final interviews. Final interviews on application to work for the Inner Circle. Real jobs, working on . . .

An interesting notion. How will I feel, going back out into space, employed by the Daiseijin for their own purposes, working for no more than room and board?

Exploited?

Maybe.

The shower cut off and she could hear Kai bumbling about, humming as he did whatever it was he did, mornings, in the bathroom. Brief image surfacing, of another morning, of coming to stand in the doorway after another sweaty, frustrating night. Kai standing in the shower, dimly visible through the sonic curtain that kept the water contained. Kai standing there, head down, hand between his legs, fooling with himself.

Masturbating like a woman. Making me cry because I hadn't wanted to do it for him.

Okay, forget about that. It's all right now.

This is it, then. Today, we find out if we're admitted to the tech team. Today we find out if . . .

In twenty-four months, the flight crews for the scoutships begin training. Two years. We've got two years to work our way in and up. Two years to get their attention. Two years to make them realize we're just the sort of people they want.

Not the crews of academic astronauts they're considering now, science explorers of the infinite. Make them realize they need real spacemen and women to take the first risks. People who've already seen the Black Sky Country.

She threw back the covers and lay naked, feeling the room's moderately cool air on her skin, though it was North American summer outside. Wish we could afford a better apartment. Well, not much longer, one way or the other.

Stretching, running her hands over her hips. Lifting her breasts, feeling little patches of sweat that had accumulated underneath. Shit. If I don't get out of this damned gravity well, I'll have to go for medwork just to do something about this fucking *sag*. . . .

Hands on her belly then, feeling hard muscle ridging there. One good thing about gravity. I don't have to exercise on purpose, even if I am sitting in a com-node bucket all day.

Hands on her crotch, feeling the remains of Kai's semen, still sticky between her legs, bits of it dried and crusty in her pubic hair. Fucking Christ. Off to the showers . . .

And away.

Scream.

Awakening agony.

Moving in slow motion.

Falling.

Falling headlong.

The horrible sensation of your arm caught, caught in the crook of two tree limbs, while your body twisted around its axis and continued to fall. *Crack.* Horrible, wrenching flash of pain like lightning and . . .

Impact.

On the ground now, looking up through the branches and leaves of the tree at sunny blue sky beyond. That . . . thing. That thing now. Cool trickle of awareness. That's your arm. See your hand? Those are your . . . fingers.

Cold wind blowing. Cold wind on the raw, bleeding flesh of an empty socket and . . .

Become. He let his eyes open on the dim space. Science Lab. *Mother Night.* Pegasus. Pholos. Kai.

Kai. Memory of the first night in the tent down on Pholos. The two of us locked in each other's arms, desire driving me onward, making the risks seem worthwhile. Glad that it happened. I would never have thought that we could have come so far, so fast. Miracle of Pholos all around giving everything a special feel. Remembering the stars that night, and the beautiful sunrise.

Stark, black inner landscape.

Those eyes. Whose eyes are those? Eyes with no one at all behind them. Empty, clear glass marbles. Look deep inside. Bubbles in there. Bits of trapped air? Imperfections?

Why do I remember them oh-so-blue?

Momentary pulse of fear.

Why can't I remember?

Picture of a girl. Asian? Chinese? Japanese? Somebody . . . dear to me. Naked girl. Sleek, shiny black hair on her head. Not much between her legs. Little tits.

Motionless.

An icon of a girl.

Who?

Tick-tock. Tick-tock.

Things speeding up.

They . . . changed me. I know that. I'm not . . . what I was.

It's all for the best. You were mentally ill, fragmented. You're better now. Image of beautiful Rosie Merah, lying beneath him as he injected the terrible plague into her. All the others, going up the line to the strange little bird in Southwark. Evil. I deserved this richly.

Who? Who the hell is *saying* that?

No one.

There's no one here but . . . me.

Looking across the mental landscape, feeling the complexity there. And who are *you*?

No one. No one at all.

No, that can't be right.

Where is everybody?

No. No wait. There's nobody here but *me*.

And who the hell is that?

He thought about it for a while. Well. Well now. Mies Cochrane, of course. Just like I always . . . sudden flood of memories welling up. No, for Christ's sake. Your name is David Gilman. What are you, nuts? David Gilman. This little boy, horny since puberty for sister Seesy's hot little crotch and . . .

Memories of the other David. No, not a *different* David, asshole. Just little David, David Gilman all grown up and . . . what the hell is *Indigo*? More memories. Oh. Oh, Jesus Christ. Oh, how the hell could I have been so stupid as to . . . oh, Christ, Seesy, why the hell did you have to . . . memories become a boiling torrent, an agonizing flood of . . . Japan? Me? This . . . little whore . . . awful stinking pigs shoving dirty filthy . . . oh, my G—

A wrenching tilt, falling into the darkness.

No. Not the darkness.

Calming down. Calming down now.

I did it. I got away. Got away from the bastards.

Escaped.

This is really what I always wanted. David Gilman and all his foolishness. Gone. That's what the ersatz multiple personalities were *for*. Now they're gone, too. I'm whole. Me. Mies Cochrane. A new person who . . . but all those memories . . . and that's wonderful, too.

A spreading warmth, through and through.

With the memories, memories of David, of . . . oh, God, even the memories of being Reiko the whore, I still have a sense of being *me*.

Only, now, it's a me I can . . . like.

Will other people like me now? Like me the way I always wanted them to? One corner of his mind still seemed isolated, something . . . critical there. Wry, almost-separate voice, going, Isn't that a little childish, Mister Mies? Nobody loves me. Everybody hates me. Christ. Are you *sure* you don't want to go eat worms?

Shock of recognition.

That's me.

Talking to myself.

Like a normal person.

Normal.

Enormous implications.

What will it be like to go forth in the world and be *just like everyone else*? Oh, my God. Just like everyone else. Isn't that what David Gilman feared the most? That he'd be just like everyone else, just like all the fools he despised? That he'd be . . . just like Mummy and Dah?

But . . . the implications. To have friends. Really have friends. Not people you tried to fool, to trick, to steal from while concealing yourself, your feelings, your thoughts and fears and petty hopes and hatreds.

How wonderful it will be to sit down with someone I trust and share with them my . . . what do I want to call it? My *angst*. To let them see my fears. To let them see that I'm . . . small. Small and helpless.

Images forming up.

Kai. Kai will be my friend. Memory. Kai under him, letting him thrust and thrust. Kai trusting him like a woman, woman who lets you in, into her body, into her heart, into her soul . . . oh, Christ. What can it be like to be a woman, a *real* woman, and have to *trust* people, trust men?

That wry inner voice again. You know it's not *really* like that, Mister Mies. Women, real women, are prey to the same fears and doubts and insecurities and hatreds as you. You know that.

Sure. Sure I do. But . . .

Memory of making love to Kai. Is that what it was? Of making love to Rosie, who'd seemed to trust him, a little bit at least, for a little while. Maybe. Maybe after they let me out of here . . .

What if they don't?

Don't worry, they will. That's why they went to all the trouble of . . . fixing you, Mister Mies.

Sure. That's right.

So feel all the warmth. All the possibility.

Go to each of them, one at a time. Tell them what you learned. Tell them why you're sorry. Tell them . . . maybe. Maybe even Rosie. Memory of making love to her, back on Earth, under full gee. So comfortable, lying on top of her, thrust deep and warm inside, her warm hands on your back, warm hands cupping your little bum and . . .

Something like hormonal warmth. Lines of pleasure flowing together between his legs. A sense of . . . it's been a long time, hasn't it? I used to like masturbating. So private. So . . . close to myself. My elemental urges. Something I could do for myself that no one could take away.

Lying there, floating, gently in the darkness. Where am I? Still wrapped in the chair? No. My God, no. I'm in my room. I'm in my sleeping net. My God, they *have* let me go. I can do anything I want. I . . . hands on the front of his pants, undoing the fastener, sliding his zipper open with a soft plastic whisper. Good thing I don't have to pee. I can just . . . do it.

Sliding his hands down inside. Inside his coverall pants. Outside the rough cotton softness of his underwear. That's it. That's it. I always like to feel those first sensations through the cloth. I . . .

Oh.

Moment of soft confusion.

Reiko-chan.

Am I Reiko-chan?

No, that can't be right.

Did they do something wrong when they fixed my memories? Was it Reiko-chan who got the planetology implant and joined the Daiseijin, got aboard *Mother Night* and flew to the wonderful worlds of Alpha Centauri?

How odd.

How very odd.

Not like Kai and Izzy and Metz to make a mistake like that. I . . .

Well. Soothing inner words. It's all right. Masturbating as woman was all right, too. Not quite the thing you treasured from childhood memory, but . . . arousing. Very much more arousing in its own way, because you grew up from boyhood to become a heterosexual man. When you masturbated as Reiko-chan, it was a little bit like making love to a perfectly compliant woman, a . . .

Putting his hands now to the top of his waistband, pulling the elastic out, sliding his fingers inside. Flat tummy, yes, though with a thicker, harder feel than Reiko's had had. Mies's tummy. Mies's pubic hair, too. Thick, long, wiry. Not Reiko's sleek little thatch.

I always liked the way Reiko's pussy felt. Could never quite connect with the fact that it was *mine*.

Fingers sliding down through pubic hair to where they would surely find soft labia, the swelling, firming flap-lump of clitoris, greedy, anxious, waiting. Beyond, wetter and wetter folds, slick with egg-white consistent fluids, fluids a man would . . .

Down and down. Down and around.

Fingers reaching his asshole.

Now wait. I can't possibly have missed it. I . . .

Feeling around.

Fingers starting to shake.

Now wait. There's got to be a logical explanation for this. It's not just that you really have gone insane. Or that, in trying to *fix* you, they fucked you up worse than ever.

Wry inner voice turning slightly bitter. That *would* be a little annoying now, wouldn't it?

Yes. Yes, it would.

Fingers searching carefully in the pubic hair.

Jesus. Jesus. It's *got* to be here somewhere.

Finding a tender little hole, *much* smaller than the end of his little fingertip. Oh, God, thank God, I . . . what the hell *is* this.

It's your peehole, doofus.

Okay, so you're not a man, peehole on the end of a long, thick hose. Well. Reiko-chan's peehole used to be just at the rim of her vagina so . . . fingers moving on. Okay, in some women, it's just a lot farther forward. David used to enjoy searching them out, sorting out the folds, peek-a-boo, I *see* you . . . fingers finding the double-dome start of asscheeks again.

Mies freezing solid.

Oh.

Images of friendship and love receding.

That's right. That's right, Mister Mies. They don't just *correct* you, when you've done wrong, Mister Mies. No. They have to *punish* you, as well.

But I. But I.

Wry voice now very bitter indeed: Still looking for excuses? Well, the only one you ever fooled was you.

But . . . but they took *everything*!

That's right.

Hiss of the door opening. Dazzle of the light coming on.

Mies looking up.

Kai.

Kai floating in the doorway.

Looking at him.

What must he see?

Mies Cochrane, floating in his sleeping net, hands in his pants.

A pathetic sight.

What's that on his face?

A look of pain?

I can't tell.

Kai floated slowly over, grabbed the netting with one hand, looking at him. Finally, he said, "I'm sorry, Mies. Really sorry."

Mies staring out at him mutely. Nothing to say? But what

about all that bullshit about sharing your feelings, about your *angst*? Well. That was . . . before.

After a while, Kai said, "Izzy, Metz, and I wanted to . . . leave you as a man. We don't think this serves any purpose."

Excuses. He's making excuses. Bastard. "What about the others?"

"Doc thinks this is best. In the end, I guess. Ginny, Rose, Linda, and Spence agreed with his reasoning."

Reasoning? Is that what they call it? So. That's eight. I didn't get a vote and Sheba's dead . . . small, remote pang of guilt—dead because of me . . . he said, "What about Andy?"

Kai grimaced. "Andy wanted to cut off your dick and balls with a cooking knife, shove them down your throat, then put you out the door."

Well, at least someone is honest. "What's become of my . . ." Can't say it. God, I can't even remember what they looked like suddenly, how they felt cupped in my hand.

Kai seemed to wince. Then he said, "Incinerated."

"Will they . . . will Doc grow me a new set?"

Long pause, then, "No."

"Oh."

Do I want to ask to be made into a woman? Surely they'd let me be . . . ghost icon of Reiko-chan floating silently within, painted eyes frozen in a mask of accusation and loathing. Brief memory of Reiko the whore plying her trade. No. No, that's not what I want.

Mies said, "Why am I not feeling anything about this?"

Kai's eyes held something that might conceivably be mistaken for compassion. He sighed. Then said, "Some of it's hypnopaedic rerouting. That'll last for a year or so. Most of it's just a solid load of psychotropic drugs. The . . . effect will wear off over the next day or so."

And then?

And then, silly Mister Mies, you'll start to feel again.

Wry, sarcastic inner voice: Oh, goody. I can hardly wait.

Kai said, "Come on, Mies. Let's go get some breakfast. Then . . . well, we have work to do."

Work. Pholos. Planetologist? What does the scientist want? Pang of emptiness. The scientist is gone.

But . . . that little surge of excitement. To see again. To see the wonderful worlds of Alpha Centauri. To see and . . . understand. Why, yes. Work. That was just the way the scientist persona had always talked about it.

He said, "Okay. I'll be . . . ready, I think. Let's go."

Showtime came of its own accord, time passing the way time always passes, without your will or connivance, whether you resist its passage or not.

Then Mies. Brief and to the point.

What do we do next?

Glad for the drugs. Glad they're helping me . . . do my job. The others, though.

Christ.

Eyes on me.

Mies on one side of the table, floated beside Izzy and Metz and Kai. The others? Clustered opposite. Ginny. Floating beside Doc. Ginny had her eyes aimed . . . elsewhere. So. Embarrassed are we? All of them. Eyes on me now. As though I'm . . . no longer human. As though I suddenly became . . . something else.

He went on with what he'd been saying. "Let me take a look at the geological context of the site. Olympos's edge is multiply stepped, plateau top dropping to a long, sloping piedmont, then downward to a broad continental shelf, and finally the sea bottom. The dendritic patterns of the former rivers begin to appear just above the piedmont, dissecting it into a number of prominent drainage systems.

"To the south, about two hundred kilometers, is a fresh crater, an inset bowl with a smooth rim, surrounded by an apron of low-lying ejecta that almost reaches the location of the new Leospider site."

Kai: "Glad that impact wasn't any closer. We wouldn't have found anything if it was."

"The site itself is composed of sixty featureless hemispheres set in a close, hexagonal array, each located a hundred meters from its neighbors. As with the previous site, it's set near the edge of the high plateau, on a strip of perhaps artificially leveled rock. Looks to me like a city of sorts. It might just be a hyper-trophied version of the manned station we visited. But if every one of those hemispheres is connected to an underground complex . . .''

Kai nodded. ''Our thoughts exactly.''

That's not what you're thinking about.

I can tell.

Goddamn it, let's just get in the lander and . . . *go*. Let's get to work. A momentary, hard pulse of anger and resentment, quickly fading away to a dull orange ember. Mies said, ''Only one way to find out. Who're you sending down with Kai and me, Ginny?''

She looked up from the table. ''That's a difficult one, Mies. I've given it a lot of thought. Izzy and Metz, of course. Spence. And Rosie. You'll need her biological expertise, I think.''

Funny. That's really funny. Can't send Andy. He might kill me. And separate the lovers. So I won't see Andy fuck Rosie. So I won't see Spence fuck Linda. Does she think I'll be jealous? Maybe kill myself? Doesn't she think I might be jealous of Izzy and Metz?

Christ. Who the hell knows what they think? The anger tried to rise again, but just as swiftly faded. Bitter humor: Thank heaven for little drugs, they work the most delightful little change . . .

Kai turned to her. ''Business as usual?''

''That's right. Everyone to behave . . . professionally.''

Professionally. Right. How will *I* behave? Unclear. Maybe I should ask Kai. To his surprise, he said, ''Well, I guess that's what's left of me now, isn't it?''

Sudden look of horror, quickly masked on Ginny's face.

She . . . didn't quite realize that I . . . know.

In the lander again, darkness around them, broken only by the bluish light showing through the windows on *Mother*

Night's hull. Breaking dock with a barely noticeable surge of inertia. Complex hole cut in the stars receding, windows dwindling, shrinking into little bluish squares amidst the star-crowded heavens. Turning now, curving nightside of Pholos rising into view, dead black bite taken out of the universe.

Mies kept his eyes glued on the dark planet out the windows. Hadn't really even acknowledged the other occupants of the lander, Izzy and Metz, chattering to each other, enjoying the ride and the idea of the adventure to come.

Two men in love. Imperturbable. Adapted to their relationship, compromises made, growth and change behind them. Maybe . . . just maybe . . .

Behind them, Rosie and Spence, each in their own little world of confusion and pain. Spence thinking about Linda, Rosie thinking about . . . me? Andy? Or are they just thinking of themselves?

And Kai. Kai the killer of monsters, the maker of me. What will happen next, I wonder, between us?

THIRTEEN

Up here, Kai thought, up in the continental highlands of Pholos, we really are in outer space. Pressure down in the microbars. No wind. No rain. No life. Except for the Leospider ruins, no sign life ever was here. Overhead, the sky was flat black, the two suns twin white disks, like holes into a realm beyond, made of some impossible, shining metal. Artifact, created by the suit interface and the faceplate optics. If I so chose, I could adjust the wavelength passthrough scan and have a lovely time inspecting their sunspots.

All around them, the black plastic city could almost, but not quite, blend in with the rugged, rounded dusty landscape of the Olympian highlands. "Funny to realize they never could have lived up here without their technology."

Bending over her sample cases, Rose looked up and said, "Even back when Pholos was habitable, this was about at the planetary stratopause level. Nothing ever lived up here."

Spence said, "If the mountains weren't in the way, you could orbit a satellite at this altitude. Of course, it'd decay pretty fast, but . . ."

Right. No synergy curve for the ancient rocket enthusiasts of Olympos. Just climb above the tallest peaks and head due east. "Might as well go inside now."

Metz pointed to a wheel handle on an obvious hatch and

said, "Their technological style changed over the . . . I keep wanting to say millennia."

"Over the ages," muttered Mies.

Kai turned and looked at him. Nothing. Nowhere. No one. I did that. Am I ashamed? No. I'd like to use the scanner on him now and see how what I created is shaping up. A slight twinge of something like conscience. We really are still tied to all the old ideas, all the crude Occidental imaginings about personality and soul. I feel as though I killed Mies Cochrane and put a dybbuk in his place. Even though Mies *was* the dybbuk.

He put his hands on the wheel and twisted gently. Which way? To the left, of course. "You notice how they followed the same thread pattern as we do?"

Izzy said, "I was thinking about that. No real reason. Just coincidence."

Rosie: "Well, we did figure out they were left-handed . . ." Double left-handed.

The door popped slightly ajar, revealing a crevice of darkness. No light coming on. Something has died. No great surprise. Two-point-eight billion years. Kai swung the hatch all the way open, twirled the matching wheel on the inner surface and watched the door latches slide smoothly in and out of their wells. "Works backwards from the inside."

Metz: "Always easier to seat a bolt than to break it free."

Kai stepped through the door and shined his helmet light around. "Airlock." Again, no surprise. This was always a high-vacuum environment.

Beside him, Izzy said, "Hooks along the wall. Some crud on the floor beneath them."

"Probably," said Spence, "the remains of spacesuits." He was standing next to Rosie now, seeming to stand too close. Am I imagining things? Kai wondered. After all, Spence and Linda have . . . worked things out. Probably better than they ever had before. Yes. And Rosie. And Andy. Only the rest of us are still adrift.

Kai put his hand on the wheel latch of the inner airlock door, stood still for a moment. "Well. Probably still air inside, given the preserved state of these . . . hell. Don't quite want to call them ruins. Ginny?''

"Here, Kai.''

Voice all business. Empty of feeling. He looked at Mies, inspecting the stillness of his features, the liquid featurelessness of his eyes. Just doing our jobs now, are we?

Suddenly, Mies said, "This is what we're here for, Kai.''

Slight, startled pang. That's exactly what I wanted him to say. Goosebumps forming on his arms. Urge to shudder repressed. We always want to manufacture our friends, rig them so they do and say the things the people in our dreams and fantasies do and say. Always resent it when they do not. And yet, when it happens, when you've made it happen . . .

Mies said, "Come on. Everybody inside. We'll have to close the outer door.'' In the end, he was the one to pull the Leospiders' hatch shut and spin the locking wheel. "All set.''

Kai turned and gave the wheel on the inner door a twist to the left. Nothing.

Izzy said, "Maybe they reversed it. Makes some sense.''

Spence: "Airlock doors in old Piazzi Belt mining habitats always have a means of equalizing pressure. Even the most primitive ones from the mid-twentieth century had dump and fill valves.''

I remember, thought Kai, inspecting the area around the door. That's how the crew of *Soyuz 11* lost their lives. Nothing. Maybe just twist it to the right. What if there's a large pressure head behind the door? I could get hurt in this flimsy suit. And, door open, the air would blast into the little room, throwing people against the outer walls. We could all get hurt. "I'm just going to give it a little twist. Not enough to separate the latch bolts, and—''

The door jumped under his hands. *Chuff.* Pressure suddenly building in the room. And the wheel felt loose now. Twist to the right. Nothing. Twist to the left. The wheel spun and the door popped ajar.

"Interesting,'' said Spence. "I don't think I've ever seen anything like—''

"Yes, you have," said Rosie. "Old-fashioned bottlecaps. Push and twist. It's the same principle."

So it is, thought Kai. He swung the door open and stepped through, shining his light around. An anteroom of sorts. Crumpled things that may once have been couches. Something like a desk. For all the . . . monstrousness that we've seen, they weren't really so terribly different from us, after all. Flight of stairs leading down through the floor. Kai started walking toward it, watching the stairwell flood with the light from his helmet as he approached.

Mies said, "You know, I think I would have been more comfortable had they just been more . . . alien. Just a little bit."

Spence said, "Yeah. As it is, it's like we've discovered a civilization of monsters from some children's fairy tale."

Kai thought, It feels uncomfortably as though he were reading my mind. Looking downward, he could see that the stairs, very human-scale stairs, were intact. Rather rounded. Sagging in the middle. Worn by aeons of footsteps. He put one foot down, gingerly let his weight shift. Just fine.

Rose said, "The atmosphere in here is very different from what's down in the lowlands. Total pressure around six hundred millibars, maybe one-fifty less than what we theorize the Frogmen were breathing in their heyday. There's some oxygen. Partial pressure around seventy millibars . . ."

Kai thought, Down near the bottom of what an acclimated human can survive on for a limited time. "I guess we don't really want to take off these suits, do we?"

Rose laughed softly. "No. Relative humidity is zero. And it's up over three-twenty kelvins in here."

Hot. Hot and dry. I wonder why the oxygen hasn't adsorbed into the walls?

She said, "Mostly nitrogen. Thirty millibars of carbon dioxide. A little argon."

At the bottom of the stairs, Kai stood looking around what had been a lightless cavern. Row on row on row of . . . what? Dull, plastic cabinets. Things like chairs in the spaces between the rows. Blank screens, made of something that wasn't glass.

Smooth stuff. Kai reached out and poked one with a gloved finger, felt its material crinkle slightly. "Still supple after nearly three billion years?"

Mies said, "Hard to believe." He bent down, inspecting the row of buttons beneath the screen. "Nothing printed on the keycaps, but still . . ."

Kai nodded, feeling the thought. "It's almost as if . . . as if we could switch these things back on and the whole place would come back to life."

"But they've been gone. For a long time."

"This place," said Izzy, "reminds me of the Daiseijin mission control center and the Cismercurian launch complex."

On the other side of the room now, Rose spun the wheel on yet another hatch and swung it open, quickly stepped through. "Jesus. Come see."

Kai said, "Ginny? Are you still picking us up?"

"Just fine, Kai. You're not really underground or anything. Just under a building." Voice cool. Cool and empty. *Am I reading those things correctly, or just imagining them? Imagining her feelings from cues I've made up?*

He stepped through the door. Vast room, going down from this little platform as well as up. "All right. So they still had their spaceships, right to the very end."

Mies stepped past him and started down the next flight of stairs.

Mies walked down the stairs, a familiar feeling, knowing the others were right behind him, walked out onto the burnished black floor of the vast underground concourse, looking around, looking upward into the shadows, black depths hardly lit at all by the feeble glow of their suit lights.

Felt, he thought, *just like the stairs I left behind me on Earth. Just the right size? Why? Simple enough. The Leospiders had little legs. But with the lower gravity, the risers could be relatively higher. Why is that? Shouldn't their leg muscles have been evolutionarily adapted to the low-gee, so they'd need the same size risers as us, relative to their height?*

No. Gravity is an absolute. Inverse-square law.

A wry smile. Question and answer. An exchange, just like in the good old days. Brief frown, faint wind of sorrow blowing through him, taking a long time to fade, however weak it had been to begin with. No. Not like the good old days. No one talking now but me. And I miss the way the scientist and I used to chatter away at each other.

Imagine what it would have been like had they been allowed to . . . stay. No more Reiko-whore—image now floating in his mind's eye, icon of a dead slut—no more Indigo eyes—supplanted, still here, by those glitteringly empty eyes of glass—maybe even no more cowering, weeping David—memory surfacing, episodes of little David, unbidden.

Just the two of us. How . . . nice that would have been.

Crackle of anger. *Bastards.* Fucking bastards. Mies felt the lump form in his throat, tried to swallow it, failed. No. Goddamn it, don't you start to cry now. They'll see. And they'll want to *know.* Fucking bastards.

The others were all around him now, looking up in wonder at the vaulted ceiling with its little scooped-out place. The high stone walls, polished until they seemed to glow with a distinct black light.

Spence said, "Those dimples up there. Maybe doors?"

Kai: "You think they launched from underground?"

From orbit, Ginny said, "Why not?"

Shivering, Mies tried to stuff all the loose feelings back where they came from. Wherever the hell that was. Participate. Try to do your job. He said, "Pretty wasteful. They'd have to let the air out."

They started walking together, toward the nearest ship.

If, Mies told himself, that's what it really is. Why do I hope it's not? Just so they'll all be disappointed, because they're all excited now? Would it serve them right? Would *that* make me happy?

Well. Am I a vindictive man?

No.

Didn't I deserve what happened to me?

No answer.

No will to answer, at any rate.

Kai stood looking up at the thing, Mies beside him, the others clustered close behind. You don't want to imagine what this is. What it might be. What you hope it is. Don't want to anticipate that it's . . .

A tall, narrow cone, of some dark gray stuff the color of moon dust. Standing on six silver-gray struts. Thin. Too thin. As if this . . . vehicle is very low mass. Six flat landing pads. Landing pads, because you know it's a spacecraft, recognizably descended from the older Leospider designs re-created by the SAE. Yet . . . somehow more graceful.

Mies said, "Those engines aren't like the ones we make."

"No." Kai walked under the ship, walked under the muzzle of the nearest engine bell and looked up. Not hollow. Not a simple reaction chamber in which gasses explode. It was filled with some kind of bright, crystalline sponge. Bright after all these years.

Voice uneasy, Spence said, "It could be something like one of those old screenlight engines, I suppose."

Could be. Back in the days before nanotech was fully in force, back before we could build reaction plena capable of containing a nuclear explosion in all its glory, all its fury, they made simple atomic rockets. A flat screen of americium metal. Hydrogen gas flowing through the screen. Exploding. Thrusting. They were nearly as powerful as the fusion engines people dreamed of building, once upon a time.

Izzy said, "Too damned expensive. That's why we stopped using them."

Even by the middle of the twenty-first century, the price of americium never dropped below five billion dollars a ton. What's that in today's money? Something like fifteen hundred million ceus. Many times the cost of *Mother Night*. The economy of the time could not afford such ships, with such engines. Could not afford to send them on one-way trips to the stars.

Could not afford to throw that much money away into the infinite dark.

Mies said, "Recall the False Dawn. Project Apollo and the Throwaway Moonships."

Rosie said, "Daiseijin has thrown us away. And *Mother Night*."

Kai said, "*Mother Night* cost no more than the price of a commercial airliner, in an economy equivalent to the Apollo era."

"Airliners used to crash all the time," said Mies quietly.

Rosie: "Is that all we are? A crashed airliner?"

Spence: "What difference does it make?"

Mies: "None at all."

Kai walked out from under the ship, wondering if they'd ever understand. Us. This ship. Leospiders and Frogmen. Humanity. We can spend the rest of eternity understanding. All we've got left is time. Going up one strut was a ladder. Not quite like a human ladder. Four verticals. Three parallel sets of risers. A wide inner pitch. Two narrow outer pitches. They had two legs and four arms. Arms mounted very differently from ours. Or from the Frogmen's. Without waiting for the others, he started upward.

Another hatch. No wheel this time, just a little pull-latch, recessed into the hull. Out of the aeroturbulence. Below the laminar flow sheath. Good design. "You getting good video on this, Gin?"

"Some signal interference. We got a lot of snow while you were under the ship."

Doc's voice said, "Given the structure, it doesn't seem like it would be that dense."

"No. Doesn't seem like it would." He pulled the latch and let the hatch swing open. *Blink*. "Well. Something still works in there." Pale pink light flooding from inside the ship.

Mies, hanging below him on the ladder now, said, "Why pink? B's light's not much less white than the Sun's."

Rosie: "They may have evolved underground. Those big silver eyes . . . maybe not well adapted to ultraviolet. Red light would be less likely to make the lipids in their eyes grow rancid.''

Spence: ''The other light we saw wasn't red.''

Mies said, ''Since then, hundreds of millions of years have gone by.''

Kai: ''And they've been indoors all that time.''

Metz said, ''Too much video. Bad for the eyes.''

Kai imagined a future species of Leospiders for a moment, Leospiders squinting like moles. It made them seem even more like cartoon characters. Up inside the airlock there was a small chamber with the usual inner hatch and a standard Leospider handwheel from this era.

Mies said, ''Hooks. And spacesuits.''

Spacesuits still hanging from the hooks. Thin stuff, like plastic tissue. Still supple to the touch. When he tried to pull one down, it clung to its hook, resisting his tugging, ignoring any twists he made, springing back into shape when he let go.

Rosie said, ''Well, at least we know they weren't proof against vacuum. I was beginning to wonder.''

Kai spun the handwheel and opened the inner hatch. More pink-lit spaceship, a corridor, with open doors visible beyond. Everything lit up. I'm beginning to feel like an intruder here. Or like a character in a ghost story. We'll find the wardroom and mess hall. We'll find half-finished dinners still warm in their plates . . .

Mies said, ''You can almost feel their ghosts, can't you?''

Metz: ''Shut up. Giving me the creeps.''

The first room was . . . nothing. Tables. Chairs. Wardroom or mess hall, hard to tell. Impossible to guess. Unexpectedly, a porthole, giving a view out into the room beyond, other spacecraft visible. Other machines. The stairs back up to the mission control room.

Spence said, ''Huh. I wonder why they didn't make the whole hull transparent? One-way, I mean, like this.''

Rosie: ''Living underground, maybe they didn't like the feel of wide-open space.''

More things hanging on hooks beyond the table, four blotchy

things, like rubber diving suits hanging limply from hooks, empty bladders. Familiar pattern, though, thought Kai, walking over. He reached out and touched one of the things, feeling its stiff texture, like thick shower curtain material. Started to spread it out . . .

"Fuck." Letting it go, feeling his stomach muscles clench suddenly.

Mies, laconic, said, "That sure did look like an empty Frogman skin, didn't it?"

Izzy, nervous: "Guess this is the dining room."

Rosie: "I would have sworn they went extinct when the atmosphere got down to . . ." She spread the first of the skins open. Arms and legs hanging down. Blotchy green-and-gray belly. A froggy face . . . "Not quite right, you know?"

No, I don't know. Don't want to think about it, but . . . Well, so they didn't go extinct. Didn't go extinct because the Leospiders kept them alive. To eat. Breed and eat, like cattle.

Quick image of a Leospider, silvery fangs in a Frogman's throat, sucking, sucking, *mmmmmm-hm-hmmmmm* . . . Frogman growing smaller and smaller still until . . . just an empty skin now. Hanging from a hook on a wall. Leftovers.

Rose said, "The face has changed character over the ages. Head is smaller in relation to the body. Eyes are reduced. Hard to tell from this but . . . maybe blind. Not much room in that head for brains anymore."

Metz gagged and turned away.

Fingering a number of flat gray disks around the periphery of the Frogman's belly, Rosie said, "These are not fang puncture marks. More like valves."

Mies reached out and ran his hand softly over the empty Frogman's flesh. "A hell of a thing to have happen to you, wasn't it?"

Kai felt a pulse of anger. Bastard. Still a little bastard living in there somewhere. Remark aimed straight at me, I suppose.

Up at the top of the ship, where you'd expect to find a control room in human technomorphology, they found exactly that. Leospider-style chairs, well-padded against acceleration stress . . . meaning, Kai thought, they didn't have anything like gravity control. Just as well, since our physics suggests it's not possible, however nice it'd be to have. Control consoles, neatly labeled in the little splats of scrambled lines the Leospiders had been using for writing, unchanged, for almost two billion years. One-way windows. Viewscreens. Some of them probably computer screens.

Rose said, "They didn't seem to have anything like the eye-bubble. I wonder why not?"

Mies: "Maybe they didn't like it. Some people don't."

People. Are these people?

Spence said, "The things we've seen. Those *seemed* an awful lot like VR."

Metz snickered. "Manufactured for us by the spieltier software. Because *we* use the eyebubble interface."

Kai said, "Ginny, can you punch up the recorded data we've spooled on the Leospider written language?"

Voice fuzzed with faint static. "Kai, I don't think we can put a video feed down to you."

"Voice reciprocal will do fine."

"All right. Done."

Kai sat in a chair he imagined might belong to the command pilot. That's right. Would've gotten a fine view from here. Nice big window. One big viewscreen. Two smaller ones that probably held data arrays. He pointed to a label. "This one."

A soft voice whispered, *"Reaction engines, consolidated fuel feed."*

Okay, so it's the throttle. He laid his hand on it. Jeez. I wonder if there's any fuel? Two-point-eight billion years? Be a fuck of a note if I blew us all up now, wouldn't it?

Spence said, "Um, *Kai.*"

He grinned, pointed to a batch of switches to his right, angled away, toward the next seat. The voice whispered, *"Main life-support circuit breaker panel."*

Okay. Probably had the flight engineer sitting next to him. As if on cue, Mies came and sat down in the seat. Kai pointed.

"This one?" A bunch of things that looked like blue glass buttons.

"Hyperpipe reflux shunt control modulus."

Um . . . "What?"

Silence. Then Doc's voice said, "Kai, the translator software thinks that . . . Well."

"Well, what?"

Ginny: "Some kind of transport system. For, uh, superluminal phase movement. That's what it says, anyway. I—"

Izzy said, "Are you saying this ship can travel faster than the speed of light?"

Doc: "I don't know. The translator doesn't really have that much data, you know."

Kai: "I'm trying to imagine how a . . . uh, 'hyperpipe reflux shunt' might work."

Ginny: "The translator has loaded up several thousand library hypertext references now. Most of them to late twenty-first-century notions about how quantum transformational dynamics could be used to violate causality."

Mies said, "That's why it was displaced by quantum holotaxial dynamics. It was wrong."

Kai said, "Not necessarily. Its map was just inadequate. Classical Newtonian mechanics wasn't displaced by Einsteinian relativity, just . . . enlarged."

Metz said, "I know: QTD theorists suggested that since you could alter a particle into any other particle by changing the vibration substructure of its superstring, it should be feasible to change its locus the same way."

"Didn't work," said Spence.

Metz: "No, because they didn't know about hyperpipes and Platonic Reality. That prevented them from seeing how they could get around the problem of Heisenberg and the ubiquity of chaotic attractors. We do, however."

Kai said, "Well, we know how to think about it. But it's hard to imagine assembling enough data processing power to make something like that feasible."

Ginny said, "It'd be easier to just convert the ship to radio waves, beam it to its destination, and reconstitute it from the data.''

Kai said, ''Not sure I'd be willing to travel that way. *Or* let myself be broken up and shoved down a hyperpipe matrix . . .''

Metz snickered. ''Yes. The good old Teleportation Paradox.''

Doc's voice, tinged with amusement, said, ''Right. 'Is it live, or is it Memorex?' ''

Silence. Then Spence said, ''What's *Memorex*?''

With the passage of time, in a human context, things wind down. Back out of the depths, tomorrow is another day, that sort of thing. . . . Mies stood at the foot of *MN01*'s boarding ramp, looking across the flat, bare ground toward the sunset. Low arc of red and orange sky surmounted by indigo surmounted by black. *Indigo*. Have I learned to hate that word at last?

No. No, I haven't. Haven't learned to hate the word, nor the people, nor the things they did, nor what they stood for. What I thought they stood for. That's the worst of it, isn't it? *What I thought they stood for.* I didn't think they stood for anything. Didn't care what they stood for. Just . . . get with the program, boy. A group of people. Somewhere to belong. Someone with whom to belong. A way to become . . . unlost.

Or even just a way to *become*.

Sterilizing 99% of the world's women as a means of saving the human race, of saving the long, possibly immortal lives of everyone now living, that's not such a terrible thing? Is it? Silence. Okay. You tell me. I don't know the answer.

Kai's silhoutte, a few hundred meters further east, superimposed against the sunset. Darker sunset now, world fading to black, stars coming out. Soon he'll be just black nothingness, outlined against the stars. A little man-thing in a flimsy white spacesuit, daring the whole of creation.

Kai who destroyed me.

No. Didn't destroy *me*. Destroyed the *others*. And who were the others? Evil spirits imposed on David Gilman, imposed on him however much he cooperated with the imposition. Indigo rules of engagement. Reiko the whore. Mies the scientist, a deliberate imposition. Personal Mies an accidental by-blow.

David Gilman. David Gilman is all that was ever *real*. But . . . rage. Hard rage. They did this to *me*! Careful. Careful now. By this time Doc's psychotropic drugs will have worn away and . . . Squinting into the gloom, darkness well-nigh complete. What the hell is he doing? Billow of translucent material against the dark horizon. Setting up the survival tent.

Memory.

Memory of Kai in my arms.

Kai indistinguishable from a woman, a young woman, slim like a girl and . . . recoiling from that. He's not a woman, you see, and . . .

Bitter, angry, biting humor: And you, are you a man now?

Memory made him suddenly aware of the hollow down there.

But, walking toward him, nonetheless.

Kai looking up. Pleasant voice, almost but not quite a baritone. What do they call that? A light baritone? "Hello, Mies. Nice night."

Silence. Then: "Camping out again?"

More silence. Then Kai said, "Sure. I've . . . gotten so I like it better. I wish I'd done more of it when I lived on Earth."

The tent suddenly inflated, growing up, taking on its slightly flattened rigid hemisphere shape. No sound up here. No air. Down in the lowlands, I'd have heard the crackle. More memory. The tent material crackling softly, breathing above them, in and out, while he and I . . .

No. Put it away.

Kai said, "You want to join me?"

Cringe of fear, but: "All right."

Inside the tent, Mies sat with his back to Kai, sat turned oh-so-carefully away, looking out through the tent material at the night, trying to relax. Still something in me, something inside, that wishes . . . that wants . . . that . . . ah, hell. I don't know.

If it was the old me, maybe I'd have an erection now, but . . .

if they were going to take the *means* away, why didn't they take the feelings as well? Goddamn you, Kai.

Kai moving around behind him now, soft rustling. Probably getting out of his spacesuit. All right. Time to go to sleep. Mies had gotten out of his own suit, was holding the thin, deflated material folded in his lap. Still wearing the coverall garment though. Well. Good enough I . . . hand on his shoulder.

He jumped. Jumped away from Kai, turning, staring, glaring at . . . oh, you fucking asshole.

Kai standing close beside him. Standing there, stark naked, looking down at him, eyes wide and dark. Kai, no tits, no hair on his slit, looking down at him, so concerned, so . . . Mies, looking at him, sitting on the floor, face level with his . . . nothing happening to me. Nothing real. But, inside . . . surge of desire. No, the old, familiar rule-sieves, no. Real desire. Real clean human male desire that I . . .

Flare of blue-white anger.

Bastards.

Staring right at that prepubescent girl's crotch, remembering what it had been like to . . . to his horror, the lips began to part, something . . . something . . . coming out. Slim. Shiny wet. Red like the dick of a dog. Sliding out a little way. Just a few centimeters. Then sliding back in, going away, leaving something like girlflesh behind. Girlflesh and . . . and my desire. Unslaked. Unslakable. Softly, he said, "Goddamn it, Kai. Leave me alone."

A look that seemed to speak of surprise. "Mies. I . . ."

"Look, I don't know what you have in mind. But you know what you did to me." He turned away, turned and looked back out at the darkness. Turned his back on Kai and felt the skin between his shoulder blades crawl.

After a while, there was another spate of rustling. Kai getting dressed? Good. He didn't turn to look until he heard the rasp of a plastic zipper, turned and saw Kai, suited up, in the airlock. Leaving.

Going away.

Leaving me.

Leaving me alone.

Mies felt himself start to cry, but it was . . . unreal. Like someone else crying. Not me at all.

Standing outside, alone in his spacesuit, soft, slick plastic cool on his skin, Kai stared up at the familiar stars, the speckled stellar patterns common to this part of the inner Orion Arm, and thought, So what the hell did you expect?

Nothing.

No one in here willing to supply an answer.

Christ, fantasies always willing to supply what reality does not. Expectations coloring what we do and say and feel until, sometimes, the real world outside our skulls seems as impermanent as the wind.

What *was* in my imagination?

I fixed you, Mies Cochrane. Drove away all your ghosts. Made you whole again. Now I've come for my just reward . . .

So what the hell did you *think* he'd do?

Did you think he'd just . . . bend over for you?

Sorry I can't be a man for you anymore, little Kai. Sorry you let Doc burn my dick away to ashes. Here, let's try this instead . . .

Is *that* what you thought?

He felt his lip curl. Contempt? Amusement? Derision? At whom? Me? The whole world? Nothing. No one. Just play-acting for the night air. Telling stories to myself. Lying to myself.

That's what we all do.

Why should I be any different?

Hell, that's the way everyone excuses their behavior. Everyone does it. Why should *I* be any different? Who are *you* to hold me to a different standard of behavior?

Silence.

No one here.

Nothing.

Not even the wind to whisper solace in my ear.

Jesus, I'm sorry Mies. But, if I hadn't . . .

No answer. Mies not listening. Mies not even here.

Subtle inner voice, his own voice whispering back: In a year or two or three, the implant montage you made for him will decay. It will decay steadily and smoothly, just the way you set it up. Kai, Izzy, and Metz. Programmers *extraordinaires. So* much better, you see, than the crude butchers from Indigo.

Image of Indigo eyes turned to empty, empty eyes of glass.

By the time what *I* made goes away, what they made will be long gone. What remains will be David Gilman. Not whole again. Not healed. No one is ever healed, truly healed, in their heart of hearts. But you'll be as whole and healed as any man can truly be. Can't you understand that, David Gilman. Can't you understand that I just *saved* you?

No. I guess not.

David Gilman not listening, either.

David Gilman not even here.

Not yet.

Up in the sky, there were little moons among the stars. Little planets far away. That one there. Ixion? Or Nephelë? The latter, I think. I'd like to go back again, take a long look around. Enjoy the peace and quiet of the ice and cold. Go back with Mies at my side. Watch him grow real again as the days and weeks and months and years unreel.

Odd, familiar feel to that thought. Familiar warmth.

Thinking of him as if he were a child now. My child. Mammalian instincts triggered, deep inside, somewhere, by what he's become. By what I've done. This new Mies didn't ask to be created. But then, no child ever asks to be born. We bring them into existence, and then we cast them into the abyss.

I wish this had been a habitable world. Once upon a time, I didn't think I cared. But then . . . but then. Had I come to Earth sooner. Had I stayed a little longer. Perhaps I would never had had the will to leave.

Hot UV sun on soft, pale white skin.

Kai stood in the middle of a tawny, scrawny desert in north-western Arizona and felt the dry wind slip across his skin, wiping away tiny beads of hot sweat almost before they could form. Sunlight glaring down out of a sky almost too pale to be called blue made him squint, looking eastward across the dry, rolling countryside of the Red Lake basin, eastward to the Grand Wash Cliffs, marking the treaty border between the property of the Daiseijin Scientific and Industrial Enterprise and the Free Associated State of the Hualapai.

Southward, Truxton Wash. Northward, pretty far away, Lake Mead and Las Vegas. Visible, humping up like a black crag in the west, the not-quite-2200-meter peak of Mount Tipton, invisible beyond, the monad-city of Chloride, the Black Mountains, the Colorado River, and Lake Mohave, the southern tip of Nevada, the dry salt lake country of California, the mountains, the deserts, and so on to the fat, flat sea . . .

All right, said an exhausted voice from deep inside. Get inside, out of this damned hot morning sun, get inside, shower off the dust, go down the elevator to the dorm and see if Ginny's in the mood for a quick one before she shuffles off to her shift . . .

But . . .

Turned around for a reason, toolbelt clanking around your hips, smaller tools jingling together like windchimes. Wanted to look back at it. Done. Almost done. Riggers were starting to pull down the scaffolding already. By the time midnight shift comes on again, she'll be standing there on the concrete pad, pristine, buttoned up, ready to fly.

Lander Prototype Number One.

Surprising no one's built something like this before. Sure, things shaped like this, a short fat cone like an old SSTO shuttle from the dawn of the space age, but . . .

I wonder how much they had to bribe the regulators to get permission to test fly it right off the surface of the Earth? Millions, probably. Right now, somewhere inside that fat white cone, technicians were tuning up a compact military fusion reactor, making sure the heat exchangers were working perfectly, scanning the engine's pressure vessel . . .

Imagine if she explodes tomorrow. The bloom of live steam

would scour the desert clean of life for miles around. They'd hear the bang in L.A.

Memory of test firing the engine, months ago. It'd made an unearthly scream like no rocket engine ever built. Somehow, a most suitable sound for the landing boat of a free-ranging starship, lander able to descend from orbit, land on an Earthlike world, ascend to orbit again without refueling.

Though, if it's an *Earth*like world, there'll be plenty of water to top off her tanks. . . .

Christ. Have I been on the ground for eighteen months already? Seems impossible, but . . . Hard muscles in arms and legs and torso, muscles sliding over each other like liquid steel, telling you it was so.

Tomorrow, I'll see the real sky again.

Image of himself in no more than twenty hours, boarding the ship as floodlights played over her sides, floodlights blotting out the stars above. Sometimes the Arizona sky was like the sky of outer space, very much like the real sky.

And, tomorrow, I'll sit in front of the flight engineer's console of *LPN1*. And then, just when the sun begins to rise, we'll fly.

Inside, Kai dropped his dusty coveralls in a hopper and walked naked into the communal shower room, picked out a nozzle and hit the handle, stepping under a fine, warm spray. The room was filling up with other techies from the midnight shift, tired men and women standing under cascading water, alone or in little chattering groups.

Nice-looking people, thought Kai. Most of them born right here on Earth, most of them with a terrestrial's remarkably stocky build. They all look just like Ginny. . . .

"Hey, Kai. Tonight's the big night, huh?"

Kai half turned and nodded at the pudgy, dark systems engineer under the next showerhead. "Hey, Solly. Yep."

Another naked man walking across the wet floor, a rather older man, pale-skinned, bald, almost like a character from an old movie, face somehow weathered and dry and . . .

Kai tried not to start, tried not to stare. Not a man, no. Nothing swinging between his legs after all. Hairless. Nothing hidden. Not much like a woman, either, though you couldn't really tell what was among those limp little folds of pale white skin.

Manlike thing walking right up to him, getting under the next showerhead, slapping the handle and getting under the spray, going, "Ahhh . . ." Then, looking over at Kai, smiling. "Nothing like a shower after a hard night's work, is there?"

Kai nodded. "Nothing like a shower anytime." *Not someone I've seen on the pad before. Don't remember him from last night, either.* "You part of flight-readiness certification?"

The man turned to face him, stood there looking him up and down, making Kai's skin crawl just a bit, making him wonder if the whatever-he-was liked what he was looking at. *Jesus, this has got to be a woman. Weird looking, though. Maybe something new? Some sort of postandrogyne perversion?*

The creature said, "Yeah. Just looking things over. Mostly making sure life-support telemetry does its job. You boys are our guinea pigs tomorrow."

Guinea pigs? What the hell . . . Then a shrug. "It's just an old-fashioned rocketship . . . ah . . ."

"Call me Doc. Everyone does." *Funny looking bald man/ woman rubbing his/her big, flat hand with plump, spatulate fingers over his/her, maybe even its, belly, just above where there didn't seem to be much of anything.*

Watching me watch him or whatever. Masculine seeming. Making me want to stick with he *. . .*

Watching me try not to look at his crotch.

Doc smiled, closed his eyes, tipped his head back under the spray and let the water sluice down over his shoulders. "Ahhhh . . . One damn good thing about being bald. No fucking shampoo."

Kai tried taking a long look between the man's legs. *Nothing like labia there. Just folded skin.* He looked back up to see the man grinning at him. Very amused. Very fucking amused. "Um. Sorry."

A short bark of a laugh. "People will stare when they see

something like me. I'm sure you have some idea what it's like."
Very sure, aiming a significant look at the most interesting
space between Kai's own thighs.

Kai said, "Um." Nothing else to say. Maybe just, "I guess
people get used to things after a while."

Doc said, "Yup."

Another spin under the spray, then he tapped the water off
and stood dripping. Nodded to Kai, to a silent Solly, and said,
"See you in the morning, boys." Walked away, favoring Kai
with a long view of slim white buttocks.

When he was gone, Solly said, "They say he had a little
accident years ago, during the development of the suspended
animation system. Apparently, he decided he liked himself
that way."

"Odd."

"Don't you know who that was?"

"No."

A long silence, then Solly said, "You're on the rotation roster
for the explorer ship prime flight crews, aren't you?"

A nod, glancing at Solly, seeing an odd look in his eye.
"Sure. I figure if we're lucky, Ginny and I might get an early
assignment. Say to Tau Ceti or maybe Epsilon Eridani . . ."

Solly said, "That was Doctor Matel. Ernesto Matel, chief
flight surgeon for the project."

Kai said, "Uh . . . "

"The one in charge of assigning the prime crews."

One long, shallow pang of dismay, remembering how he'd
behaved, then Kai thought, *Oh*.

FOURTEEN

An end to the night. The six of them gathering again. Gathering their equipment. Going back into the Leospiders' home. Going down through tunnels of endless night, deep under the ground. Finally, Kai realized, I remember exactly why setting up the SAE scanner head seems so familiar. It's not just that we've done it so many times in the past few days. It's that it has the resonance of an old, familiar task. A similar task.

Just another part of growing up, a fading part of that long-abandoned childhood. I was sent out to work on a seismic survey team in the Taxolongula Hills, back on Titan, hills looking out over the broad and featureless gray-white flatness of the Waxsea.

Hammer man. You're hammer man today, Kai. Tee-hee-hee. You little shit. Instrument man sets up the box. Hammer man lays out the cables. Plugs them in. Lays out the conduction disks. Flicks the switch on the seismic hammer. Old tech. Not high tech at all.

Some asshole probably figured it'd make us grow up big and strong.

Then, going from disk to disk, metal disks laid out on the frozen ice rock of Titan's only continent. Hit it. *Wham* on the metal disk. Hit it. *Wham* on the metal disk. Instrument man smirking as he took his readings.

I felt like I'd broken my back, all day long, before somebody took pity on me and showed me how to swing a sledgehammer, letting the dense hammerhead's inertia do all the work.

Assholes.

Ginny's voice said, "We're all set up here, Kai. Spieltier's in RAM but out of circuit."

Out of circuit. Like all the bits of Mies Cochrane we set aside. Harada Reiko. Reiko-chan. Weeping. So glad to die. But she's in there somewhere still. Merely silenced. A guilty look at Mies. Mies paying attention to what was going on, plugging in his waveguide packet. Smiling, perhaps. Perhaps with antici- pation, perhaps . . .

Did I draw that smile on his face? Izzy, Metz, and I?

Izzy seemed focused on the task at hand, but Metz . . . Metz was shying away, looking at Mies from time to time. Metz didn't like doing it. Didn't like what we did. No, he feels . . .

Hell. Hell with it. Run the scanner. Just do your goddamned job. "All set?"

Izzy waved, thumbs up.

Kai nodded at the VR controls, watched the familiar graphs appear. *Go.* Two-point-eight billion B.C., give or take a few thousand millennia. Images building. Data coalescing. Spool- ers spooling.

And then the air seemed to fill with silent, transparent ghosts.

Spence said, "Well. You'd think, with this site being so pristine and all, so well preserved and—"

Metz muttered, "Not the problem. Problem is there's just so fucking much . . ."

Izzy: "Kai, how could the data be this deep?"

A long look around at his graphs. "Simple enough. It just has to *accumulate.*"

Rosie: "They lived here for a long damned time. Maybe five hundred million years. Maybe a lot longer than that."

Kai started running the timeline back, watching more and more ghosts appear. Denser and denser images. Overlays devel- oping throughout the VR representation. Scanner head pulling more and more unified field data out of the hyperpipes . . .

Reflux. What the hell would happen if we looked down these pipes and found the backtrail of one of those Leospider starships? Would it just come popping right out at us? Time and space don't mean anything in the context of Platonic Reality. Somewhere in . . . there. Somewhere, do the Leospiders still exist?

Now, the room was filled with ghosts, ghosts like dirty linen laundry. From his orbital perch, Doc said, "This is useless. Shall we try the spieltier array?"

Silence. People looking at each other through a fog of dead souls. Finally, Mies said, "Might as well."

Might as well. Because I'm dead and at home with the dead? Is that what you're thinking, Mies? I wish you'd say.

Metz said, "We're not going to learn anything that way. I guarantee you, we're going to have to rig a much tighter focus than this if we want to sort anything from that mess."

Izzy: "We should do it anyway. Get a baseline reading. That'll help us later on. Give the rule sieve pregenerator something to work with."

Kai: "Go ahead." The world around them changed to a black-and-white image of a stained-glass window and froze in place.

Metz said, "Shit. I told you so."

Kai thought, They lived here. Lived on and on. And yet, as we go deeper into the past, as we dig our way down the long tunnel of their timeline, the data density grows deeper and deeper. As if there were more and more . . .

Mies said, "I guess, as time went by, there were fewer of them."

You guessed that, did you? Of course you would. Because they died out. If they hadn't died out, they'd still be here. They'd still be here, because they never left. Despite the fact that they built starships. Starships that could go faster than light. Starships, for Christ's sake . . . and we have starships, too. . . .

Floating, suited up, on the flight deck of the third-hand Class F Oort Exploration Vehicle, space dimly lit by red engineering lights that would burn from now until the little ship died, somewhere, somewhen far away, Kai had taken one last look around, while the ship's eyebubble core obediently filled his vision field with cascades of data and whispered softly in his earphones.

No real reason for the lights, I suppose. We could tell the bubble to turn them off after we seal the hatch, ship's windows like red eyes going out, as if the ship were dying right then, and . . .

I wonder if it'd feel bad, being left in the dark?

Silly. But everyone does that, just the way people used to personify machines before they had any sentience at all, a hangover from the days of woodland spirits and the myth of the World Soul.

Bubblesystems have no thoughts, no feelings. Nothing at all, you see, but deep-tracking rule-sieves. Still, you had to wonder if, somewhere down among all those rules, some programmer or another had planted a single bald statement: You're all alone now.

And, of course, the core had the power to amend its own rules. Isn't that just about the totality of what defines a sentient mind?

I think, therefore . . .

I think, therefore . . .

Hmm. New rule called for here . . .

I think. Therefore, I feel . . .

Nonsense.

A lot of wear and tear on the bridge of this old ship, ship once called *Alleluia III,* ship built almost forty years ago, flown out to the Oort dozens of times already, ship flown round and round, round about, plucking dark bodies from dark space, scavenging the Black Sky Country for its human masters.

Easy to imagine all the men and women who lived on these decks, ate and worked and slept and fucked in the little cabins that we've filled with our soulless machines. Most of those men and women still alive somewhere, most of them probably still out working the Cloud. Wonder how they'll feel when they hear we've sent their old friend off to die alone in the dark between the stars?

Comradeship, maybe. Maybe that's how they expect to die, out in the Black Sky Country, doing the work of Standard ARM for pay . . .

A wasp-voice in his earphones: "*Pegasus,* mission control. How you doing Kai? We're at the start of the built-in hold, tee minus thirty minutes." Ginny's voice, from where she floated at her console in the powerstation's habitat. Ginny, bossing her crew, seeing to the generator node, tracking the play of raw sunlight on the active-matrix solar cells.

Black outside the little ship's windows, here in the lee of the sunshield. Cold out there in the shadows. A fury of stars outward bound, inward, up against the black shape of the shield, a glitter of lights where men and women worked away at the powerstation, the particle beam head . . .

Ginny, tracking her data, tuning up the beam.

He said, "On timeline, mission control. We'll be buttoning her up in seven minutes."

Leaving the little ship all alone.

I think I'll leave the lights burning.

Won't take much power.

Hell, maybe somewhere between here and Barnard's Star, someone will see her go by, will see those red-lit window-eyes and wonder who's aboard. . . .

Then, later, Kai had floated with his pad crew just outside the gaping hole of the habitat's airlock door, looking back toward the ship. Not supposed to linger outside in this radiation-dense environment only eleven million kilometers from the sun, but . . .

Right. Who the hell would want to miss this? If things fucked up, they could duck inside the lock and slam the hatch. Meanwhile, they'd shut out the airlock lights, floating huddled together in the darkness, waiting.

Doc, floating next to him, said, "This ought to be a hell of a show . . ."

Ought to be. They'd fired the beam a couple of times, just to make sure it worked the way the manufacturer claimed, but . . . But nothing. Just a couple of fiery red burps, enough to bring all the systems up, get them to register on the sensors. Not enough to violate the license issued by the solar government.

This is it. Permission to ''test fire the main tensor beam out of the solar system, away from all tracked vehicles, for a period of not more than seven hours, scientific results to be reported to the government prior to publication in appropriately licensed, refereed research journals . . .''

Ginny's voice in his earphones: ''Tee minus one minute. Begin accumulator charge.''

Nothing. No ''sense of tension in the air'' or anything. But, somewhere, all the raw power falling on the sunward side of the shield was pouring into special capacitors, energy building up and . . .

Just enough extra energy to get the beam started. But . . . imagine the fucking explosion we could have. Would it be visible on Earth in daylight? Of course not. We're hanging in front of the sun. Her light would swallow the little flicker we made as we died.

''Thirty seconds. Preheat.''

The deflector coils around the beam generator suddenly appeared out of the blackness, dim shapes glowing subtly, almost like figments of the imagination, a soft, soft orange luster.

I wonder what she'll find at Barnard's Star, this poor little *Pegasus*? Dim little star with gas giant worlds and hard-frozen ice-moons that no human being will ever visit. And she'll get there in only twelve years. By then, the first crews will have left for Alpha Centauri and Tau Ceti and all the other promising stars, for *Pegasus*'s meaningful data will all be delivered in the first year of her flight, beamed back home. She'll go on alone, her target explorations no more than serendipity . . .

''Ten.''

Light at the coils brightening, distinct red shapes now, lighting up their surroundings like the bright coils of a resistance-heater stovetop in some primitive last-world kitchen.

''Fire.''

A stark moment, in which Kai listened to his heart.

Brilliant white-violet light, quickly stopped down by the suit optics, bright white light like an explosion in the heart of the coils as the accumulators dumped energy into the collimation system.

Then, with the little world of the powerstation picked out all around him like line-art images in an old-fashioned VR interface, Kai saw the beam, a thin rod of pastel purple haze, sticking out into the depths of black space.

Wave front, he thought, racing away at the speed of light, already past the orbit of Mercury, heading for Venus, then Earth, only minutes away, scale growing fast, beam growth slowing to a crawl, long hours through the realm of the gas giants, days and weeks out through the Oort, where we wandered in durance vile, then . . .

Then years. Years before a widened and attenuated beam bathes the Barnard System in mistily invisible light. And the little ship? Already moving, beam dead center in the tilted circle of the magsail, ship itself canted to one side by carefully measured vector forces. Sail and unmanned starship sliding away up the beam, accelerating at just under one gee. Falling away into the night. Falling into the Black Sky Country.

Doc said, "Hardsuits or no, the biologicals are starting to complain. We'd better get inside."

Mies. Walking and walking. This is me. Me now. Very cold now. Forget about . . . last night. Just forget about it. Forget about everything. No one cares how you feel. No one ever did. *Fool.* Worse than a fool. Yes. Very cold now. That's the ticket.

They'd followed the spiral ramp on and on as it corkscrewed into the deep rock. Kilometers of dark granite passed, and yet there was no sign of an ending. I *can* see them now. Now that the SAE has revealed them to me. Passing along these corridors in the thousands, the tens of thousands. All thinking that there was some meaning to their existence. Every one of them convinced that their actions made a difference. But what good did it do them? To disappear. Just to be gone, as a species.

Lords of creation, looking out over their world, watching as the water, then the atmosphere went away. Watched as their world died. Understand that, Mies Cochrane. Really understand what it feels like. Life is a moment to moment thing. Sliding along the timeline, you feel the directionality, the *purposefulness* of it. But when each moment is over, it is, of itself, worthless. When they are gone, when we are gone, there is truly nothing left. Even with the SAE, all that remains is a phantasm. This is the problem that has been dogging me all my life.

Finally, the ramp leveled out.

"So," Metz said from far in front. "Now we find out what they kept in the basement."

The room was bigger than any they had discovered before. They ambled out in close order, trying to take in the size of it. The ceiling was a considerable distance overhead, and though the width of the room was no more than a hundred meters, it went on and on, beyond the range of radar. Each wall was a vast honeycomb of interlocked hexagons of some light-colored metal, each hexagon about a half meter on a side.

"Good God," said Kai. "Look at it."

Izzy took a few steps, head thrown back. "What's it for?" he said. "Is this where they stored their honey? I knew they were an industrious lot, but . . ."

Rose squatted down next to the closest one. "There's *something* in here, but I can't quite tell what. It looks fragile."

Memory of the Frogman remains. Mies said, "Maybe you'd better be careful."

But she was crawling inside already, disappearing. "Whatever it is, it seems pretty tough. I've got hold of an appendage of some sort, am dragging it out. Slowly . . ."

First the soles of her boots appeared, then she let go of whatever it was, got a grip on the rim of the hexagon and pulled herself out, standing. She looked at them. "It's a Leospider corpse. Fully intact."

"Catacombs," said Metz.

"They're all full. This is where the Leospiders came to die."

Kai had gone over to the first hexagon, was peering in. "Rosie, help me get it out."

It was marvelously preserved, identical to the images from the SAE except in color, which was sort of a dull, gunmetal gray. It was not even very stiff, and, as they pulled, it came out of the erect posture in which it had been lying, and the arms uncrossed and dragged on the floor.

Metz: "It almost looks like it's asleep, waiting for us to kiss it awake."

Izzy: "I think you're getting your fairy tales mixed up again. You can kiss it if you want to, though."

"This is . . . remarkable, to say the least," said Spence. "They're here. All of them."

Kai: "I wonder if they believed in an afterlife? Mummified for the trip to heaven."

Heaven? Hardly. "The only place they've gone is into our history books."

Mies moved closer to look into its face. Lidless silver eyes, dull, flat orbs, hair and mandibles making a grotesque but quite symmetrical display. No way to read an expression, except maybe one of horror. Afraid to touch it. Look at it, moments compiled and crystallized. Lives neatly preserved like in a butterfly collection. I think they must've had difficulty coping with the idea of their deaths.

Izzy had moved further into the room. "Metz, I'm counting something over ten thousand of them. And the returns from the far end are lost in muzz."

Metz: "Thanks, Iz. Now who wants to—"

"Hey," shouted Izzy, "There's something down there on the floor."

About halfway down, there was a little pile of . . . something, not much lighter in color than the floor, partially disintegrated. In a minute they were all around it. More than anything else it looked like a headless human torso, surrounded by desiccated pieces of exoskeleton and dark, flaky-looking lumps of various sizes.

Like a dead bug, thought Mies. Like a dead beetle. One of

little David's memories. Dead beetle lying in the grass, a dry, legless husk. Little David? No. One of *my* memories.

Rosie knelt, pulling out a long pair of tongs and carefully sorting through the debris. "Looks like there was one left."

Kai laughed. "Romantic notion, that. The last of the Leospiders. No one left to preserve him, so he just fell here and rotted."

"Ironic." Mies wondered what became of the head. Maybe those shoulder-pad-like structures . . . Kai's right to laugh. Noble Leospider, why didn't you just run for it? Fly your spacecraft into the sun, go out with a bang. Or were you too afraid not to leave your little record for us to find? Looking for your own version of immortality . . .

Is this the fate that Indigo wants for *us*? Horrible thought. Worse than the screams of the starving billions? In a way . . . yes. How hopeless this poor little Leospider must have felt. The other way, there's hope, no matter how foolish.

Kai's head snapped up, gleam of life in his eyes. "Metz, Izzy . . . Let's get the scanner head put together."

Mies stood looking up at the wall. What kind of beings would build such a repository for their dead? Mies had a sudden vivid image of the last days of the Leospiders. As their numbers dwindled, carefully preserving and burying each one in its specified place, down to the last hundred, maybe. Realizing that there was no future; closing up their planetary bases, shutting down their vast resource gathering operations, coming home . . . to die. Absurd in a way, in a way, but at the same time enormously sad.

That's what I've been after, all these years. A way to stop it. Funny, seeing the inevitable conclusion of such a scenario, it doesn't look at all the way I would've supposed. Doesn't it? This *is* what you wanted. Your anger made you want to disappear and take all of humanity with you for not being what you expected. No. No, I, well, maybe . . .

"Okay," said Kai.

Superimposed on the world, a seltzer of light motes, sublimating into vapor, swirling, enveloping them, folding in on it-

self, boiling and boiling like a speeded-up convection cloud.
Metz made an adjustment, and the image solidified, coming to
a stop. There were no discernible patterns, just random smoke.

Rosie: "Is that all there is?"

Izzy shrugged. "We're trying to pull in an image from its
lifetime before the burial, but there's no structure that the SAE
can make out. This is just noise."

Kai: "It looks as if the molecular structure of the mummy's
surface is some sort of plastic."

Metz: "Can't find any signal that could be coming from the
remaining original tissue. I guess there isn't any."

"What is it, then?" Mies said. "Just a floppy statue?"

Rosie looked at him, said, "The biological structures are
there, down to the cellular level at least. This is more than just
a mold."

Izzy squatted next to it, ran a gloved finger along its smooth
flank. "Hard to say. The plastic probably incorporates most of
the original atoms, but they've been polymerized into this stuff.
We can't get a reading because the molecules are no longer
in the same arrangements, and our scanner is getting multiple
overlapping images which cancel each other out."

Kai strode over to the wall, looking at the inhabitants of
some of the other hexagons. "There were plenty of people at
the beginning of the twenty-first century who were vitrified
when they died, in the wan hope of being revived in the
future."

"Yes," said Mies. "But we don't do it anymore. We don't
have to."

Spence laughed. "That's because when we die there's nothing left to mummify. If the symbiotes go critical, there's not a
lot left to work with."

No one, Mies thought, is looking at me. No one can see
me remember.

"What we've seen certainly suggests that they were practically if not perfectly immortal," said Kai. "That puts an entirely different complexion on this gallery."

"Could the process of plasticization be reversed?" Rosie asked. "If so, maybe this is a way of . . . waiting."

"Waiting for what?" asked Mies sharply. "Us?"

Izzy, ignoring him: "We don't have enough information. But if they left some sort of molecular blueprint coded into the plastic, maybe we could decode it."

Metz shook his head. "I . . . don't think so. Probably not. I don't see how they could avoid losing some information in the process. And after a billion years . . ."

Mies looked at the strange, perfect mummy lying on the hard granite floor. "So, then, they didn't intend to be resurrected in the flesh. They just left . . . their forms. For what?"

So strange. As if the darkness between the stars had been made manifest to them. The bad news is all you are is your physical body; the good news: we can preserve that until the end of time.

Kai began preparing the scanner head to be moved again. "There must be some clues on the corpse that didn't make it. We'll soon have some answers."

Floating in the darkness.

I've lost any sense of wanting to be here, Ginny thought. Can't remember quite why I came. Visions of times past, of old, fragmented memories were arrayed against the darkness, as if presenting themselves for examination. Memories wanting me to use them as excuses. Me not wanting excuses to be made.

Anger, brief and bitter. Who am I making excuses for? Who am I making excuses to? For myself? To Kai? Or . . .

She stirred, feeling the inertial mass of Andy's body shift against her. Man breathing softly, perhaps asleep, perhaps not. Not snoring. Just breathing. Human. Human warmth. There for me. When she stirred, she could feel her thighs separate tackily, reminding her of the hour just completed.

All right, girl. Did it make you feel any better?

Silence.

Abrupt quirk of a narrow, invisible smile, self-derision, a bit of a smirk. All right, so it did make me feel better. A little bit.

Revenge against Kai for . . . for . . . betraying me? Is that what I thought he did? A sensation formed, like a lump in her throat, refused to go away when she swallowed. Yes. No. Maybe. I don't know.

Don't care. No one cares why they feel bad. Only that they *do*. Why should I be any different? But it *did* make me feel better. A little bit. For a little while. Andy's . . . a diligent lover, if nothing else. I should be grateful he's here. Here for me when I need . . .

Silly. Stupid. Unable to surmount feelings generated by simple hormones. By millions of years of animal bullshit. I try to tell myself that's all it is. That times have changed. That people have changed, but . . . I try to tell myself it's just culture. Culture and guilt and old stories and bullshit lingering from . . . Right. Fathers and Mothers and Sisters and Brothers.

Because I had *that*, I dreamed of an older world. A softer world. A safer world. A life where love meant something soft. Something other than . . . that.

Didn't get it, did you, Ginny-girl?

Andy shifted under her arm again, face stirring against her breast, sighed, rubbed against her, so she could feel the stiff bristles of his beard against her skin. Then he whispered, "Ginny. I . . ."

Oh, God. Now he'll tell me that he loves me. He'll tell me that . . .

Andy said, "Ginny, what am I going to do? I . . . think I'm in love with Rose now. I think . . ."

She felt a surge of anger cramp briefly through her. Swine of a simpleton man. Fucks me and then tells me that he loves someone else? She stuttered, then said, "I'm glad for you, Andy. For both of you." There. Said the right thing for once.

He said, "But what about Sheba?"

For just a second, Ginny wanted to scream, *But Sheba's dead, you little asshole.* . . . No. No, that just won't do. Somewhere in there, thoughts and feelings just as complex as my own. Not a mirror for me. Nothing at all like that. A man. Feeling whatever it is men feel when they feel.

Some inner voice, part of her, but not *of* her, whispered, *If they do, that is.*

She put her arms around him, rubbed the back of his head, pulling him close to her, feeling the persistent bald spot he'd allowed to develop as part of the Physical Culture religion he and Sheba had shared, when they'd shared their lives. "In the old days," she said, "when marriage was all there was, people would die. The ones they left behind would remarry. I guess guilt feelings are natural. And temporary." There. More right things said.

He said, "But it's not the old days now, Ginny. What if . . ."

Right. *What if?* She said, "Andy, if Sheba wakes up some day to find out she's been in suspended animation for a hundred years or a thousand, or ten thousand, whatever, she'll understand what it was like for you." That's what women do, isn't it? *Understand?*

Andy muttered, "You didn't know her very well, Ginny. Not as well as you should have. She wasn't very good about . . . understanding."

Another brief pulse of anger, this time at his unintentional rebuke, followed by, *Unintentional?* Are the things men say *ever* unintentional? She sighed, pressed herself to him, and said, "Forget about it, Andy. Just forget about it. Here. Fuck me again and . . ."

And felt his hands on her body, felt his quick stir of arousal, and thought, Then, when Rosie comes back up from her visit to Pholos, you can fuck her, fuck Linda . . . hell, fuck Kai, fuck old Doc, fuck anyone you damned well please. When Sheba wakes up, if she ever wakes up, she'll fucking well *understand.*

Oh, God. Why am I *here?*

Then, that shadowy inner voice: Don't you remember?

Standing there, just standing there, looking down at the rubble that had once been a sentient being, Mies thought, I too have to take responsibility for what's happened to me.

Kai said, "Let's take it back slowly until there's some sort of change."

Concentrate. Join them in their exhilaration. The air shivered and cleared, VR image taking the place of reality. On the floor, the pile of Leospider detritus was unchanged.

Is that my imagination, or is it . . . taking on substance?

The material *was* growing, swelling almost imperceptibly, husk rehydrating. Tiny jerking movements, like spasms, were visible, but so fast that they almost seemed like glitches in the SAE. The little graph in the corner of his eyes showed that these were months unreeling with the rapidity of seconds.

"Whoa!" Izzy cried. "Right there. Slow, slow. Here it comes."

Metz: "This is at least a million years later than any of the ghost images we saw."

Now it's really happening. Weeks going by in seconds. Before his eyes, the creature began to undecompose, parts reassembling themselves, reattaching, stretching and fattening. Now it was actually beginning to resemble a Leospider, head and legs, though distorted, in the right places, hair fluffing out to make a mane.

After a long minute, it had assumed the form it had in life, a complete Leospider lying on its side, legs folded under it, head thrown forward as if in sleep, almost comfortable seeming. As they watched, the thing took on the patina of life, hair thick and silky, exoskeleton showing a metallic gold-purple iridescence, the skinlike covering of its head growing smooth and supple. Suddenly, the silver eyes appeared, almost inflating, filling the little caverns in its face. Except for the dark orangish stain on its beard, it looked like every other Leospider they'd seen.

"Slower now," said Izzy. "Almost there."

Around its head, almost hidden by the rough texture of the granite, the stain could be seen on the floor around its head as a thin puddle of fluid.

Without warning, the stain disappeared. The Leospider leapt to its feet, eyes staring blankly into darkness for just a second.

Then it jumped, did a little dance, sprinted away from them in reverse time. Before they could react, it was leaving the catacombs, moving up the ramp backwards, head bobbing comically, legs almost invisible.

"Hold it!" Kai said. "Okay, forward again, real time."

Izzy: "We've got full coverage here. No interpolation routines necessary."

The Leospider was coming down the ramp, in normal speed not funny at all, in fact, Mies, thought, with a great amount of dignity. It walked halfway down the gallery of crypts, turned, looked around once, inscrutable, of course.

Mies's gaze met that of the virtual Leospider. No expression, only the great mirrored eyes unmoving, unwavering. Filled with bright hexagons, distorting at the edges. Inhuman. This was the noblest Roman of them all . . . the only Roman, in fact. All the rest . . . preserved in miraculous counterfeit all around, but . . . no more.

It looked at something in its hand, a long, sharp-looking piece of metal, reflected in duplicate in its blank stare. A blade, something like a dagger, but wider. A moment, then its mandibles began to work, and somehow, the hair of its mane and beard began to swell, standing on end as though from an electric shock. A tiny shudder, exoskeleton clicking.

"This is too horrible," murmured Rose.

The Leospider plunged the blade upward into its neck, piercing the juncture between two exoskeleton plates, penetrating a good twenty centimeters. It tugged the dagger down as far as it would go, then up again, deep into the area covered by the beard. Dark orange, the color of marigolds, blossomed in its beard hair, and it fell to the floor. The blood did not spread far, but made a halo of wetness around its head. There were a few feeble spasms, then nothing.

"Enough," said Izzy. The image faded.

Kai said. "It must have been living alone here for most, if not all of that million years."

Rosie: "What could have made it . . ."

Mies felt an irresistible compulsion, and kneeled next to the restored pile of debris. He fished around under the carcass, rocking the torso-shape, digging, then pulled forth a metal object. "Here's the knife."

For a moment, the image of running the knife into his own throat held a degree of attraction. His eyes focused on the dirty jumble of debris that was once the Leospider's head. "This is worse than we could ever have imagined."

He looked up. For a reaction? Rosie and Spence feeling distaste, thinking I can't possibly feel anything like pity. Kai? *He* knows how I feel. Why couldn't he just . . . turn me off?

But Kai wasn't looking at him now. "Reset the scanner," he said quietly.

FIFTEEN

Looking down at the thing on the floor, Kai thought, A million years. A million years of solitude. I cannot imagine. But then, I can't imagine living a million years, either. People, for all eternity, expected to live and die. Some to die and just be . . . gone, others clinging to the comforting myth of some postmortem immortality. But . . . now, we still live and die, because . . . things happen. If I were careful enough, could I live for a million years? What would that be like? No idea. Life is just a succession of days.

Mies, kneeling on the invulnerably hard black plastic floor of the crypt, reached out, as if to touch the tattered body again, hesitated with his hand just centimeters above the aeons-dead rubble. "There was a time in my life," he said, "not so long ago, when I could not have imagined a million years of loneliness." He looked up at Kai, eyes a beady glitter behind the clear plastic of his faceplate. "I can now. A little bit."

Cold chill running through him. The Mies that Indigo created, a mind of many independent parts . . . hell. Maybe it was the perfect answer to little David Gilman's skull-locked loneliness. No wonder he hates me. A voice, somewhere inside, full of mirth: Wouldn't you hate someone who used you thus? No voice. No real voice. Not even an imagined voice. We are all composed of legions within. Mies's legions were no different from anyone else's. Indigo merely gave them faces and names.

And it made him feel as though he had . . . friends. Friends he could trust.

Rosie said, "How much is a million years to a being that's lived a thousand times that long?"

Spence: "You really think this thing lived for a *billion* years?"

Mies said, "Continents are ground down to nothing in considerably less time than that."

Geological forces, thought Kai. This thing endured geological forces when it was alive. And endured them further, after it was dead. Look at it.

Izzy looked up from where he was tinkering with the scanner head. "Sure they do. Get ground down to nothing, and all the while, new continents are born."

Mies: "Only on a living world."

Rosie said, "Maybe a billion years. Maybe less. What's the difference, whether he lived a billion years, or only, say, a hundred and fifty million?"

Kai kneeled beside Mies. "Maybe it meant a lot to him. And a million years was enough to drive him mad, to make him want to let go of life at last."

Vivid memory of that death scene. How will I feel, when so many years have gone by? Can't imagine. Only my few dozen years to use for comparison. Oh, yes, I can imagine all the years of history. Can imagine myself having been born with the Pharaohs, maybe having sat around old Thinis with Scorpion and Striking-Catfish, helped them build the first empire of *Kmt*? Lived on to King Body-Divine's day and helped architect Imhotep do his math, watched his conscripts build the first pyramids. Oh, that's centuries already, four hundred long years and more from Narmer to Djoser, almost as long as the span from *Nina, Pinta,* and *Santa Maria* to *Apollo XI,* longer than any human life has yet run. Can it happen to me? Will it? Or have I already been too careless?

So Kaihotep, little striking-fairy lives on and on, lives until Alexandros comes, and Ptolemaios, and Kleopatras, and Yehoshevah the Prophet. Am I three thousand years old already? Hardly seems possible that eternal *Kmt* has died, died at last, having lived more than half the span of human history. Skip forward. Rome falls in little more time than the years I lived between Narmer and Imhotep, while, across the mountains, the Han fall and the Tang rise and fall and the Song as well. The Mongols come and destroy the Kievan Rus, and just a few centuries later, Yuri Gagarin rises into the sky.

Five thousand years, Maeru kai Ortega. An eternity. How long is a billion years? Two hundred thousand times those five thousand years. Two hundred thousand. A completely meaningless number. This mysterious little spider-man dwelt here, alone, for two hundred times the whole span of human history. And that was, perhaps, finally, no more than one-half of one percent of his life's aeon.

Standing beside the scanner head, Metz looked out at them, looked, Kai presumed, out through his piles of maps and integrations and programmer's tools, and said, "Okay. That's got it. Let's try again."

Mies said, "I wonder how he would have felt about this?"

Just about, Kai thought, how you felt when I came prowling down through the long dark tunnels of *your* mind. Mies looking over at him, the two of them kneeling together beside the corpse, as if in some horrible parody of prayer. Looking at me, Kai thought. Telling me how he feels. He stood, turning away, walked back to the scanner head, and started plugging in his waveguide packet. One last time. Is that what this is? What will we do for an encore?

Maybe nothing. Harsh vista of all the years to come. We'll be staying here. For a while. But then we'll move on. The years of my life are a flyspeck, just the barest instant in the face of all the years to come. Who were you? Can you help me understand? Understand you and your people? Understand myself and mine? He said, "All right. Let's do it."

From the ship, Ginny said, "Spieltier rolling . . ."

Then the scene exploded in their eyes.

Long, long dark corridor.
Hardly any light at all.

Soothing. Yes. Soothing this.

World of steely gray shadows seen from within steely silver eyes.

Aÿ. Aÿ alone, walking down the long, bleak corridor, feet padding softly on the shiny, immortal finish of the black plastic floor, walking through all the steely gray shadows, familiar shadows, shadows lying in their places for so long that if, somehow, the pattern of lighting changed, the texture of the floor would record where the shadows had been.

Ghosts of shadows.

A most satisfying concept.

Aÿ could feel the concept settle anew in its snug, familiar place.

Niche in my mind.

I have had this idea before.

Thought this thought before.

Thought every idea there is to think a hundred billion times.

Aÿ walking alone down the long dark corridor, walking ankle-deep in familiar dark shadows, walking past sealed doorways, walking past them as he always walked past them, walked past them in memory, memory so deep it was as if the closed and seal doors no longer existed. As if he no longer remembered who had once lived beyond them.

No longer wanted to remember. Another dreary, familiar thought, plopping down in its place.

Here I am.

Here I am.

Yes, I see you, little thought.

Little, familiar thought.

Aÿ emerged onto the observation deck, stood by his broad window, looking out at the world. Empty, silver-gray landscape. Stars overhead. No sun. Dark, empty plains, far, far below. Band of dull, dark red on the horizon, gentle arc of light, the last of another familiar sunset, familiar image settling where it always settled.

Rustle of memory, old, old thoughts stirring. A brighter sky, a blue sky, a higher sky, a sky full of life. Mighty, thrilling

Rhinotaur herds thundering on the plains below. Stone cities of lovely, lovely Frogmen. Frogmen smelling like life and love, bloodlust and food and sexual heat all rolled into one.

Oh. Oh, lost. Long, long lost.

Regret falling into its socket, snapping home.

Here I am.

Remember me?

Of course I remember. Remembering is all I have left.

"Jesus Christ," whispered Metz.

Whispering, thought Kai. Whispering as if, somehow, we might disturb poor Aÿ's reverie.

Mies said, "An inkling, that's all. Just an inkling."

Aÿ felt the familiar hollow building inside, wrapped himself in familiar misery, around that hollow, and walked on, down the next long corridor, to the next station. Long, hard, brilliant silence.

Then Doc murmured, "Of course. We adore you, O Christ, and praise you."

Another long silence, Aÿ walking his endless path, looking down at the bright aura of his own footsteps, the places he trod, endlessly, since some . . . beginning.

Rosie said, "Because by your holy Cross, you have redeemed the world."

Kai thought, Is the metaphor so important to them? Will we next chant, in unison, Most sweet Jesus, grant that peace . . . A brief pang of astonishment that he even remembered the words.

Aÿ, oblivious, gone in oblivion, walked on.

Mies said, "This is some time long before the end. He's been alone forever. Has not yet decided to die."

Ginny said, "I wonder what made him come out of his rut? Made him decide to . . . do it?"

Izzy said, "Let's roll him back."

"Back to the beginning," said Kai. A nod, a wink, a look round at all his magic controls. A swirl of color and light and . . .

Brilliant blue sky overhead.

Brilliant blue sky.

Children playing.

Laughing together.

Dancing the dancing circle.

Little black children, covered with hair.

Mossy green rocks all around them. Children playing on the hillside. Rolling plains far below. Dark gray peaks towering far above.

Mies said, "At this altitude, the sky could never have been blue."

Rosie said, "It's in their eyes. They see things differently."

Spence: "Just another spieltier artifact, then. Blue is blue. This sky should be indigo at best."

A sense of a whisper from Mies, *Indigo*, though, apparently, he'd said nothing.

Doc said, "Not necessarily. The wavelength, yes, but the neural interpretation? We cannot know."

Linda: "Then the spieltier cannot know, either. Not with all the SAE data in the universe."

Children then, children playing, on a brightly lit hillside overlooking the watered green plains below, lone adult Leospider standing on a boulder, many arms folded and intertwined, motionless, silver eyes empty and staring. Is one of these children little Aÿ? Which one? Unknown. No point of view here, just little children in rough and tumble play.

"As if," said Andy, radio linked from his place aboard *Mother Night,* "they weren't quite sentient as children."

Linda: "Are the children of any species sentient?"

Ginny, bitterness apparent in her voice: "Adults believe they are not."

Metz said, "This *could* just be an artifact of the spieltier. More easily than the rest, in fact. A minor bug in the point-of-view algorithms. I'll look into it."

Izzy said, "We're not getting much of anything new here. Let's try shifting the temporal focus a bit."

A whirl of color and light and . . .

Darkness falls.

Stars spangle the black vault of heaven.

Thick air dense in Aÿ's breathing spiracles.

Stone buildings.

Low stone buildings.

Fires leaping high from shallow braziers.

Aÿ and his cohorts standing on the platform, skyship resting behind them on cut and planed stone. The people down below. The people. People scented of . . . Hard pulse, pulse from within, bloodfoodbreeding scent of the people rising up around them, Leospiders stirring, looking down at the Frogmen gathered below, Frogmen moaning their incomprehensible chant, grinding, grinding like gears clashing in a primitive machine.

Soft voice of the gods on the dais: *Mmmm-hm-hm-hmmmmmm* . . .

Scent of blood on the night. Rhinotaurs screaming and bucking as the Frogmen dragged them forth in chains. Dragged them forth, pinned them down with sheer weight of numbers, crystal knives flashing by the light of stars and moons and torchfire . . . Rhinotaurs' screams, terror and anger and pain, turned to bubbling moans as their throats were cut and their blood gushed forth and the Frogmen dashed forward to bend and drink and cry out in imitation of the gods before them.

Grind. Grind. Chant. Chant.

Rrrrghghgh-hrgh-hrgh-hrrhghghgh . . .

Almost the same.

Almost.

But.

No one below the Rhinotaurs.

No one above the Leospiders.

Hope. No hope.

Gray-green Frogmen dragged forth then, one for each god on the dais. No struggling. No. Nor laying themselves down with a will. Not quite.

You could smell their terror.

Smell their doubt.

Am I really going to heaven?

Or . . .

Silver fangs flashing.

Soft lips sucking.

Frogmen growing smaller and smaller, liquid bright eyes going dull and empty. Empty skins lying on the dais. Soft froggy moan of the watching crowd. No sound at all from the dead Rhinotaurs, reduced now to steaming piles of meat.

Rosie whispered, "I am poured out like water, and all my bones are disjointed . . ."

Kai thought, Through it all, the will to . . . believe still survives. As if . . . as if . . .

Doc said, " . . . my tongue cleaves to my jaws, and thou has brought me down to the dust of death." Hard, brilliant silence. Fiery torches against the alien night.

Then Mies said, "You think you know. But you do not."

Silence.

Ginny: "No. *They* don't know."

Suddenly sounding angry, Metz said, "Move the focus."

Hard, brilliant joy.

Aÿ the Leospider stood alone under a dull blue velvet sky, alone and not alone. Dark and craggy mountains to the east. Shining plains far, far below to the west. Alone and not alone in the world between the worlds, the special Leospider world. I am the semimale. The seal of the sexes. And my time has come.

Sucking lips on his chest gasping, as if for air, though there was plenty of sharp, thin mountain air snug in his spiracles, diffusing through his tissues, superefficient blood robbing the air of its slim cargo of oxygen, cracking the ozone, using it as well.

Aÿ, semimale, with his thoughts dissolved like blood-borne gas.

Time.

My first season.

The brilliant joy of a semimale's lust.

Quondam female like a shadow in the hard, rickety bushes that grew round the clashing stones of Lover's Grace, talus tumbled from the cliffs above, lying, carelessly jangled on this midway cliff, jumbled above the long drop to the foothills below. Somewhere down there, if you looked, a spring jetted from the rock, from some mountain aquifer, Aÿ's newly trained geologist mind told him. Jetted out, like a spray, gathered from the mists of the air, fell and fell, perceived as a waterfall from below, so far below.

Everything looks different from below.

But the gods. Yes, the gods look downward.

Quondam female shivering at his touch.

She is ready.

Shivering.

Shivering with her own special inner heat. Coming into his embrace, silent, ready for him. Quondam female and semimale beginning their ritual dance, ancient ritual, familiar ritual, grown from instinct, grown in the long, slow pressure-cooker of culture. Dancing. Touching. Moisture rising in their spiracles. Beading on their skins, defying the eternal, freezing wind of the heights. I am the seal of the sexes. Producing nothing, but . . .

Embracing. Embracing the quondam female, feeling the heat of her estrus, shiny, hot, wet nipple protruding so delicately through the wall of her chest fur, seeming to throb against him, his breeder lips pouting, lovely, delicate, opening to take the nipple within, sucking, sucking, just the way your eating mouth would suck the blood from a meal animal.

Nameless quondam female sighing against him, squeezing against him, hot wind from her spiracles stirring the fur on his sides and . . .

Nipple pulsing, deep in his chest now.

Once.

Twice.

Explosion of delirium.

Hot fluid entering his body like molten metal.

The egg is in me now.

Safe within.

The world without hazed with shadow.

Passage of time . . .

"What the hell is happening?" whispered Spence.

Doc said, "The analysis engine isn't quite sure."

Rose: "A complicated breeding scheme, at any rate. Remember the scene we observed back at the control center? The, um, pornography.''

Kai thought, Obviously, the quondam female views these things quite a bit differently from the semimale . . .

Aÿ the semimale awakening now, stirring gently, stretching deliciously, feeling the cold stiffness of his arms and legs, the dull heat within his chest. Yes, the egg was safely within now, attached to his circulatory system, drawing sustenance from his blood, just the way he drew sustenance from the blood of a food animal.

Vision. Vision of a Frogman waiting. Submissive. Waiting to die and feed the potential life within Aÿ. Waiting to feed the egg. He arose, walked on and . . .

Montage. Aÿ before the Frogmen, accepting their worship. Aÿ feeding, Frogman dying, growing small, becoming an empty skin. Heat flaring in his chest as the egg drew life from his own blood. Grew strong, then stronger still.

Aÿ far up in the cold heights again, where the only heat was the heat within his chest. Aÿ wandering the dim, dark paths of the Stone Grove of Lover's Delight. Aÿ waiting. Waiting. Waiting for the One to come. Come to him and . . . Hard, growling throb of pure, naked wanting. Aÿ's soul thrilling to the overtones, pure hormonal overtones of the deep, deep, thrum. Egg, hot egg, seeming to leap within his chest.

This is the One!

A the semimale turning.

There!

Quasimale no more than a dark shadow among the stones. Waiting. Waiting for him. Wanting him. Quasimale's infrared organ, patch of bare black skin on his chest, sensing the heat of Aÿ's egg, the beloved parasite within.

There!

The quasimale moves with blinding speed, leaping down on the path before Aÿ. Aÿ standing motionless. Paralyzed. Without will.

There!

Quasimale crouching on all fours before him, before him on

the path, breath a roar, steady roar, drawn through his spiracles by surging, twisting muscle.

Excitement in Aÿ. Excitement and terror.

Linda muttered, "Good grief. It's like . . ."

There!

Quasimale leaping. Leaping upon him, crushing him to the ground, helpless. Quasimale's organ already huge, huge and stiff, like some horrid parody of a quondam female's nipple. Already butting against Aÿ's delicate procreative lips. Ramming, bruising, forcing its way inside.

Aÿ felt his chest muscles relax suddenly, his breeder mouth fall open. Then the quasimale's organ was within, driving, driving deeper, down into the hot liquid pouch where the fragile egg lay protected.

Fear.

What if he harms the egg?

What if the egg is crushed?

What if it cracks and spills within you?

These things were known to happen.

The quasimale suddenly grew rigid. Rigid and still. Muscles locked in some hard, shivery tetanus and . . .

Quasimale's soft, agonized moan.

Pulse.

Twice.

Thrice.

Last time . . .

Quasimale's semen spilling into the egg cavity. Hot. Hotter than the egg itself.

Rosie's voice, very soft: "Like a rape."

Kai imagined he could hear Ginny's silence.

Doc said, "During their long slide down to extinction, orangutans evolved a . . . courtship style that seemed indistinguishable from human rape. Long chases through the jungle. Female trying disparately to escape. Huge male, almost twice her size, catching her, holding her down, thrusting into her while she struggled and screamed . . ."

The quasimale suddenly relaxed, exhausted breath gushing

from his spiracles. Relaxed and fell away from Aÿ, flaccid organ pulling out of Aÿ's tightening breeder lips with a delicate, sucking pop, residual semen splashing on their fur, droplets like tiny pearls in the harsh sunlight.

Aÿ relaxed. Relaxed and blissful.

It is done.

The quasimale held him close. Whispered, "Who are you, my beloved?"

"Aÿ." Aÿ the geologist. Just now, Aÿ the breeder.

"Aÿ, my beloved. Together. Together we will find the perfect macrofemme. The perfect mother for our child."

Our child.

The egg within.

Wistful sorrow.

The egg within.

Fertilized now.

Beginning to divide.

Soon, it will need . . . more than I can give.

And room to grow.

Dry-voiced, Rosie said, "I suppose this is really no weirder than the breeding scheme of the terrestrial seahorse."

Kai remembered: eggs laid by the female in a body cavity of the fertilizing male. Eggs hatching, hatching within, male's belly bursting open to release the tiny *hippocampi,* watching his children swim away.

Izzy said, "I guess so. But . . . *four* sexes?"

Doc said, "Well, only two. The quondam female provides the egg, fertilized by the quasimale's semen. The others are, oh, really just surrogate mothers. There was even a time when humans could have gone that route, a brief fling with biosurrogatage, back around the turn of the millennium."

Metz: "Done by nature here. And it's led to an . . . interesting social order, hasn't it?"

Kai thought, Yes, I see. The quondam female and quasimale are both . . . well, malelike. The semimale and . . . whatever the macrofemme might be, more like female mammals? Maybe. But, here, the "males" are more like the human male cultural fantasy. The crude notion that the male provides the seed, and the female, the fertile ground.

Aÿ now, fetus grown painfully hard and huge and cold within, waited in the shadows, while Lÿwaar, his bonded quasimale, stalked the macrofemme through her forest of bushes and boulders. Lÿwaar, invincible on this hunt as any other.

Sudden, frightened scream.

Thrashing struggle.

Silence.

There now.

There now.

Someone crashing through the dry high-altitude vegetation.

Lÿwaar.

And the macrofemme.

Macrofemme clutched in his powerful arms.

"Isn't she *wonderful!*" cried Lÿwaar the quasimale, voice exultant.

Aÿ crept from concealment, crept from the shadows. Painfully crippled by his end-stage pregnancy. Over in a moment. Over in a moment and I'll be myself again. But, for now, the pain.

And the pain to come.

The macrofemme whimpered with fear and sorrow when she saw him emerge, saw his condition.

She must know. Must know.

Lÿwaar cried, "Get her! Get her *now!*"

Aÿ came forward, softly, gently embraced the shivering macrofemme, macrofemme held pinioned, helpless, by Lÿwaar's mighty arms. Embraced the shivering body, leaned forward, until his breeder mouth was over the macrofemme's own almost identical mouth. Kissed her gently, softly, with the lips of his chest. Kissed her. Kissed her. Felt the lips grow slack, responding to the moist hormonal saliva of his own lips.

Kissed her, open chestmouth to open chestmouth.

Extruded the fetus.

Whined with agony as it tore loose from the nurturing sac.

Smelled his own blood, blood still seeping, though the child was gone.

Felt the macrofemme surge.

Surge hard.

Breeder lips gaping and gagging as autonomic muscles struggled to swallow the child.

Safe now.

Safe my lovely.

He fell away.

Watched the macrofemme's breeder lips close tight.

Lÿwaar let her go, and they stood by, watching, waiting, while the macrofemme groveled and sobbed. "Oh. Oh," she said. "Not me. Not now. I'm not . . . ready."

But the deed was done.

Aÿ reached out and touched her gently, smoothing her ruffled fur. "Who are you?"

The macrofemme turned resentful silver eyes on him. Eyes of hate, but . . . ah, already you could see her hormones at work. She said, "Ta'or."

"Ta'or. A lovely name."

Aÿ watched as she slowly struggled to her feet, turning away, turning her back on the two males, who could do her no further harm. Hunched away into the shadows and gone. Somewhere. Somewhere out there, she'd find a lonely quondam female. Quondam female who would protect and nurture her until the child was born. Quondam female who would raise the child, feeding it from her breeder's nipple, feeding it a steady flow of nutritionally perfect unfertilized eggs, until it was ready for the crêche and a Leospider's education.

"I wonder," sighed Aÿ, "what our baby will be called."

Brusquely, Lÿwaar said, "As well wonder who your fathers were."

They came together again then, Aÿ and Lÿwaar, and made love one last time. No egg this time, nothing to fertilize, nothing to beget. But Lÿwaar's antiseptic semen would spill within his empty, bleeding cavity, soothing the birth wound, speed the healing process, making him whole once again.

Until the next time.

Whenever it might be.

"This would," said Rose, "help explain why there were so few Leospiders. A wonder they survived at all."

Aÿ in the distant, dark past, future to a still more distant past, past compassed within, holding tight to all his memories. I loved those breeding times. Times in which I felt so . . . real. Memories then of a thousand quondam females and quasimales and macrofemmes. All of them loved. Cherished in memory. Memories of a long ago time, in the dew-silver springtime of the world, of watching quondam females and macrofemmes walking together, walking together with their newborn children.

Tiny children at play.

Memories of watching, wondering: Who among them are mine?

None. And all.

Aÿ the geologist, standing guard, arms folded round his chest, folded over his closed and empty breeder's lips, watching the children play under a bright, fuzzy blue velvet sky, looking out over the brilliant depths of the Rhinotaur-Frogman plains.

The times came years apart.

Then decades.

Then centuries.

Then millennia,

Then millions of years.

Then not at all.

And, all the while, the black sky descended, the world grew cold.

I knew.

Knew it was coming.

Continental drift slowing, slowing. Volcanoes growing quiet. Eruptions ever fewer. World's geochemical cycle grinding to a halt. Carbon dioxide content of the atmosphere falling. Biosphere failing. Oxygen content of the atmosphere going down. Biosphere disappearing. All in just a few score million years.

Hardly the twinkling of a Leospider's unblinking eye.

We had forever, and we let it get away.

"Well," said Kai, "it seems that they knew."

Mies: "Did you ever doubt it? *We* know."

Kai skipped the temporal locus forward a little bit.

There.

Aÿ the geologist, down on the still air-dense, sun-bright plains.

Standing on some low crag.

Watching.

Watching while Frogman hunters chased and killed a fleeing band of Rhinotaurs. Leapt on them as they fell, cut their throats and drank their blood. Afterward, he knew, they'd offer one of their own number to him. Not many Rhinotaurs left. Hard for them to eke out a living on these dry and empty plains now. Hard for them to live, breathing this dry and, to them, razor-thin air. The last Rhinotaurs turned, turned and fought, ululating their war cries, brandishing their bronze-tipped lances. The Frogmen shot them down with guns of fire, then closed in with their knives of steel to slash and drink.

Thunder. Thunder on the horizon.

Kai turned, looking back toward some distant, nameless stone Frogman city. Column of brilliant white smoke, arcing into the sky. Bright bead of fire and metal at its tip. Running a synergy curve up into the heavens. It would be easier to let them launch from the highlands. More cost-effective. But . . . no. The heights are ours.

In any event, the orbital station project was going well. Get them up there, where they can do some good. Get them up there, onto the moons, the planets, the many troves of asteroids. Settle them on the two habitable planets of the Other Sun. Soon it won't matter that there are no more ores coming up from the depths as the ages roll by. Soon it won't matter that the surface deposits of the World are exhausted.

Nothing ever matters.

Not when you have forever to work with.

Interesting though, that business down in the antarctic.

A team of Frogmen constructing spaceships in secret. Outfitting them for a long voyage, using the very best of Leospider technology.

Running away.

I wonder where they thought they were going to go?

A gentle Leospider shrug.

Doesn't matter.

Nothing ever matters.

Just now, the Frogmen, finished with the Rhinotaurs, had brought one of their own number forward, laid a frightened Frogman at his feet. Aÿ could see the sun, the plains, the distant mountains reflected in the Frogman's huge, wet eyes, as he stooped and unsheathed his fangs.

Ginny said, "They were . . . not so much like us as they originally seemed."

Mies said, "No?"

Colors. Colors around them now.

Then black space.

Aÿ stood by the cloudship's big crystalline observation window, looking down at the pale yellow-blue-gray world, orb covering a small portion of the dark sky still, blotting out only a few square arc-minutes worth of stars, but growing larger, feeling the deck shudder and throb under his feet. The ship's engines were in need of an overhaul, would have to be taken out and down for the job before it could venture forth again. Tuned up, synchronized. When the next voyager set out for the Comet Cloud, he would feel only a smooth, soft shiver beneath his feet as the drive screamed without and drove the ship down into the darkness that lay between the world and the stars.

Such an old, cold world Our Home has become. Older and colder and grayer than when first I saw her from above, this Great Macrofemme of a world. How she sags from the breeding of her many children. Down there on the yellow plains, the children were fewer now. The gods still on their heights of course, and the Frogmen in their sealed cities. But the Rhinotaurs . . .

What will they do, now that the Rhinotaurs are gone?

Aÿ looked around at nervous Frogmen, the nervous, bustling Frogmen of the cloudship's crew.

Serve us. They will serve us.

Nervous Frogmen.

Voyage almost over.

During the long fall, in through the System of the Two Suns, they'd been his only companions, ship with forty Frogmen technicians and one Leospider god thrusting inward from the Cloud habitats, from a long new-resource survey.

The worldlets grow sparse as the distance from Two Suns grows. Not so surprising. Not so unanticipated. We grow more efficient, but the resources grow thinner and thinner. Maybe, someday, we'll work our way to the nearer stars. Or learn to pull resources from the cores of the gas giants.

Now, Our Home grew large in the viewport, as the ship slowed and slowed, falling into close orbit, bearing its cargo of twenty-seven Frogman technicians, nervous, nervous technicians, and one Leospider god. The drive shuddered to a stop, yellow plains rolling below, Aÿ floating off his feet, drifting in the air, looking down at the world. Come. Come now. They are waiting. Don't disappoint them.

Aÿ turned, turned to look at them. Twenty-seven pairs of shiny-wet Frogman eyes. Waiting. Aÿ gestured at the cloudship's captain, watched his eyes grow huge in the stark moment that followed. Come now. Come to your reward, faithful servant.

Spence said, "Goddamn. What makes them endure it? There were forty of them and only one of him. Why did they let it happen? Why didn't they all *revolt*?"

Rosie, voice quiet, said, "Why does a woman endure the beatings of an abusive husband?"

Linda said, "Some don't."

Ginny said, "And some do."

Doc said, "These, evidently, did."

Is that what we're seeing here? Kai wondered. The Frogmen caught in a trap of culture, a matrix of historical events that persisted out of . . . habit?

Izzy said, "Why does a worker tolerate the abuses of a boss? Why doesn't *he* revolt?"

Metz said, "Why does a dog tolerate the mastery of a man?"

Kai thought, Sometimes they revolt, all of them. When they do, we kill them.

Swirl of colors. Swirl of light.

Aÿ standing on his favorite cliff, surrounded by air so thin, so harsh, it could almost not be breathed, ozone burning in his spiracles, yes, but only noticeable because there was so little O_2. Mostly nitrogen. Not much carbon dioxide. Not much of anything anymore. Down there, the bright yellow plains, the bright red arc of the sunset sky. Bright, empty plains. Rhinotaurs long gone, and now . . .

Empty cities of plastic and stone beside dry waterways, that's all we have left. And above? An empty sky as well. We outgrew them. Outgrew them all. Frogman workers replaced by mechanical servants at last, not so much because we wanted it, as because it was necessary. Indestructible machines, fed by the fire of the sun. No need for a food economy to support them, support useless mouths that only saw to the care and feeding of the useful few.

Sharp *snap* of color.

Aÿ within; Aÿ with his comrades. No more splendor now. No more torchlight ceremonies under a dark black sky lit by the hard glitter of the fixed stars. Just . . . The Frogthing lay, quiescent on the table. Not waiting, no. Not sentient enough for that. Just sentient enough to live, no more than that. Not a being. Not capable of worship. But . . . yes it had the blood-foodsex scent of the real thing, which was all that was necessary. The ceremony, the . . . spiritual cloaking; that was for them, not us, for us . . .

Silver fangs flashing. Blood flowing so sweetly. Leospider lips sucking life's force within, deep within.

Imagine those silly Frogmen imagining they had spirits. Imagining us their gods. Imagine them letting themselves die and die, thinking they went on to . . . their reward. Only we, we knew better. There is no reward. Only oblivion. An oblivion

avoided so long as you live on and on. Aÿ felt his breeder lips
gape and pout as he sucked and drank. Yes. Yes this eating for
Frogblood, whether from -thing or -man, was as good as
breeding.

No. It was better than breeding.

Much better than breeding.

And it always had been.

Metz said, "When I was a boy, I had an unreconstructed
hetero friend who talked his parents into buying him a set of
girlygirl toys. Said they were better than the real thing. Said
you didn't have to . . . contend with them."

Silence.

Aÿ before them in a sucking delirium.

Kai said, remembering such toys, on Titan only the toys of
the very rich, said, "Whatever became of your friend?"

"Miggy?" A soft snicker. "I think he became a girlygirl
manufacturer when he grew up."

Aÿ was outside, standing under the black and star-spangled
sky the night that it came. Standing on his favorite rock, watching. Waiting. Somewhere, hidden in the darkness, there would
be other Leospiders, those few who really cared, watching
and waiting.

They'd known about it for months. Image caught by chance,
picked up by an automatic tracking camera whose real job was
to watch out that the automated freighters bringing home the
resources from afar didn't run into each other, or into some
still-useful world.

A spark of brilliant ultraviolet light in the sky.

Oh, it must have been there for a long time. Centuries, at
least, possibly thousands of years. But only now was it worth
noticing. What could it be? Some unusual astronomical event?
Something happening to a faraway star? No. Spectral lines
mainly characteristic of reflected starlight, mainly, in fact, the
starlight of the Two Suns. But fearsomely blue-shifted.

It was, almost, enough to generate excitement in the slowly
emptying Leospider world.

Fearsomely blue shifted. Showing a large parallax. Modest

proper motion, but . . . This phenomenon is an object, small, high albedo, moving at high relativistic speed. More or less directly at the System of the Two Suns. Something coming to us out of interstellar space.

What could it be?

Old, old theories from the dawn of civilization, the civilization of the gods, talked of starships. But . . . not practical. Not . . . economical. Not worth building. Nowhere to go worth going.

An object perhaps accelerated to high velocity by some ancient supernova explosion. An object now transiting the Galaxy of the Gods, a visitor from the outer darkness. Some lost rock, that's all. Mathematicians could work out the possibilities.

This will, they said, be interesting.

For anyone who cares.

Brilliant light in the sky. Growing. Growing over the hours.

Moving now toward the barycenter of the System of the Two Suns. It will turn through the barycenter, you see, and then recede, and then be gone. That's all. Some danger to any living thing caught between the worlds, object shedding X-rays as it burned its way through the stellar wind, as it fell through the gas-environment of the system. Not much danger to a radiation-hard Leospider standing on his favorite rock to watch.

Sky dull indigo now, the indigo of spectral twilight. Shadows forming on the bare rock around Aÿ, shadows slowly shifting, the thing was moving so fast. A bright blue-white spark, tinged with violet, followed by a long, long contrail of disturbed stellar wind, particles and gasses excited to luminescence by the energies of this transit.

Growing brighter.

Then growing dimmer.

Eventually gone, around the curve of the world.

Gone between the suns.

Gone back out into the dark between the stars.

It was a full day and more before the startling news came out. While the object transited the System of the Two Suns, it shed energies. The expected natural energies of the transit, yes, but other energies as well. Hard, very high-energy radar beams, touching this world and that, beams scattered forward rather than reflected back, forming a wall of reference data through which a lost rock, a relativistic . . . *object* would soon pass. Pass through and pass away.

It was a starship after all.

A starship of sorts.

No Frog-magical alien Gods aboard. No. Nor any sort of organic beings at all. Just a machine mind. Like the machine minds we built to replace our old, dead servants. Machine mind taking a quick peek, then gone. Now, somebody knows we're here. Who? And where? Those few who were interested, Aÿ the geologist among them, Aÿ who hadn't had anything interesting to do for a hundred thousand years, among them.

Ginny said, "Why were they surprised? Why didn't they expect this? I mean, the Leospider civilization persisted for a significant portion of the lifespan of the universe."

Mies said, "There's more than one component to Fermi's paradox. The universe is large in space as well as time."

Even now, thought Kai, we don't know the answer to the question of how densely spacetime is packed with sentient life, much less the simultaneous density figure for the number of technological cultures capable of limited interstellar travel. But, now we know that there have been three such civilizations, sequestered in a single galaxy, sequestered in a span of not more than three billion years.

That's something.

A beginning.

The live ones, the still living, must be out there somewhere.

Hope, then. Something resembling hope.

Over the ages, with nothing better to do, the Leospiders had fathomed the secrets of the universe. Had learned, indeed, all the static facts that there were to be learned. Learned them and put them away not having thought of anything they wanted to do with their knowledge.

It'll be there, they said, whenever we happen to need it.

The first thing they built was a little relativistic starship of their own. Just for practice. Just to demonstrate how it was the aliens had done what they'd done. Used it to take a look around at the stars and worlds in their immediate neighborhood.

One of the first things they found was a long-dead Frogman colony, ruins on the surface of a barely habitable planet circling a dim and ruddy K8 star that had, once upon a time, been the closest star to the System of the Two Suns. Not close now, for it had drifted a few score light-years away in the millions of years since . . .

Interesting ruins, Aÿ thought, when he saw them. Interesting ruins, on the world the Frogmen had tried to build. Why, look: they even brought along a herd of Rhinotaurs. Why would they have wanted to create a world without gods? A pity they didn't succeed. I miss the Frogmen. Miss their torches and processions and delicious sweat of fearhorrorbloodfoodsex delirium.

Image of himself descending on a live Frogman world, god descending on his lost children. How happy, how gloriously happy they would have been to see us.

Izzy said, "These were a sick people."

Spence: "Who? The Leospiders or the Frogmen?"

Kai felt a tiny pulse of surprise. Even Spence? I would not have expected . . .

Mies said, "Who are we to judge them?"

Then, the new ship, the luminiferous wave transformer that could project itself to a predetermined spot, anywhere in the universe, at precisely the speed of light. . . .

Startled, Kai said, "My God. He's talking about a ship that can . . . teleport itself."

A hard decision for Aÿ to ride such a ship. Philosophical questions, hearkening back to the questions those silly Frogmen had had about souls and spirits and whatnot. Questions that hadn't bothered the Leospiders since the days of unremembered savagery. Since the forgotten days when the gods themselves had faced inevitable death.

Forgotten, Aÿ knew, because everyone who'd faced that inevitable death had in fact died. Well, Leospiders knew, as gods always know, that there are no souls, that a mind is just a pattern of memories impressed in an electrochemical matrix. You are what you remember. Nothing less. Nothing more. So he shrugged off atavistic dread and flew the luminiferous wave transformer and died and lived again, memories intact.

And the first thing they did was chase down the relativistic probe. Chase it down, use their own relativistic engines to match velocities, universe growing heavy and rainbow-hued around them. Match velocities. Force entry. Board the alien ship.

No beings, of course. But signs there once had been.

The animus of the machine mind was tattered, fragmented, worn with age. And, for some reason, unwilling to talk to them. It tried to erase itself when they broke in, following some *ab initio* rule-sieve, but was too slow, too old, too fearful of extinction.

They killed it. Spooled it into their own machines. Took the measure of its days, which were a mere two billion years. Understood it. The animus was full of remembered images of shadowy, feathery folk, folk who lived beneath the rays of a pale, cool, yellow-white sun, under a brilliant blue-green sky. And where were the Featherfolk from? The locus was a galaxy a quarter of the way across the universe. A quarter of the way across the much smaller, much hotter universe of two billion years ago.

"Almost six billion years ago, to us," said Ginny.

They built the ship that could slide down the hyperpipes, slide across the face of Platonic Reality and back up again. Figured out where the galaxy and its star and world had gone.

And they went.

"Went where?" whispered Izzy. "And when? Doesn't this mean they had time travel as well? I mean . . . it's Platonic Reality we're using to . . . "

Kai swallowed past a dry spot in his throat, fine-tuning the temporal focus, waiting for the ship to . . . fall. Now that's a very good question. A very good question indeed, for it's hyperpipe access to Platonic Reality that we use to look into the past, past like this and . . . "Not necessarily. Or maybe just, we don't know. No one has ever proposed that it was possible to do anything more than look down the throats of the hyperpipes and use very large data-processing engines to sort out some of the information trapped there."

The past, said the ancient sages, is recorded only on the structure of the present.

Metz said, "In theory, if Platonic Reality is as we understand it to be, you could *go* to the past."

"But," said Izzy, "not come home again."

If you can come home from the past, thought Kai, you can travel to the future. "Part of the problem lies in our cultural perception of the past as a *place*. Time and relevant dimensions in space, all that old crap. But when you look down a hyperpipe, all you're looking at is the spilled relics of spacetime. Not a real place where you could go. Go physically, I mean."

Metz said, "If you *could* travel to Platonic Reality, you'd be traveling all the way to the beginning of spacetime. To before the beginning. To the eternity and infinity that underlies the necessarily finite here and now."

"Here and now," said Izzy. "Nothing more than a complex of collapsing wave functions."

Doc said, "I usually think of myself as an experienced thinker and well-educated modern man, but . . ."

Right, thought Kai. First, you have to discard what you *know*. He said, "The past is data recorded on the structure of the collapsing waveforms. The future is not a place at all, merely all the waveforms that have yet to collapse. Out there, somewhere, out of reach."

Ginny said, "If you could go into the future, which future would it be? Which set of collapsing waveforms . . . No. Stupid. I can see that's not right. If you collapse the waveforms by . . . *touching* them, they become part of the here and now. And, since the past is just stored data, you wouldn't be able to . . ."

Too complex, thought Kai. It's why we never really *get* it. He said, "Even if they thought they could travel in time, even though they were bold and cold enough to be willing to travel by electromagnetic-wave teleportation, the Leospiders were probably afraid of time travel.''

''If it's possible,'' said Metz, ''even if it really *is* possible, it probably means too much.''

Spence said, ''You think it's possible to . . . accidentally destroy Platonic Reality?''

Stupid, thought Kai. Like the past, like the future, Platonic Reality is not a *place*.

Metz said, ''How would I know? I doubt the Leospiders knew.''

Kai said, ''All we can do is see what the synchronoptic analysis engine thinks they actually *did*.'' Thinks. The engine *thinks* . . .

Light now twisting in odd directions. Interference patterns. Classic moirés. A clutter of color as Aÿ's starship went down the quantum drain and . . .

''Holy shit,'' muttered Ginny.

A sparse black sky with hardly any lights at all.

A pale gray world lit by the rays of an old gold star.

Aÿ the geologist standing on an empty gray plain beneath a cloudless, empty gray sky, by the shores of a flat, waveless, empty gray sea. All around him . . . nothing.

Aÿ the geologist leaning down, picking up a flat gray stone. Is this a geofact or an artifact? Using his instruments, scanning it. Just a rock. Old granite. No easy way to tell. Left alone on the surface of a world for long enough, even a world as dead as this one, an artifact may be returned to . . .

Well. We could use the starship's engines to read its data, but . . .

Why bother?

Aÿ the geologist, Aÿ and the Leospider gods, got in the starship and whistled down through the quantum dark, all the way home. Landed their starship, shut it down, put it away, with all the other old toys. Put it away and went back into the building emptiness of their lives.

''Fucking missed them,'' said Spence.

Linda said, ''Why should they have any better luck than us?''

Metz: "Why should we have better luck than they did?"

Aÿ, back in the past of the past, looking at row on row of cold, gray, empty, useless starships. Useless.

"For Christ's sake," said Andy, "these people had fucking faster-than-light starships! Why the *hell* didn't they just *use* them?"

Silence.

Aÿ staring, the way he did more and more often as the decades and centuries and millennia continued to slide by.

Kai said, "Where would they go?"

Andy: "*Anywhere!*"

Metz: "What for?"

Aÿ still staring. At the sky now. Looking up at the cold, bright pinpoints that had once seemed to beckon to him. No more.

Softly, Doc said, "We've gone that route from time to time ourselves. Back at the dawn of the space age, men went to the Earth's moon a few times, then they stopped going. Why? No good reason to continue. We only went *back* into planetary space, almost a century later, because we needed the resources and there was money to be made. Now? What good reason is there, for humanity to voyage to the stars? What *good* reason?"

"To save ourselves?" asked Spence.

"Save ourselves for what?" asked Metz.

Doc said, "Ask the average man for one good reason to promote humanity's eternal survival. Don't waste your time waiting for an answer."

Rosie said, "They could have tried to save themselves. *We're* trying."

Kai said, "Daiseijin's Ten Thousand want to preserve their own individual hides. The survival of humanity itself is incidental. Why don't we care about the hundreds of billions who must now perish? Why don't we care about all the trillions unborn?"

Silence. Aÿ still staring, as if frozen, etched forever against the face of night.

Then Mies said, "I didn't think you actually understood."

Kai, suddenly angry, thought, No one believes anyone who

disagrees with them has actually understood the subtleties of their reasoning. Which is why, in the end, we probably will *all* perish.

Before them, Aÿ was moving again, following the passage of some eternity beyond the edge of their perception. Aÿ, living through his past, was not alone in any present he chose to visit. Here and now . . . Aÿ and all his friends. Cloistered together, living together.

Aÿ lying with his companion of the last few million years, the same imaged layered, palimpsest on palimpsest, to an impossible depth, details reinforced through their sameness, to a crystalline clarity.

Atuhyr the quasimale thrusting deep into Aÿ the semimale's empty sac, spilling his semen, and spilling it again and again. Aÿ, sorrowing, feeling the semen coagulate and be absorbed, uselessly, over and over again.

"Why is he bothering?" asked Spence.

"Why does a woman?" asked Metz.

"Why are men so stupid?" asked Linda.

"Why are women surprised?" asked Rosie.

Kai thought, To ask these questions, these answerless questions, here and now, in the context of . . . Well. Why am I surprised that they focus, superficially, on the force that drives our lives on? Why didn't the Leospiders save themselves? Why didn't they bother? Because they thought they would never die. Unless they chose to. Unless they wanted to. We, so new to immortality, have not yet understood that.

Doc said, "Well, we know the quasimale's semen had some healing, some health-giving properties for the semimale. Maybe that's enough to—"

Kai laughed. "With their technological sophistication, I don't think they needed each other anymore. Not physically, at any rate."

Ginny, "But where are the others? Why don't we see Aÿ lying with quondam females, with macrofemmes? Are they extinct?"

Rosie: "Not likely. They weren't separate species, after all."

Doc: "The last example of a species is always one sex or the other, not both. Someone has to be last."

Scene shift, sliding into the future, Aÿ's last sexual interludes sliding away into the darkness, as if they *were* the last, never to be seen again. Aÿ and his friends walking, slowly, so slowly, lone figures, lonely figures, walking the tunnels of their empty cities. Scenes of Aÿ alone, walking the bright lowland plains of an empty-seeming world.

Mies said, "Toward the end, Pholos must have taken on much of the aspect that we see now."

Leospiders walking by ones and twos, seldom in little groups. Ginny said, "I see some that look like macrofemmes and quondam females. See that chest-nipple? And the macrofemmes were always rather stockier than the other sexes."

"Well suited," said Rose, "for bearing full-grown children."

"So why didn't they continue to breed?" asked Spence.

Kai ordered the synchronoptic analysis engine to dig for an answer, the spieltier software arrays to synthesize an image, something they could try to understand. Aÿ's imaginary voice suddenly hung over them, picked out in transfigured Leospider symbols:

We chose not to, was all they said.

Choice, thought Kai. That's what it really comes down to. Choice.

Color and light twisting in their eyes . . .

Four Leospiders together, one of each sex, surrounding a low table on which sprawled one of the genetically engineered Frogthings. A living thing, at least, thought Kai. The Leospiders weren't alone in the world they made.

Aÿ and the other three, bending down to puncture and suck, *Mmmmmm-hm-hm-hmmmmm* . . .

A lonely, mournful quality to it.

Flat, empty, dead Frogthing on the table.

Four Leospiders, satiated, sitting back, facing each other from the cardinal points of the compass. Sitting, staring, with empty silver eyes. Nothing more to say.

Colors, flickering, and . . .

Aÿ, alone in his chambers, sitting before a large, simmering bowl of pale gray gruel. Gruel calling out to him, bloodfoodsexlifelove . . .

Aÿ leaning forward, silver fangs popping out, an involuntary reflex, chattering uselessly on the rim of the ceramic bowl. Then lips, lovely sucking lips, touching the meniscus, sucking, sucking, faded pulse of joy flowing in with this ersatz Frogman blood.

"In the end," said Izzy, "they must have felt the need to . . . simplify their lives."

Mies said, "There comes a time when you no longer have anything like will."

Kai thought, For him? Or for all of us?

A twisting shudder of colorless light, Aÿ's memory growing pale as its simplified details began to thin out . . .

Aÿ alone, walking in the tunnel alone.

Were the others all gone now?

No. Aÿ meets this one and that one, here and there, by chance or design. But, in the end, we are all the same. Talking to another is like talking to myself. No reason to seek them out.

Aÿ standing, together with another Leospider. Aorÿ, the symbols said, another semimale. Aÿ looking at him. We are the last, we two. Aÿ looking at Aorÿ's breeder lips, wondered if he wished to see a quondam female's nipple, a quasimale's fructifying organ, even a macrofemme's resistant lips.

No.

Nothing left.

No more wants.

No more regrets.

This was our choice.

The end we wrote for ourselves.

A flicker of white light, like sheet-lightning . . .

Aÿ runs Aorÿ's pitiful corpse, battered and broken from the long fall, through the vitrifier, slides it into its receptacle, turns away, empty of thought. Just . . . remembering, remembering, watching Aorÿ topple away into the mist, watching him tumble end over end, silent, uncaring, listening for the distant *tock* of his impact, far, far below.

Then silently beginning the long climb down the face of the cliff to retrieve the dead body of the penultimate soul.

Maybe. Maybe I'll fall.

No. Not yet.

I still don't believe in souls.

Imagine.

Imagine if death were only a gateway to another life.

Then, no matter what, you could never escape from yourself. Never.

Horrible.

Flicker. Hardly any light at all.

Aÿ in the subterranean chamber, looking up at his sleek and wonderful starship, shiny, like new, ready to fly, whenever he chose.

One hand on the ladder.

I can go anywhere.

Two hands on the ladder.

I can go whenever I want.

Three hands on the ladder.

I don't have to stay here.

Silence.

Silence lasting a million years.

Yes, I do.

No hands on the ladder.

Turning away.

Flicker. Almost nothing.

Aÿ alone. All alone. Walking. Walking alone. Walking. For a million years. Footsteps falling, one after another, falling on shadows. Falling in light. Aÿ walking the empty corridors. Walking the heights. Looking up at the useless stars. The black sky beyond. Walking the bright plains where the Rhinotaurs roamed. The fallen cities where the Frogmen lived and died and worshipped their gods.

Waiting.

Waiting for what?

Shimmer. Nothing at all, really.

Aÿ standing in the room of dead souls, before the wall of vitrified corpses. Standing before the vitrification machine. Standing, with his . . . implement.

Now.

Now I'm ready.

To fall.

To die.

To empty the world of all its meaning.

All but that last thought.

One day.

One day they'll come.

Come and find me here.

Find me here all alone.

And when they see me, they'll know.

They'll *know*.

Please let them understand . . .

The implement strikes.

The blood begins to flow.

Fade to black.

The silence was filled with darkness. Mies looked up from Aÿ's remains, sadness welling up in him like a tide. Somehow, he thought, I never really understood that I'm not the only one who's alone. The fury, all the resentment, rising up, threatening to spill over, cooling abruptly, falling away into nothing. Useless. All my feelings useless. I can't even know if they're real. When I had friends, even if they were only friends within, we could . . . discuss matters. Sort things out. No. No that's not it. They were no more real than my feelings seem now. Their existence was just one more excuse. It wasn't *my* fault, you see, the Indigo rule-sieve told me it was the right thing to do.

What? *Me* know what's right on my own?

Memory of a day not long after they'd given him his symbiotes, told him that, if he was careful, there was no limit to how long he might live. Lying comfy in his bed, looking up at the timbers in the ceiling, wondering about what that meant. Pictured himself in some undefined future age, unhappy beyond belief, unable to recover, doomed to just . . . go on. Having to live forever with the consequences of his decisions.

Was that when I first got scared?

The others were moving again, recovering from the revelations, shaking off the feelings almost in slow motion. Anything to say? No, of course not. They're just as trapped as I am in their own little courses, are feeling the same petty emotions, wondering just how Aÿ's death affects *them*.

Kai looking at me now. Wanting . . . what? Why don't I know? Something beyond my imagining. If you know something, if you know what's *real*, why didn't you put it into me, goddamn you! Nothing. Just eyes. Staring. Might as well be Indigo eyes, for all the good they've done me.

Ginny's voice, finally: "Well. We have what we need, I think."

Doc, then: "We didn't understand, I don't think, just how important a role philosophy plays in all this. How delicate the thread upon which the fate of a species hangs."

Kai: "*We* being who, ICOPOSI? Doc, there's no need to speak in generalities. The question is, how do we send this information back to Earth? Because there's no question that this is a powerful argument for the Daiseijin case, one which will certainly tip the balance in favor of the human race's survival. Unless . . . it is suppressed."

Ginny: "That won't happen. Will it?"

Doc: "I can't say, for sure. Probably not. But, how do I put this, things have changed since we left. Even without direct evidence, it's easy to see that ICOPOSI's role may have changed as well. Indigo's plan may very well have flourished, and if so, people surely know about the existence of the sterility plague. I would imagine that ICOPOSI is now focusing on reducing the . . . imbalances that the plague has produced, trying to calm people down so that there is no panic."

Mies thought, When I see him, when I see him face to face, I feel, despite all cues to the contrary, as though I'm looking into a mirror. Why don't I *know*? Why can't I see his thoughts and *understand*? "So you're saying that the situation is more unstable now, and ICOPOSI will as a result be—"

"More hard-edged," Doc interrupted. "More likely to become alarmed."

Kai: "Damn you. You surely don't believe that—"

Doc said, "I don't believe anything. The organization has disparate elements embedded in it. There are surely those who would do anything to get this information out."

Mies said, "With the plague raging, the drama of our friend Aÿ here will seem very much more significant. If there is a panic, it will be directed toward . . . escape."

"And the Daiseijin will benefit," Ginny said.

Kai: "How deeply has ICOPOSI infiltrated the Daiseijin, Doc?"

"I am unable to say. There were operatives at all levels of the Daiseijin at the time of our departure."

Spence said, "Were there plans to monitor our tightbeam feed for, what would you call it, disruptive information?"

"That was discussed."

Ginny: "Oh, that's just great."

Doc said, "Ginny, ICOPOSI does not equate with evil. The driving force behind it is quite appropriate. It's one of the cornerstones of the Daiseijin philosophy that the human race has nearly reached a cusp, after which destruction is swift and total. Surely it's appropriate to try to prolong this period of economic prosperity. When things are so precariously balanced, virtually anything could be the beginning of the end."

"No solution?" asked Mies. "Just prolong the inevitable?"

"Mies, your *solution* was no solution at all. If you are still willing to defend Indigo's crackpot notions, you are not—"

Kai said, "No, Doc. It's clear that Indigo did help, will help in the future, by scaring the hell out of everyone. The reasons for expansion to other stellar systems are abstract, even now. Humans always look to their own interests, and as long as those interests are not directly threatened, they will not act. Indigo makes the threat *real*."

Rosie said, "I . . . see what you're saying. People will run to avoid the plague. And where is there to run?"

"More than that," said Kai. "The research necessary to defeat the plague will advance the development of true autoviroids tremendously."

Linda, voice freighted with contempt: "So every cloud has its silver lining? That doesn't make Indigo any more palatable."

Ginny: "We have to assume that the materials we send back will be received and acted upon by Hiraoka. But how much of what we saw was supplied by the spieltier software, anyway?"

Metz said, "Damn little. With the source material as intact as this, what we saw is probably what happened."

Kai: "I don't think we'll have to worry about the skeptics. Coupled with our report and analysis, it'll be good enough."

Ginny: "All right. The quicker the better. Let's see what we can do to synthesize the data and get our reports out tonight."

Kai, outside again, at the cliff's edge, under a starry, starry night, looking up at the sky. Reports completed, transmitted to the ship. Signed, sealed, delivered and . . . and what? Somewhere up there, Doc and Ginny put their personal imprimatur on our words and conclusions, begin transmitting them to . . .

Mother Night was a brilliant, irregular glitter arcing low above the southern horizon just now. Steady, hardly any air at all between us and them. Doc and Ginny. Linda and Andy. Waiting for their lovers to come home.

Waiting to go home. Return to a home that's vanished over time's horizon. Earth up there too. Sol a bright spark, one of the brightest stars. Right . . . *there*. Right where you left it. Signal proceeding, even now, past A and B, past Pegasus and Bellerophon, past Nephelë and Ixion. Carrying the story.

Is that all it is? A *story*? A lesson to be learned, a message for masses and leadership alike? No way at all to convey how . . . *real* they were. No way at all to tell them how, billions of years ago, whole races of real individual beings lived and died. No way to make them *care*.

Well, if they don't, then . . . we all die. Deserve to die. Just like the Leospiders and Frogmen and Rhinotaurs. Just like the Featherfolk who plumbed the stars and died anyway.

Soft pang. The Featherfolk tried to live. But they're gone. Empty gray world by a flat, empty gray sea under an empty and featureless gray sky. Why? Why did *they* fail? We'll never know, because the Leospiders didn't care enough to find out for us. They just didn't care.

Shadow. Shadow in starlight, shadow in shiplight, shadow from the light falling out of the windows of *MN01* falling across him. Shadow of a man. Kai turned to look. Mies. Eyes silent, glittering in the shadows behind his plastic faceplate.

Kai said, "Hell of a thing, no?"

Mies just looking at him. Finally: "Are we camping out again tonight?"

Kai felt his jaw drop slightly. Camping out? He said, "Sure. Let's go get the tent."

Mies sat on the crinkly plastic floor of the survival tent, darkness outside, shadows within, watching Kai get undressed. Slim. Slim like a girl. All right. You're ready for this. You've got to face things sooner or later.

Kai undoing his coverall, dropping it off his shoulders. Narrow chest, no breasts. Slim arms. A momentary consciousness of his own nose. Slim-looking, at any rate.

He felt an urge to drop his hand toward his own crotch. Don't. Nothing there. You won't like that. What the hell am I going to *do*? I don't want to be a woman for him.

Motionless icon of Reiko-chan floating in the darkness inside his own head. Not there anymore to help me. No Indigo eyes to tell me what to do. No scientist persona. Only memories. Memories of when I had them with me. Memories of when I walked in their shoes. Memories of David Gilman, man and boy. Only their memories to help me decide.

Only *me* to be responsible for . . . whatever happens.

Horrid image of moments to come. Of what it would be like when Kai . . . remembered image of him the night before, that wet, nasty, red . . . *thing* popping out and . . . me. He wants to use it on *me*. He tried not to shiver. Shuddered. Realized he must be shaking visibly. But . . . Kai's not looking at me now. Not seeing me.

Kai dropped the coverall over his hips, exposed slim, girlish buttocks. Just the right curve of hip, thought Mies. Just the right thing to attract me, stir my emotions, my hormones, my . . . nothing. No feeling down there at all. They took everything away.

Everything but the feelings.

And now? Kai's slim pubescent girl rear end reminded him of the way Seesy had looked when she took off her clothes before a supposedly innocent little boy, all those years ago. Took off her clothes, grinning a nasty-girl grin, smiling a dirty little smile and . . . no. No, I don't want to remember. I *can't* remember.

Kai turned around and looked at him, eyes dark, shadowed, almost invisible, certainly unreadable.

I couldn't read people, never, no matter what I could see. All I knew was what I *thought*. Memory of David. David confronted by some social situation, any social situation, didn't matter what was really going on. All David could think was, All right, now what do they *expect* me to say? Don't know. All right, make something up. Make anything up.

Christ, Seesy had pubic hair. It'd help if Kai had pubic hair. But he doesn't.

Kai walking toward him now in the shadowlight, hips swaying just *so*. Enticing. Enticing me. Enticing me to *what*? Nothing at all between his legs. Nothing at all.

Nothing left but my feelings.

Kai's eyes still lost in shadow.

I can't see his feelings.

Can't know if he's . . . feeling anything at all. Kai, perhaps, just centered on his own . . . physicality. What does he feel? A soft sliding wetness in his man-made cunt. Maybe even the building weight of . . .

I remember. I remember what it was like. The way lust would arrive, back when I was a man. That sudden feeling way down at the base of your belly, not quite between your legs, the sudden, unexpected kinesthetic reality of cock and balls and . . . like you could, somehow, sense an image of the woman's body, communicated, as though by telepathy and . . .

Mies licked dry lips. Swallowed past that now-familiar lump. "All right," he said. "I'm ready for whatever you want."

Kai stopped short. Seemed to gape like an actor in a 3-V soap opera.

Mies said, "Just . . . tell me what to do."

Long, long silence, Kai standing still, looming over him, little-girl mons just about at eye level.

Mies, heart pounding, terribly frightened, said, "Tell me what you want."

More silence, then Kai laughed. Laughed and said, "My God, Mies. Is *that* what you think this is all about?"

Pulse of confusion. Pulse of anger. People never stick to the script, goddamn it. People always . . . breaking character. Never giving me a chance to . . . understand. And regret. Deep regret. They took everything away. Not just my manhood. The things that made me *me*. The things that made me . . . functional. Took away what I chose to call Mies Cochrane. Took away Reiko-chan and Indigo eyes and everything else that let me move through a human world.

Left me with . . .

Kai reached down and put a soft hand under his chin, lifted, tipped his head back until Mies was looking at a face instead of a crotch. Smiled at him. Smiled and said, "Hell, don't you understand I can be your friend without fucking you?"

Mies stared up at him, astonished, and thought, *Friend?*

Not long afterward, Kai lay naked in his sleeping bag, looking up at the stars through the wall of the tent, listing to the soft noises Mies made as he stirred, shifted in his own sleeping bag, presumably awake, probably with a head full of thoughts.

So. *Does* he understand?

No way for me to know.

No way to know until I see what he *does*. Maybe not even then.

Do *I* understand?

Maybe. Maybe not.

I can look back through my life. Go back to all those long lost times, look back and see for myself . . . what I had. Sookiee? Maybe. Count Maxilon? Of course not. Ginny? Well, yes, but.

But you fixed things so it wasn't possible for you to know. Good old Maeru kai Ortega, descended from that horrid, horrid man, that noblest Roman of them all. Good old Kai, *husband to every wife, wife to every husband.*

And, in that context, how am I to know?

All the memories, jumbled together.

Starting at the beginning, ending up at now.

When was the last time I could have turned away?

I don't know . . .

In the long ago and far away, Kai sat in the right-hand seat of *Mother Night,* the seat before the flight engineer's console, looking out through a square window of armored glass, at a black sky flecked with a few insignificant stars. No stopdown on the windowpane, glare of coronal light blotting all but the very brightest objects in the sky.

Dead ahead, Alpha Centauri, fresh data scrolling across his vision field when he looked at her. It? Him? Body part of a male centaur, at least. *Rigel Kent.* The centaur's foot.

Other bright stars scattered round. And, over there, bright yellow Mercury. Dim white Venus, remote along its orbit. Earth a fat spark up that way, faint with just a touch of blue. Mars nowhere to be seen. Jupiter a rather faint fleck of grayish white light . . .

The ship's eyebubble suddenly figured out what he was looking at and supplied a pale spectral image of the ecliptic plane.

Soft voice, a man's voice from mission control, venerable Erasmus Hiraoka himself: "One minute."

Scroll of data, Ginny's soft acknowledgment. Kai's glance flickered at a couple of control surfaces and the eyebubble swung the window shields in, thick sections of heat shield dropping over the portholes, sealing with a distant, muffled thump. Sealed in now. Little views on the row of flatscreens across the top of the control panel, most of them views of the ship itself hanging in space, transmitted from external sources.

He said, "Bring up global."

A brief pause, while the core sieved vast amounts of data and made its complex, automated decisions, then the inside of the control room filled with outer space, a transparent view, stars every which way, seeming just out of reach, as if embedded in a now glassy hull. And ghost light flooding the back of the cabin.

Kai turned in his seat. Back there, the sun was hanging in space, silvery corona visible all around it, seeming composed of many individual rays. Black circle superimposed on the face of the sun, rather like an annular eclipse seen from Earth's surface: The sunshield of the powerstation, powerstation from which the collimated particle beam would soon flow . . .

"Ten seconds."

Kai stole a look at Ginny, was gratified to see her looking back. She smiled. Thumbs up. This is it. Ginny turning back to face her instrument panel, putting her hands on the controls mounted on the arms of her chair, Kai doing likewise.

"Five."

Somewhere out there, invisible, hanging on the ends of a dozen invisible black threads, the two-hundred-kilometer loop of the magnetic sail floated, perfectly round, shape maintained by eddy currents. All right. The technology worked well on the little one we built for the Barnard probe. And it works well in a sail just hanging in the sky, keeping its shape despite this dense solar wind . . .

"Fire."

What if . . .

What if . . .

A solid pole of liquid violet fire came up out of the black disk in the middle of the sun, reached over Kai's left shoulder, just over his and Ginny's heads, spooled itself away into the sky, pole become a mere stick, a wire, a thread, a spider's safety line . . .

Data stared to unwind into his eyes, charts and graphs, characterizing the condition of particles and fields associated with the magsail, eddy currents boiling now, extrinsic field starting to roll around the sail cable, roll like the smoke in a smoke ring blown by an expert, vector current forming right through the middle of the sail . . .

Ginny whispered, "Point-oh-five gee."

Kai felt himself starting to settle against his acceleration chair, felt his neck fall back, ever so gently, against the headrest.

Erasmus Hiraoka's voice, filled with something . . . some possibly ineffable feeling, said, "Godspeed *Mother Night*."

Ginny said, "Point-one gee."

The data in Kai's eyes told him the eddy currents were stabilized now, rolling around the surface of the sail cable at near-relativistic velocities, winding in tighter and tighter . . .

Ginny: "Point-two."

Kai put his right hand on the little joystick and applied an electrical impulse to three of the twelve support cables, watched the eddy currents shift and tangle, then sort themselves out in a new pattern. Good. Sail tipping just so, tipping just enough to keep the little ship out of the path of the beam.

"Point-three."

A quick look over his shoulder. Sun still blazing, a vast bright eye against the stellar night, but . . . The little black disk at its heart was startlingly shrunken.

We are . . . going somewhere. Going now.

"Point-four."

Kai adjusted the eddy again, halting the ship's tendency to roll around the beam. Have to keep on making that adjustment, most likely. The eyebubble core's rule-sieves, worked and reworked by a team of more than a hundred programmers, team stuffed to the gills with AI composition tools, would still be imperfect . . .

"Point-five."

A glance at Ginny. Eyes on her instruments. Shining eyes . . .

As if she felt him looking at her, she glanced up, smiled. "Point-six."

He said, "This time tomorrow, we'll be where no one's gone before."

Light in her eyes brightening to a brilliant luster like nothing he'd ever seen before. "Point-seven."

They were settled hard in their seats now, a sensation more or less like lying on your back, down on the surface of Venus. "Point-eight."

Thirty hours. Thirty hours to go. This time tomorrow I'll be very tired of lying on my back, looking up at an artificial sky, dogged by this hideous purple fire . . .

"Point-nine."

Down below, the rest of the crew was already asleep, buttoned up by technicians in cocoons that would remain sealed for the full fourteen years. Fourteen years while we ride to Alpha Centauri. And in a week . . . In a week Ginny and I lay ourselves down to sleep, put ourselves in the hands of this imperfect, impersonal eyebubble. Go to sleep, wait for the years to pass, wait for the core to waken us at our destination . . .

"One gee."

Kai throttled back, applying current that would lessen the magsail's grip on the eight-hundred terawatt beam outside, letting them ride on a steady acceleration.

Thirty hours. Thirty hours to go.

Ginny reached out, bridging the gap between their chairs, touched her fingers lightly to the back of his hand.

Yes, Kai thought, there is Ginny. Virginia Vonzell Qing-an, Captain and Master of the Daiseijin Starship *Mother Night*. Oh, Ginny, I'm sorry I put you through all this. Silence, maybe a soft distant hush, the sound of Mies breathing, sleeping perhaps, still now.

So. What good does it do Ginny to have all this locked up inside your head? No good at all. But you can make it right. You know you can. She only wants to *know*. Kai got out of his sleeping bag, stood in the cool air of the survival tent, stood naked, looking down on Mies. Eyes closed. Mouth open. The face of a sleeping child grown old.

In time, the implants will fade.

In time he'll be . . . whoever the hell he really was. I wonder if I'll like David Gilman when he emerges?

He got dressed, pulling on the coverall, sorting out the parts of his spacesuit, starting to put it on.

"Kai?"

"Here, Mies."

"What are you doing?"

"Going for a little walk."

Silence. No way to know what he's thinking.

Mies said, "You . . . want me to come?"

Silence.

"Go to sleep, Mies. I'll be back in a bit."

Mies was sitting up now, a shadow against the night. "Kai . . ."

"It's all right. I just need to . . . be alone for a few minutes. I'll be right back."

Silence, while Kai finished dressing. Then Mies said, "Alone." Palpable fear in his voice.

Conscious of the lie, Kai said, "Everyone needs to be alone sometimes, Mies." Mies just sitting there, looking at him, eyes hidden by shadow. After a minute, Kai turned and zipped himself out through the airlock.

It was the middle of the night now. Darkness complete. Not even a hint of color on the horizon. I could, Kai thought, walk right off the cliff. Stars up there. No suns. Tiny crescent moon low on the horizon, hardly more than a dim, irregular-looking star.

He stood still. Waited patiently. After a while, *Mother Night* rose, heading up into the sky at a steep angle. Kai nodded to his suit's node sensor, opening the interface, punching through a signal to the lander and thence up to the ship.

"Ginny?"

Long pause, then her face scrolled down out of nowhere,

hanging like a bright image before him, eyes wide. Wide and . . . afraid.

"Kai."

The two of them staring at each other.

Finally, he smiled and said, "Hello, stranger."

You could see the relief blossom on her face. She said, "Oh, God, Kai . . ."

Nothing to say. Why the hell am I so tongue-tied now? I know what I want to say. I know what she needs to hear. I . . .

Before he could get anything out, she said, "Welcome home, Kai. I missed you."

After that, it was easy to speak.

Early, while everyone else was still asleep, Mies and Kai made their way back down the long corridors to the hall of crypts. A was still low in the sky over the towering plateau to the east, shedding its wan light on the dead ruins, dipping everything in deep shadow.

They passed through the empty hallways, silently, conversation almost a sacrilege. Like mourners at a funeral. In a way, that's what we are. I mourn the loss of my innocence, as well. But innocence isn't, can not be, a desired goal. In the gallery, they gathered together the pieces of Aÿ, Mies using his sample collection kit, carefully placing them in a large plastic container. The last remaining small pieces and dust were vacuumed into a smaller pouch, using a scraping tool to dislodge pieces that had become fused to the floor.

Kai gripped the large, central piece of exoskeleton and hefted it, finding it lighter than it looked. He lifted it without difficulty, then beckoned to his companion. Nothing remaining of the corpse. They turned and left the chamber.

Outside, they walked to the edge of the plateau, where there was sufficient fine talus to make a rounded slope. Shadow engulfed them as they approached the cliffside, and they paused for a moment, looking up. Above the ebon face of cliff, barely visible in light reflected from behind them, A's corona was a little pink tuft. Quickly, the stars of night came out as their eyes adapted. First great Canopus and Achernar appeared, then their diminutive minions. The landscape around them grew brighter, seemingly of its own accord, and when they could see enough to go on, they continued up the slope.

When they had found a likely place, relatively flat, with no large boulders, they pulled out their collecting shovels and began to dig in the sharp broken material, until they had excavated a trench perhaps a meter deep by two long, wide enough to fit in the pieces of the Leospider body. When they had finished, Mies placed the bags at one end of the trench, and Kai fitted in the torso, wedging it down into the dark gravel until it was sufficiently buried to be covered.

Good enough. Don't want to bury him *too* deep.

They shoveled the material over the remains until it was completely buried, filling in with some finer debris from closer to the cliff face. Mies stepped back, looking at the hard, cold Pholotian gravels, wondering how long it would take the remains to erode away into nothingness. A long time, perhaps, but not nearly as long as in the cool, nitrogen atmosphere storage of the catacombs.

They stepped back from the makeshift grave, almost glad that it was nearly impossible to discern amid the uneven rubble. Kai, said in a soft voice, "Goodbye, little Leospider. You and your kind died because you chose to. It didn't have to end this way."

Improbably, a rhyme, from across the years of his life, came into Mies's head. "Itsy bitsy spider . . ."

Kai looked at him, face hidden in dimness. "Ironic. They sang that on Titan, too. Even though we didn't have spiders, we had rain."

Mies said, "The moral always seemed obvious to me: get the fuck out of the drainpipe. Silly, of course, but . . . on the Earth, the argument still goes on. People caught up in their own mysticism, arguing the merits of indistinguishable political philosophies. Meanwhile, inevitably, the rain comes."

They stood there, silent.

Mies spoke again: "It's so hard to come to terms with the

truth, Kai. I've lived my life hiding from it. Here it is all around us, though: the true splendor of the vast and incomprehensible universe. The unlimited freedom and the terrible necessity to do what must be done. Aÿ felt it too; all thinking beings must."

Kai said, "I wonder. Was it true for the Frogmen as well? The Rhinotaurs? The Featherfolk? What about *them*?"

Mies: "*Are* we all just spiders caught out in the rain? To me, it's always seemed that way."

Kai, staring at him now, eyes, as always, completely unreadable. Finally, he said, "Hell, Mies, the lesson from the song is supposed to be about how spiders persevere until they're dead, not about giving up."

Mies: "We're supposed to go on trying, despite everything? No matter what happens? No matter how much it hurts? That always seemed stupid to me."

Kai said, "And look where that idea got you. Look where it's taken humanity: to the brink of destruction. It's a fool's attitude, Mies. The one real truth about life is, it's do or die. And if you don't *do,* if you turn your back on a life of deeds, you die anyway. Just ask *him*." He gestured at the grave.

Nothing more to say.

They turned together, bright landscape flooding their eyes. Out there, beyond the Leospider castle, the far horizon of Pholos, red-brown curve with its cap of blue, nearly blinding even in the light of distant A. In the dark blank sky above, little Silenus, closest moon, its thick oblate shape moving upward, west to east like a slow, slow rocket.

Mies thought, Is it a lie or is it the truth? A lie with which to trick me? Or a truth with which to trick me? Will I ever *know*?

Together, the two of them started down toward the lander.